THE SACRAMENT

Donna and Pete,

So great to have the two of you enjoy this evening with me and my family. I hope you'll enjoy this adventure.

.... ————— ————— ....

DAVID HOUSER

.... ————— ————— ....

Dave Houser

abbott press

Abbott Press books may be ordered through booksellers or by contacting:

Abbott Press
1663 Liberty Drive
Bloomington, IN 47403
www.abbottpress.com
Phone: 1-866-697-5310

ISBN: 978-1-4582-1793-6 (sc)
ISBN: 978-1-4582-1795-0 (hc)
ISBN: 978-1-4582-1794-3 (e)

Library of Congress Control Number: 2014917359

Printed in the United States of America.

Abbott Press rev. date: 11/13/2014

For Larry Walke;
you left us far too soon.

I wish to extend enormous gratitude to the following:

Star Christman, Stuart Watkins, Rick Houser, and Courtney Goode for their collective contributions that gently corrected my path.

Stan and Jeanette Olafson, Minh, Connie and Peter Le, for sharing your family history and allowing me the great honor of sharing them within this adventure.

Michael Garrett, for your thorough, uncompromising assistance in edit, proving to me why you are one of the best in the business.

David and Charlene McColly; what a deal I scored when I married your daughter! You've provided me with unflinching encouragement, you've been my greatest advocate, and my biggest fan.

Ron and Shirley Houser, for doing your absolute best with what you had to work with! Thank you for your Faith in me. I love you Mom and Dad. Sorry, again, for crashing Mom's car!

To Michelle, my lovingly patient wife; your many strengths have eclipsed my numerous faults. Thank you for the sacrifices given freely toward this endeavor. You were *so* worth the wait!

PROLOGUE

Tacna Region, Peru, May 17, 1923

The short battle between the two sides appeared to be over, but Alessandro knew neither could declare victory that day. The Chilean army continued their quest toward dominance for more years than he could remember, but the pride of the Tacnenos remained in their fight for independence in Peru.

Leaning uncomfortably against a tree, he peered through the thin forest, reciting a quick prayer of hope that the skirmish wouldn't resume. He heard other victims from the short battle, scattered farther up the mountain; some from his side and some from theirs.

Looking down at his hands, he noticed how rough they'd become from too many years of laboring with his father's fish nets. Alessandro recalled a simpler life, sitting in his room practicing his guitar. He wanted to learn enough chords to play one beautiful song to perfection for his heart's devotion, the lovely Miranda. He closed his eyes for just a moment and when opened, his focus fell to the blood slowly exiting from his mid-section as a tear immediately welled and dropped from the corner of his eye with his first thought of dying.

Before he could allow himself to travel down that path of defeat, a rustling sound from farther down the mountain startled him into defensive action. Gripping his empty rifle, he turned toward the direction of the sound to see a man coming toward him, carrying only a backpack with his hands raised in surrender.

The stranger continued his approach, calling out to Alessandro, "This fight has seen its end. Allow me to come to you and see to your wounds." Alessandro immediately felt relaxed with the unarmed man's advance and motioned for him to proceed. He continued to stare into the stranger's face as the man returned his attention with a confident, steady gaze. Pale features, yet speaking Alessandro's dialect of Spanish confused the young Tacneno as to whom the man's loyalty belonged.

When the stranger was within fifty yards, Alessandro noticed the man's vivid blue eyes, suggesting North American or English descent. There was something kind, yet pained within the stranger's eyes that eased his own defenses. "Have they retreated down the mountain?" Alessandro inquired of the man, as the stranger knelt beside him and began tending to the wound.

"Yes, my friend. The rebels have passed beyond the base of the mountain and cross the river as we speak. We will be safe long enough to help those in need."

No longer fearing another attack, Alessandro rested his head against the tree watching the man focus on mending the damage the bullet had left. "Who are you?", he asked sharply, the intense pain shooting through his abdomen.

The man only paused before answering without looking up, "I am just a simple man of God here at your time of need, in the hope you find that which allows you to move forward."

He gauged the stranger to be near his father's age. With an intake of air and the pain beginning to subside, he pressed on with his questions. "I know many who live in Tacna, yet you're unfamiliar to me. Do you know my father, Antonio Fuentes? He mends and sells fish nets near the north shore."

The man placed gauze over the injured area before looking into Alessandro's eyes. "Your father looks to the mountains every nightfall, awaiting your return. He loves his only son with the entirety of his heart and prays to God for his safety."

Alessandro neither questioned the stranger concerning his knowledge of his deepest desires, nor did he fathom the chance encounter. He simply looked up to the darkening turquoise sky as it slowly began its turn to dusk. He listened to the stranger's gentle voice lull him into a peaceful trance. "And what of Miranda; is she there with my father watching for my return?" the young man inquired. Alessandro pushed himself up with his elbows before quickly settling back against the tree, exhausted from the momentary exertion.

The stranger gently placed a hand on Alessandro's forehead, saying, "Rest, weary one. Reserve your strength for the journey home." Checking the gauze and seeing it already soaked through, the man looked back up to the sky, as if recalling a memory, saying, "Ah, yes, the lovely Miranda. I heard a story, many years ago, of a host of angels that collected a decade's worth of beauty and descended it all upon one fortunate child; a girl from the Tacna Region. Could this be the same Miranda?"

Alessandro unashamedly smiled, answering, "This would be the one. This would be my Miranda."

The stranger smiled along with the young Peruvian before continuing, "I see her sitting gracefully upon a bench near the sea, with your father standing behind her with his hand resting gently upon her shoulder, like a father watches over a daughter. He speaks with great pride and tells her of his son's bravery in his fight for their freedom. They laugh at stories that they share with each other of better times when their Alessandro was not in the mountains fighting and lived happily with his father and many loved ones."

The stranger looked down at Alessandro, the smile slowly fading from his lips and from his eyes. Reaching down, he tenderly took the young man's hand into his, continuing, "Your father sees the love Miranda has for his son in how she speaks of him and how her face lights up at the very mention of his name. He imagines them, years later, married with many beautiful children, with tears caressing his cheek at the joy his son has brought forth."

The stranger took in a deep breath before gently taking Alessandro's head from its uncomfortable position against the tree, lowering him to the ground near the base of the tree where the grass was softest. He placed his palm upon Alessandro's head and quietly directed a prayer to the heavens for his safe journey.

When his prayer was complete, he stared at the scar upon the back of his own right hand. Closing his eyes at the memory from so long ago, he slowly shook his head at the realization of how long it had been since he considered or even looked upon the damaged hand.

Touching the scarred flesh with his fingertips, a flood of visions returned, as they always did when he touched the tender area. The stranger slowly rose, gathering his backpack, and ventured farther up the mountain into the darkening forest in search of his next passing soul.

He came to the mountain aware of the six, including the young Tacneno, in need of his attention. The other five scattered about the mountain top who wouldn't see their earthly demise, he would only leave them food, bandages, and some cauterizing agents, for their fate was unwritten and not for him to interact. The stranger didn't travel far before he found the older Chilean soldier with a punctured lung and shrapnel lodged within his spine. He raised his hands and slowed his pace of approach, preparing to assist another life enter its last and final stage.

CHAPTER 1

Becklin reaffirmed the intentions to himself one last time sitting, waiting by the window of a Manhattan coffee shop. He sighed heavily while uttering, "Doing anything right is rarely devoid of sacrifice." The phrase had been one of his father's favorites. He could only assume the expression waited to resurface at the most appropriate time.

He slowly sipped his overpriced hazelnut latte and nonchalantly peered across the street through steel-blue eyes for his new contact to appear. Perhaps he'd been overly cautious in prepping their first meeting, but with the enemies he was about to make, he preferred not to rent a message on a billboard.

Chuckling to himself, he casually set his coffee down and took in the room filled with college students, out-of-work business professionals, and various generation 'X's and 'Y's. *What a racket!* he thought, his smile turning upward at one corner, forming a snarl.

Becklin's attention was drawn to the music store directly adjacent to the coffee house. A slender man of about thirty years old, wearing a blue cap with brown curly hair arrived and he watched the man for a few seconds before confirming it as his appointment.

Becklin slung the stuffed backpack he brought simply for effect over his shoulder and began to rise. A young male college student with a wisp of thin facial hair that someday might form a goatee pounced on the possible opening, asking, "You all done with the table, sir?"

Standing, Becklin looked down from his six foot, two inch broad frame and held the young man in check for just a moment past uncomfortable. Finally, turning toward the door, he uttered, "Remember, there's a two hour limit, kid!" The college student slowly took the newly acquired seat, but didn't take his eyes off Becklin's back, making certain the table's previous occupant followed through on his departure.

Once on the sidewalk, Becklin turned right, following the gust of wind. With partly sunny skies above, he put his dark sunglasses on and began to increase his stride up the block. He watched everyone within eyesight, including any open windows and visible rooftops, memorizing the vehicles driving by, in case any circled or doubled back.

He matched the other pedestrians around him, stride for stride, considering how his military training, then his long stint with the CIA, tuned his perception of the world around him into a constant 'what if' scenario. It was a trait rarely used in his present career as a Contractor, but certainly came in handy, as of late. Funny, how while working with the Agency, he posed as a Contractor, but now that he was a Contractor, he was acting like a spy. Life had a twisted sense of humor from time to time.

Becklin blended with six others waiting at the crosswalk for the light to change, allowing them to shuttle to the other side like cattle. He continued to glance in the direction of his contact while crossing the street, then moved behind him while the man patiently paced back and forth. Becklin timed his stride so when the man he knew as Sam Noll was pacing toward him, he quietly breathed the word, "Inside," so only Sam could hear.

The reporter was taller than Becklin imagined, but the picture he had confirmed his contact's identity. If that hadn't been enough, the blue hat they agreed he would wear was definitely one of a kind. Without any eye contact or even a glance back, Becklin entered the music store, casually grabbed a random album from a center rack and headed directly for the last sound room in the back. Once inside, he pulled the 'reserved' sign out of the window, closed the shade, and placed the record onto the table, preparing it to play, before returning to the door.

He'd chosen the music store three days earlier for its soundproof listening rooms and back door access to the alley. He would have preferred a place with a third option for an exit, but he's confident he could improvise if bad turned to worse.

Sam finally entered the store and surveyed the room for Becklin among the handful of people perusing their musical selections. Becklin remained visible by the door until Sam noticed him before he retreated back into the sound room. Sam stopped in the doorway, removing his hat, sizing up Becklin. After Sam appeared convinced the guy could easily bend him into a pretzel, he silently glanced at each of the four walls. Becklin followed Sam's thought, breaking the ice with, "Yeah, closer quarters than I'd like, but I've showered and even used deodorant, so feel free to come on in."

Sam grinned his opening and decided introductions could be skipped, responding with, "I didn't think they still had record stores anymore, especially ones with sound rooms. Nice recon." Becklin hesitantly smiled, giving away the fact he wasn't used to doing it much.

Interrupting the ice breaker, the record dropped onto the player and Culture Club's, "Do You Really Want to Hurt Me?" began to play. Both men stared at the player with surprise, then back at each other before they broke into a chuckle. Sam picked up the album cover and looked it over, straight lining, "I had you pegged as more of a Jazz man."

Leaning against the wall, Becklin looked down at the floor before offering, "A man and his music are a fragile pairing."

After a short pause, Sam asked, "So, how do you want to do this? I figure it's your court; you should lay out the rules."

With the air in the room suddenly changed from jovial to serious, Becklin's expression eased into its usual stern comfort.

Without pause, showing his hopeful new ally that he'd already had a plan in mind, Becklin rattled through his checklist, "First, we go through some general Q and A; I do the 'Q'-ing, you do the 'A'-ing. After I deem this relationship sound and equitable, I'll start answering some of your questions. We meet today for eighteen more minutes, then again in two days at a location decided by me that I'll give you over this phone." Becklin removed a cell phone from his pocket and handed it to Sam before continuing, "After you receive the call, dispose of it properly." Sam looked at the phone and dismissed half a dozen silly little questions before placing it safely within his own pocket while Becklin proceeded at an increased pace, "What I want to know first is what, if anything, do you plan to do with the information you're about to receive?"

Sam gave him a blank look as though it was a trick question, before answering, "I'm a reporter. I plan to have it published."

Becklin leaned in and asked slowly, "Plan or intend?"

Sam responded quickly, "I use the word 'plan' because as you must know, I don't have the last word in what gets printed. I'm not the editor. Whether I plan, intend, or stamp my feet and yell; all I can do is write the truth the way I always have and hope my editor approves it for print."

Becklin took this in without expression and finally began to nod, saying, "You write what I tell you, and I have no doubt they'll print it. I just want to know if you *intend* to stay on this even if things get . . . sticky?"

Sam held his own with the staring competition, but decided to revisit some humor with, "Do you mean sticky, like cotton candy, or is this the kind of sticky where threats can be made and even possibly followed through with?"

Becklin kept a straight face, watching Sam before checking his watch, replying, "The second kind, only minus the threat."

Sam served up his best tough guy look before saying with some imitated swagger, "Good! Cuz I've never liked cotton candy!"

The song ended and "Time (Clock of the Heart)" began to play, while Becklin let Sam have his moment, before moving forward with what he believed would be Sam's first and immediate question. "What we're dealing with, without going into details you can figure out quickly for yourself, is two, possibly three, extremely influential United States Senators and the fleecing of America for their personal gain to the tune of forty-eight million dollars." he said without emotional attachment.

Sam listened intently but waited, seemingly knowing the big draw was about to be revealed. Becklin paused, baiting Sam to interrupt, but when the reporter didn't bite, Becklin proceeded with a little gained respect for his new ally, "I know. What else is new; politicians on the take, page eleven! But the difference with this set of criminals is they've permanently silenced two loose ends already."

Becklin's last morsel received the intended reaction from Sam before he closed with, "This, by the way, all fell quietly into my lap in a way no one should possibly know or even consider, and I would appreciate clinging to this avenue of anonymity."

Sam took in the limited information, staring down at his feet for a moment. Becklin figured his new contact already knew thieving, murderous senators sounded so ridiculously unbelievable that it could only be plausible in the nation's capitol. Becklin watched silently while Sam worked it forward mentally. If the reporter's facial expressions were tells, Becklin could only guess he had begun a short list of possible candidates in his mind and how they pulled it off without some panel of watch dogs or an over-zealous subcommittee member catching wind of it; it's what he would have done.

Suddenly Sam glanced up in the middle of his thought to see Becklin watching him intently, asking pointedly, "So, what exactly are you wanting me to do?" pushing himself off the wall and resting his hands on his hips in a confrontational manner.

Becklin followed Sam's dilemma and eased toward the right path. "First, fetter out the truth; see if what I say is true. Use your trusted contacts and fill in the blanks, and then weigh your only two options; expose them or run. I'd be lying if I said I didn't care one way or the other. I'm very much hoping you go with option number one, as I've a vested interest in burying them before they bury me."

The returned look on Sam's face spoke volumes; he hadn't considered the fact that Becklin didn't *have* a choice but attempt to expose them. Becklin knew secrets always had a way of floating to the shore no matter how much someone tried to weigh them down. Somebody always saw, heard, or already knew something and before long it fell upon the wrong ear. He was a marked man with an unknown amount of sand left in his hour glass.

Considering Sam was unsure of Becklin's background, he could only assume Sam figured there's some shady work in his dossier. At least enough respect that allowed him the foresight of knowing that even if he chose to walk away from this, he'd cement his fate of wondering if every drink had been poisoned, every stranger an assassin, or if one turn of the ignition would be his last.

Confirming Becklin's notion correct, Sam extended his hand to Becklin, and he received it graciously, pumping one strong shake to confirm their new, if somewhat tenuous bond. Without letting go of his hand Sam finished the meeting with, "I'll be waiting for your call" before he turned and exited the small room.

Once Sam was back at work the following day, he concluded toward one lone fact; he's already paranoid. After a restless night's sleep, and a haphazard attempt to watch for anyone following him to work, he sat at his desk staring at his phone, wondering if it's already bugged. Sam nearly jumped out of his seat when the phone he's intently watching rang. With a slight hesitation, he cautiously answered it, "This is Sam . . ."

Marci, the Editor's Administrative Assistant, impatiently yelled into the phone, "You were supposed to be in the meeting room five minutes ago, Sam!"

Blurting out, "On my way!" Sam slammed the phone back in its place and grabbed his notebook and jacket all in one quick motion before bolting down the aisle, cursing.

Sliding through the half-open door of the conference room, he quietly eased into the only seat left. The editor, Malcolm Vassault, sat frumpily at the end of the table in a chair larger than any other in the room, pausing in mid-sentence to glare directly at Sam. Remaining fixed on his tardy columnist, Malcolm continued his request for an update from Gene Defoe, head of the Sports section.

While Gene rambled on about what would make page one news with sports, Ira Nevins, Assistant Editor and Supervisor of Photography and Archives, sitting next to Sam, slid him a note that read, "We all wish to convey our heart-felt appreciation for, once again, your selfishness with Malcolm's unrelenting gaze of discontent."

Without looking at the short, bespectacled man, Sam wrote back, "Bite me hard, Ira!"

Sam shuffled together his jumbled notes and while Gene finished up with his update, Malcolm rushed through his last few words to maximize Sam's lack of preparation, "So Sam, now that we're finally blessed with your presence, what shall we offer our readers from the continued sagas of your humble article?"

Sam met his editor's gaze for just a moment before realizing he didn't have a shot at backing him down. Prepared to do his expected dance, Sam's deep-seeded ire for the man got the best of him. Adjusting what he planned to say, Sam instead replied offhandedly, "Actually, Malcolm, I was hoping to catch you privately for five or ten minutes to discuss a new lead I'm working."

The air in the room stymied in everyone's throats while Sam's reply sank in with each staff member, and all eyes suddenly locked on his every gesture. Sam smiled inwardly, knowing full well that no one made an appointment with the editor unless they're dying, leaving the job for greener pastures or, the rarest of all, landed a front page Pulitzer Prize-winning story.

Malcolm chewed over his tardy reporter's request, while Sam surveyed the room. Some of his colleagues were staring at Sam, some watched Malcolm, but Sam noticed all were holding their breath to see which way the scenario would play out. Meanwhile, Sam maintained his poker face, feeling a bead of sweat creep down his back. With nothing more than a nod, Malcolm moved on to the political page while Sam breathed a thankful prayer. The general pace of the rest of the meeting was hastened as no one really listened to the individual updates. Everyone wanted to follow Sam once the meeting quickly concluded and he and Malcolm made their way out the door, turned right, and entered the office at the far end of the hall.

With a final glance back toward the meeting room before stepping into his editor's office, Sam made eye contact with Ira, being the last to abandon the vigil. With his notoriously pained look of someone about to receive terrible news staring down the hallway, he's left wondering what his colleague had up his sleeve.

Inside the Master's Chamber, as his fellow writers liked to call the Editor-in-Chief's office, Malcolm offered Sam the seat across from him on the sofa, away from his desk, before turning and walking over to his small makeshift bar. Sam took in the room, having never been graced nor cursed to find himself within its storied walls. He's focused on the eclectic mismatched splattering of art on the walls when Malcolm finished pouring himself a drink without offering Sam anything and followed his line of sight. Pointing with his newly filled scotch in his hand, he offered, "Got that beauty in Singapore. Paid seventy-two for it, but it should have gone for ninety!" Sam nodded, still staring at the painting with a new-found appreciation for idiots with too much money, but decided to leave it alone.

Malcolm finally moved toward the over-stuffed chair across from Sam, unbuttoned his jacket, allowing his oddly shaped gut its desired freedom. Malcolm slid low into the seat, using his stomach like a table for his drink. Sam waited while his boss stared at him.

He'd had enough dealings with the man to know he preferred to open his conversations. Finally, after a slow sip from his scotch, Malcolm squinted at Sam before exhaling, "So, whadaya got?"

Between checking if all of his windows and doors were securely locked, Sam spent four hours the previous night following up on his assumptions, theories, limited amount of facts and political contacts for his story base, then another two hours on exactly how he would present the basics to Malcolm. Sam knew the story definitely had legs, but giving Malcolm too much information up front could jeopardize his own involvement in the long run. Also, Malcolm had proven to be unreliable with other writers' contacts by not honoring their desire to remain anonymous, so Sam decided to baby feed him parts of what he knew and allow Malcolm to assume more than what Sam actually shared. "I've been working a story for a few weeks and I think I'm at a point where we'll need to bring legal in on it to cover our butt" he spit out dispassionately like they were talking about the weather.

Malcolm sat up so fast he seemed to have forgotten the drink making a nice water ring on his shirt, asking, "Legal, huh? What exactly are we dealing with and whose pool are we relieving ourselves in?"

Caught off guard at Malcolm's sudden brand of humor, Sam chuckled, reflecting for just a second how he'd never seen an animated side of his boss before. Interesting, Sam thought, how the prospect of increased circulation brought about a person's lifted spirit. Sam stared unfocused at the floor in front of Malcolm, as if to be shooting from the hip, even though he practiced the speech for nearly forty minutes.

With a quick, deep intake of air, he began, "My source has painted me an ugly picture of greed, politics, and murder on the hill." Malcolm tilted his head to the right from the sound bite and waited for Sam to continue. Sam looked about the room before continuing, "My contact tested me with having to figure out who the two victims were, and I've confirmed the two deaths, both under their own investigation in separate districts; one written-off as accidental, the second, a robbery gone bad and both seemingly unrelated to each other. Also, I have active leads in place with the money, which is in the ballpark of forty-eight million dollars, and counting."

Sam reengaged eye contact, taking a short breath, proceeding, "Last, I have a shrinking list of candidates behind the whole scam. I'm not ready to share them yet, but let me tell you, when you hear their names, you're going to give birth to a medium-sized farm animal."

Sitting back slowly, Sam reflected on his perfect pitch and timing. He even inwardly smiled at his impromptu use of the farm animal line at the end.

Malcolm got up from his seat and discarded his glass onto his oversized desk, with his back to Sam. After staring out his window for a moment, Malcolm curtly stated, "I need a name."

Sam, expecting this response, threw out, "How about George Washington?"

Malcolm spun around without any hint of finding humor in Sam's quip. With hands on his thick hips, Malcolm pushed harder. "I mean it, Noll. I want to know who's on the list and the name and background of your source or this story dies in this office."

Sam hesitated before responding in anger, My story! My control! he thought defiantly. He hadn't expected Malcolm to go for the throat so quickly, and the longer he waited, the more ground he risked losing, so Sam decided to initiate Plan 'B'. 'B' was a real gamble, but he'd worked it over several times to hopefully cut off any dangerous routes it could take. Sam exhaled, concentrating on two words, *slow down*.

He looked down at his feet and began a slow, building laugh. While waggling a finger at Malcolm, he said, "Nice try, but you'll have to do better than that. I've already seen just a glimpse of how deep this story will go, and Malcolm, it hasn't even been touched yet."

For effect, Sam now resourced the extended finger, beginning to check off a list, continuing, "Two deaths; two innocent individuals murdered and made to appear accidental and unrelated, with me and only me able to connect and explain." Another finger joined the first. "A whole bunch of money rightfully belonging to the American people that seems to have been stolen and divvied up between a couple of crooked politicians."

Sam gave Malcolm a third finger metaphorically, continuing to build the drama. "Third, we have my personal brand of investigative reporting that has afforded me a large following of readers, along with an impressive group of enemies who secretly take pleasure in my attention directed toward targets other than themselves. And, last, it's *my* contact and I've promised this person to do absolutely everything within my power to keep him or her from harm. It's a promise I fully intend to keep."

Perhaps the last finger was a stretch, as the thought of him physically protecting Becklin from some unknown danger was, in nearly any situation, laughable. Glaring back at Malcolm, he believed he managed to sound convincingly unshakeable. After an uncomfortable moment and just before Sam's face began to cramp from trying to look intractable, Malcolm's expression gave way to either a crooked smile or a sneer.

Sam was content with either.

Malcolm turned away and retreated to the comfort of his massive desk, but swung around quickly, stating, "I'm giving you three weeks to confirm the pieces to this puzzle and I will, at that time, insist upon names of those involved, either living or non-living. You can have your private little 'Deep Throat' for now, but if this lead turns south, one way or another, I'll be knocking on doors with my own set of questions while you pound the streets looking for employment."

Sam rose and headed for the door without looking back, assuming he'd just been dismissed. With only three weeks, he needed to catch up to his boasted position before Malcolm pulled the rug out from under him.

CHAPTER 2

Sam sat uncomfortably at a restaurant bar still a bit unnerved. He took brief looks to his left, then right, wondering who might be watching his every move. Since leaving the office, he'd been making good headway with the abundance of information his contacts had fed him, but he's pushing the envelope in his attempt to keep it quiet. Sam took a long draught from his beer and thought, just inhale, exhale, then repeat.

So focused on trying to remain calm, he was startled when his girlfriend, Katie, touched his shoulder from behind. Jolting to his feet, Sam struck his bottle of beer in the process, but Katie caught the beer before it tipped over. Showing appreciation, Sam joked, "Nice save."

With a look of concern, Katie asked, "Are you okay?"

He shook off the jitters, finishing off the last two sips in one gulp, replying, "Sure. Yeah, just have some stuff on my mind from work and got distracted. Thanks for pulling me out of it, though," leaning in to kiss her.

The hostess approached, stating, "If your party is here now, Mr. Noll, your table is ready."

Sam turned to the hostess, saying, "Great!" Turning back to Katie, he inquired, "Are you ready for dinner?" Katie nodded as Sam gestured for her to take the hostess' lead before they navigated their way through the dinner rush to their table.

"Wine for starters?" asked the hostess while Sam politely held Katie's chair. He looked down at Katie for guidance, moving to his seat.

In response, Katie answered, "Yes, two house reds, please, Cabs preferably."

The hostess smiled, informing them, "Great, I'll let your server know and she'll have them for you right away. I hope you enjoy your dinners," before turning and walking away.

Sam beamed Katie a grin. Being more of a hops and barley guy, deferring wine selection to Katie had yet to disappoint. Katie took in the room, then turned back to Sam, whispering, "This is a nice place, Sam. What's the occasion?" Sam smiled mischievously and let the question go unanswered as he began to innocently peruse the menu. After the wine arrived, Sam held his glass up until Katie looked up and noticed him waiting for her. "Oops, sorry! You can dress her up, but can't take her fine dining!" she responded, grabbing her glass and mirroring his.

Sam started to become embarrassed until Katie held his eyes, giving him one of her special smiles, which did the 'calming' trick he'd grown to love. Sam cleared his throat, softly reciting, "To private moments and tender memories. May they last a lifetime," as their glasses touched.

Sam watched Katie sip her wine, appreciating how the warmth of it immediately invaded her body. Sam took an appreciative taste before Katie revisited her line of questioning, "So, tell me, what's with all the romance? Don't get me wrong, I love this surprising side of you with the wine, sweet toast, and dinner reservations. Did you get a big promotion or something?" Sam tried not to laugh at her stubborn resolve to uncover the truth. He had no doubt Katie would make a great reporter . . . or interrogator.

Katie innocently poked fun at Sam with, "Since I know where you stand on the whole marriage thing, I can only assume you won't be proposing, which is okay with me."

Sam stared at her blankly, asking, "Marriage 'thing'? I don't have a 'marriage thing'."

Katie chuckled, replying, "Sure you don't; as long as one of the people isn't you, or should it be persons?"

Sam answered out of reflex, "It should probably be 'individuals.' That's not the point. Why do you feel I don't want to get married? I'm curious now."

Katie tried to backtrack, "Oh, Sam, it's not a big deal. I'm not ready for marriage either. I mean, we've only been seeing each other six months."

Sam interjected, "Seven, actually."

Katie looked upward, doing the math in her head, "Okay, seven. Anyway, Sam, I just want you to know I love being with you, getting closer to you and seeing where this is going, regardless of *where* it's going. I just want you to know the last thing I would ever want to do is put any kind of pressure on you about anything."

Sam found himself speechless and wasn't certain how to proceed. His evening with Katie had detoured, and he felt trapped in a corner. Typically, the next words to come out of his mouth were always the wrong ones, but something had to fill the increasing gap. Before he had the chance to flail away, Katie saved the moment by throwing him a line of escape with a subtle shift in subject. "I don't suppose we're celebrating that you found a new roommate for me? Now that would be cause for some serious indulgence."

Sam exhaled his private gratitude for her unknown 'Hail Mary' before relenting, "Well, you'll have to be the judge. It's nothing really. I want you to think about something." Katie looked up from the menu, giving him her full attention, before he proceeded, "I was just wondering, with your roommate moving to Italy for two years and with you always complaining about how run-down your apartment building is, that, well, maybe you'd consider moving in with me; and Spalding, of course." Katie returned Sam's offer with a blank, emotionless stare. After only a moment of silence, Sam filled it in with, "Wow, Katie, you could clean up playing professional poker with that look."

Katie finally smiled broadly at Sam's admission of discomfort before saying, "Sorry; I just honestly didn't see this coming."

With a sheepish look down, still unsure of her answer. Sam added, "So, did I just step in it, or are we still okay?"

Inadvertently still holding him over a barrel by not answering his question, Katie blurted out, "Oh, Sam, I'd love to move in with you two." Sam didn't attempt to hide his show of relief, finally releasing the breath he'd been holding. Katie chuckled at Sam's expense before adding, "Are you sure about this, Sam? I don't want to get all excited about it and have you go and change your mind on me."

Sam leaned in to Katie, took a commanding breath, and softly replied, "I can't think of any reason you shouldn't, and I can't stop thinking of all the reasons you should." Katie met him across the table and kissed him deeply, softly.

Once back in their seats, they both quietly basked in the euphoric moment, before they're interrupted by the arrival of their server, "Are we ready to order?"

Sam smiled up at the waitress and then back at Katie, "Yes, I believe we are!"

Back at his apartment, Sam stood next to his bed smiling to himself while unbuttoning his shirt. He replayed in his head the bits and pieces of conversation and the thrown-together plan for Katie's upcoming change of address. Katie told Sam she couldn't wait to phone and update her sister, so they called it an evening, deciding she wouldn't spend the night; she'd be spending her share of sleep-overs soon enough.

Her excitement, he believed, was genuine and he found himself a bit giddy as well. Then, a dark cloud descended upon his momentary happy disposition as he removed his hand from his pants pocket and pulled the ring box from within.

He opened it and admired the simplicity of the gold ring and small faceted diamond, assuring himself again that Katie would absolutely love his selection. Yes, it had only been seven months, but Sam felt closer to Katie than anyone before, and he knew she was more than just someone special. She was perfect for him.

Opening his sock drawer, he looked at the ring one last time before closing the box and stuffing it into the back of the drawer. Perhaps tonight wasn't 'the' night. They'd have hundreds of other opportunities since she's moving in. The impromptu back-up plan worked out just fine, he convinced himself. He'd know when the time was right and gain a better idea for when she'd be ready. In the meantime, they'd get to know each other's pet peeves and cute little idiosyncrasies.

Turning to the mirror above the bureau, he stared at his reflection. "This is a much better way to go," he advocated to himself.

Israel, August, 1940

El Padre slowly walked up a cobblestone street, his head tilted slightly up, as if following distant music, but the faint, sad tune only he could hear. Mid street, he stopped and turned right, venturing down a short, narrow alley and without pausing, entered a windowless entryway to a side house anyone else would easily miss. He stood inside the door, allowing his eyes to adjust to the dark room.

In Hebrew, a voice, small and weak, penetrated through the blackness, "I have nothing to steal . . ." The words were left in the air unexpected of a response. With his vision acclimating to the dim light, El Padre saw a small bed straight ahead and a frail man lying within its blanket. He carefully moved across the uneven wood floor closer to the man in the bed in an attempt to feel his inner need, the thing which might bring him peace. The man surprised El Padre with a sudden, robust voice, "I have nothing but what I came into this life with; my soul!"

The old man cackled to himself and El Padre smiled with him, closing the final two feet to the edge of the bed. He took the man's hand and softly said in the man's language, "Your soul's protection is my only desire."

He watched the old man lift his head off the bed slightly and look up at him in fear, then quickly ease back into his pillow, a calm solace engulfing his being. "So, you're the boatman for the neshoma, then?" the old man asked, pressing his eyes closed.

El Padre continued to hold his hand, softly replying, "I am the one who has been sent by the only true reality, inviting you to bask in the Divine light for all eternity."

The old man smiled broadly with tears of joy beginning to well in his eyes. "I happily . . . accept this gracious invitation . . . with a humble heart," he confided, as the shortness of breath began to labor his speech.

Still unable to achieve any semblance of what the man required from him to find serenity in his fading moments on earth, El Padre knelt close to him, inquiring softly, "Has your life brought you contentment?"

In response, the man turned toward El Padre, and with tears now gently following one another in a wet line down his cheek, he stated in barely a whisper, "My wife . . . whom I adore . . . patiently waits. Let me . . . make her wait, no more." The old man's smile slowly relaxed, exhaling one last time before relinquishing his being to eternity.

Once passed, his eyes remained on El Padre. With his free hand, El Padre caressed the final tears from the old man's cheek and tenderly closed his eyes. El Padre placed the man's hand onto his chest and removed the blanket, spreading it onto the floor. Gently lifting the lifeless body, he placed him onto the middle of the blanket, covering him entirely. Moving toward the small kitchen, he opened several drawers until locating the candles, which he placed around the body. From within his pocket, he retrieved a small box of matches and went about lighting the candles, completing the proper Jewish ritual of caring for the dead.

Upon lighting the final candle, he's startled to find a boy of nine or ten now visible from the illumination of the candles sitting, watching motionless, in a chair in the far corner of the room. Surprised by not having perceived the lad before, El Padre stood and inquired, "Boy, who might you be?" The boy didn't answer, but returned El Padre's steady gaze for a moment before looking down at the old man shrouded within the blanket. El Padre followed his gaze to the old man and suddenly understood. "This is your grandfather, I believe. Is that correct, boy?" he asked. The boy stared at El Padre again and slowly nodded. He finished his consideration with, "And you have been assigned as the shomerim to guard over your grandfather when he passed, is this also true?"

The boy finally spoke, but without fear to his young voice, "Is his soul now with G-d?" following the correct manner in speaking of God taught to him through Jewish law.

El Padre looked deeply into the eyes of the lad before answering, "He is; and with your grandmother, whom he also loved greatly."

The boy further intrigued El Padre when he bravely asked, "Must you take me now, as well, since I've seen you?"

El Padre moved toward him, smiling, answering exaggeratedly, "I feel it is not your time. You have a duty to fulfill far beyond this day of mourning, and to remove you prematurely could alter the very threads of existence."

The boy looked up at El Padre, unruffled by the depth of their conversation, asking, "When shall you come for me then?"

El Padre squinted quizzically at the boy before finally responding, "Time weighs heavily upon your side. The scales favor a blessed life ahead for you. Do not worry yourself with circumstances beyond your or my restraint. For now, show respect for the kavod ha-met and aid in the comfort for the nihum avelim. Tomorrow shall take care of itself. Do you know who your village's chevra kaddisha might be and where he lives?"

The boy stood, revealing a birth defect that caused a deformation of his left hand, answering El Padre, "Yes, I know where to find him." He ended this with a long look upon his grandfather.

El Padre, following his line of thought, responded to the boy's unspoken dilemma, "I shall remain in your stead, as keeper of he who has passed on, until your return."

The boy once again looked into the eyes of the man who appeared to be the incarnation of Death and graciously smiled his appreciation. With the first sign of any emotion, the boy returned his attention to the bundle on the floor, saying with a weight well beyond his years, "My grandfather requested me to be his shomerim. Since my grandmother's passing and the destruction of our synagogue, we spent many hours here, hiding from the Germans, studying Hebrew. We feared each morning would be the day we would be found, but he remained with me, even though his health began to fail and others begged him to escape farther north."

Tears began to flow freely from the young boy's eyes as he spoke less from request but rather matter of fact. "I loved him with all that my heart allowed. He must be treated with the highest respect." The boy then purposefully walked across the room and out the door without looking back, leaving El Padre staring at the closed door.

Finally, he took the unoccupied seat left by the man's grandson, emptied his mind of all things, and looked down upon the body of the boy's grandfather, preparing to recite the Kaddish. After the moment of silence, El Padre spoke softly, slowly, in a revered cadence, "May His great Name grow exalted and sanctified in the world that He created as He willed. May He give reign to His kingship in your lifetimes and in your days, and in the lifetimes of the entire Family of Israel, swiftly and soon. Amen."

CHAPTER 3

Sitting at his desk at home deep in thought, Becklin stared at the phone next to the picture of his long deceased parents. After collecting his thoughts with what he'd say on the phone, Becklin glanced at the picture and wondered if they would be proud of him or of his 'patriotic' work in the past. Dad, he believed, would have accepted the things he'd done with a certain measure of guilty pride, but his Mother, being such a stout Methodist, would simply pray for his lost soul. Part of what he did, a part he constantly pushed back down for fear of it showing weakness or distraction, he did for them. In some way, he hoped there would be a deeper wisdom or understanding in Heaven that allowed clarity from narrow-mindedness, judgment, or doubt. Becklin saw a world run by evil, greedy men, and though his part in the fight against the evil was small or, even perhaps, insignificant, it's all he could do.

He smiled from the memory of a parable of the hummingbird and the forest fire. As the hummingbird flew back and forth from the small spring to the vast forest fire, dropping all the water it could carry onto the flames, the other forest denizens called out, "Humming bird, what are you doing?" The hummingbird simply responded, "What I can. I'm doing what I can."

Becklin shook the emotional thoughts of parents and parables and refocused on the job at hand. He dialed the number by memory and only waited two rings before it's answered. "Sixteenth Precinct, how can I be of service, sir or ma'am?" the desk sergeant recited.

Becklin responded in a slightly distressed manner, "Yes, I was the victim of a mugging last week. The detective, um, I have his name here somewhere . . ." Becklin shuffled some papers around on his desk, "Ahh, here it is, a Detective Bodnovitz. Do you need my case number?"

The sergeant quickly replied, "No, I don't need it, but Detective Bodnovitz doesn't come on shift until three, sir. Would you like me to direct you to his voice mail or is there someone else who might be able to assist you?"

Sounding anxious, Becklin replied, "Um, his voice mail would be fine, please. Thank you very much. I appreciate your help." Without further communication from the sergeant, Becklin was transferred to an outgoing message from Detective Bodnovitz to leave a short message after the beep.

Becklin hung up without leaving a message and grabbed his cell phone, hitting the speed dial for the phone he gave Sam Noll. After one ring, Sam answered, "This is Sam. When and where?"

Appreciating the seriousness given the circumstances, Becklin kept his response short as well "Eighteen-eighteen McColly Avenue. 2:15 p.m."

Sam paused briefly before acknowledging with, "Oh, really?"

Smiling at Sam's response, again gaining further respect for his choice of contacts, Becklin asked wryly, "I take it you know the address?"

Sam chuckled over the phone, "You certainly do like surprises, don't you?" Without a need for a response, Sam hung up.

Becklin moved to the master bathroom upstairs and began to change his appearance for their upcoming meeting, reflecting on how he decided on Sam as the right reporter for the assignment. He had breezed through the limited information on the web and performed the usual background check on him for any red flags. He knew Sam graduated from Cornell with degrees in Journalism and Theology and worked at two small papers before moving up to his current gig.

Sam's style of writing was what tipped the decision his way. A lot could be interpreted through how someone wrote, as true character always had a way of seeping into the written word. There didn't seem to be an arrogant bone in his body; only confidence. He had no interest in writing what others deemed to be the current trend; he followed his own path, which seemed to please a majority of his readers. There's never an infusion of some underlying, ulterior motive, nor did he venture down a path without doing enormous research. He simply wrote the unbiased facts and allowed readers to come to their own conclusions. The fact that Becklin simply liked the guy was an added bonus.

Staring at his altered reflection in the mirror, Becklin nodded his approval before checking his watch and deciding to make his way to the meeting place. He didn't want their arrival times too close together, just on the chance someone might notice. Perhaps all of his preparation and subterfuge were excessive, but in the realm of self-preservation, when it came to the subject of survival, overkill was always considered more acceptable over being killed. The cold thought of making one fatal mistake or relaxing any of his instincts followed him out the door toward his appointment downtown.

Sam slowly walked up the steps to the Sixteenth Precinct, taking a breath before opening the door. Odds favored he'd run into an officer or detective he'd crossed paths with through his line of work, so Sam had a prepared story for hanging around the station. Once inside, he scanned the entrance, front desk area, and waiting lobby, but it appeared he's first to arrive. This unnerved Sam more than he cared to admit, being Becklin hadn't seemed to be the type to run late.

The line at the front desk took a momentary break from angry victims for the desk sergeant to look up long enough, noticing Sam.

"Well, well, well, what have we done to be blessed with a visit from Mr. Noll?" he asked sarcastically.

Sam spun around from his search, quickly smiling his response. He moved closer to the desk, whispering in a secretive tone, "Actually, I'd appreciate it if you didn't mention I was here." The desk sergeant leaned in to adjust to Sam's hushed reply while Sam looked around before continuing. "I'm sniffing around for a story on abuse of new officers, you know, within the lower ranks. There's a nasty rumor of new recruits being mentored into the whole 'blue shield' ideology of 'you watch my back; I watch my back' and how it harbors a rift between old school versus rookies; should be a real eye-opener!"

The desk sergeant moved back into his seat and looked around quickly, stammering, "Uhh, well, good luck with that, Mr. Noll. But I have no comment on whatever you're talking about. I've gotta get back to work now. Have a nice day." He immediately grabbed the phone and began dialing while Sam walked away feeling assured he wouldn't be bothered by the boys in blue for several weeks.

After roaming around the lobby for a few moments, Sam decided to move to the waiting area just around the corner from the entrance. Once seated, he scanned the room again, this time looking at the variety of people waiting to be heard. The only thing seemingly tying them to commonality was their dwindling patience. An attractive, older Eastern Indian couple entered the fray. With only single seats available, they stood for only a moment before a man with long, black hair, Yankees cap, and large bandage by his left eye offered them his seat, allowing them to sit together. After showing their appreciation, the man with the bandage picked up a section of the newspaper and walked toward an empty seat next to Sam.

Once seated to his left, the man opened the paper, saying to Sam, "What this waiting room really needs is some good Culture Club music, don't you think?"

Sam took a slow, appreciative look at Becklin's disguise before turning forward again, saying quietly, "I can't decide if you look like a roadie for some grunge band or Frank Zappa reincarnated. The bandage is a nice touch; pulls the attention from the hair."

Easing quickly into business, Becklin asked, "Did you lose the phone?"

Sam adjusted his mood in the attempt toward serious with, "Swimmin' with the fishes."

Becklin followed further, inquiring, "And the SIM card?"

Sam looked the other direction, answering, "Blender; pulverized." Becklin nodded his approval while Sam turned to Becklin, adding, "Was that 'fish' line right? Is that how you say it?"

Becklin turned the page with his paper, replying, "I wouldn't know. I'm not with, nor ever have been, connected to the Italian mafia."

Disappointed, Sam continued, "Oh. Well, the phone is at the bottom of the Hudson."

Becklin made nearly an unnoticeable gesture with his right hand, and a new cell phone appeared on Sam's left knee, which he casually slid into his jacket pocket. Becklin, still speaking through the paper, quietly murmured, "Same drill; one call and done. Got it?" Sam slowly nodded as a large man in suspenders got up and walked in front of them on his way to check on the progress of his internment.

Both men watched the large man for a moment, though Becklin's ability to look at someone without actually looking at them allowed their intentions to be less obvious. Once the man was deemed safe, Becklin resumed their conversation. "Who have you spoken to about this so far, and how much have you shared?"

Sam tried to duplicate Becklin's audible level, but with little success. "The only person who knows is my editor, Malcolm Vassault. I told him what little I knew; about the two unconnected murders, the stolen money, and that it's being run by somebody way up the political ladder. He's letting me pursue it, but wants quick results. He's giving me three weeks to turn it in, or else . . ."

Sam let his boss's threat linger and waited a moment while Becklin pondered before he finally asked, "Can Vassault be trusted?"

Ouch! The one question Sam didn't want to answer. Finally, Sam admitted, "He's a worm of a man and fought me pretty hard on the specifics at first and pushed for names of those involved, but I think his main concern is geared toward increased circulation. This story is the kind of thing that keeps the press rolling, and he believes I've got a good lead, otherwise he wouldn't have cut me loose, right?"

Becklin softly responded with "Hmm," then silence again. Sam waited patiently, before Becklin shifted gears forward. "So, what's next? What are your questions for me?"

Caught off guard, Sam only had to think for a second before diving in with, "Just exactly how *did* this thing drop into your lap, as you put it?"

Becklin turned another page of the paper dropping his volume one more octave "Did you find out who the two victims were?"

Sam looked up at the ceiling, recalling the information. "Yeah, a finance guy named Gregory Haskins and some administrative assistant from North Carolina named Yvonne Draski."

Becklin kept the direction rolling with, "Yvonne and I knew each other. We met on one of those Internet dating sites. We'd been exchanging messages and decided to take the next step and meet for dinner. She was spunky; soft brown hair and big brown, caring eyes; a nice girl. After dinner, we decided to have a glass of wine. She was telling me about what she did for a living and how she worked out of three offices, North Carolina, D.C., and here in New York, then, out of the blue, she brought up how the last guy she'd met online had been killed two weeks previously and hoped I would have better luck surviving our first date."

Becklin paused before slowly turning briefly to look at Sam, then quickly returned his attention to his paper before proceeding. "I've . . . done some things in the past, professionally, that tend to revisit me from time to time. If she hadn't mentioned what she did for work, then tell me about the guy being killed so closely together, I probably would have missed it, but let's just say the training

I've endured a lifetime ago has left a lasting divot on my back nine!" Sam didn't quite follow the golf analogy, but felt validated about Becklin's questionable past and supplied his ally with an agreeable nod.

His disguised contact continued. "Anyway, the two comments nagged at me for a couple days before I decided to look into it. I did some research and read up on who the guy was and what he did, and after some digging, it turned out he financed large sections of a company in the running to build the new ship terminal on the coast of North Carolina. In fact, they were his largest account by far."

Becklin disgustedly shook his head before proceeding. "Then along comes Yvonne, innocent Yvonne, looking for love in all the wrong places, and who does she get hooked up with? The money man for a company trying to build a shipyard that's being organized by Yvonne's boss, Senator Kyle Sinclair. Yvonne was about three times removed from working with the Senator directly, but the connection must have scared too many pocketbooks, which put a containment order in place."

Sam stared at the newspaper as if it wasn't actually there, asking, "And by containment, you mean . . . ?"

Without any emotion to his voice, Becklin furthered Sam's imperious education with, "They covered their tracks before any damage could be done; they silenced both of them so that nothing would impede their big plans of hedging their financial future. Damned shame, too; she was a sweet girl. I liked her."

Sam got an idea, blurting it out before using his filter. "Wait a minute. If she was under surveillance, wouldn't they know you met her and figure out who you are?"

Realizing his voice went beyond the acceptable level, Sam calmed himself down before Becklin responded, "I doubt very much the people on Yvonne had the kind of clearance needed to take a peek at me. All they saw was a lonely building contractor showing a romantic interest in their girl. They don't want to eliminate every person connected to either of them in fear of attracting a huge, bright spotlight on their big, bad business. I believe they think they got away with it Scott-free. And let me tell you something, Sam, I really want to sink their boat!"

Sam stared at the man behind the paper, again wishing he could throw him a little emotional support, but he reconsidered knowing it wasn't exactly the right venue for the two to start bonding in public. All he could do at this juncture was work hard on the story and break it as soon as he could. Emotional support could come later, if they survived. Sam moved away from the dark side with, "You had mentioned politicians, meaning more than one. Who else do you think is involved?"

Becklin rattled the paper and paused for a moment, in case the noise might have drawn someone's unwanted attention. After scanning the room, Becklin resumed. "That, I don't know. But to pull open the government purse strings for a new mega shipyard for the world's import/export business would require more than just one senator sitting on the Committee of Ways and Means. I'm just hypothesizing, but I would say you'd need someone inside the Appropriations, Banking, and Commerce, and maybe even someone involved with the Surface Transportation Board if they plan to profit off the back end as well."

Sam's face grew immediately pale, looking up from taking notes. Sam received a look from his partner in anti-crime with Becklin adding, "I know, Sam. But it's not why I selected you for this cat-n-mouse job."

Sam looked into Becklin's disguised face for any hint of enjoyment, and after seeing none, decided to believe him. Staring forward for a moment, Sam asked, "So, you know all about my 'history' with the STB, then?" He didn't turn toward Becklin for the answer; he didn't need to. Sam recoiled with just a fractional memory from exposing the drug ring within the railway system three years previous. Sixteen people indicted, along with two ranking board members who would still be serving time during

Sam's retirement party. He still had nightmares of two eighty-plus-year-old men with walkers crashing his retirement party pumping lead into his going-away cake. Ahh, the life of those who pursued to expose the guilty; how grand and exciting.

Sam realized Becklin wasn't risking his hide for Sam to wallow in his own past and turned to Becklin, asking "Okay, I'll start connecting the dots and shake a tree or two and see what falls on my head. When can I expect a call? You can give me just a ballpark. I'm not trying to sound clingy."

Becklin gave Sam one of his rare, uncomfortable smiles, answering, "Tuesday. I'm thinking something in the afternoon."

Sam slowly got up to leave, whispering, "Then it's a date!"

Ten minutes later, Becklin slowly rose from his seat, laid the paper down, and sauntered out of the waiting area and down the hall to the bathroom. After stalling at the sink and giving his hands a slow, thorough washing, he exited the men's room and picked up his pace, preparing to leave the building, only to walk past the Detective he'd scheduled to meet.

Becklin cursed the poor timing under his breath. While slipping out the front door he heard the desk sergeant calling for Detective Bodnovitz, as the detective began ascending the stairs. Once out the door and down the front steps, Becklin discretely shed the baseball cap, long hair, and bandage, depositing the wig and bandage into the trash receptacle on the left, and the hat into the matching trash can on the right. Picking up his pace heading north, he slid his dark jacket off, carrying it over his arm.

Before getting a safe distance from the precinct, he heard a man yelling at him while pulling the Yankees cap out of the trash. "Hey! That's sacrilegious!" Wiping off the hat and placing it on his head, the Yankee fan walked past Detective Bodnovitz, who'd just arrived at the sidewalk to locate the mystery mugging victim. Yelling over his shoulder, the man with a new hat exclaimed, "Damn Mets fans! They need to stay on *their* side of the river!"

From across the street, a man in a black leather jacket and dark stocking cap stepped out from a depression in the building. He watched as the detective finally gave up on locating anyone matching the desk sergeant's description and returned to the precinct. After looking down the sidewalk in the direction Becklin had gone, he made a call on his cell phone, following Becklin.

CHAPTER 4

Sam sat on the edge of his sofa, staring at the blank screen of his laptop. His dog, Spalding, a mixture of gray, black, and white Border Collie, laid upside-down, asleep next to him. His first thought when the story arrived on his doorstep via the mysterious Mr. Becklin was to follow the money. Find the money, and everything else would come together. It sounded a lot easier than it actually was, though, as politicians on high had nothing but time to figure countless ways to hide their blood money from the people who elected them. They could move, exchange, withdraw, and redeposit their greedy sums a thousand times a day, thanks to the Internet and wire transfers to various discrete banks in thirty different countries.

All someone needed to do was find the initial deposit; the thirst quencher that put a big, fat smile on their target's face, allowing them to truly believe all the broken laws and severed promises they swore to uphold were worth their thirty pieces of silver.

Of course, locating this hypothetical pile of cash would require knocking on some extremely sensitive doors and fluffing a number of high-powered feathers. It would take time and resources Sam wasn't privy to, but over the course of the three days since first meeting Becklin, Sam was struggling with a different angle of attack.

Sitting there, playing the entire scenario out inside his head, Sam broke through a big mental block and rode the moment of clarity. He slowly reached over to the end table and grabbed the phone to call Ira, without disrupting Spalding's slumber. The money would be, as it always was, the bad guy's bargaining chip for a plea deal, so forget the money trail. To get the party rolling, he wouldn't require much of anything. All he needed to do was turn the fan on high. The crap was already waiting.

Ira answered on the third ring, "Ira Nevins, Archives."

Sam spoke quickly, "Ira, it's Sam. Any chance you could locate a number for me? I'm talking about someone's personal cell number; someone . . . politically tenured."

Ira's slow way of processing information bothered a number of colleagues, but Sam was used to it, always giving him some measured patience. After a wheezy sigh from the other end of the line, Ira relented, "What's the name?"

Sam rattled off, "Kyle Sinclair" as if it were just someone whom no one had heard of before.

This time, Ira was quicker with his thought process, shrieking into the phone, "You mean, *Senator* Kyle Sinclair from North Carolina? Chairman for the Ways and Means Committee; *that* Kyle Sinclair?"

Sam couldn't help but enjoy hearing Ira become emotional, since it hadn't happened since Watergate. Sam calmly brought Ira off the ledge with, "Ira, I wouldn't ask for it unless I was absolutely certain of what I was getting myself into."

Ira dropped back down in volume and pitch, responding dryly, "Forget about you, Sam. I'm more concerned with *my* participation!"

Sam waited only a second before closing in on him, asking, "So, can you get it or can't you?"

After what seemed like an unusual amount of consideration, even for Ira, he snapped back with, "I'll have to call you back. It's not exactly something I have here on my rolodex!" which was followed by an immediate 'click' from the phone, ending the conversation.

Sam laughed to himself at the impending setup. It started as an innocent experiment back in college. In his third year of Philosophy class he tested an idea that some people were worthy of trust and

others were not. He discussed the theory with his professor one day
after class and with his consent, began a test of trustworthiness which
resulted in an average of eighty-nine percent unable to keep a secret.

The same situation applied to the workplace, though, and after
getting Senator Sinclair's direct number from Ira, Sam was willing
to gamble his fate on it. Chuckling to himself, Sam grabbed his hat
and jacket, asking his audience of one, "We should at least see if the
old theory remains true, shouldn't we?"

Spalding lifted his head from the sofa in response to his owner's
inquiry, tilted his head to the right, and offered a low, muffled,
"Woof" before Sam headed out the door laughing at his perception
of Spalding's agreement.

Sam nervously waited, holding the pay phone while it continued to
ring endlessly. Only a crooked, self-righteous senior senator from North
Carolina would put someone through this many rings, Sam thought.

At last, a young woman picked up with, "Senator Sinclair's
assistant, may I ask who's calling?"

Caught off guard, Sam paused before saying, "No, you may not.
Would this be Victoria Young, Chief Assistant to Senator Sinclair?"

She curiously responded more warmly, "Um, yes, this is she.
How may I help you, sir?"

Sam moved the phone receiver directly under his mouth with his
gloved hand to ensure every word was enunciated correctly. "Let
the Senator from North Carolina know that I can almost hear the
ships rolling in the money to port with the sounds of ka-ching, ka-
ching!" Immediately, Sam hung up, pulled his cap down a bit lower,
stuffed his hands deeply into his pockets and calmly flew the scene.

Vietnam, 1971

From his vantage point, El Padre paused from writing in his
journal, taking in the leafy, rolling hills before him. Completing

his weekly additions to his leather journal, he placed it back into his backpack while finishing his lunch of bread and dried meats. Slowly, he stood, stretching his back in an attempt to work out some of the soreness from a rocky night's sleep and took a long drink of water from his canteen before stowing it away. He'd successfully avoided a small band of V.C. the day before and, though he knew he could stay clear of any complications, he needed to get moving if he's going to find the squad he sought before nightfall.

Vietnam, this time of year, wasn't in the top of El Padre's list of countries to visit, but he appreciated the temporary break from the rain. Unfortunately, there's war here, and with it, there's death. He's drawn toward it like a moth to the light. Just before beginning his descent of the small hill, El Padre crouched, reacting to a sound coming from below near a crop of shrubs and rock, not fifty yards from his position. Attempting to ascertain which side of the battle was being represented, he caught a glimpse of the black pyjama uniform commonly worn by the Vietnamese.

El Padre watched the man fall and remain there for a moment long enough to convince El Padre that the man was injured. With his eyes closed, he placed his focus on the resting man and confirmed the injuries to his leg and right arm. Knowing the Vietnamese soldier wasn't at risk of expiring from his wounds, El Padre drew on the man's desire to continue his own journey east and away from his position above. Once the man began to rise, the rifle strap slipped off his shoulder and in the effort to retrieve his weapon, he turned and looked directly at El Padre sitting atop the hill.

Forgetting his pain from the injuries, the man immediately drew his rifle in the direction of the stranger and laboriously rose to meet the enemy. El Padre raised his hands, and in the man's language and dialect, declared, "I mean you no harm, my friend. I am not a soldier nor do I carry anything to cause you further injury." In response, the Vietnamese soldier looked down at his bleeding arm before staggering slightly from his attempt to hold the rifle steady.

El Padre began to cautiously approach the man, but the soldier yelled in Vietnamese, "I'll shoot you!" El Padre stopped, looked into the man's eyes, and realized he's only a boy of about fourteen or fifteen.

El Padre lowered his head slightly and, in a calming voice, said, "I have bandages and cleaning agents that I might use for your arm and leg. I only wish to take away the pain and infection and help you continue your journey. May I approach?"

Appearing unaccustomed to hearing his native tongue from a white man, particularly one willing to heal his injuries rather than inflict them, the young soldier surprisingly dropped his defenses and nodded his invitation for El Padre to advance.

Once he approached the young man, El Padre extended his arm for the boy to brace himself against, leading them both over to level ground and assisted him down onto the soft ground.

Understanding the young man's obvious lack of trust, he proffered, "I require items from my backpack. May I retrieve them?" The soldier nodded his consent, his attention turning from El Padre to his bleeding leg and arm. While removing the first aid items from inside his bag, he reached into the front pocket to pull out some of his bread and meat and handed it to the young man, who wasted no time devouring all of it. El Padre said with a grateful smile, "I take it you were hungry, then?" as he began to work on the soldier's arm, cleaning it carefully.

With food now occupying the emptiness of his stomach and less blood being lost from his body, the Vietnamese man began speaking comfortably, stating, "I've been traveling for one day and a half. No food nor water, only this gun and two injuries as company. I was separated from my older brother and six others after we came across a small band of American soldiers. There was much fighting and many were shot, including me. I escaped with two others, but they both died from their wounds. I covered their bodies and slept between them, hoping to slip past the enemy the next morning. Thankfully, I didn't see anymore Americans, but neither did I see my brother nor our fellow soldiers. You're the first person I've seen since the exchange of fire."

El Padre began working on the young man's second wound, only to realize the bullet remained inside his leg. El Padre gently placed a hand upon the young man's shoulder and explained, "The bullet remains lodged within the wound on your leg. I can remove it, but it will not be easy and will be quite painful. There is a chance you may lose consciousness during the removal. Do you still wish that I assist you?"

With little choice and unable to proceed further with the injury to his leg, the Vietnamese soldier consented, saying, "Don't let me die. I must find my brother and return him home."

Already knowing his brother had been killed during the skirmish, El Padre agreed to finish the work on the leg and keep him from harm. Once the young man was strong enough to travel, he'd encourage him to return home and tell his family of their eldest son's bravery in the face of certain death and let the memory of him carry on for many, many years.

It wasn't necessary for him to know the cruel fashion his brother was killed or even that his own injuries were inflicted by his compatriot's weapon. War was their constant existence, and how a man died wasn't nearly as important as how a man lived. El Padre would catch up to the squad at a later date, or perhaps he wouldn't.

The need for him in this country seemed endless, and he's certain there would be countless opportunities for his unique gift. He helped the young man, not out of pity nor promised servitude. El Padre believed in divine intervention and witnessed it far too many times to dispute it. Over the years he'd become acutely aware of the smallest examples of that which lied between. The young Vietnamese soldier turning and seeing him had purpose, and not even El Padre would intervene predetermined events, nor fill the gaps with his wasted curiosity. He knew what his calling was and to some extent, where, but never exactly why.

El Padre's thread of life was long and rarely crossed others who were not at the end. When the opportunity presented itself to engage with those allowed to carry on, he reveled within those precious moments and took a restrictive immunity to impress upon them the value of their life. Whether the young Vietnamese soldier chose to cast aside his fight and strive for a deeper responsibility or die another day for his country in this continuing conflict or the next was unknown. For now, he'd live another day and continue to exercise his free will, and El Padre's responsibility was left to hope for the best.

CHAPTER 5

Sam knew his contradictory weaknesses all too well. He trusted too easily, but kept people he cared for at a distance. He bravely fought for those around him, yet could rarely apply such tenacity when it had to do with personal affronts. His present conundrum had to do with his appreciation for letting things play out, yet far too often allowed his impatience to rush the events. He's the perfect patsy, he thought.

Sadly, to make matters worse, regardless of knowing all these facts he's unable to help himself. Just like a gambler with money in his pocket, Sam had to push his luck. Instead of staying home and waiting for his plan to play itself out, or better yet, going into the office to quietly keep a pulse on the action, he needed to bear witness first hand.

Unfortunately, Ira did Sam an inadvertent disservice. Not only was Ira able to attain the senator's private number, but going above and beyond, as he's known for, afforded Sam the senior senator's complete itinerary for the week. Sam changed clothes, checked his watch, and started for the door, convinced his commitment to the First Amendment and the people's right to know would keep him from personal harm.

With only a hesitation of self-reproach, remembering how ignorance could manifest itself into blind faith if the person closed his eyes hard enough, Sam pushed aside the momentary doubt, grabbed his keys and exited out the door toward his half-plan.

Standing inside the dark entry of a closed bookstore, Sam watched from half a block from where Senator Sinclair was preparing to leave a dinner meeting with various members of his staff at an upscale Chinese restaurant. Taking the liberty of occasional peeks in the direction of the front door to the restaurant, Sam began to feel for the first time his feeble attempt of surveillance was perhaps a bit over-zealous.

When a dark sedan rolled up in front of him and the front passenger window opened only three inches, Sam moved his previous consideration to assurance. Waiting for the scene to play out, Sam remained frozen, unable to keep from staring at the cracked window. Realizing he looked like a stationary silhouette at a gun range, he finally allowed an exhale, when an unknown man's voice summoning him, was the only thing exiting the window's three inch gap. The calm, beckoning request luring him to the car allowed Sam a chance to collect himself as best as possible, realizing if they wanted him dead, he'd already be a chalk line.

Leaning closer to the car, Sam peered in, unable to see who was in the car or even how many occupants resided within. The man's tranquil voice again asked politely, "Would you like to step inside the car, Mr. Noll, or rather have our chat as we presently are with me inside and you curiously leaning in?"

Sam stood in reaction to the offer, giving it a moment of respectful consideration. Once inside the car, he'd be completely at their disposal to do with him as they desired, but his curiosity of just exactly who 'they' were moved his feet closer to the sedan, pulling open the back door to get in.

The driver stared straight forward, seemingly content to remain oblivious to anything taking place around him. The only other passenger was the man who invited him into the car. He appeared to be in his early forties, with dark hair, dark suit, and an unmistakable clean-cut look that reeked of smooth politics. Though Sam couldn't recognize him, nor had he ever seen him out stomping the governmental pathways of the continental United States, he figured he's extremely connected and well financed.

Sam's attention remained fixed to the back of the front passenger's head when the car slowly pulled away from the sidewalk without anyone making any inquiries or suggested destinations. Finally, the man in front turned around to face his backseat traveler. His face was clean shaven and flawless, but beyond that, unremarkable.

Without providing animation to his expression, the man in black stated, "There's no need in trying to size me up, Mr. Noll. You don't know me, because our paths have never crossed before tonight. I will tell you that we're in opposing fields, with drastically different hopeful conclusions, and that's all you'll need to know about me."

During the brief pause, Sam verbally stuck the man in black, with, "I can't even know your first name? Come on! Mine is Sam; what's yours?"

With a straight face that didn't appear to falter for any reason, the man offered, "Albert. You may call me Albert."

Sam smiled from the back seat, thinking that it's probably the last name he would have picked for the guy, before returning with, "Cool! Albert; that's a good name for you. It suits you."

Albert returned Sam's approval with an unemotional, "What we're here to discuss . . . well, allow me to reword that, inform. Yes, to inform you would be more prudent in this situation, since you, Sam, are *not* in the driver's seat, as you may have observed."

Sam looked down and chuckled, saying, "Now, Albert, that's a well-constructed statement, both literally and figuratively. Are you certain we aren't in the same line of business, cuz you seem to have quite a way with words?"

Ignoring the rhetorical question, Albert proceeded. "You, my friend, have been traveling down a path that can neither be substantiated nor proven. All you're doing is causing a slight bump in the road and possibly harming the chances of a great man following through on an even greater mission."

Sam returned a look of dismay at Albert's comment before responding with, "Great mission? Are we talking about the same Kyle Sinclair?"

With a hint of impatience, Albert replied, "Yes, the man is not only a frontier in development, but aside from infusing over twelve hundred jobs into a distressed region, he'll be announcing his intentions toward a fact-finding mission, starting in the Midwest."

Sam dropped his head in disappointment, verbalizing the conclusion, "He's running for President in the next election."

Albert followed it up with, "You, Sam, are to be the first member of the media to be the recipient of this, as yet, unbroken story, as well as the opportunity for you to have exclusive rights to unlimited personal interviews, within reason, with the Senator as he prepares for his run. Of course, that is, as long as you 'cease and desist' any further advancement to this wild-haired notion that Senator Sinclair is anything but the upstanding American we all know and love."

Before Albert, or whatever his real name was, finished his offer, Sam had already recognized it as nothing more than a sales pitch with a heavy payment plan. Immediate decline could result in a negative counter offer, which Sam quite possibly would be forced to swallow, if he was still able to function the act of swallowing.

Getting into the car was to be blamed on Sam's curiosity of who's behind the great curtain, but getting out of Oz was going to rely on his answer to the offer. Access to a man running for President had its 'up' side, but this particular candidate was someone Sam didn't care for, and certainly didn't want running the country. Regardless of his obvious faults, Senator Sinclair was a popular Congressman and had done a great deal for his state. Sam, although, had been given a rare glimpse of the politician without his mask, and therein was all the truth needed to tip the scale.

Sam cleared his throat, staring out the car window, as freedom passed by in a blur, and began his response slowly. "This offer, I assume, has an expiration date?"

Albert, who hadn't taken his eyes off his backseat occupant since he first turned around, expected the question, answering, "Twenty-four hours, Mr. Noll. And at that time, or hopefully before, we expect to hear from you, but please don't use the previous cell phone number. The Senator is a busy man, as I'm sure you can imagine." Albert extended Sam a business card. "Here's a number where I may be reached, and that way we can keep this conversation's substance between us, where it belongs."

Sam inspected the card, but it only had a boldly printed phone number with no name or address, not even a company logo. The irony of Albert giving him the understated card wasn't lost on Sam, chuckling as he said, "Well, Albert, I must say, whatever business you're in, you should look into better advertising personnel."

The sedan pulled up to the front of Sam's apartment, mutely emphasizing the adage, "We know where you live," While Sam stared out at his building's entrance, Albert added, "Oh, and Mr. Noll; sorry to sound overly melodramatic, but let's keep this visit between us, and only us, shall we?"

Sam opened the car door, pausing before getting out, answering, "Yeah, right."

Watching the car slip into traffic, losing itself within the metallic yellow and black of cab drivers and other city dwellers, Sam breathed a sigh of relief for surviving the brush with never being heard from again. With his moment of continuing existence past, he sprinted into the building and up the several flights of stairs as his concern turned to Katie, stopping at the door to take a deep breath for the appearance of being under control.

Once inside, he scanned the room for anything out of the ordinary before being startled by Katie coming out of the kitchen eating ice cream out of a coffee cup. Sam closed the gap, taking her into his arms, holding her tightly. Katie simply let him hold her without question. The answers could come later, and if the ice cream happened to melt, Sam would happily get her more.

Pennsylvania, 1984

With the church relatively empty, El Padre sat contentedly mid-row of the auditorium. With evening mass still three hours away, he found much pleasure in the quiet solitude inside the place of worship before it became filled with so many looking to give praise and receive absolution. El Padre believed a church was, without doubt, the best place to be closest to God, and during the most difficult of times, often searched out refuge from various holy places. Whether it was a temple, synagogue, stake, or shrine, he'd bowed at them all, allowing his own faith to entwine with others, knowing no matter where he knelt, he's always heard.

Certainly, thinking back, there'd been many times in his long life that he'd experienced a simple, makeshift lean-to transform itself into a cathedral of God when the heart was right. Buildings were but four walls and a roof, giving the occupants temporary protection from the elements, but a place of worship gave them so much more; hope, direction, understanding, and unconditional love for a lifetime and beyond.

The priest from the church interrupted El Padre's meditation, quietly entering from a front passageway near the raised platform. He watched the church's leader carry a small stack of papers and a Bible that he stowed away inside the podium for later retrieval.

El Padre applied his gift with just a thought, emitting a gentle suggestion for the priest to return to his private chambers without noticing him. When a notepad fell to the floor from the podium's inner shelf, the priest turned, looking up to see someone sitting alone in the empty auditorium. Responding to his unspoken question, El Padre replied, "No, Father, I am not one of your parishioners. I am only a man in search of divine intervention in a world filled with self-righteousness and greed, enjoying the quietness of the moment in your church, with your approval, of course?"

The priest stepped off the platform, approaching El Padre, responding, "Naturally, all are welcome, as this is no more my church than it is yours, endowed to us by the good Grace of our Heavenly Father. Do you know Christ, my son, if I may ask such a personal opening question?"

El Padre considered the matter and lowered his head, answering humbly, "Our paths have seemed to intersect more than not through the direct witness of His work. I know of His desire for us to be with Him, though we all have transgressed and certainly come short of His Grace."

Approaching the pew where the visitor sat, the priest nodded his agreement and took the seat in front of him, sitting sideways, continuing on the topic, saying, "Yes, Christ's love is beyond our comprehension, and it's because of that love that He died on the cross for our sins. Do you know He died for you, my son?"

El Padre looked up slowly and met the priest's question, looking deeply into his eyes, before finally answering, "Each day I awake and welcome the new day He has provided and all that He has in store for me. The air that I inhale, the food that I partake, even the clothes that I wear, are simple gifts from Him allowing me to go about my work. Not one sun has seen its setting that which I have not thought about His great sacrifice. Not one."

The priest looked intently at the man seated behind him, and studied his face for a moment before offering, "You appear to be a godly man, sir. May I ask your name?"

El Padre lowered his head once again in reverence and simply answered, "I am just a vessel, guided by the light, traveling from port to port in the hope of bringing peace and comfort to those who require it most."

The priest accepted the response without pressing the issue further, commenting, "It's a selfless path you lead, my fellow believer, and the journey must be long and weary for you with so many in need of such reward. Surely, if it's as you say, the Lord must hold you in great favor."

El Padre flinched from the words, suddenly realizing he'd given the priest more information than he need hear. Attempting to maneuver the discussion elsewhere, he asked, "This sermon you intend to deliver; what, may I ask, will it offer your congregation?"

The priest smiled, answering, "I always hope for absolution as they enter, but I accept their humbled recognition of His existence by the time they leave."

El Padre stood, retrieving his coat from the back of his pew before stopping and looking down at the priest still sitting, commenting, "Courage and faith must breathe the same air, walk the same path. To have one and not the other is like eating food without experiencing its taste." The priest just stared up at El Padre with a confused expression, so El Padre fed him a little more direct insight with a bit less depth, saying, "Never settle, Father. It has been my experience that the fear of the unknown is often more than enough incentive for God's children to find immediate desire for penitence."

The priest watched El Padre exit the church in silence as he began to wonder just who exactly he'd been speaking with.

El Padre entered the bright light of midday and squinted at the cloudless sky. He mentally chastised himself for contributing so much to the conversation with the priest and tried to understand why he felt the need to speak so openly. His private affairs were his own burden to carry, as were his blessings when he gave praise.

The priest's comment of being held in high favor with the Lord for his selfless deeds, for some reason, burned deeply, and El Padre struggled to ascertain its cutting edge. He believed in his endeavor and placed his trust that what he did, he did not for glory, but for divine righteousness; he's a tool, nothing more. One didn't extol the plow, but rather the plower, knowing the plow was but the instrument of the gifted hand, and to consider just rewards for services rendered made him feel as though his life was nothing more than a worker awaiting his expected commission.

No, the contemplation of such material rewards was but a downward path toward self-righteousness and sin, which he chose to avoid many, many years hence. How odd, though, to have felt temptation after so many miles ventured. The long-faded memory of the enticement brought a slight chuckle to El Padre before he continued down the city sidewalk.

Becklin was already lost in thought, bent over in his entryway, lacing up his running shoes. Running had been his constant in a life filled with trying to remain inconsistent. It allowed his mind a certain chance for clarity, enabling him to figure out his toughest dilemmas. He wasn't on the pavement yet, and he'd already made progress. He'd deciphered where the leak was, but needed time to conceive a plan to ferret out the proof to exploit the person or persons responsible for the leak.

Becklin exited his house and moved onto the sidewalk at a casual walk, adjusting his breathing for a long run. He took into account how listening to each word a person used, and how they stressed certain phrases, had always been his best source of beneficial information. Becklin knew that Sam had picked up on something, yet he wasn't sure of, nor did he understand, what he knew, but that didn't keep him from unintentionally relaying his doubt to Becklin at their last meeting. Sam's responsibility was to follow the lead and run with it; Becklin's was to cover Sam's six and clear his path. His friend hadn't filtered it out yet, but he would. It's time, though, to find out what Sam's editor knew, because odds were in favor he had ulterior motives for being alarmed by Sam's impending story. Picking up his pace, Becklin decided all he needed to do was figure a way to get to Malcolm, and then he'd make him talk.

At about the third mile, Becklin noticed his breathing was becoming much more labored than usual and his instincts kicked in immediately. When he suddenly veered off the running path to take a short cut to the emergency room, he nearly knocked over two female joggers beside the park's sidewalk, stretching before their run.

He had no time for apologies. If what he's experiencing was indeed the beginnings of heart failure, he needed to be on a gurney with some form of medical professional standing over him within eight minutes or he was dead. The closest hospital was only three minutes away, but he needed to be conscious enough to explain his condition. With the pain building within his left arm and the dryness to his mouth, he's certain it's some sort of fast-acting poison he either ingested or absorbed, perhaps by a liquid or powder.

Then, as the first wave of painful convulsions hit him, he suspected what they used to get to him; his running shoes. It had to be. He was borderline obsessive-compulsive when it came to covering his tracks, but running was his one Achilles heel, so to speak. With the hospital in view, Becklin dropped to the sidewalk across the street from the entrance. Lying on his back, while people tried to assist him, he's unable to speak, struggling to kick off his running shoes. In a violent rage he forced himself up from the ground with people trying to help him stand, and half crawled, half stumbled in his stocking feet toward the automatic sliding door.

Once inside, the trained hospital staff responded immediately as Becklin collapsed in the entryway. He's lifted onto a gurney as two nurses, an orderly, and a doctor started on his vital signs, wheeling him into the first available exam room. Becklin tried to speak, fiercely grasping the hand of the orderly, squeezing with all his might, but could only focus on his dwindling heartbeat that's easily heard within his ears, slowing its pace to silence. He could hear a gentle voice echoing inside his head, even while he tried to force his own desperate words to escape.

The medical team reacted on impulse to his going into arrest and began CPR until the paddles were charged and the current was run through his chest. After three desperate attempts to bring him back, the doctor called for the time of death.

With no identification and no one able to explain what happened or who he was, the staff covered the unknown man wearing a runner's outfit, but no shoes.

CHAPTER 6

Sam walked into his office building wondering if his new friend, Albert, was watching him through binoculars from twenty stories above. He hadn't gotten to bed until after two, catching Katie up on all of the sordid details of his recent business, breaking his usual detached effort when working on a difficult story. She listened calmly and even nodded at the appropriate times, but as he allowed the story to unfold, he wondered if she was rethinking her moving in with him.

After he'd finished with his description of his meeting with the secretive Albert, which explained his needy arrival in the kitchen, Katie took his hand and pulled him into her arms without saying a word, holding him like never before. Katie was his girlfriend, and Sam was truly beginning to understand the depth of that responsibility and commitment. Katie, he knew, already had it figured out, but for Sam, the experience was just beginning to unfold.

On his way up, alone in the elevator, Sam took out the phone Becklin had given him, checking it for any missed calls for the tenth time. He needed to tell him so much, but most of all he wanted to be sure his friend was alright. If the bad guys knew how he's involved, then odds were they knew about Becklin, too. Once at the safety of his desk with only his comfortable animate objects surrounding him, Sam quickly eased into his rigorous task of unloading onto his laptop the information from his notes, printouts, and memory into a timeline for future reconfiguration for the first draft.

When in trouble at the paper, the normal operating procedure was that one was quietly summoned to either the conference room or a supervisor's office. In the extreme cases, such as guilty of plagiarism, insubordination, or personally causing a negative spike in the company's stock, it's handled within the chilly confines of the editor's office. This was followed, typically, by a security escort from the building. But, when the editor-in-chief silently arrived at someone's desk and stood over the work area like it were already a cemetery plot, one could make the deliberation that their proverbial goose was cooked, without the pleasure of enjoying a last meal.

Sam was in the middle of a prepositional phrase when he felt an undeniable sensation that danger lurked ever so close and chose to explore the feeling by uncharacteristically looking up from his fingers to see Malcolm staring down at him. With his thoughts still lingering on his article, Sam, in his fuzzy state, casually asked, "Can I help you with something, Malcolm?"

With an angry, but controlled response, Malcolm theatrically turned an about face and headed back down the aisle, bellowing in a loud, pretentious voice for everyone to hear, "My office, right now!" Assuming a call had been made from someone connected to Senator Sinclair's office, Sam left his typed sentence dangling and followed his enraged editor down the hallway, thinking with contempt, *Sure, Albert, let's keep this between you and me, sure!*

Entering Malcolm's office at the end of the corridor, Sam considered suggesting the helpful addition of a sign for his door, reading *Dead End!* With Malcolm already pompously seated behind his desk, Sam withstood his editor's woeful glare and quickly took a seat in one of the two padded chairs that faced the desk. Sam finally looked into the face of Malcolm and decided he wouldn't allow his editor to non-verbally brow beat him into a confession. He'd need to spill some evidence of any professional misconduct before Sam felt the need to share. After an awkward moment of silence, Malcolm began with a standard fishing expedition opener, asking, "Do you have any idea why I requested to speak with you?"

Sam gave the question more than enough respective consideration, granted it's about as leading as one could get, before stating, "I can only assume you wish for an update on the progress of my story."

Malcolm started shaking his head *no* before Sam could finish his answer; then, between clinched teeth and rising in crescendo, Malcolm asked, "I want to know why the hell you feel the need to embarrass your colleagues, this newspaper, and its owners by instigating an unauthorized liable course of action with political reverberations we could feel for decades? I've been on the phone with people who don't desire to call the likes of me, but find themselves forced to lower their standards to see that you're restrained immediately. Do you have any idea the repercussions your little investigative stunt last evening has caused? Not to mention the owner's personal request for your immediate walking papers."

Sam stood defiantly. A slap on the wrist was one thing, but dismissal was completely uncalled for. In an angered response, Sam fired back, "Now wait a damn minute, Malcolm. All I've done is follow a lead, same as anyone here would do. The information is solid and everything my contact has relayed, I've personally followed up with and proven valid. You've got nothing here substantial except a dirty senator attempting to bully his name out of a damaging story."

Malcolm remained in his seat, taking a second swing with renewed vigor, hinting to Sam that this was exactly how he enjoyed his closed-door conversations, saying, "And, let us discuss this unknown source, since you're kind enough to bring him up. Who, precisely, did he say are the co-conspirators involved in this multimillion dollar scheme? If there's been any kind of senatorial conflict of interest, why hasn't some young subcommittee member tried to make a name for themself or, better yet, someone from across the aisle, yell, 'bloody murder!' just to embarrass their counterpart?

Let me tell you why. Because this entire fabrication was created by someone, most likely your spy friend, with a personal grudge toward Senator Sinclair and fed to you with the enticement of two nobodies being killed."

Sam took a step back and looked at Malcolm with his mouth opened in disbelief. He knew Malcolm could verbally spar with him all day long without need for lunch break or to catch his breath. More important, Sam also knew that he's no match for Malcolm in a face-to-face debate. Malcolm retained his pit bull demeanor, waiting for Sam's next anticipated argument, but Sam decided he wasn't going to give it to him.

Regardless of his poor math skills all through school, something wasn't adding up, and until he could figure out what exactly that was, he needed to let Malcolm believe he's in full retreat. Sam remembered some good advice from his past that had served him well, even though he didn't recall who to thank for the wisdom of *sometimes you have to give a little to get a little.*

Sam knew he's right about his theory, but decided he couldn't move forward with his investigation while thumbing through the want ads for another job. Playing into Malcolm's ego, Sam sheepishly requested, "Let me ask you this question, Malcolm. Is there anything I can do to salvage some dignity and keep my job?"

Malcolm's surprised expression evolved from a rattlesnake about to strike into a prosecutor hearing a surprising guilty plea. His immediate Cheshire cat grin response gave Sam the hope he's looking for. Malcolm began his slow rolling turn of Sam over the spit, while reluctantly mumbling, "Well, maybe I can speak to the owners on your behalf and see if I can smooth things over with them. After all, as stupid as it was, what you did I believe you did for the paper. I think I can get them to focus on your dedication rather than the way you went about it."

Sam forced himself to over-dramatize a show of relief, following it with a heartfelt, "I appreciate anything you can do for me, Malcolm. Thank you." Sam began to rise, but Malcolm cleared his throat roughly enough to resume his writer's attention quickly giving Sam the thought, Oh crap. He isn't done with me yet!

Malcolm opened a thick file on his desk, slowly leafing through it, stating frankly, "But after this debacle, I'm forced to make some . . . adjustments."

Sam froze in place, inquiring, "What's your definition of 'adjustments,' if I might ask?"

Malcolm looked up from the file and answered with no show of emotion, "Tomorrow, Sam. Everyone can hear about it tomorrow at the 9:00 a.m. meeting. See you there."

Once freed from his meeting with Malcolm, Sam rushed to the front desk to hopefully find resolution to his nagging curiosity. Sitting at her desk, the receptionist, Melanie, saw Sam coming her way. She didn't even try to hide the reaction of grabbing her small mirror to ensure she looked her best before turning to say, smiling, "Good morning, Sam. Malcolm wasn't too hard on you in there, was he?"

Sam played off the dramatics of his boss with, "Oh, he just has such a unique way with people. He missed his calling as a life coach!" Her giggle lasted a bit too long so Sam saved her some embarrassment by asking, "Hey, what time did the big guy show up today? I have a bet with Bobby in classifieds that he came in at six."

She pouted her disappointing look at Sam and answered, "Sorry, Sam. He showed up right before you came in at around eight." She perked up with the offer, "Do you want me to tell Bobby it was six? I don't mind."

Sam returned his answer with a devilish grin, saying, "I'm tempted, but no. He'd find out and kick my butt! A bet's a bet!"

Obviously trying to keep the conversation going, Melanie said encouragingly, "You'll win the next one, I'm sure of it! Is there anything else I can help you with?"

Sam began shaking his head *no* before he considered one more issue to address, asking, "Oh, do you know if the owners were at the game last night? I was watching the Yankees on ESPN and thought I saw them in the crowd."

Melanie smiled back, answering, "No, Sam, they're still on their Caribbean cruise. Why? Are you trying to get their seats for a game this week? I could call their Assistant, and see if anyone else has them."

Sam responded warmly, "Oh, no, thanks Mel. I was just thinking the camera panned a glimpse of Mr. Alan eating a ballpark dog."

Melanie repeated the offer, "Well, just let me know if you change your mind about the tickets. I wouldn't mind calling about it for you, no problem, okay?"

Sam waved his thanks, returning to his desk deep in thought. So, not only had Malcolm lied about all the phone calls he'd been dealing with, odds were the owners weren't even in the loop. The real slip up was a chilling one for Sam to consider; Malcolm knew his contact was a man, which was something Sam had been careful not to let out. The 'spy' comment came as a shock, too, and with the addition of an overzealous performance of protecting Sinclair, was leading Sam to believe his editor knew a lot more of the story than Sam did.

The rest of the day went by in its expected useless fashion. With nothing to do but fume over recent events, Sam busied himself by allowing Ira to enlist him in the mundane responsibility of assisting him in photo selection for pages five and six of the world section. The only benefit about the delegation was he could talk privately with Ira and bounce an idea or two off him. In Ira's office, once a majority of the pictures were narrowed down, Sam slid the most recent morsel of troubling circumstance, saying nonchalantly, "So, it sounds like we can expect big changes around here come tomorrow."

Ira, bent over the small meeting table, paused from his close inspection of a three by five glossy of Muammar Khadafy and peered at Sam over his glasses before stating, "I wondered how long it would take you to bring up what's bothering you."

Sam gave Ira a look of pure innocence, replying, "What are you talking about? I didn't say there's anything bothering me."

Ira offered Sam the closest semblance of a smile, which always seemed to appear as if constipated, before continuing the conversation with, "Oh Sam, you've never, in all the years that I've known you, been able to hide your multitude of never ending emotions that easily display themselves upon your brow. So, let us cut to the chase, as they like to say, but skip the idle chatter about tomorrow's meeting, as I am, as usual, left in the dark just like you."

Sam kept up his clueless facade saying, "Honestly, Ira, I haven't a first guess as to what you're referring to."

Ira dropped the photograph onto the table and stood to face Sam, continuing with, "Oh, please. Everyone this side of the Mississippi either heard or has been informed of your call to worship from the angry troll. I'm of the few who cares not what may or may not have transpired within those bloody walls at the end of the hall, but what I am curious about is what lingering effects my friend left that office carrying. So tell me, Sam, what is it that bites at your heels?"

Defeated by his friend's intuitive deduction, Sam relented, "Okay. So maybe I'm a bit transparent when it comes to whatever is on my mind, but that doesn't mean I'm an open book!" Sam waited for Ira to agree with him, but his statement was left to echo through the room with Ira staring back at him, so he proceeded, "I've been working a story . . ."

Ira cut in dryly with, "Everybody has a 'working story,' Sam. It's a newspaper."

After a good, long stare, both men assumed their respective seats, Ira behind the desk, Sam across from him, and prepared for a lengthy heart-to-heart. Ira waited as though the presses could cease forever, allowing his friend to collect his thoughts before the sharing began. Sam opened with, "Ira, I need you to clear something up for me."

Ira formed a pyramid with his hands and rested his chin upon the point, responding with, "I'll do what I can, of course."

Sam began to slowly shake his head with disgust, speaking through clenched teeth, "How do you work day in, day out with that self-serving, manipulative, jackass-of-a-midget, slothfully loathsome excuse for a human being without vomiting everything from within you or throttle your hands around that second chin of his and choke the very life out of him?"

Ira kept his deep thinking pose and pale expression, simply responding, "Who are we talking about?"

Sam broke into a much needed fit of laughter, as Ira's impenetrable composure and dry sense of humor eased him away from his tempered state. When Sam's enjoyment settled into a chuckle, he added, "Seriously, Ira, you seem to take all of his petty idiosyncrasies that drive the rest of us insane as if you're immune to it. I know he treats you worse than the rest of us. How do you do it?"

Ira sat up trying to appear to be all of his five foot six inch height, straightened his glasses, and stated smugly, "I submit to the balance of all things, which is Karma, and I rely upon the existence of Fate, in that which what you spurn shall return."

Sam nodded his understanding, asking, "Who said that, Aristotle? Or was it Freddy Mercury?"

Ira gave Sam a blank look in return before answering, "Neither. I just did."

Sam exhaled heavily, got up from his seat, and began walking around Ira's office, continuing to vent his frustration. "I just can't get my mind around why Malcolm lied to me about the reasons for pulling me from this story. Everything was solid, and I was covering our legal backside as well, or at least I was until last night, but heck, that shouldn't have even been a blip on the radar with our slew of lawyers."

Ira interrupted Sam's rambling, pleading, "Sam, slow down and back up. Start from the beginning and walk me through this."

Sam returned to his seat, took a cleansing breath and began filling Ira in on the whole situation. He started with the first meeting with his contact, Becklin, and his thoughts about his curious background from the onset. Sam followed that with the connection established with Senator Sinclair, his run-in with 'Albert' and his story getting sacked by Malcolm, who seemed to know more about the lead than he should.

Sam closed with, "Something just didn't ring quite right in my meeting with Malcolm, which I confirmed with Melanie this morning. There's no way he had time to hear about my extracurricular activities last night and talk to the owners, who happen to be on vacation, unless he knows one or more of the players involved with my story."

Ira looked down for a moment, tapping his fingers on the desk before looking up at Sam over his spectacles. Sam gave Ira a furrowed look before quickly giving in, asking, "What? What don't I obviously know that you have prior knowledge to, and yes, I promise you'll never, ever be indicted for contributing whatever it is you're about to share."

Ira relented, even though they both knew he would, saying, "What do you know about Malcolm's past; I mean, his work history?"

Sam tilted his head, working out the chronological order in reverse. "I know he came over from D.C., working for that weekly magazine, *Executive Privileges*, which went under not too long after the embezzlement charges. I remember the media frenzy and all the witty headlines about a magazine having such an ironic name. And, before that, I think he was working on the Hill as a Congressional Aide to, now who was the Senator . . ."

Sam paused in thought, in an attempt to recollect the name, but Ira facilitated his lack of memory, answering, "Senator Glendale Schubert of the great State of North Carolina, and, at that time, the Senior Senator from North Carolina."

Sam snapped his fingers, chiming in with, "That's right! He was the one who took Sinclair from being the new state rep and groomed him as his replacement when Sinclair was beginning his climb up the Hill. But I don't see the connection to Malcolm if they worked in separate camps."

Ira sneered, responding, "Because that, my young, innocent friend, is where the mud doth thicken! Once the younger politically aspiring representative sponged every last drop of knowledge he could, he put into play a scheme to replace the Senator, by enlisting the support of a particularly disgruntled Schubert Aide, who was all too contented to help with the shoveling. Conveniently, or as luck would have it, depending on your angle of perception, Senator Schubert opted not to run for a sixth term, citing an indefinable illness, paving the way for Sinclair to fill his wingtips."

Sam fell back into his seat from the revelation, as Ira let the bastard union sink in, before inquiring, "Why don't I remember any of this from the news? It should have made the front page of every politically based circulation!"

Ira removed his glasses and held them up to the light for inspection in preparation to clean them as Sam had seen him do a thousand times whenever he wanted to punctuate a particular theme he's building toward. Eventually, Ira proceeded, saying, "Because it was nothing but hearsay, and you know what hearsay results in, without corroboration?"

Sam dropped his head like an obedient student, finishing the adage, "Slander, to the tune of millions."

Ira completed his cleaning and returned his glasses to their rightful place, before concluding. "That's right, and I've seen far better men than Senator Sinclair bankrupt greater companies than the likes of you or I have found employment. Our little ferret found guided refuge at *Executive Privileges* until it went under, then with one phone call from his 'Daddy' on high to the newspaper's owners, who, mind you, are at the top of the Senator's election contribution list, and poof, we're blessed with a new editor, for our bestiality pleasure. Sorry, Sam, but Malcolm pushed Sinclair's speed dial button before you were even down the hall from your first meeting."

Sam leaned forward in his seat, putting his face into his hands, trying not to lose his lunch on his shoes. The only words he could produce were, "No! Oh, please don't let this be, no!" Ira moved around the desk and took the seat next to his friend in an attempt to show some semblance of support. He knew Sam was internally placing the final piece of the puzzle together to see the whole picture, frame by frame.

By initially going to Malcolm with his lead, he most likely placed things in motion to kill Becklin. Sam had, until that moment, held out hope that his contact caught wind of danger and went into hiding, but neither of them could have predicted being blind-sided by a stacked deck from the very beginning. With blood already on their greedy hands, other than an odd number, what was one more dead body?

The thirst for revenge was so close to boiling over that Sam could nearly taste the metallic essence of Malcolm's blood, but he wouldn't be surprised one bit if Sam ripped him open and found no heart.

Sam looked at Ira and then toward the door. He knew Ira was unable to physically hold him back from storming out of the office and wreaking vengeful havoc upon their editor. Before Sam had the chance to act on his knee-jerk response, Ira slapped him squarely across the left cheek. It wasn't the hardest slap one could give another, but effective, all the same.

Sam stood quickly and glared down at Ira with his fists and jaw clenched, unable to speak. Ira, rising, matched Sam's stare, in a somewhat, convincing manner, until Sam's sensibility had time to catch up and filter itself between them.

The two quietly sat back down next to each other as Ira kept watch for him to bolt for the door, in case the slap hadn't been enough. After the silence began to be an issue, Ira disrupted the uncomfortable moment, saying, "I don't need to verbalize that he isn't worth it, correct?"

Sam slowly turned and faced Ira, responding, "Didn't you just verbalize it?"

Ira patted Sam's leg, before standing and moving back to the safety of his desk chair and answered, "Yes, my friend, I suppose I did."

Sam rubbed his eyes with both hands in a feeble attempt to clear his life of colossal greed, senseless murder, and hidden agendas, as well as the people who committed the transgressions. When he reopened them and saw all was unchanged, he asked his friend, "I don't know what to do, Ira. It's not in me to do nothing, nor do I have the ability to expose them all without getting myself killed. Where is the path that leads to justice in this situation?"

Ira looked out the window at the traffic creeping by, contemplating the dilemma for only a moment before turning back to Sam, asking, "If you want to survive these circumstances, and reckoning is truly what you seek, would you be willing to sacrifice the glory?"

Sam answered without any need to think about it. "Absolutely. I didn't get into this business for the recognition, just the truth. And, if they killed Becklin to secure their blood money, I want them all buried." Ira nodded his understanding, then reached for the phone and began to dial. Sam, watching him intently, scooted forward in his seat, asking, "What are you doing?"

Ira deadpanned, "I'm making a phone call. Now sit back and just listen."

CHAPTER 7

Ira sat alone in the back of a dingy bar. A large, tattooed bartender with a pierced loop in her left nostril brought him a vodka gimlet with a chunk of lime wedge dropped in as an afterthought. Afraid to touch the table in fear of what disease he might contract, Ira carefully picked up his drink with the use of a paper napkin and tasted the concoction, only to make a sour face and return the glass to its place on the table.

A man appearing to be in his mid-thirties, with dark hair and a hint of Hispanic ethnicity, entered the bar and cautiously scanned the room, looking at each patron before seeing Ira in the back, facing away from him. Approaching his table, he asked, "Back to the door, really? Don't you know what kind of neighborhood this is?"

Ira half rose from his chair, extending his hand in greeting, responding with, "Carlos, so good of you to meet me on short notice. You haven't changed a bit."

Carlos accepted the compliment and his hand with a shake, returning his greeting with, "Well, Ira, the call was a bit mysterious, to say the least, but you've never called me for anything trivial before. So, what's up?"

Before they began discussing the matter, the bartender returned, noticing a new thirsty customer, asking, "What can I get you?"

Carlos responded politely, "Rolling Rock, if you have it; Coors Light if you don't."

She smiled at him, saying, "Rolling Rock it is." Turning to Ira, she asked, "How's your gimlet?"

Ira looked up at the large woman, dryly responding, "Devastating."

She smiled and headed back behind the bar, saying, "Good. I'm glad you like it."

Carlos chuckled at his friend's candor, saying, "Well, I see you still have the talent for charming the multitudes. How's the grind been treating you since I left?"

Ira exhaled deeply in preparation for his response of, "Oh, work is what it is, tedious and unfulfilling. I still, from time to time, find myself daydreaming about my quiet, little place with a view of the river."

The bartender dropped off his beer, while Carlos gave Ira a look of irritation, stating, "Ira, it's a cemetery plot, and not something you're supposed to be excited about. There's therapy for depression, you know that, right?"

With a shocked impression of catching only a fraction of the conversation, the tattooed woman looked at them both, then quickly withdrew to her post. Ira looked over his shoulder, watching her walk back, mumbling to himself, "Well, it is quite peaceful there."

Carlos shook his head as a sign of giving up on the subject, then changed the topic, asking, "So, tell me; what can I do for you?"

Ira showed more enthusiasm than usual, replying, "Remember six years ago after you'd started at the other paper, and you did me a favor for that one guy?"

Ira stared intently at Carlos waiting for his memory to fill in the vagueness of the question. Carlos cautiously looked about the room, then back at Ira, answering plainly, "Yes, I remember."

Ira nodded at Carlos' understanding of the similar situation and continued with, "Good, then I was hoping you could assist us with this . . ." while sliding a thumb drive across the table to Carlos, who quickly took it and placed it into his pocket. The two took quiet sips from their drinks with Ira making the same face in response to his drink as before.

The small talk they exchanged quickly thinned to periods of silence, covering only non-work-related topics. But with so little in common to talk about, Ira struggled to keep the conversation sputtering for Carlos to finish his beer, even though Ira just wanted to leave the filthy bar. He smiled inwardly, watching Carlos try to hide his anxiousness to see what front page story was on the thumb drive. Once Carlos finished off his drink, they parted, promising to get together more often, with Ira realizing it most likely wouldn't happen.

After leaving the bar, Ira realized that in his hasty preparation for his rendezvous with Carlos, he had forgotten his briefcase at the office. Not wanting to leave it overnight for someone to rifle through and steal his prescription for hypertension, he decided to return to the building and retrieve it. Before crossing the street to his building, he noticed a dark sedan, similar to the one Sam had described, sitting idle in front of the entrance.

Ira kept his pace steady and his head down, not looking back toward the building. At the end of the block, Ira prepared to cross the street toward the southwest corner of the news building. With a quick, subtle glance toward his office window on the first floor, Ira noticed two muted lights moving behind the shades from within his office.

When the crossing light turned, Ira proceeded and stole one last look toward his office before reaching the other side. Instead, his attention averted to the building's front entrance, just as two darkly clad, serious-looking individuals exited. Both men slid into the waiting car before it hurriedly sped away.

Ira watched until the taillights were no longer visible before turning around and heading home, deciding the janitors could filter through his briefcase to their heart's content; he had more medicine at home.

❊   ❊   ❊

Sam arrived at work earlier than usual the following day, after Ira's secret liaison. With so much going on that's out of his control, Sam wore the uncomfortable reality like a soaking wet suit. Hanging around the first floor, waiting for Ira to make an appearance, Sam remained out of view, just in case someone wondered why he's loitering about the dungeon rather than his lofty nest several limbs up the tree.

Ira walked through the lobby wearing his trademark trench coat and head staring down at the progress of his feet. Sam smiled his elation knowing he could finally hear what transpired the night before.

Ira didn't see Sam until he was nearly on him and responded to the unexpected visit with, "Oh, hello, Sam. How are you this morning?"

Sam refrained from his desired inquest, not wanting anyone on the floor to suspect their actions as anything inappropriate and followed Ira into his office, answering, "Fine, fine. I just wanted to go over a few things with you before the meeting at nine. Do you mind?"

Assuming Ira was playing along with the discretion, Sam stood by while Ira responded, "No, not at all. Come in and have a seat while I settle in." Once their privacy was secured, Sam began to unload with his first question, but Ira raised a hand, halting the conversation's beginning, asking, "So, how's the little lady doing?"

Sam froze, unsure what Ira was up to, until his friend pointed for him to sit down and rolled his finger to keep the small talk going. Sam immediately responded to the prompt, answering, "She's great, really great. Since she moved in, I can't seem to find any of my stuff in the bathroom, but other than that, life is good."

Scribbling onto a notepad, Ira replied almost in an out-of-character, perky tone, "Cohabitation seems to suit you."

Sam read Ira's note, as he wrote the words *bug infested*, then stared into Ira's bespectacled eyes in disbelief. Ira once again prompted him to keep the conversation rolling with Sam asking,

"So, I wanted to touch base with you about this meeting today. Do you have any idea what it's about?"

The two finally worked out a system of suitable timing of when Ira wrote, Sam talked; when Sam read, Ira assumed his side of the dialogue. Ira hurriedly filled out another page, updating him on the most recent crisis of the paper's late night visitors. Once completed, Ira spun the notepad around for Sam to read, with Ira returning with, "Well, I know we'll be going over every department's budget shortfalls and upcoming data contributions. Malcolm mentioned to me he wanted to end the meeting with a list of adjustments, or at least that's how he explained it to me. I guess we'll find out together at nine."

With Sam finished, he spun the pad back to Ira, saying before heading to the door, "Okay, well, save me a seat in case I'm late. See ya!" While Sam exited out the door, Ira read the words from Sam, *Lunch, 1 pm today at Skinny's.*

The call to order for the nine o'clock meeting came without further incident, and Sam quietly breathed a sigh of relief when he entered the conference room to find several chairs far from Malcolm still vacant. He didn't foresee any mad dashes for the man's throat in his immediate future, but it's good to have some distance between them for any last minute reconsideration.

Ira, already seated in his usual spot next to the king's throne, sat without any show of emotion, busily jotting down last minute notes to report. Sam felt an immediate need for Ira to look at him and acknowledge they knew something no one else in the room did, but pushed the immature thought aside, knowing he's allowing his emotions to run high, forcing his logic to run low.

Without any fanfare, Malcolm shuffled in, taking his seat at the head of the table. While everyone found their seats, he simply offered, "Good morning, everybody."

Most grunted their knee-jerk response, except for the brown-nosers, who energetically replied with a, "Good morning, Sir!"

Sam glared at each of them, screaming inside, Don't you know he's an accomplice to murder? Realizing how useless it would be, he refrained, as it's just their nature to be ignorant of recognizing any form of integrity.

After clearing his throat, Malcolm began with a bang, informing his audience, "Some of you will be leaving this meeting today wondering if you really want to remain employed here."

With everyone in the room suddenly wide awake, Malcolm paused to look around the room at each staff member, appreciating the evidence of their deeper level of attention by the big eyes staring back. Sam looked directly at Ira and got his earlier wish, with Ira already staring back. He wasn't one hundred percent certain, but he believed he noticed a slight shake of a *no* from his friend and could only assume to the meaning of Ira's head movement.

Malcolm slowly proceeded with his 'shake the tree' announcement, lowering the boom on nearly every department, leaving few untouched in one way or another. By ten, he managed to switch four supervising positions, eighteen columnists, two bloggers, and adjusted the workload of thirty-seven staff members from heavy to over-loaded.

The best was saved for last. Sam, lost within his good fortune to have been left out of Malcolm's version of musical chairs, didn't notice the music stopped when Malcolm started in with, "And, Sam, I have something new and exciting in store for you. I believe you're going to enjoy this interesting project!" Sam knew every eye was suddenly on him, and before the beads of sweat began to well up on his brow, he came to the immediate conclusion that Malcolm's opener was provided for him and him alone. Malcolm didn't want Sam fired; he wanted Sam to quit.

Ira walked into Skinny's Restaurant shortly after Sam. They waited for the hostess to find them a table in the back so they hopefully wouldn't be seen by anyone they knew during the lunch rush. Once seated, Ira immediately began complaining to Sam about being seated too closely to the kitchen entrance, and as if he had planned it before hand as punctuation, a waitress nearly knocked his menu out of his hands from the swinging door. Sam chuckled at his friend, asking, "Would you like to switch seats?"

Ira scooted his chair closer to the wall, replying, "No, I'll be fine. I just didn't plan on this being a full contact lunch."

Appearing concerned to facilitate a quick turnover in patronage, the waitress arrived before they had a chance to peruse the menu, asking, "Would you gentlemen like to hear the specials, or do you already know what you want?"

Ira beat Sam to a response with, "Is the term 'special' accurate?"

Confused by the question, the waitress simply stared at her new customer until Sam saved her from the growing dilemma, adding, "Yes, we'd love to hear the specials for today!" She happily responded to the return of her scripted comfort zone and rattled off the short list. Sam chimed in with, "I'll have the club with fries, just water to drink."

She returned her attention to Ira, who behaved much better, this go around, answering her silent prompt with, "The half turkey sandwich on whole wheat and cup of soup, vegetable beef, and a water as well, but I'd appreciate a straw. And, please, be a dear and keep the cook from plastering any salad dressing on the bread. Use force, if need be." She walked away smiling, but her body language suggested otherwise. Sam rubbed his temples from what already was turning into a stressful day. Ira watched his friend and replied, "I admire the way you showed great restraint in the meeting, Sam. If you had reacted any other way, he would have had you for an early appetizer."

Sam looked up from his woes, asking his friend, "So, you knew what was in store for me before Malcolm performed his slice-o-matic act?"

Ira answered, "I had just come from his office before you showed up at the conference room. He couldn't wait to see how you would react and had to gloat about it prematurely to someone.

People like Malcolm are incapable of keeping what they consider as major triumphs to themselves without imploding. They require an audience and enormous amounts of positive feedback."

Sam squinted at his friend, asking, "So, you're telling me you were patting his back, saying, *Gee, Malcolm, this will be fun to watch?*"

Ira shook his head back at his friend, stating sarcastically, "Oh, Sam, you know how rarely I touch other people!"

Sam laughed at Ira's humor as the waitress returned with their waters. Once his chuckle faded, Sam added, "Well, it's not as though I didn't know it was coming, but the switch in storylines is so extreme, I can't help but wonder if he's trying to set me up for failure."

Ira pondered the situation briefly, responding, "Oh, I'm sure he has your future at the paper in his cross-hairs, so to speak, but as you know, I communicate with the owners more regularly than he, and I would venture to say Malcolm would have a difficult time having you sacked."

Sam perked up, asking, "So, what you're saying is the owners actually like me? They really, really like me?"

Ira sneered at his friend, returning with, "Let us just say that on a scale from one to ten, you're somewhere on the scale." Sam accepted the non-committal response before Ira continued, "But one thing you should know is this; the Allens, in their infinite wisdom when it comes to business investments, have less than a grade school understanding for financial contributions. They, unfortunately, coughed up one of the largest donations for Senator Sinclair during his first two election campaigns. If he were to go down by the hand that fed him, it would, no doubt, bring the paper to its knees. The story has to be broken by someone else. I'm sorry, my friend."

Sam stewed over the predicament as they sat in silence, now understanding why Ira was so quick to pass the story off to Carlos. It was nothing more than a catch-22, with nothing but bad in all directions except to pass the buck. Sam asked, "So, you think the information fell into the proper hands then?"

Ira hesitated before taking a sip from his straw and answered emphatically, "Without a doubt in my mind."

Sam shook his head, saying, "I don't know. It's just hard placing something this big into the hands of someone I don't know."

Ira leaned in, waiting for Sam's eyes to meet his before stating, "He's capable, Sam. He'll bring it home, don't you worry."

Sam held Ira's complete attention and asked, "Why him? Why not somebody from D.C.? I would think the news would travel quicker, closer to the vein. I mean, geez, you know that guy has been my nemesis for as long as I've been at the paper!"

Ira paused from his reply long enough for the waitress to deliver their food and slid the bill toward the little man's side of the table. Ira just stared at it as if it were a mouse until Sam snatched it away. Not allowing an opportunity to go by without poking fun at his friend's expense, Ira responded, "My, you nabbed that awfully quickly for a man who came so close to unemployment!"

Sam chuckled between chews, saying, "I'm not ready for a permanent vacation quite yet!"

Ira winced at Sam's resolve, then answered, "As far as the question of selection, Carlos has proven his worth before, without disappointment. And the simple fact of the shared animosity between the two of you made him perfect for securing plausible deniability. And, in regard to the location, it needs to be here, as my trust is restricted to our own city limits. The Hill is a quagmire of greedy predators deprived of soul. And, the media there, only feed off the regurgitated soot that drips from the mouths of the politicians. Trust is simply a topical word used during election years and on campaign trails."

Sam stared at Ira and finally declared, "Alrighty then, I guess I won't be asking for your vote anytime soon!" Sam tried to squeeze Ira for additional details from the meeting the previous night, asking, "So, did he even ask who did all of the research or leg-work for the story? Did he even care who my contact was, let alone what happened to him?"

Before taking a bite of his sandwich, Ira glared at Sam with what little patience he had left on the subject and replied dryly, "Perhaps, if you would prefer, I could slip him a note after school today with two little boxes inscribed with the words, *Do you like my work? Yes or No Circle one*! Or maybe you'd like to know what he was wearing?"

Sam moved off the subject and on to the next matter, asking, "Well, what about your visitors last night; should we call someone or something?"

Ira blankly stared at Sam for a prolonged moment while he finished his meal. Finally, Ira responded with, "First of all, they are more *your* visitors than *mine*. Second, *I* will contact the appropriate specialist for this delicate situation. I can circumvent our dim-witted editor and have the listening devises removed discretely. Perhaps the next time you decide to go after someone, you can opt for someone less connected."

Realizing he'd reached the end of his interrogation and their abbreviated lunch break, Sam checked his watch, then reached for his wallet to pay the bill while Ira stared back at him, sucking on his water. Not wishing for further insults, Sam rose from the table and followed Ira out the door, pondering the difficult task ahead of getting up to speed on a new story, with the bonus of a disgruntled, disapproving editor to impress.

CHAPTER 8

Sam woke early Monday morning. For several days in a row, one constant thought continued to invade his day, and he believed that until he found an answer, he simply wouldn't rest. The unknown had a strangely tempting attraction even when one of the possible scenarios was something difficult to bear. Sitting in the living room in his pajama shorts and white t-shirt, Sam dialed his cell phone and almost hoped for no answer.

On the forth ring, someone did. "This is Detective Brice, Homicide."

Sam closed his eyes and forced the words to escape from deep within. "Hey there, Michael. This is Sam Noll. Gotta minute?"

The room outside the morgue was chilly and in response, Sam pulled his coat a little tighter around his body. Waiting for his longtime contact from the homicide department, Detective Michael Brice, to clear the way with the coroner, Sam contemplated whether the room was truly as cold as it seemed or whether the magnitude of what he's about to do dropped the temperature just a bit. Detective Brice returned with a bespectacled, large nosed man in a white coat. "Sam, this is Dr. Stockton. He's the Chief Medical Examiner."

They shook hands as Dr. Stockton stated in an unemotional, nasally voice, "Charmed. I sure hope this is your guy, because I'd love to get this one off our books."

Sam immediately stopped shaking the man's hand and simply stared at him with clenched teeth.

The detective quickly placed his hand onto the Medical Examiner's shoulder, leading him into the next room and away from Sam before the doctor needed his own coroner. "So, you say there wasn't any trace of foul play with your John Doe?" the detective asked as their conversation trailed off past the closing door. Sam paused a moment before following the two into the morgue, letting his emotions show a little restraint.

With a deep breath, Sam concluded that his anger couldn't be with a coroner just hoping to confirm the identity of an unknown victim. That would be misguided and unfair. Sam had acknowledged a deep-seeded anger that had been building inside for quite some time. With the smug, guilty face of Malcolm walking around free continuing his damage without receiving his just desserts, as well as the possibility of something tragic happening to Becklin, exploding his fury on an innocent bystander wouldn't help matters. Best he kept his focus of vindication where it truly belonged and let this man do his job. One more deep, cleansing breath and Sam lifted his head bravely to see what needed to be seen.

Through the door, he joined Michael and Dr. Stockton standing quietly next to a table that had been pulled out of a stainless steel wall of numerous other small three by three drawers. They both stared at Sam with a matching look of 'ready when you are . . .' before Sam nodded his agreement.

The first thought going through Sam's head when the doctor pulled back the white sheet was, Don't let it be him. Please! but, with one glance, Sam's heart and mind confirmed what his eyes saw; his secret contact and new friend with a questionable past lying coldly before him.

Sam stuffed his hands into his pockets and looked at Michael. The detective gave Sam a knowing stare, but waited for Sam to verbally confirm what all four men in the room already knew. "That's my friend, Becklin. Yeah, it's him, Mike," Sam uttered.

With one last glance before the sheet was returned, Sam closed his eyes and thought, I'm sorry, my friend; you deserved a hell of a lot better, before walking toward the door with the detective. Sam placed his hand on the door knob to open it, hearing the table retract back and the stainless steel door clasped shut behind him before opening the door and walking out.

Walking down the corridor, Michael let the silence engulf the two of them, giving Sam time to settle up with his painful thoughts. Sam appreciated the fact how the detective rarely forgot that just because he dealt with these situations regularly, didn't mean everyone else ran on his disturbing wave length.

Dr. Stockton interrupted their slow, respectful cadence when he swung the door open and called after Sam, "I'm sorry, but I have one question that maybe you can clear up . . ." Sam gave Michael a short, questioning look, but the doctor went ahead with his untimely interrogation, referencing a clipboard with "Your guy came in without shoes; running jacket, t-shirt, shorts and socks, but no shoes. Any idea why?"

Sam's expression changed from irritated to clueless in a span of a heartbeat. He quickly turned back to Michael, both staring at each other for a second. Without a response for the Medical Examiner, they both continued in the direction down the hallway and jumped onto the elevator with the doctor yelling after them, "What about the shoes . . ."

Sam waited impatiently across the desk while Detective Brice finished his phone call. "M-hmm, that's right. No, he'd definitely be wearing tennis shoes; running shoes. Pretty expensive ones, you know; something you wouldn't expect on the guy." After the detective listened for a prolonged moment, he looked up directly at Sam, saying into the phone, "Ya don't say? Yeah, Donny, that's it. That's what we're looking for. Can I get that faxed to me, like A.S.A.P.?" Another pause, before he said, "Thanks, Donny, you've been a huge help!"

Once the phone met the cradle, Sam ended his silence, insisting, "Tell me, Mike. What is it?"

The detective fell back into his desk chair like he's pushed back, scratched his head, and finally explained, "The first three districts I called were dead ends, if you'll excuse the pun. But the last one, the eighteenth, had a homeless *woman* drop in an alley the same day as Becklin. My guy at the eighteenth nearly skipped over her since we were looking for a man, but he recalled her turning up with men's running shoes about four sizes too big and it sort of stuck in his craw."

Sam met the detective's level of anticipation, asking, "So we were right! Becklin ditched his shoes knowing they were causing his attack or whatever ended up killing him . . ."

The detective finished the scenario, adding, "And the bag lady grabs the shoes, thinkin', lucky me! and sports 'em for an hour or two before meeting the same outcome."

Sam took it to the next obvious direction, asking, "Do we have the shoes and can we test them?"

Detective Brice was ready for the question, replying, "Donny at the one-eight is already on it, but we won't have any results for five to seven days; backlog at the crime lab. Until then, I'll have both M.E.s run additional tests on your friend and the bag lady for anything unique in their blood. They won't give me any crap since we've got so much to go on. Anymore on Becklin, other than what you told me?"

Sam thought for a second before answering, "I wish I could, but the guy was beyond private. Do you think your buddy at the F.B.I. will be able to dig anything up on him?"

Michael made a questionable look, answering, "If not, I have him plugged into the system that's monitored by N.S.A. and C.I.A., so if he belonged to either of them at any point, it'll get flagged and they'll come knockin'. They just knock real soft."

Sam stared at the floor by his feet and remained silent for a moment before standing slowly, saying, "Well, I guess we've done all we can for now. We'll have to wait for everyone else to do their job."

The detective stood, extending his hand to Sam, stating, "Thanks, Sam. I appreciate what you've done."

Sam shook his head, but deflected the graciousness, saying, "No, thank *you*. You've done all the leg work on this."

Detective Brice raised a hand to stop Sam, countering with, "Sam, you're clearing two cases; one for us and another over at the eighteenth by following up on your friend. I'm sorry what happened to him, I really am, but at least we're on the path to nailing someone for what they did. That's more than we typically get to do in a month!"

Sam took a humbled stance and simply attempted to end his visit with, "Well, I hope to hear from you about what you find out. Can I count on that?"

The detective smiled broadly and patted Sam on the back, answering with sincerity, "Absolutely, Sam. I'll call you as soon as I hear anything." Sam turned to go, but Michael grabbed his arm to get Sam's focus once again and reiterated, "You're the adhesive that put this whole thing together, Sam. I think it's worth repeating, because I want you to know I mean what I say that I'm truly sorry how Becklin went down, but you're doing him a righteous by not letting it happen in vain. Wherever he is right now, Sam, I gotta believe he's smiling over your efforts."

With that, Sam felt, for the first time, a fraction of satisfaction or possibly some level of resolution over the loss of his friend. Sam left the detective's final comment with a smile and a curt, "Thanks" before turning and walking away from the detective's desk.

On the morning the story broke concerning Sinclair and his crooked side business, Sam arrived at work bright and early anxious to see his editor's reaction, wanting to keep an eye on his progressive mood swings from beginning to end. Ira had relayed the heads-up from Carlos the night before that it would be run as a three day front page headline account from Monday to Wednesday, starting with Sinclair's nefarious rise into politics, including the questionable ousting of his predecessor, the late Senator Glendale Schubert. Sewing all the pieces together that he had assembled left Sam with a slightly detached feeling, but he's unable to deny Carlos' ability to maximize the damage.

Senators Wilma Hodgkins and Carl Melner were also implicated as co-conspirators to the brazen scheme and were joining Sinclair in the feeble attempt at a low profile. Becklin had been correct in his early assumption, as Senator Melner was next in line as the Chairman for Appropriations and Hodgkins was a sitting member of Finance. Sinclair had all his ducks in a row. The sensation of murder, corruption, and abuse of power would engulf every news channel, radio station, and newspaper for weeks.

With Sinclair and his exploratory committee building steam stumping around the Midwest, a larger than normal host of media attention remained in tow, and the breaking story would easily cause a flurry of additional sub plots to pester the hopeful candidate. Sam begrudgingly had to be impressed with his nemesis for the way he unfolded the entire story. Carlos' detailing of Becklin's huge contribution made Sam's friend appear to be the unfortunate hero who paid the ultimate price for his involvement, which put a big smile on Sam's face that would remain for a long, satisfying moment.

Drop kicking the dirty politician out of Congress and ending his selfish need to be President was only part of the plan. Sam needed to bear witness to Malcolm's demise as well. He's the one who set the sorted matter into motion, resulting in Sam's contact and friend to be killed, and that's something Sam refused to allow to not be reciprocated. By eleven, Sam began thinking old Malcolm had phoned in his regretful inability to show up to work, and by one, began considering that perhaps he's away on business; but after checking with Melanie at the front desk, she confirmed no word from the boss, no planned trips, and no answer on any of his numbers when called. Sam decided he'd have to wait for his thirst for revenge to be quenched another day.

On Tuesday, Sam's attention span became terribly erratic, as there's still neither word nor sign of Malcolm, and on Wednesday, Senator Sinclair, now in full duck and cover mode, began avoiding anyone with a camera or microphone in an attempt to get his affairs in order before the indictments started flying.

By Thursday, several of the newspaper's Executive Board members started showing up at the office, unannounced, and went about their close-lipped business dashing in and out of Malcolm's office as if they were all collectively trying to figure out what an editor was required to do during a regular day. Ira was often at their heels, but refused to make eye contact with Sam's inquisitive stare. It took every ounce of Sam's resolve to remain focused on his new article, when all he wanted to do was ask, where exactly was Malcolm?

Eventually Sam smiled to himself, knowing he didn't really care. Malcolm could be swimming his escape to Cuba or flying one way to the jungles of New Guinea, Sam figured his life of bullying, snitching and wasting fine, New York air had finally come to an abrupt, illustrious end.

To cap off Sam's roller coaster week, he received a call from Detective Michael Brice. The call was loaded with information that shocked and astounded Sam, yet in the same respect, did not. After hearing from both coroners concerning the additional blood tests and results from residue from the tennis shoes, it was determined and adjusted in both death certificates that the deaths were homicides. The residue turned out to be a rare and exotic powdered toxin that, once absorbed into the blood stream, caused a restriction to the main aorta, increasing the heart rate dramatically, which resulted in heart failure within forty-five minutes.

Just before the detective was preparing to head home, he received a late visitor from Langley, who couldn't fill in all of the gaps concerning the mysterious life of Becklin, but did allow enough light to ensure the existence of their own investigation being conducted concerning his unfortunate homicide. In addition, the tight-lipped informant relayed that Becklin had a well-financed family who would welcome him home in interment in Arlington.

At the end of the work day, Sam straightened up his desk for the first time in months, loaded his leather case with homework, and decided to pick up a nice bottle of wine on the way home for him and Katie to celebrate.

Minnesota, 1987

As the cool autumn air slowly carried its brother, fog, in tow, El Padre leaned against a large elm tree, watching a black and white stray cat chase a small mouse down a street. The mouse attempted, unsuccessfully, to scale the curb and escape capture while the cat playfully swiped at its prey several times before its intended pounce. Before finishing off the attack, the mouse worked its way far enough down the street gutter to avoid capture by slipping into a drainage pipe. The cat remained next to the opening, pacing back and forth, waiting for the mouse to come back out. Leaving his place by the tree, El Padre crossed the street, informing the cat, "My friend, I believe you have a long wait ahead!"

Down the street, then left for two blocks, he continued down the route as though he'd traveled it every day, even though this was his first visit. At times, the appointments conveniently crossed his path; other times he's required to seek their own skein, no matter where that took him. Either way, the result was constant, with the only variance being the soul.

Entering the hospice, he walked past the woman at the front desk. She nodded her greeting, before returning her attention to the chart she worked on for the morning watch nurse who would be coming on duty in five hours. With a breath of suggestion from El Padre, the gentle thought of someone visiting so late seemed to slip away. It simply disappeared into the host of unimportant bits of information, such as her high school locker number or what she wished for blowing out her candles on her eighth birthday. His position within her memory was replaced with a feeling of contented purpose with her life and hopefulness toward her future, allowing a rare smile to find refuge upon her face.

Down the hallway and through the slightly opened door at the end on the right, he followed. The night light at the base of the left wall glowed softly, giving El Padre a shadowy view of the small room and its occupant. First a stir, then a sigh from the young man as he pulled the covers away from his hairless head. Staring up at El Padre standing at the foot of his bed, there was another sigh, followed by a slight questioning tilt of the head.

Assuming the silent inquiry, El Padre moved closer to the teenager and rested his hands on the side rail, saying gently, "You have fought such a brave and fearless battle, Douglas, and I have come to take you home. Your entire family, countless friends and loved ones continue their prayers even as I stand before you, and wage war against this disease with all that is within them, and it is time for them to rest as well."

Only left with one arm, Doug pushed himself up in the bed with what little strength was left. He again met the eyes of El Padre, but with a steady determined gaze that built a lump in El Padre's throat. The strength that he'd witnessed over the years of someone facing death with such brave composure never ceased to affect him emotionally.

El Padre's eyes welled up with love and respect as the young man whispered, "I haven't once asked God, Why? Why, Lord, me? I've believed in His purpose in all things. When I was diagnosed with this disease when I was ten, I prayed for my family. When I lost my arm, then sight in my right eye, I praised God for the time I had them. During hours of chemotherapy and recovery from its effects, I thanked God for my church and all those who came to visit, praising Him for their love for me and mine for them. At last, after nine long years, this disease has run its course and I'm ready to be received by the loving embrace of God Almighty himself."

The young man held back emotion, taking a short breath, continuing, "But, I humbly ask, being an angel from our Creator, to give me a glimpse of the reason I was chosen for this difficult journey? I regret nothing, and please don't think I hold anger toward anyone or anything for the path I've traveled. But I consider so many things I was denied. I would have enjoyed falling in love or traveling to foreign lands, playing sports and hearing crowds cheer me on as I break tackles and run for the end zone or hit a game winning home run, rounding the bases toward home."

A pause, as Douglas dropped his head, shamefully, before continuing, "It may sound silly, but these weaknesses I cannot deny, and I want to put them to rest so I can face my Gracious Savior with a pure and thankful heart."

El Padre let tears stream openly down his cheek as the fearlessness and continued faith of the young man moved him even further. He replied, "You give me more credit than due, as I come to you being far less than the angel you deserve, but what I do bring, I pray might suffice your final request."

El Padre hesitated with the brief consideration. Why not just a glimpse? he thought, before resting his scarred palm gently upon the young man's forehead. It was a rare event when he was so moved to share his personal strife with another living soul, but where was the harm in connecting with a departing spirit?

The young man settled back into his pillow, the weight of El Padre's hand slightly stiffening his body from the light jolt coming from his hand. Doug's eyes opened wide, though the only thing he was allowed to see was the world from El Padre's past as he quietly narrated into his ear, "My sweet child, you have pleased the Lord well. You have faced an overwhelming challenge and soared above it with your humbled bravery and courageous strength. In this short life here on earth, you have performed greater than any athlete could ever have hoped, leading hundreds of souls to finding a Faith in God. From the sidelines, thousands have witnessed your story and heard of your tale and cheered you on from great distances. The stories of how you undauntedly gave of your limited time and burdened energy to help the children from your church's youth group, as well as your work with the foreign student exchange at your school, has been told by students and missionaries in sixty different countries. In spirit and in thought, you have been nearly everywhere."

El Padre smiled through the tears, continuing, "And, as for love, you have given and received more than most do in several lifetimes, and it is this love that will continue with you into heaven. So, now it is time for you to round third as you listen to the cheers from so many fellow believers who have you to thank for their redemption, and come on home; you'll be safe, at last."

El Padre removed his hand, taking the young man's in his. Doug's eyes slowly came into focus, though his eyelids became heavy from the final moments before his departure. Doug returned to his stare toward El Padre, but now there's an essence of amazement within the fixed gaze. He struggled to find the right question before settling with simply, "How can this be, and why?"

El Padre only offered a slight shrug and a brief smile before replying, "Do you not agree that God works in His own mysterious way? I have learned over the years that when one clears the path before their feet of questionable doubt and meaningless endeavors, it allows one a clarity of purpose and a heightened sense of priority. You and I have chosen similar paths, but as you have seen, yours began much more productively than mine!"

The young man's eyes began to close and his breath became shallow. Doug squeezed El Padre's hand with the small amount of life force that remained, asking in just a hush, "What of my family and friends? Who will be there for them once I'm gone?"

El Padre responded to the question by leaning over the bed and gently kissing Doug's forehead, saying softly, "They will have the Faith that which you led by example. They will carry this strength until you meet again." El Padre's hand released its grasp as the young man's eyes slowly turned from blue to gray to opaque. Gently, respectfully, El Padre closed Douglas' eyes and offered a short prayer of thankfulness for the young man's unmatchable winning season.

CHAPTER 9

At home, Sam was bound in servitude to the kitchen, preparing dinner. He recalled how his first response over being pulled off the ship terminal story was to go nuclear with his defense. After an hour or two of taking deep breaths discussing the matter with Ira, Sam begrudgingly agreed to let his revenge move to the back burner, for now. Unsatisfied with Malcolm's disappearance without having to face the ugly music he conducted just didn't feel right or fair, even if the worm was history. Ira had patiently listened to Sam rant and rave about all things foul, but when Sam transitioned his frustrations toward the loyalties of the paper's ownership, Ira made him hit the brakes. Ira was, as always, his moral compass, and it didn't hurt that he's chief liaison for the paper's legal team, who let their emphatic positions on the subject be known in no uncertain terms.

When it came to working a good lead, Sam didn't back down from a fight if the cause was worthy, but he clearly understood where the line was drawn. He just needed a reminder from time to time, and Ira, ironically, was his best slap to the face. Now that the story belonged to Carlos, he knew he'd just have to live with the fact that it's out of his hands. Someone else was exposing the entire scandal and that was that.

Sam finally realized he wasn't only mourning the loss of his friend, Becklin, but also his chance at breaking a huge story. In the big scheme of things, he knew he had to let go of all the animosity and anger toward everyone involved in his decision. Becklin was gone and someone else was reaping the benefits of his labor; so what? He did everything he could to get justice for his friend and there would be other stories. Life was sweeter with no regrets; time to move forward.

Time in the kitchen was an essential part of Sam's preliminary work when facing a new, difficult assignment. Mincing the garlic, crushing the dried oregano, and adding them to the sauce for the spaghetti, he mulled over the barely scratched surface of his recent dilemma. Thus far, what little he'd gathered from the reports in the file was that there's someone out there, old; at least one hundred and thirty years young and looking better than Dick Clark in his fifties, globe-trotting the world searching out the unfortunate ones, knocking on death's door. By comparing all of the data, it appeared that this ageless perplexity possibly didn't assist in the victims' demise, but, for some unusual reason, seemed to be on hand exclusively for those about to die. In some cases, no one could possibly have predicted the deaths.

Sam ran through a brief checklist of questions he already had growing inside his curious mind; who was he? Why did he do it? How did he know the person was about to die, and where did he get his information? When will his duty be completed? Who, when, where, why and how; all the basic instigating queries required of a good reporter. Sam had never doubted his abilities since he began reporting. He studied law in college, thinking his curious mind was best served protecting the innocent, but his desire to delve ever deeper constantly drove his law professors to near legal action during class.

He remembered one special professor, Dr. Theodore Lyndon, who took him aside after a heated debate concerning a death penalty case and asked him the one question he'd never asked himself, "Would being the best attorney make you feel complete?" Sam knew the answer almost without full consideration and two weeks later switched his major to journalism.

From his first job as a reporter at a small, eight staff paper, he seemed to find an ease of direction to the center of the story, similar to driving down a road and catching all the green lights. Something, though, was missing from the El Padre equation, and that's the piece to the puzzle that drew him in, as well as his readers. All Sam needed to do was figure out what that one thing was.

He combined the three pans he's diligently maintaining and a smile slipped across his face acknowledging the gentle, penetrating surge of excitement only felt from his kindled intrigue. The front door opened and Katie entered with Spalding, with a loud, "We're home!"

"There you two are. I was just beginning to think you stole my dog and scrammed!" Sam called out toward them.

Katie unclasped her brown hair, letting it fall around her shoulders before responding from just inside the door. "Are you addressing me or Spalding? What time did you get home?" Katie knelt by the entry, unleashing Spalding, watching him sprint to his 'daddy' in the kitchen.

She could hear Sam babying his precious six-year-old 'puppy' as he answered, "About three hours ago. How was the park?"

She tilted her head up, sniffing at the process taking shape in the kitchen, then looked at the haphazard piles of scattered paperwork around the living room. She smiled and shook her head, saying when she entered the kitchen, "The park was fine." then leaning on the entry, added, "So, what's the new story?"

Sam innocently looked up from the floor where he's wrestling with Spalding, then returned his attention to the dog before calmly replying, "Am I that transparent or are you really that good?"

She strolled past the two boys on the floor, took a glass from the cupboard, and filled it with tap water, straight lining, "It's not that you're completely transparent, but there are times when you're blocking the mirror, and I can still fix my hair!"

Sam got up off the floor with a blank look and moved next to Katie as she smiled back wickedly. He began filling her in while rewashing and drying his hands at the sink. "Sorry I haven't mentioned it yet, but I've sort of been . . . reassigned, temporarily, or so my previous editor has led me to believe. I'm still working the three weekly segments, as well as covering bi-line politics when needed, but my main article has been completely flipped. Unfortunately, this hand-me-down lead has long-term potential between the lines, I just know it."

Katie rested against the counter and sighed her empathy before asking, "What happened to the story you were working on? And what happened to the contact you were working with? It sounded like he was a big help."

Sam stared at his hands within the dish towel and contemplated just how much he should share concerning the circumstances and disappointing outcome of his friend Becklin, but decided to soften that part, throwing down the dish cloth in frustration, adding, "Dust in the wind. My contact disappeared, so Malcolm pulled the plug a while back."

Katie moved in and rubbed Sam's shoulder consolingly, offering, "I'm sorry, honey. There's no way to move forward without the contact?"

Sam shrugged and replied, "I had to make a decision, so it's out of my hands now." Sam shook his head to change the subject, stating, "I don't want to go down that road again. It just infuriates me. Besides, I believe the story always finds its own way to be told, one way or another."

Katie moved back to the sink and tried to change the mood with, "So, what's the new assignment? Who are you going after this time?"

Sam happily changed his expression from frustrated to excited, explaining, "Out of the gate, I thought this whole thing was some kind of morbid joke; a story about some ageless guy traveling the world in search of people on the cusp of death knocking on the pearly gates, with him being the gatekeeper. All I could see was a short story with a lot of holes and me getting yanked off my previous lead. But, I gotta tell ya, even though I'm just getting started on it, everything I've read seems pretty factual."

Sam rushed toward the living room, saying over his shoulder, "Let me show you something . . ." He's back in a flash with a pile of papers from the clutter he was working from. "This is a copy of a letter from a Peruvian freedom fighter to his sister in Bolivia from late 1923, during a war for the independence of Peru. He describes a man around fifty years of age with dark curly hair and a scarred right hand aiding six of the badly injured, leaving the other five to fend for themselves. He believes the man to be a local priest or perhaps something more sinister, but comments in the letter . . ."

Sam shuffled through two pages until he found the section to reference, "Here it is, ' . . . and the stranger desired not to deliver assistance to any of us who survived, only granting solace and comfort to those who succumbed to their injuries. Strange, my dear sister, how desperately I wanted his help. If it had come, I believe this letter would not have been written.'"

Sam looked up from the pages and saw the interest in Katie's eyes from the single entry and became increasingly excited that the single quote already had her drawn in. She scratched the back of her head, asking, "What else do you have?"

With a victorious smile, Sam pulled down two wine glasses from the cupboard and placed them onto the counter next to Katie. "Pour the wine, I'll plate up the food, and we'll meet back at the table. I don't have a lot of answers yet, but what I've found out will knock your socks off!" he declared without abandon.

Sam and Katie sat on the sofa with Spalding asleep between them. Sam placed the final entry into the neat, organized pile on the coffee table before them while Katie blankly stared at him, forming her first question. "The obvious question is, why does he do it, right?" Sam played devil's advocate and mischievously shrugged his response. Katie bit at her lip moving forward with her questioning. "Is it to finish them off? Is he trying to get something from them, or is he just taking their souls?" Sam gave her another shrug, which resulted in one of her playful slugs to his shoulder, adding, "Come on, smart guy; tell me what you think he's doing!"

Sam chuckled at his girlfriend, taking in a long, thoughtful breath, before answering, "I don't know, Katie. It's just too early to figure one way or another."

Katie rubbed her chin, which Sam knew to be an indication she's putting her full thought into something, before offering, "So, what you're leading me, the hopeful reader, to believe, is that somewhere out there this mysterious guy seems to show up and speak only to people who, within the succeeding twenty-four hours or so, die from anything from war injuries, tornado strike, or . . ." She placed a hand on Sam's arm, turning to look at him. "What was it that one guy from St. Paul died from?"

From memory, Sam smugly recited, "Acute myocardial infarction waiting for a light to change at the corner of White and Lombard. It's often due to the occlusion of a coronary artery."

Katie stared at Sam for a quick second, then asked, "What's an occlusion?"

Sam continued down his path of educated superiority. "It's an obstruction, or, in this case, a blockage of blood to the heart."

She continued staring at him before saying, "You mean it was a heart attack?" Sam slowly nodded, followed by a hint of self-reproach. Katie removed her hand from his arm and turned back to the pile of files once again complete upon the coffee table, asking, "Well, why didn't you just say he had a heart attack?"

Sam answered her sheepishly, looking at her with his head down. "Then I couldn't have impressed you with the big medical words I researched!"

Finally, Katie let him off the hook with a warm, all-was-forgiven smile. Since their first date, Sam melted from receiving that particular smile and thrived off it. Everything became right in the world when she smiled like that. He took her in his arms, looking into her eyes. His heart desired to express exactly what he felt for her at moments such as that, but the words remained hidden, and eventually the opportunity was once again lost. Katie moved in, tenderly kissing him, as if to say, it's okay. I know what's inside. She stood, looking down at her muted boyfriend still sitting on the couch, befuddled with his lack of simple expression. "So, what's the name of the article?"

Sam tilted his head, replying, "As yet, undetermined."

With a half-smile, Katie returned saying smartly, "Odd name. I think it needs work!"

Sam threw a sofa pillow in her direction, which she easily dodged. Spalding awoke and obediently retrieved the pillow, dropping it onto Sam's lap, awaiting a second toss. Both he and Katie laughed at Spalding's response to their horseplay, before Sam reengaged the subject. "Just before his questionable departure, Malcolm gave me the opportunity of naming it and, if approved by, I guess, either the board of directors or Ira, would let it run. I just haven't come up with anything, I don't know, poetically effective or eye-catching."

Katie blurted out, "How about 'Death Comes Easily'?" Sam stared blankly at his girlfriend, but before he could respond to her idea, she stated, "I'm going to jump into the shower. I know you've got more work to do, so I'll just see you when you come to bed."

Sam watched her saunter down the hall toward their bedroom with Spalding in tow. He realized Katie wasn't just rare in her understanding of his emotional struggles; she seemed to be perfect for him. Now, if he could just figure out what it'd take to be perfect for her, he'd be on to something enduring.

Sam had considered pulling the ring out of his sock drawer so many times over the last few weeks, but had allowed one reason or another to change his mind. In hindsight, he's even more grateful for the way his planned proposal went awry. Sam was seeing sides to his girlfriend he never would have noticed had she not moved in, and the recent nuances of her personality deserved long, respectful consideration. Living together had opened his eyes to a new dimension of their relationship, and he wanted to slow things down to be sure it flowed in the right direction, naturally.

Even though Katie was recently giving subtle hints of possibly being ready to take the next step in their relationship, whatever that might be, he had, so far, managed to smother the embers. At some point, though, he'd need to face the issue of progression or find a bigger extinguisher. The momentary consideration of how much his intentions had changed over such a short span of time flickered at the edge of pursuit, before the thoughts sputtered out, turning away his emotional opinions and returning to his homework.

Sam rested his head on the back of the sofa and did his best to push aside thoughts of unknown things to come. He shifted back into work mode and began his plan of attack. He often organized a methodical three step launch so he could set things in a direct, forward motion. It consistently impressed the higher-ups when he rattled off a preconceived game plan whenever they required an update on his progress. Sitting up and moving to the edge of the cushion, he grabbed his laptop from the floor, then rifled through his briefcase until he located a spare flash drive. He scribbled the words, 'Best of Mozart' onto the drive, figuring he didn't know anyone close to him who appreciated classical music, keeping his private notes safe, but accessible.

After sliding it into the back of the computer, Sam began working out an order of concentration, breaking it into three sections that he labeled as Sightings, Research, and Interviews. He began with subheadings under the Research section, transferring his handwritten notes into a list of books and various articles from numerous periodicals, starting with accumulating additional information on Peru. He started researching the history of the country and how the Tacna Region became such a major part to its battle for freedom as well as how the area had fared since. Sam rubbed his tired eyes in an attempt to force himself to continue his work before switching over to the Internet.

After compiling three pages of notes, Sam had a wayward thought and changed direction by typing 'Sightings of the Incarnation of Death' into the search engine. Scanning down several pages, he came across a book by a Professor from Fordham University called, *The Rights of Visitation* and wrote down the information for later use. Out of nowhere, Sam stopped writing and looked up with a belated thought, saying out loud, "Death Comes Easily . . . that's pretty good."

CHAPTER 10

The following day, Katie burst in through the front door of the apartment like a bundle of pure excitement. After tossing her gym bag onto the floor near the entry, she yelled, "Sam, where are you?"

Sam peeked around the corner from the kitchen doorway holding a screwdriver in his hand. "I'm in here doing manly things!" he joked as she ran toward him for a kiss. Once her greeting was administered, Sam gave her a skeptical look, asking, "Wait a minute, you were only gone for two hours and that felt like a 'gone all day' kind of kiss. What's up?"

Katie gushed, unloading a little more of her high energy. "Mom called. She and Dad are flying over to finally meet you and stay in New York for a few days!"

Sam fought the initial facial reaction of a wince and forced a smile to take charge of his expression while Katie watched his every tick like a gambler at a high stakes table. Evidently the bluff took hold, giving him time to add, "All the way from Washington State? How great is that?"

Katie gave his arm a tug as her response reached a higher pitch, "I know! I can't believe she got him to agree to fly, you know, since he absolutely hates flying!"

Sam considered his next inquiry and knew that 'how' he asked could determine whether they'd ever have sex again, so he allowed an extra second or two tick away before diving in slowly. "So, when do we get to see them?"

Katie's reaction paid off dividends for Sam immediately. Jumping into his arms, she shifted her enthusiasm to an even higher level, as if it was at all possible. Muffled by her face in his neck, Sam thought he heard the words, "Two weeks." The two playfully collapsed to the floor, with Sam taking the brunt of the fall, letting all of Katie's nominal pounds use his slightly softer frame as a buffer. Laughing, even though he may have injured himself upon impact, Sam held his girlfriend close to his chest, enjoying the simplicity of the moment. Who could ever have imagined the amount of pleasure he's able to feel, deep inside, from just making her happy. It's a win/win system that he'd only just begun to comprehend.

The two were interrupted when Spalding decided a referee needed to join the fray, nuzzling his snout under Katie's arm and placing his head between them, just in case anyone felt the need to pet him.

Then, the moment was gone.

Katie punctuated the end of the play with lifting herself off the floor and stating on her way to the shower, "Oh, you're going to need a new dress shirt or two for when they're here. Maybe a nice pair of slacks, too. Black."

Sam remained on the floor like a wrestler who'd just been pinned in less than thirty seconds, wondering what in the heck just happened. Spalding moved over to his owner and panted his hot breath over Sam's face. Unappreciative of the smell, Sam rolled quickly to one side, saying to the imaginary referee, "Fine! I give, I give! Consider me tapped out!"

Omaha, 1992

Hospitals and nursing homes carried a great deal of care and consumption of attention from El Padre. The gentle hum of so many souls whispering for his company bode a sweet sorrow upon his own heart. The draw to his appointments affected his every sense and to calm the enticement from within was to satisfy their calling.

Odd, how his reputation depicted him as something evil. Death was a mere awakening. Some awoke from a bad dream to the pleasantness of life; others stirred from a good dream to the realization that they lived in an unpleasant existence. It wasn't his misdeed or his merit for the choices one made during one's time. He simply heeded the call and offered his service, allowing those about to leave this place an inner contentment, a freedom of restlessness and serenity from the heaviness of life.

Walking down the hospital corridor, his musing was interrupted by a janitor placing signage of 'caution ahead,' preparing to mop the hallway. El Padre's thoughts shifted to the similarities of their tasks; both quietly and inconspicuously laboring to clear a path for any and all who were destined to follow their intended course, only for both to begin, once again, repeating the same responsibility, over and over again. The janitor, in his defense and at the very least, was allowed to offer a semblance of warning to those who passed, even if it's rarely heeded.

Past the rooms and down one flight, El Padre reached his destination and entered the nearly empty cafeteria. A young man and woman sat close together at a table in the middle of the room. They shared cups of hot coffee and a rare moment of quiet, speaking softly and staring at each other showing every sign of a new and budding relationship. El Padre casually purchased his own refreshment and walked unnoticed across the expanse of the room. Navigating past a table, he tripped over a chair, tumbling to the floor, and spilling his drink in the process. The couple reacted immediately and rushed to assist the man as they'd done numerous times in their short careers as nurse and doctor.

With what appeared to be only a bruised knee and pride, the two invited the stranger to join them at their table. "Are you visiting a loved one?" the young woman asked while El Padre attempted to dab away the wet spots from his shirt.

He looked up from the question and the young woman noticed the unique shade of blue to the older man's eyes, catching her off guard by the gentle calmness of his face. El Padre smiled back, replying, "Yes, I am here out of servitude, and I patiently wait for the right time to make my visit. The door was not yet open, so I thought I might come down here and wait for the appropriate moment to make my presence known. I take it by your capable assistance that you both work here at this place of care?"

The young man was first to respond, answering, "Yes, we started about the same time last year. My name is Paul. I'm a nurse in the ICU, and Wendy here is one of the emergency room physicians. Personally, I think the best one this hospital has to offer!"

Wendy smiled bashfully at Paul's biased submission, playfully slapping his arm, saying, "Oh, stop!" Wendy returned her attentions toward El Padre, asking, "Is the person you came to visit improving?"

El Padre looked down briefly before explaining, "Sadly, I feel it will only be a matter of a few short hours before . . ." Both doctor and nurse silently nodded their respectful understanding of the man's unfinished comment and impending loss. El Padre added, "May I ask you both a rather personal question?"

Paul looked at Wendy with the question but, without any hesitation, she answered for them both, with, "Of course." The kindly gentleman might be unknown to her, but there's something comforting about him; something fatherly.

With a hesitant look down and then a slow shake of his head, El Padre inquired, "How do you both cope with the constant realization that someone you spoke with, took vital signs from, or even a patient you checked in on during your rounds possibly won't make it through your shift? How do you deal with returning day and night, one shift after another, knowing you will likely look long into the face of death?"

Paul looked again toward Wendy, letting her field the question. Confronted by the depth of the inquiry, she took a thoughtful moment before placing an arm around Paul, answering, "We were both raised in a strong church atmosphere and, for me, faith was embedded into my being long before I could even walk, with my father being the pastor of our church. He unfortunately passed away when I was only fifteen, but until then, he touted to everyone who would listen that he knew his baby girl was going to be a doctor and save lives. When I started college, going into the field of medicine was nowhere on the radar, but he kept his influence rolling down from heaven. Math and science came so easily for me, and during my sophomore year, a guidance counselor asked, 'How about medicine?' That was the first time I seriously considered becoming a nurse, and once I got there, I thought, Why *not* a doctor? After eight more years and a small fortune in school loans, here I am."

Wendy offered a shrug and a smile, concluding with, "So, to make a short answer long, I have faith that this is what I'm supposed to be doing and that this is where I'm destined to be. I may not be here next year, and perhaps I'll switch to some other specialized practice down the road, but either way I know I'm supposed to help heal those in need."

She extended her pointer finger to the middle of her palm, adding, "We learn in our first year of med school that sometimes people die on your watch. Sometimes people will die while your hands are inside of them trying to help them continue living. Sometimes, regardless of your efforts, people die. You can't let it tear you apart, nor can you allow yourself to become detached, either. I've seen far too many doctors and nurses with eyes that are vacant of feeling. I can't do that. I have to see the person before me as a breathing, laughing, crying, and even angry human being, just like me. I refuse to simply tell another person they're sick and then leave him or her in a confused wonder. I choose to explain why they're sick, what exactly is going on with them physically, then explain in detail what can be done about it. There's an enormous difference in talking *to* someone and talking *with* someone, and I believe it's that small difference that allows me to face each new day." Paul just stared at his girlfriend until she returned his look and asked, "What?"

Paul just smiled broadly and hugged her tight, replying, "That was way better than what I was going to say!" He kissed her on her cheek and they turned back to El Padre as he watched the two, masking his heavy heart with a smile.

He rose quietly and thoughtfully patted the chair in preparation to excuse himself of their leave, saying, "I am grateful for your assistance in my misjudgment of walking past the chair, and I am thankful to have met you both." Beginning to turn, he hesitated and looked back deeply into the young woman's eyes, saying, "Please forgive me if this seems presumptuous, but I believe your father couldn't be more proud of you." He turned, leaving Wendy's eyes welled up with emotion and speechless, while Paul just held her tight, watching the kindly gentleman exit the cafeteria.

Climbing the stairs to continue his bidding, El Padre prayed for strength for Paul, for Wendy's family, and even for the man who would shoot and tragically kill Wendy later that evening. Fate drew people to a certain place at a certain time for a certain reason. Some of those moments could be for the good, while others simply snatched a precious innocent life over twelve dollars that one individual had and another individual wanted. It's these examples of senseless loss that El Padre's heart constantly wrestled, testing his resolve all his days.

Sam lounged at home on his sofa wearing his Mets cap, holding a baseball in the palm of his hand while the television blasted the play-by-play to the game. With Spalding asleep next to him, he stared off at nothing, his mind nowhere near the living room, apartment, or even the ballpark. After six well-received installments of his *Death Comes Easily* article, he had slowly come to the conclusion that the basis for the article had become a bit overdue. Before he could proceed with any further haunting stories concerning additional victims of El Padre, the readers required an origin.

On his laptop were four solid paragraphs building his story concerning the original El Padre sighting from Southern Peru. Only feeling slightly content with his opening, Sam contemplated his next paragraph, finding himself frozen within the muck of uncertainty trying to put into words an area he'd never actually seen.

He knew, down deep, that he carried a bit of prideful swagger when it came to writing about places of interest in his articles. He further admitted to himself taking pleasure when one of his readers expressed appreciation or paid him a compliment for his ability to explain some place that they, themselves, had visited and held dear. If vivid adjectives and analogies were used to form a great story, then including the sights, sounds, and even smells often placed the narrative over the top.

Reading his own words for the fourth time, Sam knew it's flat and lifeless, and he's quickly coming to the conclusion that there's only one way to give the article its deserved existence; he needed to be there.

With the Board of Directors in their sixth week of active duty taking turns shuffling around the office in an attempt to keep the newspaper rolling, the fact remained that, without a full-time editor, the odds were slim for Sam to get a travel voucher signed off. Like a grade-schooler looking forward to a field trip, the only way he could get on that bus was with a permission slip, and forging a parent's signature in this situation wasn't an option; then the idea took sudden form. "Forge one," Sam said out loud. Spalding looked up with a sleepy stare and wagged his tail in response. Sam looked down at his loyal friend and gave him a big kiss on the top of his head, before turning his new scheme over from different angles.

Ira made his way down the busy sidewalk with his head down, as usual, and entered the paper's building with an overdramatic push of the door, as if it weighed a thousand pounds. Making the turn down the hall and approaching his office, he came to a stop before looking up at Sam waiting for him.

Sam smiled broadly, saying, "Not bad, Ira. You only made it halfway down the corridor this time before sensing I was here. Nice job!" Ira ignored the opening morning banter, moving in beside him to unlock his office. Sam acknowledged Ira's lack of desire for idle chatter by filling in his friend's half of the dialog, mimicking Ira's voice with, "Oh, Sam, you're such a juvenile. Why don't you run along and play in the street."

With still no response, Ira mutely walked past him and into his office, so Sam continued his impression, saying, "And while you're at it, pick up my breakfast. I want a lightly toasted bagel with low-cal margarine on one side and cream cheese on the other, cup of coffee, two sugars."

Ira removed his trench coat, hanging it gently on one of the protruding bars extending out from the coat tree, straightened a pen back to its twelve o'clock position on his desk, and looked up at Sam, stating, "I don't care for the cream cheese, but the other items would be appreciated; and it's only one sugar." Sam smugly moved to a chair in front of Ira's desk, as Ira sat, proceeding with, "And I do not, nor ever have, sounded like Peewee Herman when I talk, and I'd be quite pleased if you refrained from any further attempts at imitating me, thank you very much!" Sam took his turn at being silent until Ira positioned himself comfortably behind his desk before he asked, "So, what do you want that you feel the need to bother me so early?"

Sam didn't try to play innocent and simply conceded that they both knew he's looking for a favor. Sliding forward in his seat, he dove in with, "We're in agreement that Malcolm is long gone and never to be heard from again, right?"

Hearing the name caught Ira's full attention, clasping his hands together, resting them on his desk, he replied, "Definitely in the capacity as editor, at the very least, but yes, I would say we've seen the last of him . . ."

Ira left the response trailing, knowing he's being led down Sam's guided path, but curious enough to follow. "So, if Malcolm and I had a closed door meeting the day before he up and disappeared concerning my required trip to Peru for my story's research, at his insistence, by the way, with our temporary dilemma with being editor-less, would I go through one of the acting editors, Melanie, or you for my voucher approval?"

Ira didn't change his expression, seeing Sam's sinister plan unfold. Sam continued to watch his friend just stare back at him without blinking, while turning the question over in his mind like a Rubik's Cube. Finally, Ira's eyes refocused on Sam, answering, "Acquire a blank travel voucher from Melanie; I'll call her in ten minutes to say that you'll be picking one up. Fill it out and backdate it for when you had your meeting with Malcolm. Bring it to me later today, and I'll get it approved."

Surprised by Ira's lack of argument in being an accessory to his alleged misrepresentation of the truth, Sam hesitated before making his exit and asked, "I've got to know, Ira, why?"

His friend turned his focus on some paperwork to his left, before responding, "Malcolm was a peevish, self-absorbed little man who used his position as editor in a negative way every chance he possibly could. Helping you with this small indiscretion, we hopefully can close the final chapter on his reign here, perhaps on a positive note. Anyway, if not for you, I guess I'm doing it a little for me. I could have and, most assuredly should have, stood up for you more when Malcolm began his campaign of vengeance directed at you." Ira turned to look at Sam and asked, "I hope you can forgive me."

Sam smiled his response, followed by saying, "There's nothing to forgive, Ira. We've kept our friendship under wraps all these years for obvious reasons, and Malcolm couldn't dish out anything I was unable to handle; certainly nothing worth exposing our united front. When we get our next editor, I hope you continue treating me, publicly, with the careless indifference you've always been known for!"

Ira winced one of his rare smiles, saying, "Thank you, Sam. I certainly hope I can live up to those lofty expectations."

At home, Sam sat on the edge of the bed, awaiting Katie's return from her last aerobic class. His usual anticipation of seeing her walk in the door, still sweaty and exhilarated from exertion was dampened by the knowledge that he had to relay bad news. For a split second, he considered postponing passing on his schedule update, in case her endorphins led them under the covers, rather than on, but he quickly ruled out any deception, knowing it would only add insensitivity to Katie's growing list of his selfish attributes. He looked down at Spalding lying next to him with his usual expression of, *I know exactly what you're thinking and I'm still your obedient friend.* It didn't remove his lingering guilt from the thought, but he patted Spalding on his head for the effort.

Nearly on cue, the sound of keys at the door stiffened his resolve, preparing for the ensuing letdown. Katie walked into the apartment with her usual fashion of dropping her gym bag by the door and searching out her two boys. When she found them hiding on the bed, her expression turned to concern, asking, "Is everyone okay?"

Sam stammered his response, "Yeah, sure, um, at least to my knowledge everything is fine. Why do you ask?"

Katie moved to the bed, taking a seat next to Sam, replying, "The air in this room is all wrong; don't you feel it? It's like a gloomy kind of sensation."

Sam looked around the room before turning back to Katie and just stared at her. He considered how contentment, and to a greater extent, happiness, was a fleeting thing, and the number one culprit to its own end were words. Knowing his selfish actions and desire to follow his story would cause a negative impact toward Katie's dynamic of their relationship, he struggled for the perfect words of explanation to break the streak. The unattainable words could then allow the progress of how she conceived they're moving forward to proceed; but, being human, and a flawed male version at that, Sam blundered ahead to the Fate he needed to place his foot within. "Katie, about your folks' visit . . ." Sam tentatively opened the infliction.

Katie turned her full attention to Sam's next sentence, and when one didn't present itself, she coached him by leading with, "Yes, what about it?"

With his foot already through the door and the fire exit no longer an option, Sam stared at Katie for just one last innocent moment before barreling head-first into the chasm of no return. He cleared his throat for no other reason but to stall the inevitable before admitting, "An opportunity came up to fly to Peru to follow the original lead to my El Padre story, and with all the chaos going on without having a full-time editor, I need to take advantage of this window."

Short and informative, Sam considered. He hadn't rambled, nor exaggerated any of the facts. How could she not respect the delivery?

That's when Sam opted to look up to face the music, only to notice Katie's face turning a medium shade of red and moving quickly to crimson. Her fists were clenched and her jaw was set with little muscle spasms fluttering from her ears down to her chin. Sam wasn't sure, but he thought her eyes even changed color, but chose not to inquire about it. The only word that came out of Katie was a curt, "When?"

Remaining on his decided path of full disclosure, he responded, "The day after tomorrow."

Katie blinked once, taking it in, referencing the calendar in her head before adding, "And for how long?"

Sam sheepishly replied, "Probably ten to twelve days."

Katie stormed past Sam on her way to the bathroom, saying over her shoulder, "Well, isn't that convenient!" When the bathroom door slammed shut, Sam stared at it like he expected it to carry on the conversation. When it didn't, he turned and headed for the kitchen for a long, quiet dinner for one, as Spalding remained on the bed, choosing to stay neutral.

In the early morning hours, before much of the city considered their first cup of coffee, let alone waking up to the sound of their annoying alarms, Sam quietly carried his bags out the door for his long trip to Peru. He hesitated there before letting it close all the way, glancing down the hallway to the bedroom where Katie gently slept. Sam wondered if he should make a belated effort to try to smooth the fissure that seemed to be growing between them, but decided waking her that early would only make things worse. He considered the adage, "time heals all wounds" and scoffed at the thought that it should've enlisted a bold disclaimer.

He'd been given the appropriate silent treatment for the last day and a half from Katie, with only short, terse replies when directly questioned. With a heavy sigh, Sam decided it's best to let her sleep away his departure and hope to let a little time and distance heal enough to maybe build a bridge.

The fifteen hour flight to Peru would be the longest flight of Sam's life, in more ways than just time on a plane. He checked his watch, shook his head once in frustration, and let the door close. The taxi wouldn't wait forever and neither would the plane. The decision had been made six days previous when he concocted the whole scheme and he couldn't let their untimely fight spoil his chance of improving the continued progress to his story. He'd make it up to her somehow when he got back. He wasn't sure how, but he'd hope for enlightenment between now and then.

Hearing the apartment door close, still lying in bed, Katie opened her eyes, rolled over to Sam's side of the bed, and cried herself back to a restless slumber.

CHAPTER 11

The multitude of connecting flights were much longer and lonelier than Sam expected. At each terminal, disembarking for short layovers, the following plane he boarded seemed to get smaller, causing him to wonder if he'd land in southern Peru on a hang glider. When he's able to have his phone on, he checked for calls or texts from Katie, but his phone seemed to have joined her icy, muted response to his latest self-centered act.

On one hand he understood her staunch position, especially with the unfortunate timing of her parents' visit. On the other hand, he believed she'd see through this 'little' episode and remember she'd been one of his main avenues of encouragement with pursuing the story. He continued to remind himself that time could heal all wounds, but when one multiplied the strain of time with distance and Katie's anger, the effect usually required someone like Einstein to figure out.

Walking off the small plane, Sam breathed in the balmy air the rugged landscape of Peru offered him. Glancing around in his foggy state, he took in his first impression of the border city of Tacna. With little time to research the area, he resigned to the fact that he'd require some trustworthy assistance from the locals if he wanted to be pointed in the right direction so he could gather the accurate information for his story.

The small amount of sleep from the restless crowd on the longer flights had left him a bit punchy. He concentrated on the basics of keeping the left foot following the right, struggling to remain in single-file formation following the other passengers to the terminal building. Food and a bed, and hopefully food again were his first three priorities. Everything else would seem surmountable after nourishment and sleep.

Waking from one of the deepest sleeps he'd ever had in his adult life, Sam stumbled to the mirror to make sure his head wasn't as thick as it felt. He peeked out the balcony window to a beautiful sunny day and squinted from the jolt of additional sensation. He vaguely recalled paying for the taxi ride from the airport and checking into a hotel the driver had suggested. Also, the previous night's dinner was a blur, but he clearly remembered the four Acholado Pisco Sours he consumed. This embedded memory, no doubt, had much to do with the bartender rambling on and on concerning the entire history of the drink, with his extremely biased, yet subtly over-the-top, confirmation of pride that the drink originated in Peru; *not* Chile.

A shower would help shake away the cobwebs that had taken refuge within his head, and perhaps a hearty breakfast would further his recovery. The lukewarm water did more than expected, as did the exercise from racing back and forth in the small stall trying to minimize the areas hit by the low temperature burst of water. Once he got the routine down of a little water, a little soap, then a little more water, Sam covered the main areas in only eight minutes; extra cologne and deodorant would have to bridge the gap.

Breakfast was brief at the hotel; just bread and jam with a bitter coffee, but with his belly still a bit delicate from the previous night's Pisco sours, sometimes less was more. Lunch would be the adventure, he confirmed to the bland hotel furniture.

He opened his computer and started compiling notes from his visit thus far. With the long, boring flight and his hazy recollection of the prior evening, he only managed to amass one and a half pages and read it over a few times in the hope to elaborate on some of the highlights. After the second reading, he realized there were no highlights and decided he could use the notes as filler, if he needed it. Sam reminded himself that he couldn't be discouraged by momentary uninspired writing, and that creativity was a flighty beast and could return by the simple act of opening a door for another person.

He recalled learning in school how external stimuli were the key components to triggering imagination, just as the slightest sound affected our dreams when we slept, but just to pad the odds, he decided to avoid anymore bartender concoctions.

The warm sun greeted him upon exiting the hotel. Carrying with him only his voice recorder, note pad, and small digital camera, his virgin outing, he decided, would be short and light. With the hotel's location only three blocks from the main hub of Tacna, Sam ventured out to scour the vegetated strip in the desert that was Tacna and, if he found the need to return for more hardware, his room wasn't far. He'd arrived with only two names of descendants who survived the battle of 1923, and his confidence was surprisingly high that he'd find what he's looking for; once he figured out exactly what that was.

At the crosswalk, Sam stopped, looking for signage allowing him to cross. When he came to realize there were no instructions, he decided to follow the chicken and bravely cross the road. Out of nowhere, a taxi suddenly bore down on Sam just before he reached mid-crosswalk. He half dove, half leapt to safety as the driver blared his car horn at the near miss. Sam dusted himself off, checked his equipment, and stared after the car that almost took him out. He breathed a venomous curse as the taxi propelled itself farther down the road looking for its next unwitting victim.

A young boy of about nine or ten interrupted Sam's vengeful thoughts, saying in broken English, "Street danger in day. Best run when go."

Sam turned to look at the lad, noticing for the first time that the boy was sitting in the shade on a three-legged stool, balancing his weight so that he didn't fall over. Sam smiled at the friendly advice and asked, "Don't the cars stop for pedestrians?" Sam saw the look of confusion on the boy's face from his lack of understanding of the word 'pedestrian,' and added with a gesture of patting his hand to his chest and pointing back at the boy, "people; you and me?"

The boy looked upward and to the left, appearing to consider how best to reply in his limited English, before simply answering, "No. Drivers no stop."

Sam laughed at the young man's response, which led the boy to join in the laughter. Sam asked the lad, "What's your name?"

The boy leaned forward, gracefully sliding off the stool, letting it fall to the ground, answering, "Me? I'm Arcapi!"

Sam repeated the name, "Arcapi?" watching the young man's reaction to whether he pronounced it properly.

The boy smiled enthusiastically, hearing his own name, before braving the question, "Who you?"

Sam couldn't stop smiling at the boy for some reason, politely responding, "My name is Sam. I'm from New York. Do you know where that is, Arcapi?"

The boy gave Sam a defiant look, stating, "New York, Si, I know. Senorita Liberty, Yankees, Big Apple!" Sam laughed at the response, easing the boy back to his grinning mannerism. The young man continued his questions with, "Why come to Tacna? You cross border, travel to Chile?"

Sam gave the boy a curious look, replying, "No. I came to Tacna to find someone. I write for a newspaper."

The fact that Sam wrote for a paper seemed to be discarded by the young Peruvian, but he did latch on to the fact that Sam was looking for someone, quickly responding, "Who you find? I know all."

The young man's eager desire to help forced Sam to hesitate from years of being so guarded by living in New York, but he decided there wouldn't be any harm in letting the interested lad take a shot at speeding up his search. Sam pulled out his notebook and read the name, "Manuela Esperanza, daughter of Roberto Esperanza."

Sam looked up to see Arcapi staring up the street as if he's no longer listening. Sam was about to ask if he heard the name, but the young man pointed in the direction he's watching, saying excitedly, "My grand mama walks there, now!"

Sam turned quickly to see an elderly woman enter a shop near the Plaza de Armas. He returned a look of disbelief to Arcapi, asking, "Your grandmother is Manuela Esperanza?"

Smiling hugely, the boy nodded agreement, following it by saying, "Come, we go see." Before Sam had time to react, Arcapi bolted down the sidewalk toward the plaza.

Sam shook off the amazing coincidence and trotted after the young Peruvian with an increased feeling of anticipation. He nearly giggled out loud, passing an enormous monument of some military leader of a battle long ago.

After being escorted to their table by the exceedingly pleased owner of the restaurant, Sam sat across from Arcapi and watched while his grandmother, Manuela Esperanza, indulged his every whim with the backdrop of soft Latin music playing overhead. She cleaned a smudge on his cheek from some unknown encounter Arcapi had with the earth, telling him in near perfect English that he needed to come over that evening for dinner, being she hadn't seen him in two entire days. Her thick, black and silver hair was bound up in an overflowing bun, and her face carried a constant display of quiet wisdom that seemed to engulf a calm for anyone within her vicinity.

Proud of his consistent eye contact he gave when interviewing, Sam found an added pleasure meeting Manuela's steady gaze, due to her astounding beauty. When she was younger, her father must have kept very busy chasing off suitors.

Agreeing to be interviewed by recorder, Manuela insisted she treat the three to a pre-lunch snack of something called sweet pastel de choclo before she headed back home for a busy day of cleaning and cooking. The restaurant was nearly empty, due to the early hour, which suited Sam just fine, having fewer distractions.

A light, warm breeze drifted through the open-aired dining area, with gentle scents of flowers and some unique spice Sam couldn't recognize. Manuela turned her attention to Sam while he's considering the aromas of the city, and he smiled at his own embarrassment, saying, "Sorry, I just can't ever remember feeling so relaxed in such an unfamiliar place. I find it odd how peaceful this city is."

Manuela leaned forward and stated, "Perhaps your soul has needed to travel."

Sam gave the intriguing thought an extra moment before referring to his notepad, turning on his small voice recorder, and asking, "Now, you've lived your entire life here in Tacna, is that correct?"

With a nod, Manuela replied, "Outside of six years in America, yes. My father fought for our freedoms and would not have desired to leave the city he so bravely protected. He instilled within us his strong patriotism and pride … " With perfect timing, she gracefully slid her arm around Arcapi, whose attention had begun to divert to the happenings on the street outside the restaurant, and his grandmother's nurturing arm snapped him back to the conversation. ". . . that he insisted we pass on to our own children, as well as our children's children."

The server and proprietor dropped off a platter of what looked to be corn pie in the middle of the table with three small side plates before the owner of the restaurant rattled off what appeared to be an expression of disappointment in his not seeing Manuela for a long period of time. Sam watched her receive the show of respect elegantly, reconsidering the owner's display of admiration he previously horded for himself and began to detect a level of reverence toward Manuela and her family. Curious by this, Sam slightly adjusted his questions about the family's past to its present with, "Manuela, can you tell me where Tacna's civic pride originates?"

The question actually received a brief look of surprise, which she softly contoured back to her usual tranquil presence. After a delicate bite from the small portion on her plate, she gathered her thoughts for the loaded question before asking, "Do you believe in a higher purpose, Mr. Noll; perhaps Fate or a specific Faith?"

Familiar with people answering his questions with questions, Sam allowed Manuela to do her own version of adjustment, answering, "Well, I was raised Baptist. Is that what you mean?"

She smiled, and added, "Religion is an invaluable channel, but purpose is what religion and belief should yield. Take me, for example. I wanted to go to college in America for as long as I could remember. My father wanted me to learn English, so he sent me to a school on the East Coast. After six years of working two jobs and going to school, I received my Masters in Education. I took this education and brought it home to Tacna, and was the English teacher for thirty-three years."

With a graceful wave about the room, Manuela proceeded, "I have seen hundreds upon hundreds of Peruvian children become bi-lingual and take their skills to incredible heights throughout the world, with many returning home to be teachers as well. I had a purpose before I was even born to help my people; I simply did not know how. So often, we waste much of our time and effort wondering what will come of our lives, when all we really need to do is trust in our purpose. The people of Tacna believe, with all of their hearts and within the depths of their minds, that they have such purpose. And our lives are a constant adventure toward that assured goal."

Sam remained silent from her story while Manuela returned his stare. Finally, Sam relented, asking, "Other than trust or Faith, are there any other paths to finding one's purpose, you know, like a shortcut or back door?"

Manuela's laugh was rich and pleasant, and Sam smiled to himself for simply causing her amusement. "I believe you understand what I am speaking of, even if you have yet to know your own path." Manuela moved her hands under the table and leaned forward, stating in a more serious tone, "Now then, I find it hard to believe you have traveled all the way down here to simply enjoy our pleasantries and to be enlightened of our sense of purpose."

Sam returned to his notebook, feeling his lesson from the teacher had concluded, and replied, "El Padre. The legend seems to have continued far beyond the battle in which your father witnessed his, shall we say, unique ability of selection."

Manuela smiled as though she had already known Sam's intent, replying with, "The legend is part of our people's resolve; if our patriotism is borne through the efforts of our ancestors who bravely fought for our independence, then El Padre is a symbol of our continued search for our life's intent."

Sam nodded his understanding, following with, "And your father; according to what I've read, was injured by gunfire from a group of Chilean soldiers, is that correct?"

She took a slightly pained expression when speaking of her father. "Yes, he was wounded in the shoulder and a bullet went through his leg. In fact, the Chilean soldier who had shot him was lying only twenty meters from where he was hiding, with neither having the means to inflict further damage upon one another. For a time, they spoke their words of anger and difference, but as time waned, their conversation conformed to their families and their strong desire to return home alive. A level of respect or understanding was acknowledged by both men, and their words became those of support and encouragement toward the other."

Sam interrupted the story, asking excitedly, "What was the name of the Chilean soldier?" preparing to write the name in his notepad.

Manuela answered without pause, "Xavier Molina from a small village north of Santiago. He was only two years younger than my father. His soul was taken that day by El Padre while my father watched."

CHAPTER 12

Sam recognized the lump forming within his throat and slight tingling sensation from deep inside when he became increasingly curious by a single piece of relayed information. The best avenue toward extracting illumination for a good story was slow, controlled breathing and sticking to a mental list of three to five most suitable questions he often seemed to form automatically inside his head. It's a pattern that had worked successfully over the years, but something nagged at him to keep from interrupting Manuela with questions and simply let her speak. If she didn't cover all of his requests, he could prompt her once she was finished.

Sam moved the recorder closer to Manuela, politely asking, "Will you tell me the whole story?"

She smiled and, for an instant, Sam thought she might say no, but, she settled in to her seat and began the tale of long ago. "Are you familiar with the War of the Pacific?" Manuela questioned as an opening.

Sam replied with a hint of embarrassment, "No. It sounds vaguely familiar from my limited research, but I can't recall any specifics."

Unfazed by his lack of South American history, she explained, "The great battle of my people took place from 1879 to 1883. Much like your Revolutionary War, it defined and shaped all Peruvians, especially those living in Arica and Tacna. The conflict was over land rights, as many guano and nitrate deposits were found throughout Tarapaca, Tacna, and Arica, and as the reason for most wars, one country had it and another wanted it."

Manuela broke for a drink of water, sat back, and crossed her legs before resuming, "By the end of the battle, Tacna and Arica were acquired by Chile, and their fate was to be determined in 1893 by plebiscite, which is a public opinion election. But this did not happen. Many small skirmishes and fights continued between Chile, Bolivia, and Peru until a compromise was established between Chile and Peru in 1929 giving Chile control of Arica, and Peru re-acquiring Tacna. Yet, even with this agreement in place, the hostilities remained."

Sam's pen ran out of ink and Manuela paused. Sam shook it twice before giving up on it and retrieving a replacement. He looked up at his patient interviewee and blushed, declaring, "Sorry; occupational hazard."

Manuela smiled warmly before picking up where she'd left off, "During the period of disagreement concerning Tacna's future, in January of 1923, my father was called to fight. He never explained whether it was my grandfather, a friend, or nothing more than civic pride that influenced him into battle in the mountains, and it was many years before I was born. I can only imagine that he did not wish to direct blame toward anyone but himself for his decision to join the fight. Many men fought bravely for ideals they believed were pure and many men died proudly. Many were Chilean, as well as Peruvian. Some were Bolivian. Death knows nothing of borders or reasons for wars; death accepts the proud, the greedy, and the pure of heart alike."

Arcapi, who had been relatively composed during the interview, whispered into his grandmother's ear. Manuela smiled and said to him, "Very well, my child, but do not forget about dinner tonight."

She kissed his matted head, and Arcapi slid off his seat, starting for the door, but stopped in his tracks and returned to the table. Extending his hand to Sam, Arcapi offered, "Very good we meet.

See you!" With that, he escaped out the door and merged into a passing group of youth across the street on their way to play soccer.

Manuela watched until he was no longer in sight. Sam commented, "He's a unique child. Polite, extremely sharp, and quite advanced socially for his age. I can only assume your skills of education have continued beyond retirement, perhaps?"

Turning back to the table, she smiled, letting the question remain unanswered, stating, "The boy will grow to be a man too soon, but for now, he is my little Arcapi." Sam just smiled at her joy and hopefulness, giving Manuela a moment to relax back into her narration.

She picked up as though she marked the place in a book, continuing with, "It was May of 1923, and my father and four other Peruvian fighters were asked to deliver a message one day's journey into the highlands to a lieutenant training a small group of soldiers. Before they reached the lower hills, they were flanked and attacked by a group of Chilean soldiers coming up from the south. My father and the other men fled up into the hills as the fighting continued for several hours."

Manuela gently slid forward in her seat, her narrative's intensity increasing. "Two armed Bolivians joined their fight halfway through the skirmish, giving the Peruvian soldiers a renewed strength in believing they would survive. They fought bravely with limited ammunition and held the higher ground as, one by one, his men were being wounded. He, too, had been injured, as you know, but instead of abandoning his men or their duty, he remained with them. The fighting diminished and darkness came and the remaining Chileans retreated back down the mountain. My father and one of the Bolivians began to crawl their way to tend to the injured. For those mortally wounded, they gave them solace. For the men they believed would survive, he and the Bolivian soldier gave them earnest hope and encouragement. Once they finished with their own people, they began assisting the Chileans, beginning with Senor Molina, though he insisted my father help others first."

Sam gave a noticeable look of indignation as Manuela suspended her story to ask, "Does this fact bother you, or is it that you find it hard to believe?"

Sam thought a moment, then answered, "I guess a little of both. I can understand, after several years, passing a Chilean on the street and saying hello, but helping them immediately once the bullets stop flying . . . it just begs to be questioned."

Manuela beamed at Sam her all-knowing smile, as though she expected his objection. He sat back and awaited another lesson in human character. "My father was a principled man. He greatly admired the example left by Peruvian Admiral Miguel Grau of the ironclad Huascar. He was an honorable, well respected captain of our Navy who, during the first year of the War of the Pacific, proved his chivalry on numerous occasions, such as in the Battle of Iquique, by rescuing his enemy's crew after the opposing ship had been bested. He even sent a respectful letter of condolence to the widow of the defeated Chilean Admiral Arturo Prat, along with her husband's sword and personal effects. These character traits rang deep within my father, so it was second nature for him to see to the enemy's needs, once his own men were tended to."

Sam shook his head, more from respect than speculation, saying, "It sounds like your father, just as Admiral Grau, was a great man in his own time."

As if there needed to be one more sample of evidence, Manuela added, "Just in recent years, Miguel Grau was recognized as the Peruvian of the Millennium, which was decided by popular vote."

Sam held up his hands in a show of defeat, replying, "I give! The man was and still is loved and adored by his people. Your father chose quite a man to be his role model."

Manuela leaned in, placing her hands onto the table with her palms down and, in a teacher-to-student like tone, replied, "I press this issue of strength of character so that, in your writing, it is made abundantly clear that the people of Tacna, as well as all Peruvians, weigh heavily upon the heroes of our past. Our heads are held high, because we not only have a history of fighting bravely, but in our defeats, we hold ourselves accountable to show dignity to the bitter end."

Sam was held by Manuela's intense stare, knowing his consent to her request was the only thing to release him. He slowly began to nod, answering, "I'll do as you ask. But I want you to know that I'm doing it because I believe it's not only relevant to the story, but because it's the underlying subplots to this account that I came here looking to find. El Padre and his growing legend is a drawing story, no doubt, but the understanding of the people involved gives each individual tale its own unique perspective."

She sat back contentedly and took a sip of her tea. Once the cup was returned to its saucer, she returned to the story of her family's past. "My father knew Senor Molina's injuries would most likely take his life, but he treated him as though he would return to his home. My father had crawled back to his backpack for more clothing he was using as bandages when he heard someone coming up the hill. Through the brush, he saw a man approaching the wounded Chilean soldiers and appeared to be assisting them. Fearing him to be an enemy, he remained in hiding. He observed the man curiously avoid those to have the better chance of survival and approach only the men close to death. My father said the man did this without a glance, as though he already knew who would not survive."

Sam's anxiousness got the better of him, uncharacteristically cutting in. "Please tell me your father spoke to El Padre?"

With a sincere expression of disappointment, Manuela answered, "I am sorry, but no. When El Padre came to Senor Molina, my father watched intently. He strained his ears in an attempt to listen to the words they spoke, but only heard very little. It was when the unknown man reached for his backpack that my father noticed the badly scarred hand. The light was fading in the hills, and my father remained unsure to whom the man showed allegiance, so he stayed behind the cover of the tree.

The man began speaking softly, gently to Senor Molina, and my father believed he heard the Chilean soldier cry out, 'May these things truly come to pass, as you say.' And with that, the man placed his left hand upon Senor Molina's head, as his body slumped gently to its lifeless position on the ground. My father wept at his passing, but continued to watch the strange man. With his hand still resting on Senor Molina's head, he lifted his face to the sky and appeared to pray."

With a slow shift to the back of the seat, Manuela uncrossed her legs, and proceeded, "Once finished, he rose and walked past the tree my father hid behind, venturing farther up the hill to kneel beside one of the Peruvian men my father traveled with and repeated the same scenario of dialog, hand to the head to relinquish the spirit, followed by the prayer. My father watched as the stranger disappeared up the mountain and farther into the darkened woods. His curiosity finally gave in, and he crawled back to Senor Molina's lifeless body, offering his own peace for the man's soul.

"Once it was decided to make their way back down the mountain, the Bolivian who had helped my father check on the injured, Senor Mateo Gutierrez, agreed to deliver the message to the lieutenant at the Peruvian training camp, completing their assigned mission. After parting ways, not more than one hundred meters down the slope, my father found the body of the youngest soldier who had accompanied him, lying peacefully near a tree. He recalled the young soldier's expression appeared to be smiling before slipping into his final sleep."

Sam interrupted, asking, "Do you remember the name of the young Peruvian?"

Manuela whispered softly, reverently, answering, "Alessandro Fuentes. He was only seventeen years old and lived right here in Tacna, on the east side of the city. His father and my father knew each other well, so naturally, it was upon my father to break the sad news of his death."

Sam made a note in his pad to reference later, asking, "And what of the Bolivian who delivered the message? Did anything ever come of him?"

Enjoying her interviewer's direction of questioning, Manuela smiled and asked, "Do you ever miss a stone unturned, Sam Noll?" Sam bashfully grinned and let the question remain unanswered. Manuela, though, didn't wait for one, proceeding with, "Senor Gutierrez found his way to Tacna some three years later. He and my father corresponded during those years and he chose to leave his country and move here with his family. He and my father remained close friends until the day they died."

Sam switched gears in the story by asking, "Sorry to jump around in the story, but I wish to revisit the part about when El Padre tended to the dying soldiers."

Manuela smiled warmly, responding with, "By all means, I know the story quite well, so I do not think I will lose my place."

Sam proceeded with his thought. "You say the stranger placed his left hand on the men he assisted, but did your father mention anything else about what occurred while he touched them; anything at all?"

Manuela took a thoughtful moment, retracing the story she'd known from her father's repeated account; then a curious look slipped across her face that formed into a mischievous smile as she looked back at Sam, sharing, "How strange that I have not thought of this in so many years. I can only assume I have left it out only due to its trivial nature."

Sam didn't want to press her, but finally disrupted her pondering with, "What? You're killing me here! Left what out?"

Manuela reengaged into the present, shrugging her response. "Again, it isn't much; it's just that I forgot that my father would describe the way the stranger treated the soldiers he tended to as if . . ." Manuela paused, wishing to word it properly. "As if he was performing a Holy Sacrament. He said it was as though he was giving them their last rites." Sam sat back heavily while Manuela proceeded, "It was why they began calling the stranger El Padre."

San Diego, 2001

Sitting at his regular table at his usual cafe, Nick scanned the room with one of his rare moments of interest beyond his own existence. His attention fell upon a family of four, consisting of parents, son, and daughter. He inhaled a regretful breath, long overdue, staring mesmerized by the completeness of the party of four as they dined, laughed and conversed with one another.

He quickly turned away as though the thoughts would cease with the absence of what had initiated them. His eyes betrayed his casual demeanor, locking their gaze upon his ring finger that, decades past, bore his band of commitment. How drastically his life had changed since then.

Some, though not many, would say the alteration had been for the better, as he never would have seen so much of the world and certainly wouldn't have accumulated the wealth, but there's always the still, quiet murmur deep within himself, whispering its same sad tune of what could have been. Being a devout, practicing realist, Nick knew that every living, breathing sack of flesh walking the earth had regrets, so why should he be any different in this regard? His reasons for leaving his ready-made family twenty-three years earlier had been wrestled into submission long ago.

He set his jaw, pushing his thoughts toward his current dilemma of whether a supporting character of his recent novel should live or suffer a horrendous death. About to stroke his full beard, as he often did when deep in thought, a gentle voice interrupted his subconscious habit, asking, "Might I bother you for your salt, as mine seems to have been exhausted?"

Nick turned to notice the kindly gentleman sitting to his right for the first time, grabbing the shaker, responding, "Of course, not a problem." handing it to the man, adding, "Sorry. I didn't even see you sit down."

Making abundant use of the salt, the gentleman replied, "I could see you were working something out." He stopped his shaking long enough to gesture with a finger to his own head. "Up here." With a brief smile that started with upturned lips, then lighting up within his blue eyes, he held Nick's stare for only seconds before returning to his feverish dispensing of salt.

Nick continued watching the man devour his stuffed potato and side of broccoli. A peculiar desire began to build inside him to continue the conversation. "So, I appeared to be deep in thought, then?" Nick contended while the man worked over his final bites.

Slowly, the man politely dabbed at both corners of his mouth with his napkin and took in a contemplative breath, as if he was grieving his final meal. Turning to Nick, giving him his undivided attention, he stated, "My friend, when I see the look of consternation upon the face of another, I feel duty driven to offer my ear. I make this offer without pretense or subterfuge, as that would only contradict its pure intention. May I ask what trouble seems to grasp your thoughts?"

Nick chuckled at the question. He began to mentally venture down the path of an honest answer and felt compelled to speak it aloud. "Since I decided to become a writer, I've squandered so many precious moments bellowing forth the useless tirade of my chosen field. So many constantly repeated questions from faceless people asking the same subject, and all of it followed by my gleeful acknowledgment to share the secretive insight of every established author; the story of 'Me'."

Nick let out one further sly chuckle before proceeding, "And, by chance, you come to sit beside me, a complete stranger, asking me to talk about what troubles *my* thoughts." Nick slowly shook his head back and forth, staring at his discarded plate, not yet retrieved by the waiter, asking, "Allow me to inquire this from you; can a man step beyond redemption and be consumed for eternity by his self-absorption?"

El Padre appeared unfazed by Nick's turn of interrogation, but instead leaned in and simply replied, "My friend, a wise man like yourself must realize that forgiveness can only be received from the one who has been harmed, and the request must be presented by a pure and humbled heart. Salvation is never beyond our grasp."

Nick stared at his half empty wine glass, turning it in his hand, asking quietly, "And what if one of these who was harmed is no longer with us?"

El Padre met the solemn question with a sobering response of, "The dead care not about forgiveness. They have far too much to contend with to concern themselves with our petty grievances here on earth."

Nick turned at the dark response and intently observed El Padre, trying to deduct just whom he's speaking with. After a pensive scratch to his beard, Nick dove in further. "Does your wisdom care to advise me further?"

El Padre smiled at the question, deflecting the compliment, saying, "Whatever wisdom I may, or in particular circumstances, may not possess is a direct blessing from He who is most worthy."

Nick's eyes became slits, humorously inquiring, "Are we speaking of the Oracle, Buddha, or the Wizard of Oz?"

El Padre smiled back, adding, "If God's wisdom may, in some way, be utilized through me, feel free to convey your curiosity."

Nick scooted closer to El Padre, lowering his head in a secretive fashion, and his voice dropped several octaves, struggling to produce the precise wording. "Many years ago, before I chose to become a writer, I had a wife and a son. Kathleen . . . that was her name."

Nick took a brief sip of his wine before going on. "She had been married before, and the brief unity bore a son; a bright boy." His face lit up with the next thought. "He took to me immediately, and I to him. He was a wonderful child, and she a devotedly beautiful wife. It was nearly blissful, the three of us."

Darkness descended upon Nick's countenance before pressing forward. "I was an assistant editor for a large literary agency in Boston, but believed I was capable of writing something better than what I was reading. So, I began to work on an idea for a novel during my few spare moments, but life has a way of consuming even the briefest of stolen minutes when you're committed to family and career. My mind began to wander during evening times set aside for my wife and son, and at work I spent so much energy on my own manuscript that my workload began to suffer."

Nick shook his hands in frustration at the memory, continuing, "When I tried to stop or take an extended break from writing, I became insufferably dispirited, to say the least. For some writers, if you're not riding the inspirational wave of creativity, you feel out of place or less than adequate. I'm one of such writers; it's nearly like an addiction to a drug, always anxious for the next journey to see how high it will take you. I saw my career and my family as anchors around my neck, pulling me under and keeping me from swimming to the other side. So, one morning I left for work, only I kept driving for four days until finally stopping once I reached the other ocean."

El Padre remained silent and attentive, but during the short break, seized the opportunity to ask, "What is the boy's name?"

Nick nearly started from the question. Staring at El Padre, he asked back redundantly, "I didn't tell you his name? How odd. Michael is his name, though no longer a boy, I must admit. He should be celebrating his twenty-ninth birthday today."

El Padre intently stared at Nick appearing momentarily lost in his thoughts. El Padre closed his eyes, asking softly, "Please tell me, my friend, if Michael were sitting across from you at this very table, right here, right now, what exactly would you wish to say?"

Nick obediently looked at the chair facing him through dreamlike vision cast from El Padre's focused will and stared in disbelief at his late wife's son, Michael, as tears welled in his eyes. Nick's unsettled guilt pushed him back into his seat, but his eyes refused to let go of the image before him. He reached across the table and Michael extended his hand and met him halfway. Feeling the softness of the young man's hand, Nick brought it to his face as he wept openly.

El Padre gently placed his hand on Nick's shoulder, whispering, "Tell him what you feel. Share with Michael how much you've missed him."

Nick managed his emotions, looking deeply into Michael's face, saying, "My son, my dearest son, I beg for your forgiveness. In my selfishness, I deserted the only true happiness my life has ever known. Please believe that I loved you and your Mother so very much, but I became weak and wrongly blamed everyone around me for my inability to prioritize what mattered most. I regret my poor decision that kept me from watching you grow up; to see with my very eyes how you became a man. I should have adopted you as my own. I'm sorry I failed to be there for Kathleen when she became sick and suffered from her illness."

An emotional intake of breath before Nick proceeded, "I should have been there holding her hand, telling her that I loved her and that I would take care of you. For all of these things and so much more, I plead with every ounce of hope and desire within me for atonement. Will you grant me this tremendous gift?"

Broken down and humbled, Nick lowered his face to the table and respectfully waited for the answer, knowing he deserved nothing in return. He didn't have to wait long before El Padre's voice spoke softly into his ear, "Lift your head, for you are now fully prepared to seek that which you require for peace."

Nick sat up quickly and immediately looked across the table at the empty chair. Turning to his right, he began to inquire, "Where did he . . ." but stopped in mid-sentence seeing no one there.

Arriving to remove Nick's plate, the waiter asked, "Would you care for another glass of wine?"

Still staring at the empty seat next to him, Nick turned to the waiter, still trying to figure out what had just happened, and slowly replied, "Um, no thank you." The waiter began to move away before Nick asked him quickly, "Pardon me, but wasn't there a gentleman recently sitting over there?" gesturing to the table El Padre temporarily possessed.

The waiter followed the gesture, staring at the empty seat, looked back at Nick, answering, "I'm not sure. I just came off break.

The waiter who covered my tables might know, but he just ended his shift and went home. Is there anything else I can do for you?"

Nick slowly looked back at the chairs across from him, then to his right, before turning back to the empty place where his plate was. There, sitting alone, was a small piece of paper inscribed with a Boston phone number. Nick picked up the note, glancing back toward the waiter, contentedly replying, "No, I believe I have everything I need."

CHAPTER 13

Sam made his way toward the commercial section of Tacna. He'd made plans to meet Manuela for a follow-up appointment once he'd written the first installment and to see if she'd found someone to guide him into the mountains. Unfortunately, his second possible descendant he'd come to interview was in the late stages of dementia. The elderly man's son had been extremely gracious, offering to assist in an interview, but Sam had declined. A father and son trying to hold on to a past slipping away, little by little, deserved its respective freedom from exploitation.

Knowing colorful animation never replaced the real thing, Sam intended to venture up to the area where the skirmish of 1923 occurred to get a feel for the lay of the land, but being directionally disadvantaged, he asked Manuela to seek someone with personal knowledge of the area. They'd agreed to meet at a small cafe that her friend operated. Sam arrived punctually only to find Manuela already seated, chatting with a woman near her age, which Sam assumed to be the owner.

Approaching the table, Sam watched the woman speaking with Manuela turn his way, smile her greeting, and excuse herself. Sam set down his leather case, saying in place of a greeting, "She didn't need to leave on my account, Manuela. I hope I don't already have a reputation to duck and hide from."

Manuela smiled graciously as Sam took his seat across from her, responding, "In this beautiful city of ours, you will find a sense of deserved tranquility, a rare type of kindness to all and a passion for singularity, but in the very same people you will also see a sovereign oneness toward our freedoms which come from our not so distant history of fighting for our independence."

Sam shifted his weight in his seat and tilted his head curiously, replying, "The people of this beautiful city are gracious and open, but I'd be fibbing if I didn't admit to coming across one or two locals whose greeting may have been deemed as perhaps a bit 'frosty.' But, coming from New York, I simply appreciated them for making me feel at home."

Manuela smiled at Sam's sense of humor before attempting to explain, "In your country, your freedoms were settled more than two hundred years ago, allowing you, your parents, as well as your grandparents, to be raised in a democracy which allows you to achieve whatever dream you wish to fulfill. Many born and raised here in Tacna before the fifties carry with them a deep-seeded suffering of uncertainty passed down from their parents, always wondering if we must travel down the disruptive path of fighting for what is ours once again."

Sam could only offer her a look of questioning perplexity, struggling to understand an example of strife he'd never had to suffer through. Manuela tilted her head appearing to contemplate a better example to assist his understanding. Finally, she wagged a finger at him, continuing her explanation with, "In the 1930's, every American felt the reverberations of the collapse of the stock market, yes?"

Sam shifted back into comfort mode firmly, if not mentally, returning his feet back upon steady ground, answering confidently, "You're talking about the Great Depression that was triggered by the stock market crash of 1929." Manuela nodded, but remained silent, allowing Sam to catch up with her as he proceeded, "Okay, I'm curious how you intend to connect the two dots of America's Great Depression and the people of Tacna's cautionary sense of character."

Manuela spread her hands out onto the table, palms down, before returning to her teaching mode, explaining, "In your country's time of depression, it has been well documented by historians the reflex of consumer loss of confidence, increased unemployment, and the acquired custom of hoarding every cent saved or earned as nearly everyone's wealth and savings disappeared. The activity of placing great importance on decreasing any and all waste was obviously imbedded deeply into the adults and children of this time. A time where the purchase of three potatoes was needed to feed a family of six for perhaps three meals or where the gift of a single bag of week-old bread was considered a virtual gold mine of treasures celebrated by the entire family.

Easing back in her seat, Manuela proceeded to connect the two theories. "This philosophy transcended from that generation to the next, leading many parents to raise their children with a fierce habit of saving money for the questionable future. It is this concept of exaggerated concern or fear that they are unable to restrain because it has become a means of survival, even though they have become financially secure. The same is with the people of Tacna. Instead of a concern toward money, we feel an insecurity of freedom, taking our liberties seriously, yet are ever watchful of the horizon for Chilean ships or invading Bolivian armies. Perhaps this unsettling awareness can one day find its peace, and maybe Arcapi's children can live free of such feelings. I can only hope and pray."

Sam considered the comparison for a moment before reaching over and gently grasping Manuela's hand. Startled by the contact, she lifted her eyes to his while Sam held her attention for only a breath before asking, "There was a second version to America's repercussion from the Great Depression. Are you familiar with it?"

She only shook her head once, slowly, without disturbing their link. Sam let a crooked smile slip into his expression before continuing, "For many of those inflicted with the sudden poverty of working for pennies and scraping together the entirety of the family's savings for things we now take for granted, caused an opposing reaction. The children of that generation vowed to never let their own children want or need for anything. They raised them to appreciate the finer things in life, buying them a brand new car when they received their driver's license, new clothes at the start of each school year, or pushing them toward sports and scholastic achievements, not leaning them into the responsibilities of working after school or weekends. They pamper their offspring so they never have to feel the hunger, want nor need from the imprints left by the emotional scars of their own childhood."

Sam evened out his smile, moving forward to the punch line, stating, "And, just as there's a counter to my country's time of despair, so, too, is one for yours. I see how you are with your grandson, and I can only imagine you were the same with your daughter; displaying an abundance of love, compassion, and most of all, fearlessness."

Manuela sat back from the examination and looked toward the door, as if contemplating a hasty exit, struggling with her own influence on her offspring, but Sam retained his grasp upon her delicate hand and could see that her eyes began to question his direction. Sam brought his right hand to join the left, holding her hand softly and pushed toward his closing. "To inundate your family with a civic pride, coupled with a reassurance that no man can take away their personal freedoms, can only allow them to walk down their intended paths, or as you put it, 'their life's purpose,' with their heads held high, believing there is nothing they can't achieve." He squeezed her hand slightly to get her to return his gaze. It worked, and he added, "And I'd take that family gift over a new car any day."

Manuela released the building emotion with a deep laugh at Sam's perspective, letting go of each other's hands and sitting back at the same time. A brief silence seeped in, and Manuela quickly cleared her throat before abruptly changing the subject. "Oh, I spoke with my friend about a guide and gave her your number like you asked. You should hear something later today. She sounded quite hopeful."

Sam nodded, smiling, before responding, "Thank you for calling her, as well as allowing me to take so much of your time. Your interesting history and the stories of your family have been a great help with the article."

He started to add something else, but caught himself. "What is it, Samuel? You seem to have one more question to ask, no?" Manuela asked innocently.

Sam looked up at her with an innocuous grin and held the silence for only a second before asking, "I've noticed a certain reverence or respectful awe from many who live here concerning you and your family. I'm curious if you acknowledge it or will admit to its existence?"

Once again, Manuela looked toward the door for relief from the direct line of inquest, but then turned back to Sam with a darker shade to her otherwise sunny disposition. "To understand the acknowledgment of respect in this country, one must comprehend many generations of unequaled display of courage and honor," she almost whispered across the table, causing Sam to lean forward as if they're exchanging top secret information.

"Go on. At least, until I begin to show an expression of some form of dim-witted understanding. Then you can stop!" Sam humorously retorted, which eased Manuela's demeanor somewhat.

"I'm not certain I can even explain it effectively, but I will try," she responded. Sam only nodded, allowing her to take the floor, continuing with, "This show of respect comes not from any one occurrence, nor anything a single individual in my lineage has done, but by many. My heritage leads back to the early 1700's, to include those who survived the earthquake of 1784 and our descending from the heroic libertarian, Francisco Antonio De Zela. We grieve our family's loss each year on the anniversary of our five brave ancestors who, on one fateful day, offered their lives defending our nation on the front line during the War of the Pacific. And we pay homage to numerous heroic tales of distant relatives whose names may not ring familiar or be inscribed into any history books, yet are immortalized within our hearts."

Manuela subconsciously centered her necklace's pendant before continuing, "It is this proud, unshakeable lineage of patriotism that you most likely detect, borne through the devastation of losses and carried forth by the vision and fortitude of victories. To live here, is to accept our courageous past, but to have been born here, carries the burden of never forgetting the sacrifices so many gave. Our path and the lives we are allowed to freely choose, need to be a constant reminder that what they forfeited must be for a greater good."

Sam blankly stared at Manuela, unable to properly express his admiration for her explanation. Recognizing a hint of appreciation, she filled in the silence with, "I can only assume we have reached the end of our interview?" gesturing with a slow nod toward Sam's voice recorder.

Sam reached for his device, turning it off, stammering a response, "Yes. I think that pretty much sums up what I was looking for." Stuffing his notepad and recorder into his leather case, Manuela reached across the table, grasping his arm, freezing Sam's movement. He slowly looked at her weathered hand on his arm and followed up her sleeve, shoulder, and, finally, her face, as her intensity found its extent, softly stating, "Please remember this, Samuel; there is purpose in all things and I have great anticipation for your journey ahead." With that, Manuela Esperanza released his arm, rose gracefully, turned, and walked out the door.

CHAPTER 14

Unable to pawn off one last aerobics class while her parents were visiting, Katie sat on the subway heading home. Staring at the back of the seat ahead, the only thing she focused on was her anger toward Sam. With only two days left before her parent's departure, she cursed the thought of his gallivanting around Peru, smiling with every experience, while she juggled their life back at home, taking care of Spalding, giving away her classes and trying to fill her parents visit with an overload of activities. The brief thought of keeping herself from slipping into her 'martyrdom' mode whispered from its secretive place within her mind. Impulsively, Katie grabbed her phone, filtering down to her analyst's number, and pressed the green 'call' button.

Waiting for the connection, she privately admitted her 'analyst' was actually a psychologist, but referring with terms or titles not as desperate sounding allowed her to feel in control and self-assured. Making appointments to help her cope with her self-esteem, anger, and anxiety issues, Katie, also, affirmed to her meddling self-criticism that adjusting what someone was called, as opposed to what they actually did, was the easy decision of the lesser evil. What truly mattered were the results, and she believed she'd come a long way in the last four years of off-and-on appointments.

Once she squeezed in the 'meeting' and confirmed it into her schedule, the sheer fact of having someone to unload on immediately let her feel less drained and hopeful, like ordering food when extremely hungry; knowing it's coming gave one an unexpected second wind to endure until it arrived.

Katie's father hadn't masked his displeasure in Sam's sudden need to fly south, adding to her anxiety. Unable to defend the actions of her boyfriend, Katie was left to simply stomach her father's lengthy tirades concerning his belief that Sam was only interested in the milk and had no interest in buying the cow. Her comparison to the cow in the analogy was, no doubt, going to take up a chunk of her next fifty minute 'meeting' with her 'analyst.'

Once she's back at home, Katie read Sam's article to her parents after dinner, thinking it would fill her with anxiousness and pride. Instead, it left her feeling empty and detached. Throughout their daughter's enthusiastic interpretation, her parents remained silent. Once complete, though, her mother was unable to grasp the futility in searching the world for someone connected to so much death. Her father, on the other hand acknowledged the good writing, and with his long career as a military man, admitted his enjoyment concerning the parts having to do with fighting and war. After a pause, and not one to leave a subject on a positive note, he found a way to segue Sam's column to a lack of commitment and carelessness of character in young men of today's generation.

As usual, the short spat ended before any real ammo was brought out, with their preemptive agreement to disagree; something that'd become their awkward attempt at getting along within close quarters.

Unaccustomed to the negative verbal exchange, Spalding escaped to the kitchen, waiting for Katie to use him as an excuse for an escape outdoors.

At the park, Katie and Spalding's walk was more like a half marathon. With every light pound from her running shoes upon the paved sidewalk, she slowly transferred the anger from her verbal contest with her father to where it truly belonged; the merry traveler and absentee boyfriend, Sam.

Sam had done a rather convincing job assuring her that the timing of his trip to Peru had been purely happenstance and certainly not premeditated in the least, but, over time and meticulous replay in her mind, the whole story was beginning to smell rotten. After giving Spalding a break from the exertion, and while he utilized the 'puppy' fountain to quench his thirst, Katie stared at the fountain with eyes unfocused while her maddening thoughts, at last, found its complete circle. The basic point of contention she'd been struggling with, was that he placed his article above her and their relationship.

The real kicker that bridged the missing emotional link was her deep, unspoken resentment she had toward her father and his past military career, which moved her and their family nine times before she reached her senior year in high school. Never once had he asked what Mother, Katie, or her siblings wanted or thought; it was simply time to go. Never once had her father explained why they were moving or how long they would be at the next location. It left Katie with a youthful history of too many half-friendships, of short-term pen pals who after a second move, no longer wrote, and a spotty memory of which state or military base she learned how to swim, started wearing make-up or first kissed a boy.

Her therapist had spoken so many times about transference and all of its deceptive forms, but just like the doggy fountain before her, one could lead the dog to the fountain, but if nobody pushed the right button, the puppy went without.

For the first time in her life, she found herself *wanting* to let go of her anger toward her father, *wanting* to acknowledge it wasn't him, but rather the career he chose. Most likely, her father had sat down with her mother long before Katie was born and explained what type of life was ahead of them. After all, she was still by his side after thirty-four years of marriage. Didn't that say something about understanding?

She and Sam had been together quite a while before the article sprang into existence. She had seniority. Since they'd never sat down and verbally applied a few ground rules concerning their relationship, Sam had allowed his life to remain at status quo, fitting Katie's needs in at his leisure. Just because her moving in started out as Sam doing her a favor certainly shouldn't mean she's enlisted to carry all the emotional burden and responsibility of the relationship. Katie smiled as the water fountain came back into focus. Bending over to show Spalding a little affection, she realized she was through running.

With three more Peruvian-based segments to the article completed and sent off to Ira, and confidently finishing up the fourth, Sam decided a little celebration was overdue. The venture into the mountains with his guide, Thomas, two days previous answered many of the gaps he'd been hoping to fill. With his excellent English, taught to him naturally by his high school teacher, Senorita Esperanza, Thomas provided Sam with an unbiased, if not humorous, interpretation of his country's past.

During their hike through the desolate landscape, his recollection of several side-stories not only reaffirmed Manuela's account of her father's part in their history, but also opened the door to one additional bi-line for his piece. What truly made the trip worthwhile through the abruptly changing climates and arduous ascent was what he found at the site. The location of where the small battle took place had been preserved over the years by a local government-funded organization. Small plaques honoring each individual who fought and died, regardless of which side they represented, were placed in various locations on the western face of the small mountain.

Once the terrain gave way to an area of level ground surrounded by few trees, Sam stopped in front of a large hand-carved sign telling the tale of the unexpected battle of Cordillera del Barroso. Looking around the area, he could almost visualize the surprise and immediate reaction of Roberto Esperanza's small band of young fighters scrambling for protection toward the trees encircling the open field. Without the prior knowledge of what took place there, anyone could notice the plaques or quickly read the large sign and continue on their way, completely unmoved by its meaning or place in Peruvian history.

Sam left the mountainside that day with a strong feeling of respect, admiration, and pride toward humanity for how the survivors chose to set aside their differences and help one another. Their simple show of civility in such desperate circumstances was humbling to the point of numbness as he considered how they met on that barren hill as opposites, but so quickly evolved into compatriots fighting one enemy; death and its ability to take them from their families.

Since his first night in Tacna, now nine days past, Sam had avoided the 'strong stuff,' opting for a beer or two as refreshment. Now, he decided it's time to get to the bottom of the Pisco Sour difference between Chile and Peru, and in doing so, would toast to the bravery of men from so long ago.

The rare, short message from Sam letting her know he's stateside and what time he'd land in New York caused a strange flutter of emotion within Katie, like a disturbed bee hive. The resolve she'd committed to burned deep inside while she finished up on the treadmill. Every mile of the revolving rubber surface under her feet brought her closer to their heart-to-heart discussion. With her parents safely returned home and life's routines settling back into their proper places, her focus was able to shift and compress directly toward Sam. Picking up the stride while running in place, Katie played through her opening, basis of reasoning, and confident finale one more time for good measure.

The briefest thought of sympathy for the eventual blind-siding flickered the edge of consideration, but she ignored its imaginary raised hand, substantiating the need to inflict her will for the good of the relationship. Knowing Sam wasn't one to argue about their personal life, the little chat would be quick and painless.

The man could venomously debate about the decay of morality in American society or the varying religion nuances between pygmies in South Africa, but when it came to matters of the heart, Sam was consistently mum.

Katie had suitably prepared for the one-sided conversation with four simple topics and a flowing, but brief, strategy that brought about a smile at its conciseness. Now, all that she required was a shower and the return of her boyfriend so they could put the subject to rest once and for all.

Walking in the door and dropping his bags in the entryway after such a long, exhilarating adventure, being greeted by an overly excited Spalding erased all exhaustion from the lengthy return flight. The happy welcome carried him into the kitchen with his dog at his heels, not allowing his master out of his sight just yet.

Sam opened the fridge, reaching in to grab a beer. Katie emerged from the bathroom and into the kitchen wearing a tight fitting black dress, hair and make-up prepared flawlessly, and nails freshly polished from hand to toe. Sam and Spalding stared at her without a proper word or bark to offer. The two remained stupefied, giving Katie her first introduction to her planned checklist; flood his senses. She broke the silence, offering a simple, "Welcome home."

Sam, realizing his mouth remained gaped, released a humbling, "Wow! You look absolutely breathtaking." With a quick slap to his forehead, he added, "Nuts! Did I forget about plans for tonight? With the long flight and getting in late, I'm totally brain-dead."

Katie moved closer, answering with a laugh. "No, silly. I just wanted to make your welcome a little . . . memorable."

Sam lifted an arm as she slipped into him while he closed the fridge door, saying, "Memorable? This staggering image will be burned into my heart, mind, and soul for all of eternity!"

Her welcoming kiss was soft and slow. Quickly, she released him, withdrawing from under his wing, and leaving Sam with her soft impression before Katie proceeded in a hush, "I thought we could have some wine; a little celebration of the returning, conquering writer."

Sam physically shook the fogginess administered from her kiss in time to respond, "Sounds great! What smells so good in the oven? Did I walk into little Italy?"

Katie struck a match, lighting two candles on the table, before answering, "There's crab manicotti next to the fresh baked bruschetta waiting in the oven. I've been keeping it warm until you got home."

Sam opened the oven for a peek and inhaled the warm, delightful aroma, turning back to her, saying, "Now this is how to welcome somebody home! I'll bring these over and pour the wine."

The meal didn't disappoint. Every forkful was accentuated with the backdrop of Katie, candlelit and glowing. The combination of the wine and the view were beyond intoxicating. The two settled into the living room with their wine glasses topped off and melted onto the sofa. "That's got to be one of the greatest meals of all time." Sam breathed out upon landing. "The wine, the dinner, your dress and dessert; it all just couldn't have been better."

Katie looked back toward the kitchen, then returned her attention to Sam, replying, "But I didn't make any dessert."

Sam smiled at her mischievously and reached for her with both arms, giving her the punch line that he believed he'd set-up, "Well, I guess we'll just have to think of something appropriate for a colossal meal like that!"

Katie caught up to where Sam's mind was headed and put his plans on hold by saying, "Whoa, cowboy. We haven't even had a chance to catch up on what either of us have been doing for the last two weeks. So, put the horse back into the corral and simmer down. This is the first opportunity I've had to just talk with you. There's plenty of time to ride later."

Sam pressed the back of his head into the sofa, responding childishly, "But I don't wanna talk. I'm a cowboy! I wanna ride the range!" Katie playfully hit him in the arm, which signified to Sam the subject was decidedly over for now. Sam sat up, begrudgingly evolving into an adult once again, and in a humorous huff responded, "Fine. We can talk, I guess."

Katie took a sip of wine before opening with, "So, the column seems to be finding an audience. I've heard it mentioned on a program last week, and I hear people talking about it at work and on the subway. It sounds like it's taking off."

Sam became enthused with this subject matter and responded by scooting to the edge of the seat, replying, "Really? It was mentioned on a program? I hadn't heard about that, but yeah, the feedback has been alright; not record breaking, but moderately surprising."

She let him bask in the moment of editorial success for several seconds before asking, "And do you have any upcoming trips on the horizon? You know, any leads you'll have to fly off for?"

Not wanting to leave his limelight quite so soon, Sam responded after a pause with, "Hmm? Oh, no. I don't think I could repeat this last scenario. I'm going to have to build any further stories, for the time being, either on short day trips or from the comfort of my desk, via the World Wide Web."

Katie put on a face of mild disappointment, responding with an appropriate, "Oh, well, that's too bad."

Sam gave her an amused expression, asking inquisitively, "Since when are you disappointed by my lack of travel? Is there a new male yoga instructor I need to worry about?"

Katie smiled reassuringly, but then replied snidely, "No, but there *is* a new cute teenager working the counter at the yogurt shop on fourth. Just think of all the free yogurt I could get my hands on!"

Sam laughed along, but then stopped, wondering if there's any truth to her admission. He shook off the doubt and added, "Anyway, so what's up with you pushing me out the door? And just after I get home from a trip we can both admit was untimely."

Katie waved at him dismissively, responding, "I'm not trying to get rid of you; I'm glad you're home. It's just that I know how much weight you place on writing from experience and not being able to 'be there' will take away from what you wish to convey to the reader."

Sam stared at his girlfriend for a bemused moment before concluding, "I don't think anyone could have stated exactly how I feel about this issue as well as you just did. Not even me!"

Katie simply smiled from the compliment, proceeding with, "All I'm trying to say is, when you're gone, I know, in a small way, you're following your ambition of writing the very best article you possibly can, given all of the external circumstances you're faced with. For instance, with me, my job is here in the city. I have my job and I have us and I work hard at both, to make every effort toward noticeable forward progress with each of them. But it's difficult for me, you know, with a different set of external circumstances to carry the weight of both; to make them work."

Sam continued nodding and listening, but knew his attention span light was blinking low. Clearly, Katie noticed it, as well, quickly moving forward, stating, "Sam, what I'm trying to say in a roundabout way is, I know when I first moved in, it was more out of convenience than from a place of commitment or level we had reached in our relationship. I understand that, and to a certain point accept it. But I refuse to be the noose around your neck or the one pulling on the leash, trying to hold you back."

To stress her sincerity, Katie placed a hand on Sam's leg before continuing, "I know we've talked about how I have a hard time with you being gone and not hearing from you, but I feel as though I'm the one keeping this relationship afloat. Your article seems to come first and foremost in your life right now, and I wish you could talk less about death and dying and more about us and our life together. I need you to unplug from work when you're here and act like you actually want me around other than to cook, wash your clothes, and walk Spalding."

If there had been any fade to Sam's ability to listen attentively, he managed to discover a much needed second wind. Mentally, he shuffled through several responses, discarding all of them due to their lack of depth. Katie had brought up some serious topics that obviously had been weighing on her mind for quite some time. To respond lightly would only belittle her feelings and possibly enrage her in the process, but what should he comment on first? Several inquiries immediately push to the forefront, but there's no way he's going to start pelting her with questions he's already supposed to understand. Sitting there quietly wouldn't clear up his ignorance of what she meant by 'external circumstances' or why she felt someone was wearing a noose, and had she referenced him somewhere in there as a dog? Before Sam could settle on one front to address, his time for a response ran out on him, even though it was all he'd been working on.

Katie pushed herself off the couch in one easy thrust and spun around to stand over Sam, saying through clenched teeth, "Nothing. You have nothing to say then?"

Sam looked up at her sheepishly, offering, "Yes, I do. It's just so much to register. I mean, it's a lot to process."

Her hands moved to her hips in a defensive manner, and Sam knew immediately that it didn't matter what had come out of his mouth; it would have been some form of bait. "Oh, so what you're *trying* to say is that I'm high maintenance." she asked pointedly.

Sam waved his hands, trying his best to hit replay, saying, "No, no. Not you. It's the array of subjects you bring up; they're all important, every single one of them, and it's just difficult deciding which one to cover first."

Katie jumped crisply on the opening, seething. "Okay, so not only am I high maintenance, but I'm too complex and difficult. Got it!" Sam dropped his face into his hand rather than toss his girlfriend any further slow pitches for her to knock out of the park. The evening started with such good intentions, and he's unable to back-track to where exactly he screwed up. In case there's any doubt on whether intimacy was still on the table, Katie added, "And for the record, my body is *not* a 'range' for you to 'ride,' and being that you're such a gifted writer, you probably should have gone with 'beautiful hills and lush dale'!" With one more spin in the opposite direction, she headed for the bedroom and slammed the door behind her.

Sam winced a stare down the hall, rubbed his head, and extoled to himself, "And then comes the bill for dinner!" before fluffing a sofa pillow and making himself comfortable on the couch.

The next morning, Sam was up early from a restless sleep. Evidently, when one male was evicted from the bedroom, all males had to follow suit, so Spalding spent half the night on half the couch, leaving Sam with little room for comfort. With Sam's special coffee made, the previous night's dishes cleaned, and the kitchen straightened up, Katie emerged from their bedroom puffy-eyed and hair disheveled. Sam nipped his first thought of comparison to her previous night's kitchen entrance and opted to go with simply handing her a cup of brew just the way she liked it.

Once her first sip of caffeine was administered, Sam unloaded. "Listen, I have no idea what exactly happened last night. First, you make us the most incredibly intimate dinner I've ever enjoyed, then not one right word comes out of my mouth. Please believe me that I want to be the best boyfriend I can possibly be, but I'm going to screw up from time to time. I want to share the cooking, the cleaning, and the laundry. I'll walk Spalding anytime you don't want to. I know my work takes me away every once in a while and, unfortunately, I can't help that. But I'll promise to be here when I'm home, and I'll try to keep our life and my job separate. I don't want you to have to pull my leash. I want to already be by your side."

Katie held the cup with both hands, listening while she savored the warmth from the hot coffee. Finally, a small grin and a sparkle to her eyes returned, simultaneously with the release of Sam's held breath. Before he got ahead of his emotions, he quickly asked, "Now, is that smile from the caffeine kicking in, or am I going in the right direction?"

Katie slugged him in the arm before setting her cup down and putting her arms around him, replying into his ear, "I'm sorry about last night, too. I can't blame you for how you reacted from the way I dumped absolutely everything I've been dealing with while you were gone. That was completely unfair."

Sam pulled her to arm's length and shook his head, saying, "No, it's alright. The timing for the trip was awful, and I left you to deal with way too much without me. It's my fault." Another smile from her and they silently agreed to let it go and share the blame.

After breakfast, Sam got ready for work and kissed Katie in an exaggerated fashion before heading out the door. Ascending the stairs, something nagged at his subconscious concerning the fight the night before, and the feeling preoccupied his thoughts the entire way to his office. A sensation of something lost or tainted was all he could cypher, but exactly what and by whom was still murky. One thing for certain was that he needed to put more energy on the story at work, allowing him to be more attentive at home. Not sharing his El Padre ghost stories simply had to become a way of life. There would be a 'work Sam' and his alter-ego 'home Sam.' Maybe utilizing a pair of horn-rimmed glasses could help him recognize one identity from the other.

Uganda, 2003

Preparing his soul to speak to the heavens, El Padre pondered to himself how the word 'massacre' was so desperately over-used in modern language of any dialect. As a noun, it became exceedingly descriptive, and when used as a verb, even more venomous. He recalled, years ago, passing by a high school teenager in a letterman's jacket calling to a teammate how they massacred another football team the previous week. At the time, El Padre gave it little consideration. Odd, how easily a small amount of perspective could open one's eyes.

Under his scarred, weathered hand lay a small child of Uganda, beaten and broken, sucking his final gasps here on earth. "You are loved, child. You are so deeply loved," he uttered as the boy's eyes dilated, struggling to focus on El Padre. "In Heaven there is a place prepared for you, and God, the Father, waits to take you into His open arms. His home has many mansions, and you shall sit upon his lap and receive His unconditional love forever and ever." With a last, gentle squeeze from his hand, the boy slipped away, but the peaceful look upon his face drew a lasting, deep emotion from El Padre, and he wept at the loss. Anyone staring at the scene before him, of women violated and murdered, of children slaughtered without consideration, and men killed for the simple act of trying to protect their family, would reserve that devastating word for conditions far beyond their petty, care-free lives. No, the word, 'massacre' should be left for those who sadly monopolized its true existence.

CHAPTER 15

At work, sitting in the staff break room, Sam skimmed through a book he picked up at the library. Flipping to the back, he inspected the dated picture of the author from when he wrote the book in 1982, jotting down notes about the man as he read the short bio on the author. Checking the table of contents page, Sam turned to the section referenced in his research and began reading aloud an excerpt at the bottom of the second page. "He appeared to be neither ghost nor apparition of any sort. He stood before me, a man, not unlike any other you might pass on the street. Upon his right hand, he bore the scar of death itself, but beyond that, his features were aptly forgotten."

Sam opened his computer and searched Professor Efram Bashalbowitz's name. Reading that the author was no longer tenured at Fordham University, he looked up the college campus' three addresses and their phone numbers. After calling two of them with no help and being transferred four times before being disconnected with his third attempt, Sam put down his cell phone and contemplated his next move.

Ira entered the break room, nodding his greeting to Sam before preparing himself a cup of tea. Sam watched Ira meticulously clean his cup with a slow reverence before filling it with a measured amount of bottled water and placing it into the microwave oven to heat. While he waited, Ira turned to face Sam and finally stated dryly, "If you intend to research all of my curious idiosyncrasies, you'll require a much larger notebook."

Sam stopped staring and quickly offered, "Sorry, Ira, I wasn't really watching you; I was just . . . I don't know, putting together a game plan in my head. You were just the unfortunate backdrop."

Ira removed his cup from the microwave, replying sarcastically, "Perhaps you should have opened with calling me an 'unfortunate backdrop' and concluded with the apology. It at least allows me to pretend to be appropriately kind."

Ira started to exit the break room, bobbing his tea bag to the beat of his footsteps, but Sam quickly interrupted his escape with, "Ira, before you take off, can I ask you a question?"

Ira returned to the table, responding before he took a delicate sip from his beverage, "You mean, in addition to the one you just shared?"

Sam let the snide remark pass and simply continued with his inquiry. "I don't suppose you know anyone at Fordham?"

Ira looked over his glasses at his friend before returning his attention to his tea, answering, "This won't be anything like what happened with a certain ex-Senator from West Virginia, would it, because the firm, emphatic answer will be no!"

Sam smiled at Ira's mention of the past indiscretion, but recovered quickly to put the proper face on it, replying as he held up three fingers, "Absolutely not; Scout's honor!"

Ira deadpanned his response with a quick glance at Sam's pledge and a slow shake of his head, "Sam, those *aren't* even the correct fingers. For goodness sake, you can't even lie properly."

Sam inspected his fingers, shrugging before changing his hand gesture, dividing the middle and ring fingers, adding, "Well then, how about, 'live long and prosper'?"

Ira ignored his attempt at humor, set down his cup, and scribbled a name and number on Sam's notepad. "Here's the Dean of Admissions contact information, but do not, under any circumstances, mention my name. I want nothing to do with, nor have any connection to, whatever it is you're scheming."

Sam stared at the written information Ira provided, then looked up at his friend, asking, "Is all that information just rolling around there in your noggin waiting for someone to request it? I mean, geez, Ira, I can't say that I've ever personally witnessed you reference an address book or computer for anything I've asked. It's like you have it all memorized."

Ira returned Sam with a blank stare before finally replying, "Some people never forget a face, while others can figure complex mathematics in their head; my gift is contact information. If I hear it once, it just stays with me like that awful cologne you're wearing today. Let's just hope the cologne finds a shelf life." With the parting shot, Ira shuffled out the door.

With Ira's helpful assistance, the call to the Dean provided an appropriate connection allowing Sam to reach one of the professor's old assistants. After explaining who he was and why he wished to speak with the retired professor, the staff member happily gave him Efram's current address, with the only request that Sam pass on his greeting and well wishes.

Sam apprehensively considered his endeavor at hand, walking down the sidewalk to meet the retired professor. Most people under the age of eighty-five unconsciously avoided nursing homes, or as society preferred to label as assisted living facilities. Even people in their mid-eighties would probably choose to avoid them, if they were properly asked. He couldn't quite put his finger on the reason for the aversion, but attributed it most likely to the typical medicinal odors, heartbreaking sights, and the over-bearing reality that every life had its eventual end. Walking up the sidewalk toward the entrance, Sam considered how at every stage in life it seemed to be simple human nature to avert the fact of our own mortality.

The facility that Professor Bashalbowitz called home, by contrast, greeted its guests and visitors with a warm and inviting front lobby replete with a large fireplace, comfortable leather seating, two plasma screen televisions, and dark mahogany book shelves with hundreds of books. There's no bothersome smell, as Sam had expected from his limited experience and, in fact, the only aromas he picked up were of fresh-cut flowers, a hint of leather, and whatever delicious fare the kitchen was creating for the next meal.

Approaching the nurse's station, just beyond the lobby, Sam was immediately greeted by two smiling, attractive women who appeared to be nurse's aides coming from opposite hallways. "Can we help you locate someone, sir?" asked the shorter of the two.

Sam returned their pleasantries with, "As a matter of fact, I could use a point in the right direction. I'm looking for Efram Bashalbowitz."

The two ladies exchanged a look and the taller aide responded, smiling, "That would be *Professor* Efram, as he insists on being addressed." She pointed down the blue carpeted corridor to the left, instructing him, "The little cutie is down this way on the right, room 111. Would you like me to show you the way?"

Sam smiled his consideration, but followed it with, "No thank you. I think I can find the room now." Following the directions, Sam turned, saying, "You ladies have a nice day."

The door to room 111 was slightly ajar, but only by about four or five inches, so Sam chose to knock rather than barge into the gentleman's privacy. A hearty reply greeted him, stating, "I've taken the damn pills, ladies; now will you please let me alone?" Sam pushed the door open wider and peered into the half lit room as his curious expression was met by a bespectacled angry-faced little bearded man with white hair seated in an over-stuffed recliner with a thick book sitting open on his lap. The man's look immediately switched from irritation to surprise, stating, "Oh my, I was expecting the peccadillo twins. I know they're out there somewhere plotting my next enema."

Sam hesitated at the door, inquiring, "Professor Efram?"

The elderly man reached to the end table, placing his book on it before responding, "Yes, that would be me. Are you here for blood, urine, or stool? I'd prefer you came back after lunch, though, I'd say around two, as I'm a little short on all three." This was followed by a long, wry chuckle which made Sam laugh right along with him.

Once they both ended the shared laugh, Sam replied, "Sorry for showing up unannounced, Professor, but I only received your address late yesterday from your last assistant at the University, who, by the way, wanted me to send you his greetings." The elderly professor continued staring blankly at Sam, remaining either dumbfounded or in an effort to size up his new guest. Sam, hesitant to keep talking, gave in and added, "I wasn't sure how to get in touch with you by phone, so I took the liberty of stopping in."

The white-haired man looked Sam up and down before saying, "Well, let us start with your name, shall we?"

Sam moved closer, answering, "Oh! My name is Sam, Sam Noll. I'm a reporter."

Efram looked intently at his visitor, confirming, "You're the one who writes the article, *Death Comes Easily*. I've read your column. Would you care to sit?" Sam took the seat gestured by the small man as he watched Sam try to appear casual in the close quarters. Sam felt nothing but discomfort under the intense stare of the wise old man and wondered how he could have adjusted his appearance from brittle and helpless to piercing and intense in such a short span of time. The old man broke the silence, asking, "So tell me; do you chase the ghost by choice, or is this simply an assignment handed to you out of distaste?"

Sam blankly stared at the space between them in disbelief, asking, "What makes you think following this story was a punishment?"

Efram looked to the ceiling, consulting the off-white tiles before answering, "You've covered politics, business dealings, and crime of various types in the past, but as of recent, the patronage of death has occupied your interest. The shift is quite radical for someone so intent on exposing the weakness of man, so you've either angered someone in the ranks above you or experienced something monumentally life-altering. I place my bet on the previous."

Still considering the comment about his need to expose the guilty, Sam caught up to the Professor's choice and grimaced a response before adding, "So, the assignment wasn't my decision, is that what you wish to hear?"

The old man smiled at the admission and cheerfully answered, "*How* one comes to a door isn't as important as *what* one does at the door. Some enter, some just knock, and some fear what's on the other side so much that they never even rattle the knob!" Again, he returned to the raspy chuckle with Sam delegated to just observe the odd little man enjoy the sound of his own wisdom. The professor settled back into seriousness and looked into Sam's eyes, stating, "I further presume you're here because you've read my book, am I right?"

Sam leaned in, answering, "Not all of it, as it was a difficult read for someone of my particular mental density, but yes, I read the chapter that referenced a, shall we say, chance meeting."

The Professor slammed his hand down on the arm of the chair, saying vigorously, "I knew it! I just knew someone would finally want to know about Danny!"

Sam raised his hand for the old man to stop and back up, asking, "Wait a minute. Danny? Why do you call him Danny? Is that what he said his name was?"

The little man stared back at Sam and reacted strangely to the question, then simply replied, "Oh, no. That's just what I've called him over the years; Death-bed Danny. It just seems appropriate, for some reason or another. He never bothered to introduce himself to me, and I don't believe you and I would be speaking right now if he had."

Sam asked anxiously, "In the book, you don't describe what he looks like, other than the scarred hand. Do you recall anything about his appearance, anything at all?"

Professor Efram scratched at his snow white beard and returned his attention to the ceiling as Sam waited patiently. Finally, the old man looked back at him and began with, "I'm an old man, both inside and out. I've lived a privileged life among many who fell to less fortunate circumstances."

He paused, kissing his fingers, and lifted his hand toward heaven. Sam watched the elderly man's show of respect as Efram proceeded, "Being a professor of a fine university such as Fordham allowed me the freedom to explore and further my understanding of life's last and final stage. I was a young boy when I met our friend, Danny. Perhaps, being so youthful, meeting him when I did may have had a deeper effect than had I been mature, as age makes our hearts grow cold and grays our transparent view of life. We're so very impressionable in our early years; we believe more, feel more, and love with absolute purity. But, nevertheless, the impact I sustained has lasted my existence."

Musing over his long past childhood, the elderly professor inadvertently began massaging his left hand with his right. Sam noticed for the first time the clustered fist at the end of his left arm, realizing his hand had either been severely injured, or most likely, he'd been born with a birth defect. Sam, again, gave the old man his moment of reflection before the professor eased back into the conversation. "His hair was dark with little gray. He stood perhaps your span, maybe an inch more. There was little light in the small room, as I was unable to see him until he lit several candles."

Sam interjected, asking, "He lit candles?"

The Professor smiled at Sam's question replying, "He knew the proper ritual for caring for those who have passed on. It's Jewish custom to also wrap the body in cloth or a blanket, which he also did." Sam nodded his understanding and waited once again for the man to proceed, but didn't wait long for him to chime in. "The discussion which transpired, as best as I'm able to recall, mainly concerned the safekeeping for my grandfather, who had expired under his watch. He didn't seem to know I was in the room until the glow of the candles exposed my presence in the corner of the room. Until then, I watched in the darkness while he treated my grandfather with true affection and dignity, which touched my heart with great pride."

Sam jotted down notes on a small pad he'd earlier removed from his pocket and looked up to ask, "So, how did he leave?"

The Professor stared at Sam for a moment before saying, "He raised his hands high over his head, spoke the word, *Abracadabra*, and disappeared into a cloud of smoke!" Sam squinted his eyes at Efram while the little man laughed at his own joke, but then finally answered, "He left through the door, just as any man would do. He kept watch over my grandfather in my stead as shomrim while I retrieved the Chevra Kaddisha from our village." Sam blankly stared at Efram until he realized Sam was uneducated in Jewish law. "Sorry, I forget at times others are not in harmony with the tongue of an old Jewish man." He said with a wink and a smile before continuing, "According to Jewish custom and traditions, which is called Halacha, a close friend or family member is chosen as the shomrim to stay with the departed to guard over the body until a member of the Holy Society, or Chevra Kaddisha, arrives and prepares the body for burial."

Sam wrote furiously on his pad in the attempt to keep up with the Professor, not worrying about correct spelling. Stopping for a question and a break from writer's cramp, Sam asked, "So, did he remain until your return?"

Professor Efram's face paled slightly, and his expression slipped to somber, answering, "Upon exiting, leaving him in my stead, I stopped and waited. With the soul removed and his responsibility fulfilled, I needed to make certain he truly intended to remain. My grandfather was all I had at that time in my life. My entire family, including my mother, father, an older sister and brother, as well as my mother's parents, had all been taken away by the Germans to a fate I dare not think about. When I decided he had chosen to remain, I moved closer to the door to listen,"

Sam was left to just watch as the elderly man looked as though he might break down, but the professor bravely pressed forward, stating, "And, I could hear him praying over my grandfather." With tears slowly cascading down his cheeks, he conveyed with embarrassment, "Oh my, look what the past has made me do! So many years gone by, and that simple act of reverence affects me still."

Sam grabbed a box of tissue from a bookshelf and offered them to Efram. The old man took two tissues, chuckling at his emotional out-pour, adding, "Well, I guess the peccadillo twins can add these tears to their collection of samples!" Both men laughed at the remark, taking a small break from the interview.

Sam looked around the room for the first time since arriving and studied the man's life displayed throughout the room with his honorary plaques and framed certificates, numerous books on religion, psychology, and of course, death.

He rose to move closer to a crop of photos on the wall to his right, but hesitated first, looking over at Professor Efram for his approval. The gray-haired man smiled his consent, adding, "Please, be my guest. A picture on a wall begs to be remembered." While Sam looked about the numerous items on display, Efram filled the space with tales of his heritage. "My grandfather had come to Israel from Kiev. After watching two of his friends killed by the Russians during the Kiev Pogrom, he took my grandmother and ascended to the Holy Land during the second Aliyah. They established themselves in an agricultural settlement called Petah Tikva, but due to the area being swampland, malaria took many lives, so they temporarily moved south until after the swamp could be drained in 1893."

Sam moved in and inspected each one, stopping when he recognized a man standing next to Efram who looked to be in his fifties. The photo showed the two men shaking hands and staring intensely at each other. Sam turned back to the Professor, inquiring, "The gentleman in this photo shaking your hand; I can't quite recall where I've seen him before."

Without the need to look up, Efram answered, "His name was Jacob Von Stublich. He was a member of the Einsatzgruppen; an

SS death squad that took away my parents, my grandparents, and my older sister before my brother and I managed to escape from Poland. My brother was caught a week later outside a small town about twenty miles east of Warsaw. With the assistance of two families from our village, I made my way to my grandparents' village in Northern Israel."

Sam turned toward him with a horrified look, waiting for the explanation.

Efram sighed before taking on the heavy unspoken question, but finally relented, saying, "The trouble with hatred is that far too often it eventually channels itself into action. Even if it's left alone, pushed down deep inside one's self, it'll manifest into something that can only do harm."

The wise, old professor dropped his head momentarily, before saying with a hint of regret, "I had such anger. Von Stublich had written a book describing what he had gone through being half Jewish and half German, carrying out his orders during his time on the death squad. When I saw the book in a store window with his arrogant face displayed for everyone to see, I vomited right there on the sidewalk."

Sam began pacing the small room as he listened intently. Efram shook his head slowly before proceeding with the dark memory, "The author was visiting Boston on a book-signing tour, so I took a flight the next day to confront the murderer. I sat in the back while he spoke of his personal torment and infliction of torn loyalties throughout the war. He spoke of his six years as a prisoner of war and how he found peace through the realization of his wrongful ways. I sat there, numb to his tales of finding truth through conviction and when he was finished with what I deemed as cheap propaganda, I followed him to his hotel, then up to his room."

Sam returned to his chair, sitting stiffly on the edge as though he was approaching the cliffhanger to a thriller. The Professor hesitated, then turned toward Sam, asking, "You didn't happen to bring anything to drink, did you?"

The sudden downshift of excitement jolted Sam back up in his seat like the abrupt end to a roller coaster ride, fumbling for a response. "Hmm? Drink . . . no. I'm sorry, but I didn't think it would be allowed. Is it allowed?" The cackle returned and echoed off the four walls, ending in a deep, congested cough from the little man. Sam half stood, unsure what to do, asking, "Can I get you a glass of water, Professor?" As he continued to cough, Sam looked toward the door considering calling for some assistance, but the Professor held up his hand, hindering his intention, while Efram's coughing began to subside.

Slowly, Sam sat back down as the bearded man stood on shaky legs and waddled toward the small kitchen, saying, "Water is nice . . ." He opened the cupboard under the sink, slid the trash can over, and pulled out a yellow bottle of Pine-Sol. He closed the cupboard door and pulled two glasses off the drying rack next to the sink. Returning to his chair, he finished with, "But nothing quenches a thirst like good old Pine-Sol!"

Sam examined the bottle as it went by and noticed the liquid's unique color, asking, "I've never seen dark brown Pine-Sol before. How old is it?" The Professor held up the bottle for closer inspection and replied confidently, "Twelve years." Once both glasses were distributed, Efram held his glass up until Sam joined in the toast. The Professor looked beyond the ceiling toward the heavens and said with reverence, "To the many who have walked with us for too short a time. May God bless the taken and forgive those who did the taking, l'chaim." They took their slow swallows in unison. Unaccustomed to hard alcohol, Sam tried to muffle his reaction to the kick of the whiskey, but the effort only amused Efram into a chuckle, adding, "I call that the Pine-Sol after kick; probably from the residual at the bottom of the bottle!" Sam looked at his glass with horror as his reaction caused another bout of laughter from Efram.

CHAPTER 16

Settled down, the old man became serious again in attempt to return to the previous matter, "Now let's see, where were we before we cleaned our pipes, so to speak?" he said with a wink.

After one more cough, Sam was anxious to try out his voice, to see if the burning sensation removed his ability to speak. Helping the little man back on track, Sam offered, "You were following Von Stublich to his room."

Efram's eyes became slits, focusing his memory before finally responding, "Ah, yes! The gun in my pocket truly felt cold and heartless as my emotions at the time . . ."

Sam interjected, "Gun? You'd brought a gun?"

With an expression of mild shock from the interruption, Efram stared back at Sam before continuing as though a question wasn't brought forth. "Have you ever held a gun without looking at it? It has such an unusually powerful affect to your senses. They're quite a bit weightier than they appear on television or in the movies, and I can't help but think that their purpose adds a few ounces."

Professor Efram rubbed his legs, getting back to the story. "Once Von Stublich opened his door, I positioned myself directly behind him, keeping my hand on the gun in my right pocket. Before I could pull the pistol from my jacket, the door was pulled wide open and two small children rushed toward Von Stublich's legs, followed by a lovely woman, who embraced him warmly. My immediate reaction was to step back and simply watch in amazement as he was welcomed back to the hotel room by his loving family. It was his wife who noticed me first, asking her husband to introduce us."

Efram looked at Sam and smiled impishly, adding, "For the first time, Von Stublich looked at me, and I saw in his face an appearance of innocence, struggling to recollect who I was. I stepped forward, released the death grip I had on the pistol, and extended my hand, introducing myself, stating that I had been moved by his story and simply wanted to meet the man. After I made my final show of appreciation and apologies for the inconvenience, Von Stublich escorted his family back into the room, but asked me to wait a moment before leaving. Closing the door to the hotel room, he turned to face me again, but his face had taken on a darker emotion and I saw fear and doubt for the first time."

Sam wiggled forward in his seat, anxious to hear the story play out, while Efram moved toward the end. "With less cheerfulness, he asked to walk me out. Unsure of his adjusted intentions, I agreed as we walked silently down the hallway to the elevator. Once the doors slid together, Von Stublich pressed the button for the eighteenth floor, suggesting we have a drink upstairs at the bar before I took my leave."

Efram sighed and took a moment to put his thoughts into words before continuing, "I knew from the moment I saw his children and wife that any ability to take his life dissipated. He became a human being; someone real and loved and obviously had the capacity to show love. He achieved a sudden existence by opening that door. We sat there with our drinks for a long time, wondering what the other was thinking. He was the first to speak, mentioning how strange the way two people should meet. Shocked by his candor, I admitted I didn't find it strange, at all and that I listened, followed, and now here we were sharing a drink."

Efram shifted back to narration, explaining to Sam, "Another quiet moment passed as we exchanged uncomfortable glances, until I felt the need to ask how he figured out I wasn't the fan I admitted to being. The cold stare he gave the question was followed by thoughtful consideration before telling me he'd seen the look of far too many faces of those he'd taken everything they held dear not to have recognized it. He asked, respectfully, 'I can only assume it was family?' My eyes welled up with long suppressed emotion with the mere thought of my parents, sister, and grandparents, my brother, as well as my stolen youth."

Efram removed his glasses as the memories flooded in once again. He grabbed a hanky from his pants pocket to wipe his building tears. Sam felt his own emotions choke up within his throat, silently watching the elderly man struggle with his devastating past, unable to deliver any proper words of comfort. Once he collected himself, Efram continued, "I went from blaming him for everything I had lost to accepting him as a survivor of that terrible period in our history. We were both forced into impossible choices during extraordinary times; he with his cross to bear and me with mine. Hating him for who he was made me no better than someone wanting to exterminate an entire race for no other reason than being Jewish."

Both men sat back heavily into their chairs like they'd just completed a long, difficult journey. Sam continued to stare at the little man, but with a renewed level of respect. Efram broke the silence, adding, "I've learned so much in this long life I've led, from books, from other professors; even from my students. But what amazes me most is how the lessons I experienced through pain and trial have, by far, benefited me the greatest. Funny how we proactively search for understanding and knowledge, yet it's what besieges us and that which attempts to tear us down that actually forms our character."

Sam internalized the words from the Professor, his thoughts momentarily slipping toward the loss of his mother as Efram's innocent statement cut deeper than he could bear. Sam pushed his thoughts away from the painful memory, rising in preparation to depart. Extending his hand to the gray-bearded man still sitting, he offered, "Professor Efram, I'm unable to fully express my gratitude for taking the time to talk. I came to see you for information about your friend, 'Danny,' yet I leave here with volumes. This has been incredibly insightful, and I'm excited to get to work on my next article."

Efram received Sam's handshake, looking into the eyes of his young interviewer and simply stated, "Forgiveness, my son, is like a shovel; to get anywhere with it, you have to grab the handle and dig." Sam smiled at the man's amusing offering as he began to turn and release the handshake, but Efram didn't let go and his grip became tighter, pulling Sam's attention back into the conversation. He stared into the professor's face as Efram's eyes became piercing black beads penetrating the very edges of Sam's obtrusive consciousness. Sam was left waiting for only a moment before Efram continued with, "But once you've dug deep enough; and you'll know when you've dug deep enough, bury whatever you believe caused you pain and walk away."

The simple analogy hit Sam right in the heart, reflecting upon his mother once again and flinched from the cold, sharp truth. How the wise old professor knew his suffering was beyond Sam's comprehension, but he swallowed hard before turning away, attempting to hide his flush of emotion. Efram released his hand and gently shared, "Forgive me for my boldness, my young friend, but I felt the need to do so before you left this meeting."

Sam once again turned to face Efram with only a fraction of control returning to his demeanor. Sam cleared his throat, asking jokingly while moving closer to the exit, "Are my innermost feelings so obvious that a man whom I hardly know can so easily read them at a glance? Please enlighten me how you can sit there and kill me so softly with your song?"

Efram looked to the floor, smiling, before he replied, "I find myself humming that song from time to time. It's always been one of my favorites; the original version, by the way!" Sam joined him in a chuckle, leaning against the wall near the adjoining kitchen. With the ten foot space between him, Sam folded his arms in a show of limited patience for an answer to his question. While waiting, he once again saw the smallness of the man and reminded himself that looks could be ever so deceiving. Just as he finished the thought, Efram asked, "Let us come back to how I came to ask and allow me the opportunity to dig a bit deeper, with your consent, of course?" Sam raised an eyebrow in response and Efram quickly added, "Wouldn't you agree that a location to a place is nothing but an address without directions?"

Unable to argue with the mind of a man such as Professor Efram, Sam gave in and answered, "Fire away!"

The little man scooted so forward in his chair that Sam thought he might slip right off. With his toes finally touching carpet, Efram stopped and placed his hands under each leg in preparation for his inquisition. Sam flinched from the anticipation of what he's about to endure, momentarily cursing himself for agreeing. The first question surprised Sam even more than he'd dreaded, as Efram stated more than asked, "Your mother passed while you were still quite young, is that correct?"

Sam shook his head in disbelief, but still answered, "Yes, near the end of my first year of college."

"How did she die, Samuel?" he quickly retorted.

Through gritted teeth, Sam answered, "Ovarian cancer."

Efram's head slowly swayed back and forth in genuine sadness, offering, "I'm sorry, my friend. All forms of that ugly disease will be one of my many questions I hope to have explained when I see our Maker."

Touched by his sensitivity and yielding to his own desires on the subject, Sam simply nodded his agreement before Efram pressed on. "So, please let me know if I'm mistaken with my additional deductions." Sam just stared at the man, hoping his silence was enough consent, for now. Evidently, the Professor understood, proceeding, "You opt to write as opposed to any other form of communication, because you find this avenue safe with its relative distance. You work diligently toward the end result of restitution for evil men, risking personal tragedy or harm in doing so, by the way, in an attempt to answer an inner calling to place light on all things corrupt. And last, there's something incomplete with the stories you produce, like a subconscious effort to keep yourself removed from what you experience. I believe that once you delve deep within and release yourself into your writing, you'll find the true gift you've been blessed with."

Sam couldn't decide whether he should be angry with the man or thank him for his insight, and after the pause in the conversation neared awkward, he forced himself to fill the gap by ignoring the comments altogether, saying, "Professor, again, I thank you for your time and sharing your experiences." With one quicker handshake, Sam turned and left the man in his chair before he's required to face anymore reflections. Sam knew himself all too well already.

Walking out of the room and leaving the assisted living home, Sam consumed his regret like the whiskey from under Efram's sink; only this burn didn't clear with a cough or the passage of time.

He could go back, attempt to explain himself, and have left things just a bit more cordial, but he knew he wouldn't. He knew he couldn't. Burdens were funny things, Sam pondered. One carried them no matter where they went and just when one started to forget about them, they clipped the happy moments like a sedative. The only good thing about them was that the airline companies hadn't thought of a way to charge us extra for them. If they had, Sam would've gone broke.

When he begrudgingly chose to be honest with himself about his feelings, which was extremely rare, his issues could be fixed in just five minutes; five minutes with his mother to let her know how much he loved her. Thank her for her inspiration, for her determination and for her sacrifice. All the modest things he denied her allowing her the simple gift of passing on in peace.

Sam visibly shook off his musing and pushed it to the dark closet he preserved within the back of his mind and decided to move on to matters he *could* do something about. The information obtained from the Professor had proved to be invaluable once he got his fingers to his keyboard. The background notes he'd jotted down concerning Efram's family and tragic demise would capture the readers' hearts and leave a big lump in their proverbial throats, begging for more. Sam nearly got dizzy from the switch in emotions, chuckling with anticipation from the combination of mortal and immortal, conveniently sewn together in another fine example of literary brilliance. Sam laughed at his lack of humility and readjusted the thought, Okay, fine. Maybe 'brilliance' was a stretch.

Sitting at home on the sofa with Spalding half-on, half-off his lap, Sam allowed the interview with Efram to playback in his mind. With Katie not due home for two more hours with back-to-back classes and his article nearly finished, Sam rubbed his eyes, trying to force away the sting beginning to let him know sleep was soon a requirement. Reading over the last paragraph, his inner 'nag' alarm began its steady pulse, forcing Sam to halt the progress and deal with the growing issue.

Exploitation in his business had always been a sensitive gray area for Sam. For all the years he'd been writing, he truly believed he refrained from crossing the line he'd drawn long ago inside his consciousness. Other writers, many whom he knew and even worked with, couldn't see the line behind them even with expensive binoculars, yet with the demands of his competitive occupation, he held true to his standards; but when his exuberance started bumping against his integrity, his internal smoke alarm consistently seemed to rescue him from the edge where the flames of immorality comfortably took refuge.

Efram had shared a great deal with him, some of which Sam held as private and confidential, even though the retired professor remained on the record. Editing out the portion concerning Efram's early intentions with Von Stublich wouldn't take anything away from the story, but could shine a dark light of disappointment to a number of Efram's past students, marring a life filled with so many great achievements.

The Professor had certainly paid enough without adding the public display of a momentary weakness concerning something that, eventually, hadn't even happened. Once the article was complete, edited, and ready for print, Sam decided he'd send an early copy with a thank you note to Professor Efram and hope the way their meeting ended hadn't harmed the opportunity of a second shot at his floor cleaner. That should pave the way to a possible second visit, with or without his note pad in tow.

CHAPTER 17

With the far too early sights and sounds of morning meeting Sam on his slow walk to Macie's Bakery, he couldn't help but let his investigative mind run wild. Instigating the early quandary was why Ira called him at home the previous evening and insisted, rather than ask, to meet him first thing.

The paper had slipped into a functional form of chaos with the interim manager seemingly adhering to every command from the Board. It escaped his understanding why Ira needed to have one of their secret meets unless it's dire news, which Ira knew to be the straw that made the camel come to the stream.

Sam cursed under his breath for not already having his first coffee, as even his adages were coming out confused.

The smells of the bakery slapped Sam's attention right in the face, and his stomach responded to the scents with the rumblings of an angry, unfed child with hypoglycemia. Ira approached him just before he began to salivate over a fresh tray of croissants that emerged from the back ovens. "I thought we could grab a pastry, some coffee, and slow walk our way to the office," he suggested, trying to steal Sam's attention from the baked goods. Sam finally peeled his focal point from the warmth and pleasantries of the racks of doughnuts to Ira's frigid, uncomfortable topic of unknown origin. Quickly selecting their breakfast and coffee, payment at the register, and exiting the bakery into the onset of an early morning drizzle, Ira spilled the headline before they passed three doors, "We've got a new editor."

Sam stopped mid-stride and mid-chew of his apple fritter, slowly raising his head to stare at Ira, who took a peevish sip of his steaming cup, watching his friend's reaction with only a slight hint of enjoyment. Sam finished his chewing and asked, "So, what is this," raising the remnants of his pastry, "my last meal?"

Ira rolled his eyes at Sam's theatrics before continuing, "They went out of town; your old stomping grounds, in fact. A guy named Tom Walters, from the *Chicago Herald*. Have you heard of him?"

Sam stopped his progress and breakfast for the second time and repeated his reaction to Ira's information flawlessly, mid-chew and all. Noticing his friend had ceased progress once again, Ira stopped and waited for his comment, looking up toward the dispensing clouds. Sam slowly approached Ira, telling him, "Tom Walters is my Cousin Bea's editor, or at least was. She adores him, but Bea has a screwy list of attributes for admiration selection. I met the guy once; arrogant, over-bearing, and short-tempered. Picture the bully from high school all grown up, and you might come close. Geez, Ira, I thought after Malcolm we could look forward to a little positive Karma; you know, a bit of sunshine after a torrential downpour. We aren't even going to have the pleasure of a pretty rainbow!"

Ira paused, probably to ensure Sam was finished ranting before adding, "I've never cared for rainbows. They're just too colorful for me." Sam glared at Ira for a prolonged moment before Ira turned, continuing down the sidewalk.

Inching their way toward work in silence, Sam asked a sensitive question he'd been pondering for some time. "Did the owners or Board members ever consider you for the job, Ira?"

This time it's Ira's turn to cease their forward motion. Ira stared down at the small cracks in the sidewalk for a long moment before lifting his balding head to address the question. "It's an odd thing, your question. I'd be lying if I said the opportunity never crossed my mind, but regardless of my feelings or experience concerning the job, the answer is no. I was never given a meeting to express my interest. You've been the first to even suggest I could be capable of doing the job. Regardless, I believe it's for the best. One can easily fall into the ravine when overstepping one's boundaries."

Sam briefly watched Ira to be certain he really was alright with the situation before asking, "Who said that, Napoleon?"

Ira gave his friend one of his irritated glares before answering, "No, Samuel, it was just me."

To change the subject so that Ira didn't dwell on the negative anymore than usual, Sam asked, "Do we know when he starts, because I'll want to make myself pretty scarce?"

Ira shook his head slowly. "No word yet, but I don't think it'll be soon."

Sam looked back at his friend, asking, "Why not?"

With a dramatic shrug, Ira answered, "Editors typically have large incentives at the major papers to keep them on the payroll until a suitable replacement can be found. Often it's a binding contract or written agreement to ensure a fluid transition to keep the stockholders placid and the papers selling."

Nearing the building, Sam tugged on Ira's jacket to halt their entry before adding, "Hey, I just want you to know I think you could have done the job better and more efficiently than anyone. You would have been my first choice, easy."

Ira almost stepped back from the unexpected compliment, stammering uncharacteristically with a response. "Oh, well, Sam, I just don't know what to say to that."

Sam chuckled at his friend's rare loss of words, replying, "You don't need to say anything. I just think what I said needed to be said, that's all." With that, Sam walked ahead and entered the building with Ira in tow. They went their separate ways, with Ira to his first floor 'dungeon' and Sam heading to the elevators for the thirteenth floor.

Arriving quite a bit earlier than he's accustomed, Sam rode the elevator alone contemplating the day ahead and the recent update of a new sheriff coming to town. The ride up was suspended at the fifth floor when the doors slid open and Tom Walters walked into the suddenly shrinking compartment with his attention fixated on some paperwork he's carrying. Sam discretely shuffled to the far left wall of the elevator in an attempt to become invisible.

Tom briefly looked up to see his selection already pressed before turning to notice his elevator-mate for the first time. Sam remained committed to watching his shoes dry, trying to pretend not to notice the tall male occupant three feet in front of him. Tom cleared his throat and Sam knew it was a lame attempt to get him to look up, but Sam didn't bite. Finally, Walters asked, "So, you work on the thirteenth, then?"

Sam took his turn at the throat clearing and just grunted his response of, "Uh-huh."

Tom didn't let the grunt suffice as the entirety of Sam's side of the conversation and pursued the staff member's identity, asking, "So, what's your name and what do you do here?"

Sam let out a heavy sigh, looking up and thinking to himself, Walters, you're such a putz! Really, you couldn't lower yourself to introduce yourself, first? Sam stared at Tom for a fraction of a second to see if he recognized him from their one and only meeting. When there wasn't a flicker of acknowledgment, Sam was finally forced into admission, extending his hand with, "My name is Sam. Sam Noll. I'm a columnist here at the paper."

Tom shook the offered hand vigorously, responding, "Glad to meet you, Sam. Name is Tom Walters. Been hired here as the new editor-in-chief. Probably didn't know. Most weren't in the loop." Sam internally shuddered in disgust, recalling Tom's annoying habit of short, curt sentences. It was as though he didn't feel the need to bestow the listener the complete version of his wisdom.

Sam opted to play along; not in an attempt to gain favor from his new boss, but instead to simply pass the uncomfortable time of close quarters with the passing floors seeming to slow with each second. "Malcolm isn't the editor any longer?" he straight lined convincingly.

Tom reacted appropriately, "Malcolm? You been under a rock, Noll? That boy is either floating on or under a boat somewhere. Nope, I'm the new sheriff in town!" Sam nearly snorted a laugh at the inside joke that only he got with Tom's self-proclaimed title that Sam had already considered.

The saving bell of their arrival to the thirteenth floor came just in time before they exited the elevator with a quick 'We'll see each other again' nod. Sam hurried to his desk, grabbed his leather bag, and decided to adjust his schedule by moving up a trip to the library he'd been planning for the afternoon. The office suddenly had become the last place he wanted to be, and since a storm of house cleaning was about to begin, the less seen, the less considered. No, Sam figured if he flooded Tom from afar with incredible feats of penmanship, he could remain employed and shoot for a small degree of personal satisfaction as well. Ira would have to find out on his own that the sheriff had already ridden in.

"Katie, are you home?" Sam yelled while setting his leather case down by the entry.

"In the bathroom; how long do you need to get ready?" Katie replied. Sam stopped in his tracks and his mind raced through his social calendar, only to find it empty and vacant. The lack of response brought Katie slowly out of the bathroom. She faced Sam at the other end of the hallway holding what looked like a crayon. With little emotion, Katie filled the void with, "'Ready for what?' Are those the words you're afraid to ask, Sam?"

Sam flinched from her amazing show of psychic ability, but decided to appear unmoved and attempt to play it off. "No, not at all. I've been looking forward to this for a while. I was just trying to decide which shirt to wear. What do you think, the dark blue or the gray?" he asked innocently.

Katie turned back to the bathroom, and Sam honestly thought he pulled it off as Katie asked over her shoulder, "I thought you hated these art openings?"

Sam shrugged, stating nonchalantly, "A little culture won't kill me, right?"

Katie poked her head out of the bathroom, responding coldly, "Well, since we're going to Victor and Patricia's, rather than the art gallery, how about you wear the oatmeal shirt I put out for you with the pleated black slacks lying on the bed?"

Sam closed his eyes and cursed the entrapment, thinking, No, it definitely won't be culture that will kill me. It'll be suffocation by foot in mouth! With that, he obediently headed for the bedroom to change for an evening with the Spensers; or was it the Stensons? he struggled to recall. Sam needed to figure it out before they left, feeling it would be best not to aggravate Katie any further and try to have a pleasant evening at her friends', whatever their name was.

Back at their apartment building, Sam tried his best to catch up to Katie, but she was already up the stairs and on their floor. He swore under his breath, starting up the first flight for not remembering the umbrella that Katie had asked him to grab on their way out the door. The partly cloudy skies turned ugly while at the Stevensons', and since the distance was only twelve blocks, they'd decided to walk. Unfortunately, their evening out coincided with an opening at the Met, so there wasn't a taxi to be hailed. Frustrated, Katie stomped off for home, leaving Sam standing in the rain, still hoping for a miracle.

On the long, slow march up the stairs, Sam used the idle time to allow the evening's lower points to echo through the stairwell along with his footsteps. The steady cadence and rising crescendo from the resonance off the walls played well to the mental recap of the evening's building plot. Forgetting the umbrella simply graced the night-out with its remorseful, final straw. It seemed the only positive aspect of Sam's involvement in the evening was that they arrived on time; not the first and certainly not the last, with their entrance meshed somewhere in the appropriate middle.

The evening's festivities took a speedy nose dive as people he didn't know began speaking to him. If he had simply nodded and attempted to make small talk, he could have punted through the entire night, but the very first person to approach him shoved a platter in his face, asking, "Have you tried the pâté?" When he agreed to sample it, his instantaneous negative reaction insulted the hostess nearly to tears.

If that hadn't ostracized him to a corner, he then entered a conversation with two men that began well enough, but when one of the gentlemen asked what Sam did for a living, the man started insulting the paper Sam worked for, calling it 'excellent fish wrap.' In retort, once Sam learned the man was a defense attorney, he began making similarities of the profession to prostitution. Shortly after, the man left the party angry. Katie finally intervened and placed Sam on a three foot leash, cutting off his sentences once he hit a verb. When a conversation he was spectating turned to the subject of death, Sam severed his ties that bound and reengaged himself back into the party.

In hindsight, Sam considered a saying one of his professors used back at college that went, 'when you lay out the tracks, you may as well start preparing for the train wreck!' Katie probably saw the oncoming train, Sam now recalled, excusing herself once he went to full steam. In his own defense, he couldn't let the other gentleman continue spouting off such ridiculously erroneous statements in regard to what Islamic beliefs were for their afterlife. When he declared his judgment on all Muslims by the actions of the few, Sam simply felt obliged to enlighten him on what the true followers and believers of the Koran held dear. If only someone had mentioned he was arguing with the CEO of Katie's company. Sam knew the man was going to be at the party, but thought he would be much older and a little more open-minded.

Finally at the front door to their apartment, Sam hesitated before opening it and focused his will to express humility. Once inside, he could hear Katie in the bathroom, most likely drying off from the downpour she endured on her sprint home. Sam looked down at the puddle formed at his feet, kicked off his shoes, and tiptoed into the kitchen for a dish towel to pat himself moderately dry.

Katie arrived in the kitchen doorway and leaned against the frame, watching Sam without expression, drying her hair with a towel. With one more self-dosage of the humble pill, Sam offered, "Katie, I don't know what got into me. I had every intention of being the boyfriend you'd be proud to have accompany you tonight. I don't know who *that* guy was. I'm sorry for ruining your evening."

Katie took Sam's apology with a nod, pushed herself off the entry, and began to turn toward the bathroom, but paused without looking back, saying, "I miss the times you didn't have to try." Sam deflated a bit from the comment and stared down at the counter, silent.

Katie turned back to face him, but Sam couldn't force himself to meet her gaze as she added, "Do you realize not a day goes by that you feel the need to slip the depressing subject of death into the conversation? And I'm not talking about when you're at work; I'm talking about just you and I, out to dinner or walking Spalding at the park. I love what I do, Sam, but I don't drag exercise into every topic I share. There has to be separation; a time to clock out and leave it at the office, you know?"

Sam offered a quick glance up to let her know he's listening, but slipped his attention back down to the caulking between the counter tiles. Frustrated, Katie turned and retreated to the bathroom, leaving Sam to wonder if he truly could turn off the work light and leave it off.

The next morning, Sam walked into the kitchen and stopped in his tracks, having to double check whether he's in the right apartment. Katie stood in front of the table adding the finishing touches to, what appeared to be, an assortment of delicious breakfast fare. Sam salivated, scanning the spread on the table of scrambled eggs, French toast, sausage links, oatmeal, juice, and coffee before looking at Katie and her proud expression. Sam scratched his head before asking, "I was expecting cold porridge! What gives?"

Katie's expression turned from youthful excitement to bashfully apologetic, answering, "Well, I gave last night a great deal of thought, and I think I may have been too hard on you. Nothing you did was done out of malice; I mean, you didn't say or do anything you haven't been known for."

Sam took the criticism with a humorous wince as Katie continued. "And even though my boss might keep my personnel file handy on his desk for a while, just in case his mood turns sour, he was wrong in expressing his mistaken ideals so adamantly. You never told him he wasn't allowed to have his take on the subject; you simply offered another opinion. But I stand firm on what I said about the whole 'death issue.' And, if you can try reeling it in just a bit, perhaps an attempt at less time away from home, I think we can find half an acre of happy middle ground."

Sam crossed the room and snuck behind his girlfriend, hugging her from behind and rested his chin on her shoulder, saying, "I'll also take this agreement to an additional level and promise to remember the umbrella when you ask!"

Katie pushed off toward the kitchen, responding with, "Don't ruin a perfectly fine breakfast, Sam Noll. I worked too hard on this meal to let your jokes rekindle my anger!" In response, Sam zipped around the table and pulled Katie's chair out for her, making a grand gesture with a wave of his arm. Katie smiled, sat down and stated, "Now, that's more like it!"

Once seated, Sam began passing plated items to Katie, but his mind was racing on other things. His relief concerning the cease-fire with Katie would be fleeting as he considered the brewing pressure of the next issue to come. He couldn't decline the trips nor would he stop thinking his way through each piece of his story. His job wasn't like hers, where he could stop jumping around when the music ended. There's always another song immediately following without the luxury of another instructor to take over. All he could do was slow down how much he shared with her, but he found himself conflicted about that as well. Sam committed himself to this relationship when he asked her to move in, and to keep things from Katie wasn't really being honest.

Katie looked up while she applied maple syrup onto her French toast and asked, "Sam, is everything alright?"

Jolted back into the present and out of the future, Sam smiled and lied, "Oh, I was just wondering what we should do today; any ideas?" While Katie began suggesting a walk in the park for the three of them, Sam shuddered inside at just how easily the little fib exited his lips. Is this how it starts? he asked himself with a thought.

Not expecting any logical reply, Sam tuned back in as Katie closed with, "And maybe we can start on that photo album we bought in November. I know we have enough pictures to fill several pages."

Sam smiled softly, answering, "Sounds like a perfect day!" After he took a bite of his eggs, he added with a smile, "This is absolutely delicious; best ever!"

Mississippi, 2005

Walking into the bar, Billy Dawkins nodded his typical greetings to the usual crowd spread about the room, many of whom having the singular tie of being supporters to the cause. Removing his hat and wiping the last bit of sweat off his brow from a long day of manual labor, Casey, behind the bar, placed Billy's first beer at his usual seat. Both men offered each other a grunted greeting; a custom that hadn't seen interruption for several years.

Born and raised in Mississippi might have limited Billy's scope of culture, but the comfort of knowing he would die for his beliefs gave him a deep pride and confidence that would never force him to drop his head in shame. The patrons in the bar and the people throughout their part of the town carried the same gritty assurance that they'd fight for their homes, their jobs, and their freedoms.

Taking the first sip of the reward from his completed workday, he smiled at the dream of an all-white town, an all-white country, and an all-white government, absent of conspiracy, abuse of welfare, and arms-wide-open borders; a nation no longer begging to receive virtually anyone's tired, poor, and huddled masses yearning to breathe in the simplicity of choice. Don't worry about any type of insurance coverage, paying taxes, or stealing our dissipating jobs; we'd take care of you until the country we'd built with our bare hands and fought for with the blood of our ancestors collapsed under your financial burden.

By the time Billy finished his first beer, he was bristling with his comfortable mechanism of anger that'd burned within him since he couldn't remember when.

The quiet stranger arriving two seats down didn't spur Billy from his fit of delusion, but rather went about the business of watching the news on the elevated television behind the bar. It wasn't until Casey inquired from the man what he'd like to drink that Billy turned to notice him. In response, El Padre inquired of Billy, "Do they have good wings here?"

Billy chuckled, replying sarcastically, "Sure, if you don't mind 'em burning ya twice!"

Both Casey and Billy laughed at the man's expense, but El Padre answered, "I'll try your wings then, but just water for now, please." The request silenced them both as Casey simply walked away to place the order and fetch his new customer his tap water.

Billy, unabated, sized up the stranger as though the option for him to remain was entirely his decision. He began with a few qualifying inquiries, asking, "So, where ya from, mister?"

El Padre coolly let the question hang in the air before turning to him once again, replying, "I have spent most of my life in a number of different areas. To choose precisely where I am from would pose to be rather difficult."

Billy stiffly sat up, inspecting the visitor more deeply, inquiring, "Well, you certainly don't talk like someone from around here. Where's that accent from, then?"

The water arrived and Casey remained with his arms crossed in front of him. After a slow sip from the water, El Padre set down his glass and offered both men a look of unintimidated innocence, responding, "The dialect you inquire of is a product of numerous years abroad and from time spent with countless races and an infinite variety of languages. My accent is that of the entire world." Satisfied with the grand, if vague response, Casey scoffed his reaction, plopping another beer in front of Billy before retreating to the kitchen to check on the food order.

Billy, on the other hand, sustained his careful watch of the curious new arrival. Deciding to let the subject drop, Billy moved on with his cross-examination, leaning in as he asked, "So, what brings you to Waveland from such distant lands? If you're here for the storm of the century, sorry to tell ya, but you're thirty-six years too late, as this new one looks to be fadin' out."

El Padre smiled at Billy's humor, replying, "Your weather does not interest me, but the people of this town certainly do. I have met several of your city inhabitants and find your town pleasant, indeed. To be greeted warmly by all whom I passed on the streets and walkways, in the grocery store, and even during my visit to Fred's Department store, there is a balance of affection and respect for any and all who find themselves blessed to visit here."

Billy blankly stared at the stranger's fixed composure of bliss after describing the town Billy only barely remembered from his youth. The anger slipped back into Billy's heart, moving upward through his lips, his voice beginning to grow louder while he chastised the stranger, "Who do you think you are, mister, I mean, really, a balance of affection and respect? This town hasn't seen balance of any type since before 1980. I swear there isn't one family, person, or dog who would agree with feeling blessed. What the government doesn't take, the illegals grab for themselves. Then the part that the bleeding-heart government took from us, they give to the illegals, too. So don't come here preachin' your 'love of fellow man' speech, cuz everybody here gave at the office, before the office laid us all off."

Three of Billy's compatriots rose from their seats unsure if their friend would need any help removing the bothersome intruder. Several other patrons whooped and hollered at Billy's fiery retort. El Padre looked over Billy's shoulder at the three waiting for a sign to intervene, raising a hand toward them, gesturing for them to return to their seats to which they numbly adhered.

Billy spun around to witness the taming before turning back to the stranger, asking, "What the heck was that about? You think you can tell my friends when to sit or stand like they're a bunch of circus animals?" Feeling provoked, Billy angrily stood to face the stranger. El Padre turned in his bar stool and grasped Billy's thick arm before he could wield it like a weapon. Billy immediately experienced his entire body tighten and was unable to maneuver away from the hold. "Let go of my arm!" he cried out. He looked about the room, as everyone else remained engulfed in their own conversations or varying forms of business, not noticing his struggle. He yelled to the entire bar, "Hey, you idiots! Get this guy off me!" but no one reacted or even turned their way.

With one command from El Padre of "Sit," Billy obeyed without thought or argument. They once again assumed their original positions of facing each other seated at the bar, with El Padre releasing his grip.

A heavy sigh from El Padre, before he proclaimed, "It is a rarity for me to utilize such rudimentary means, but in your case, I felt it was quite necessary." Billy simply listened, unconsciously rubbing his arm. "What I wish to tell you, you may not share with any other. The consequences would be perilous." Billy nodded slowly, unsure exactly just who he's sitting next to and why he's the unlucky one stuck next to him.

El Padre turned forward, away from Billy's now attentive gaze, as his chicken wings arrived and he continued while eating them.

"Your life choices have been difficult and beleaguered. The pool of options since the loss of your father left you to struggle on your own, inviting desperate, small-minded men to take control of any possible hope for a productive life. They brainwashed your ideals through angry, hateful music, and molded your core beliefs with one-sided language to fit their own clandestine plans, building you up to fulfill duties they, themselves, were in fear of accomplishing. But do not believe they know your heart, nor have entirely broken your will. You are the son of Ezra and Tamara Dawkins, who bore you out of pure, unconditional love and raised you to be strong and faithful to the one true righteous leader. And he wears no brand or symbol of bigotry, but carried the burden of the original cross that all others fail to take up. Let not your past define who you are, but allow this new future to awaken that which has slept far too long and determine the path you truly desire to walk."

Billy's thoughts were flooded with memories of his parents, long forgotten, and he began to sob openly at the renewed emotions of their painful loss. A warmth never before allowed began to grow deep within Billy's heart. He slowly ceased his tears, acknowledging the beginning of change by lifting his head to stare at all things in a new manner. A curious smile dawned quickly across his face as he fought back the need to giggle. Once he grabbed control of his freed emotions, Billy set his jaw with a new mission rapidly forming; not from anger, ignorance, nor someone else's tainted philosophies, but directly from his heart. Billy silently left the bar while the stranger finished his meal.

Walking through town and away from Waveland, El Padre watched Billy courageously working with the other town's people in their attempt to prepare for oncoming devastation, eventually sacrificing his life to assist and save others regardless of their skin color or place of origin.

CHAPTER 18

Sam walked into the office building with a meager offering of a heavy sigh for so early in his day. Melanie had called him just before leaving work the previous day, informing him he's scheduled for a 7:30 a.m. meeting with the new Editor-in-Chief, Mr. Walters, in the conference room. Without any significant background on the new editor-in-chief, Sam knew he's walking into this meeting pretty much blind. Regardless of whether this would be just a meet and greet or a ball-busting, fire-up-the-troops type of coming together, he'd simply have to grin and bear it.

To his surprise, he wasn't going to achieve any revelation solo. Sitting alone already in the room was Ira. Sam smiled a big grin, but stopped when Ira returned it with a disparaging expression. Before he had a chance to inquire what's up, Tom entered the conference room, coffee cup in one hand, a full file in the other, and closed the door. Sam spun around like a caged animal attempting to solve the dilemma of entrapment while Tom fluidly moved across the room toward the big chair at the end.

Still standing, Sam recognized Tom's effort at gently breaking the ice, stating, "First thing, this ridiculous throne has gotta go! Bet ol' Malcolm had a short man's complex." He took the regular seat across from Ira and set the thick file down hard in front of him. Tom took a sip of his coffee, but stared at Sam while he sipped, then moved his focus to the chair next to Ira. Sam quickly consented to the unspoken request, sliding into the chair, setting down his notepad and pen, and folded his hands out onto the table.

Tom opened the file and flipped through several pages until he came to an item that interested him, saying, "Ah, here's something. I have a trip to Peru, signed off by all the wrong people for all the wrong reasons." Sam and Ira simultaneously sank three inches into their chair. Moving deeper into the file, Tom stopped again. "And what's this? Mr. Noll has the rare opportunity to one of the biggest stories of the decade, and somehow all of his hard work gets mysteriously stolen by one of our paper's toughest competitors?"

Tom looked up at his shrinking captive audience before going back to his page turning, followed by, "Now this one absolutely takes the cake. Here's a bill for an expensive security company to de-bug an office and Mr. Noll's desk. According to this invoice, they removed eleven extremely hi-tech listening devices." Tom slid the invoice across the table, asking Ira, pointing to the bottom of the bill, "Is that your signature, Mr. Nevins?"

After a moment of hesitation, Ira could only nod yes. Tom dramatically withdrew the bill of lading, adding, "And yet, not a word to our attorneys or any of the Board members. Heck, you didn't even alert the owners, whom you conveniently have on speed dial." Ira darted a look up and glared momentarily at Tom, but Tom didn't even flinch from his set expression. Ira dropped his head and returned his attention to the table top.

Sitting there, watching his friend be punished along with him for what were his actions, Sam felt a fire begin to ignite deep inside. Knowing he most likely was about to be fired, the very least he could do was throw himself on the grenade and try to save Ira. He leaned in and placed a hand out flat onto the table for support, but before he could open his mouth and let the first defensive word fly out, Tom pointed a finger directly at him, freezing Sam preemptively with one word, "Don't."

Sam physically sat back from the contraction chastisement and crossed his arms defiantly, letting Tom proceed. "Do you think for a second, Mr. Noll, that I can't see you as the common denominator here? Mr. Nevins has simply done what he could, when he could with proper intentions and with this paper's best interests in the forefront. If I was intending to fire him, he certainly wouldn't be sitting here." Both Ira and Sam relaxed a bit from the news of Ira's reprieve, before Tom honed in on Sam. "But you, Mr. Noll, are on thin ice."

Sam gave the last statement a brief thought. Tom evidently didn't want to fire him, either; or at least that's what Sam could decipher from his new boss' few tells. Sam decided to stand his ground as he typically did in this format; he opted for an attempt at humor, asking with a straight face, "So is this ice cracking or is it holding my weight?"

Tom allowed a short, almost unnoticeable smirk, but Sam saw it and mentally did his best effort of a touchdown celebration inside his head. Tom closed the file like a dark chapter to a scary book before shifting his weight in his seat, replying, "Let's just say your name will be on my mind for a long time and leave it at that."

Ira squirmed a bit in his seat, drawing Tom's attention, which froze Ira immediately, but unfortunately for him, it's too late, "Mr. Nevins, until further notice, I'll insist on everything that passes your desk to be forwarded to mine. If it doesn't have my John Hancock on it, it ain't flyin'. Understood?" Ira, again, simply nodded his agreement.

Tom returned his attention to Sam and, with the steady stare, also returned a little fear into Sam. Tom rapped his fingers on the closed file for two seconds, taking in his prey. Sam focused on keeping his face from turning gray and nothing else. Finally, Tom said softly, "Mr. Noll, I don't have a good feeling about this article you're working. I understand the numbers have climbed a bit, but I don't see it sprinting like we hoped. I'm thinking seriously about scrapping it."

Sam looked to Ira for a boost of support, but with his head still down attending to his recent wounds, Sam figured he's deservedly on his own. Sam drew a deep breath before adjusting to the new direction of his fight. It wasn't lost on him that, at first, all he wanted was to be off this assignment, yet here he was ready to fight for it. The story had become his own; at some point and for some reason, he had made it personal.

Throwing feel-good fluff at his new editor wouldn't work. Tom had been in the trenches far too long to fall for smoke and mirrors. Sam chose an angle he never would have considered had he been prepped for this battle; he spoke from his heart. "We can't end this story. I can't end this story. Have you read the letters the people have been writing in?"

Tom looked down briefly, and Sam managed to either see that Tom was caught unprepared for the question or that he had read them and knew where Sam was going with his argument. So, Sam pressed forward with just a hint of acquired confidence. "Everyone has lost someone; everyone. The whole idea of El Padre, whether he's good or perhaps, maybe, a bit evil, is the comfort of knowing someone was there when their loved one passed. That somebody held their hand in the final moments so they weren't alone. Think about who you've lost. Isn't there someone you cared for who, when they died, you thought deep inside how much you wish you could have been there, by their side, letting them know everything was going to be alright and that they were loved? I have someone. I think about her with every story I write, and I feel closer to her with every lead I follow up on. Please don't take that away from me and from so many others who feel the same. I'm begging you, don't take her away again."

Sam barely held back his emotions, waiting for the one-man jury to convene. Ira simply stared at his friend, but Sam didn't even notice, as his attention was fixed on Tom.

The heavy exhale from Tom hit Sam like a 'Not Guilty' verdict.

A slow smile slipped across Tom's face with his body motion following suit of giving in before offering, "Fine. We'll see where this takes us, but I want my hands in this. No more flying to Peru unless I deem it absolutely necessary. We have a budget for things like this and there are limits, so when you come cryin' to me for airfare to Swahili and I say no, that's why!"

Sam turned quickly to look at Ira, but his friend was already on top of it. "Actually, sir, Swahili isn't a place. It's a language. It's a Bantu dialect of the coast and islands of eastern Africa. Also, it's the official language of Tanzania."

Sam smugly nodded his agreement, turning back to Tom. Their new editor-in-chief halted his rise from the chair and glared at his two staff members. Sam immediately lost his smugness, and Ira returned his attention to the table. Tom made his exit, but turned, informing the two, "Tomorrow, Wednesday morning. Eight o'clock sharp. The three of us are going to hammer out a game plan for the story. No more running all over the place; it needs some organization. Bring everything you have and we'll work out some sort of arrangement. Until then, get to work."

Like two fifth graders hearing the last bell before summer vacation, Sam and Ira grabbed their belongings and high-tailed it out of there, thankfully thinking how there's still work to go back to.

Beatrice Jackson sat impatiently outside her boss' office like a claymore mine waiting for any type of contact. The slow-building rage consumed her, seething a fiery breath, checking her watch for the tenth time during her eighteen minute stay. If admitting one's problem was the first step to recovery, then Bea, as everyone called her, was a full-fledged 'temperholic,' and she seriously doubted her meeting with her editor, Gloria Staples, could be labeled as a step toward a cure.

Being summoned to a meeting upstairs with the new boss had the condescending air of being called to high court by her mighty highness. If Queen Staples expected a curtsy upon entering the throne room, Bea would tell her where she could bend over.

Gloria was thin and pretty with long, flowing dark hair, feminine and well respected for her business mind, and Bea hated each and every one of her positive attributes. Bea, on the other hand, was Gloria's polar opposite, tipping the scale at one hundred and none of anyone's business, with short cropped dishwater blonde hair and an unmistakable fixed expression of someone ready for a fight, be it verbal or physical, your choice.

For two weeks Bea had managed to avoid the new monthly one-on-one meetings that Gloria force-fed her entire staff. Bea thoroughly understood her boss' desire to meet face-to-face with her staff. The over-bearing need for absolute control was the only thing they had in common, but when the meetings began morphing into 'fireside chats,' as it'd been jokingly labeled by the other columnists, Bea found every opportunity to be unavailable. This plan had functioned successfully until last week when Gloria's administrative Assistant cornered her, of all places, in the ladies bathroom, where they hammered out a confirmed appointment.

The exchange was punctuated with just a slight hint of an 'or else' ultimatum from the secretary, which mentally added her to Bea's growing 'Skinny Bitches I'd Like to Slap' list. So here she was, waiting on the time-out bench for twenty-three minutes for her moment to glean a little radiance from the sun. Bea privately scoffed at the fact that she usually preferred the shadows.

At last, without the expected celebratory public display of coronation, Gloria's door swung open, as three bloggers from the newspaper's political section filed out with their heads bowed in a confused, humbled silence. Bea had noticed the after-affect numerous times before as the typical post-Gloria experience; broken, disregarded, and emotionally unsatisfied.

Bea nodded her greeting to them while they sauntered past, only to be the beneficiary of a 'Sorry, but you're next' stare from each of them. Gloria herself appeared at the door entrance in a black pin-striped pant suit, gray, starched shirt, and expensive shoes, looking more masculine than usual. It was common knowledge that Madam Staples dressed her mood, and the dark suit was a discouraging start.

Once the three rejected bloggers were out of ear shot, Gloria broke the silence with, "Beatrice, so good of you to be able to make this meeting. We have so much to catch up on!" Before a response could be offered, she turned on a heel and returned to the comfort of the lioness' den, leaving Bea to assume she'd been called to worship and to follow in tow.

Once inside the office, Bea remained standing awkwardly in the middle of the room with her notebook in hand, waiting to be directed. Gloria finished her follow-up notes from her recent clarity session and looked up to notice Bea standing in doubt. She chided an off-handed remark of, "Oh Bea, just sit anywhere. You know we aren't big on pomp and circumstance around here" which she followed with an odd little laugh for effect.

Bea sat in the left chair across from the desk, thinking, Oh yeah, Gloria, since when?

Bea made herself comfortable while Gloria pulled a medium-sized file from someplace below and began going through it, page after page, not making a sound. Just when Bea started to feel she's keeping her from other things, Gloria looked up at Bea and stated, "So, your hits continue to climb, I see."

Thrown off for just a second, Bea forced a response before her mouth was ready to work and stammered a comeback of, "That's correct; well, sort of. I mean, the numbers are only an inaccurate gauge, they're not something you can count on. But, yeah, I try not to follow them too closely."

Gloria stared intently at Bea for a moment, and Bea did her best to appear as if she wasn't actually on any heavy medications. Gloria dismissed the odd comment and moved on, turning another page, continuing, "And we haven't had any further episodes of your personal vendetta with anymore silly little diatribes concerning conspiracy theories between the banks and the Senate Committee on Finance? I hope the paper doesn't need to revisit *that* swarm of bees your article caused the legal department last year."

Bea bit her lip and took a breath, thinking, you just had to poke the bear, didn't you, Gloria? Bea felt her anger immediately surge from her gut to her throat, where she'd been known to do the most damage to her career. She swore an oath to herself that she would not, could not allow the woman to instigate her fury. The glaring fact that Gloria hadn't even been on the payroll when Bea's article hit the stands, in and of itself, should've kept her from bringing up the entire subject. It'd been discussed and approved for print by the previous editor, and that's all Gloria needed to know.

Bea mentally slapped her forehead to remind herself that she had a game plan for today's meeting, too, but she needed the right moment to plop it on Gloria. Bea realized she's just staring back at Gloria's open-ended question and also knew the inquiry was simply a test from her editor, and for one of the few times she could remember, Bea opted for the high road, saying, "Our talented legal team needs to be challenged every now and then, don't you think? I mean, after all, why do we acknowledge the envelope if we aren't going to push it a little."

Gloria appeared taken aback from Bea's quick change in demeanor and took her turn to struggle for the next word. Bea, considering herself on a good roll and priding herself at being every bit the opportunist, moved in on the conversation gap left by Gloria with, "Now, what I have on tap is an interview with the Director of Homeland Security."

Gloria waited a second for the punch line that never arrived before re-engaging into the dialog with, "Rebecca Turner? You intend to meet with Rebecca Turner?"

Bea beamed her first smile since, well, longer than she could remember, before answering, "The one and only. We have a meeting the day after tomorrow in New York."

Gloria gusted a managerial atmosphere back into the room, stating, "Now, Beatrice, you know that any travel expenses must be pre-approved by the supervising editor, and the last time I checked the door plate, it was me."

Not to be usurped of her momentum, Bea shifted gears once again, keeping her boss off her step with, "Really, Gloria? Do you honestly want to jeopardize the first, and possibly only, interview from the first woman to not only head up the largest federal department in the country, but also be the first high ranking female to carry a higher approval rate than the President of the United States? Not to mention, her chances in the next Presidential election, which I intend to inquire about. Seriously, are you that insecure about your door plate that you'll let travel expenses get in the way of a huge story?"

Gloria's blank look signified her mind was racing with visions of the possible headlines the unique opportunity could provide, and in her uncertainty was where Bea finished her off, saying tactfully, "But, if all you want is a request, then here it is; may I *please* go to New York and do this interview? Pretty please, with saccharine and low-cal whipped topping on it."

With no accessible avenue but to relent, Gloria was once again allowed to make the final decision, even if it's not of her own creation with, "Fine. Go to New York, but you'll stay at the Holiday Inn Express. No Embassy Suites this time. And watch your per diem. According to my records, last time you ran way over your limit."

Grabbing her unopened notebook and heading for the door, Bea tossed one last tidbit over her shoulder. "I'll do you one better! I can bunk up with my cousin, Sam, and that'll cut down on meals, too!" Out the door she went, wondering how long it would be before her next high court summons with her editor.

Once at her desk, Bea dialed the number by memory, impatiently tapping her pen on her desk while waiting for the call to go through. Her female office neighbor in the cube to her right yelled over the divider, "Bea! Quit with the damned pen! Why can't you start smoking again?"

Bea didn't even show her neighbor the respect of turning her direction, but yelled back with, "Eat me, Sarah!"

Sarah stood and peeked over the divider, looking down at Bea on the phone, asking sarcastically, "Geez, Bea. What blew up your skirt?"

Bea finally looked up at her neighbor, stating, "Just came from Madam Staple's funhouse and didn't like the ride."

Sarah responded apologetically with, "Oh." After she sank back down to her desk, she asked over the barrier, "Did she bring up your Senate Finance and Banking article from last year?"

Bea, feeling the painful experience all over again, responded sarcastically, "Yes, Sarah, she did, and thank you so much for asking."

Sarah offered one last sentiment with a quiet little, "Sorry."

Finally, Sam picked up on what seemed like the twentieth ring with, "Sam Noll."

Bea unleashed her excitement over the phone without taking a breath, saying, "Sam, my boy, care to receive a visit from your favorite cousin from Chicago? I've got business in New York and hope I can crash with you and the little lady."

Sam let out a small chuckle on his end of the line at the rare show of positive energy from his cousin. "Who is this?" he asked jokingly, following with, "I don't have any happy relatives in the Midwest."

Bea conceded to her cousin, admitting, "Okay, okay, sorry for being in a good mood. I promise I'll be grumpy my entire time in your city limits. Heck, I'd probably fit right in!"

They both laughed and Sam asked, "When can you be here?"

Bea answered with, "I plan to fly in tomorrow around two for an interview on Thursday. Can I stay till Friday?"

Sam instantly responded with, "You can stay as long as you want, cuz. How did you pull off a visit on such short notice; not that I mind?"

Bea looked around and lowered her voice in case any eavesdroppers were listening in, stating, "I pulled off a major coup in my boss' office just now and dropped a bomb of an opportunity.

She didn't know what hit her. I swear, the woman either completely fears me or simply can't suppress her unbridled curiosity. Either way, I've scammed a trip to the Big Apple."

Sam laughed at his cousin's undaunted sense of dominance before replying, "Well, Katie and I are the lucky ones out of this elaborate scheme you've put into play. Do you need me to pick you up at the airport?"

Bea replied, "No, I think the paper can foot the bill for a taxi. I'm looking forward to meeting Katie. Is she still into reds?"

Sam shot back with, "I hope you're talking about wine! Yes, though it's evolved into blends. But whatever you pick up, don't let it be a Pinot. Her palate claims it tastes like Kool-aid."

Bea laughed through her response, "Got it. No Kool-aid. See ya tomorrow around four."

CHAPTER 19

There's a first time for everything, and getting to the conference room before Ira had never happened. In celebration of the event, Sam decided to sit in Ira's usual chair, with never having the opportunity before. Once he spread out his array of files and bulk of data on his article, Ira shuffled in and stopped at the door, watching Sam finish settling into his position. From the door, Ira simply stated the obvious, "You're in my chair."

Sam sat up and looked at the back of the chair, replying, "Oh, there wasn't a name on it, so I assumed it was for anyone."

Ira moved slowly forward into the room, responding with, "I would appreciate very much if you could move your items to any of the other available seats as I've been occupying that chair for longer than you've been able to chew gum."

Sam pretended to be preoccupied with his papers, answering, "Sorry, didn't hear you say, 'seat saved.' Besides, I like this chair! It's like it conforms to my boyish figure. I think I'm going to stay right here!"

Ira moved five feet closer before replying between gritted teeth, "I'm going to count to three . . ."

Tom entered the conference room with his own papers and coffee cup, interrupting the standoff with, "For gosh sakes, can you two stop acting like four-year-olds for five minutes. Nevins, just sit in the big chair. Jeez!" Ira quickly moved to the chair next to Sam, refusing to sit in the big chair, but continued glaring at Sam while he sat. Tom shook his head at the two, adding, "This is like dealing with my kids from my second marriage; only a divorce and a ton of money won't get rid of it."

Both Sam and Ira decided to switch to their professional faces showing they're ready to begin. Tom accepted their sign of putting their immaturity behind them with a grunt of, "Alright then" before opening a notepad and sliding it over to Ira and stating to Sam, "I want you to start listing each sighting, minus those you've already covered in previous articles. I want dates, if you have them, and locations. Ira will dictate the list and I'll throw out my questions and any input as we go along. So, let's get started."

After three hours of going through all of the leads, Sam stretched his arms and yawned from the nonstop labor. Tom checked his watch, saying, "I've got another meeting, so let's break for lunch and be back here at 12:30 sharp."

Tom was up and gone before either Sam or Ira could respond, leaving them to stare at each other. Ira finally asked, "Why didn't you stretch and yawn an hour ago? I've had to use the facilities since we started."

With that Ira quickly left as well. Sam called after Ira from his still seated position, "Well, who's bringing me lunch?"

Back in the conference room, Ira and Sam waited patiently, watching Tom stare at the ceiling, leaning back in his chair with his hands folded behind his head. Neither wanted to interrupt his train of thought that'd been going on well past sixty seconds. Brief, stolen glances at each other became a game as Sam turned toward Ira with his eyes crossed, trying to get his friend to laugh.

Tom leaned his chair forward in time to catch Sam red-handed and cross-eyed, replying, "For gosh sakes, I hope they stick!" Sam turned red, but chose not to comment on his guilt as Tom proceeded with the culmination of his thoughts. "Okay, here's what we've established so far; a guy appearing to be in his early fifties, stocky build, and a scar on the back of his hand roaming the earth possibly taking people's souls, finishing them off or giving them their last rites."

He glanced up at his audience, and Sam offered an agreeable nod, so he continued. "Doesn't mingle with the living that we know of, 'cept the Jewish guy from Fordham and the priest at his church."

Another look up followed another nod of consent. "Here's what we need; this guy, ghost, or incarnation, has to have talked to someone else other than these two. We get a sketch artist over to that church and the retirement home, pronto. Have the two composites compared and we run the sketch with your next story. People skip over pictures of criminals in the paper all the time cuz the bad guy is already caught. Give 'em a sketch of somebody unknown, somebody we're looking for, and people start phoning in their ex-brother-in-law, quiet neighbor, or scorned lover."

Sam tilted his head inquisitively, asking, "But what does that have to do with finding the actual El Padre or future leads?"

Tom smiled, responding, "Circulation. Nothing slicks the wheels of the presses like the unknown perp. Everyone is gonna be on the lookout for this guy. We'll flush him out."

Sam shook his head while Ira just watched him. Finally, Sam advised, "Won't that inundate us with bogus leads to follow up on? I'm solo on this gig, and I'm carrying three other articles to boot. There's no way I can handle the volume you're going to dump on me."

Tom tapped his pen on the table for a moment of thought before suggesting, "Let's just see how much we get in return value before you go jumping off a bridge with your panties in a bind." Sam rubbed his temples with his boss staring at him. Finally, Tom asked, "Okay, you won't hear me ask this again, but what else is bothering you?"

Sam glanced at Ira, then back at Tom before diving in. "I understand we're in the business to get people to read our publication, but I can't do it without any shred of integrity. This article should be a cause for reflection and a moment to honor those who have passed on, not a sideshow or gimmick to sell newspapers. The mystery of El Padre and what he does is the draw, but the connection that everyone dies and the hope it isn't done alone is what will keep them reading. My background and studies are exactly what this story needs to enlighten the reader about other religions, theologies, and customs different from theirs; that people mourn and show their respect for the dead with varying degrees of practices and beliefs."

Tom sneered with a tilt of his head, drawing Sam to press harder. "There are 238 nations in the world with approximately 270 major faiths or religions and over 4,200, if you include every sub-group. With each religious body, culture, or movement they have their own take on death and dying. Along with all of these varying beliefs are numerous embodiments or personifications of death. For instance, the Hebrews believe in the Malach HaMavet, also known as Azra'il, meaning the 'Angel of Death.' The Hindu's take on the Grim Reaper would be Yama, or Yamaras, who rides a black buffalo carrying a lasso to drag the souls to Yamalok, the Underworld of the dead. My favorite is the Greeks' Thanatos, the Hellenic myth of the one who hands the deceased over to Charon, the ferryman from the land of the living, crossing the River Acheron to that of the dead. The Japanese believe in Shinigami . . ."

"Enough," Tom cut in with a hand slap to the table. Ira dropped his pencil from the abrupt interruption, and Sam ceased his sharing of knowledge, offering only a steely gaze toward his boss. Tom stood and began to pace with his arms crossed in front of him and one fisted hand to his chin, while both were once again left to simply observe the man and his thoughts.

Tom stopped and grasped the back of the chair with both hands, staring down at Sam before saying, "Fine. Fill their minds with religious babble. I'll give you one person to help with research and any back-draft. But if your numbers nosedive or even take a dip of half of a percent, I'll pull on your leash so hard you'll have your tail hanging out of your mouth for a week." Sam felt his face flush a little, but was pretty certain he retained his steady glare.

Ira scooted his chair an inch or two away from the heat as the two faced off. Once appearing satisfied with his distance, Tom bellowed toward him without taking his eyes off Sam, "Nevins, know what collateral duty is?"

Ira sat up in response and quoted, "Paralleled responsibility, often without increased compensation or remaining at the same pay grade."

Tom turned to Ira, grinning as he added, "Congratulations, Nevins. You've been randomly selected." Tom stood, straightened his tie, and grabbed his jacket from behind the chair before heading for the door, saying, "Now, I've got a meeting uptown and you two have a lot of work to do, so you'd better get to it." With that, he was gone.

Sam turned to Ira, as his friend's face was in his hands. In an attempt to add a little levity to the situation, Sam joked, "I'll call the engraver and have them add this to your name plate. You call payroll and let them know there won't be any changes to your pay." A sour look was all Ira could muster at the moment, as Sam added, "So, does this make you my assistant?"

North Dakota, 2004

Though the scope of the reservation spanned many miles of stark, desolate territory, El Padre's destination was certain and predetermined. A heavy heart carried him among the crops of trees and smoky trailers that he passed, scattered along the meander of countless gravel roads that made up the self-ruled territorial dominion. A young girl was laughing and playing with her brother for her final time here on earth, and the sadness he felt was nearly unbearable. Her calling echoed off the large pines, and the draw toward her death forced him to continue his slow, steady pace placing one foot in front of the other like a heartbeat.

Dusk began to shade the land of so many trees, but still he proceeded forth, knowing she'd require his presence soon, very soon.

Another mile, then another, El Padre began to clear his thoughts of what should be and focused on what was as he took in the area around the small trailer. A metal jungle-gym leaned rusted and forgotten just beyond the home, along with several broken plastic toys from earlier years of usefulness. The sad metaphor caught his breath, as well as his emotions, just before a young Native American girl of thirteen exited the front door. She stared at the arriving stranger, appearing to try to produce some form of recognition. When none came, she began to turn quickly to the safety of the home.

El Padre froze her escape with one word, calling out calmly, "Saffron," The young girl turned back for a second chance at familiarity while El Padre slowly approached closer with her continuing to look into his eyes for recognition.

"My father is on his way home!" she challenged, but remained on the three-stair steps leading to the entrance.

El Padre stopped his progress and folded his hands in front of him in a show of nonaggression, replying, "Yes, and I wish I could speak with him at great length, but the reason for this visit is solely for you."

Her curiosity took hold and she asked hastily, "Me? What do you want from me?"

El Padre moved toward a discarded wooden spool sitting, turned over, in what could only be suggested as the front yard. Turning it flat-side down, he set one foot upon it, placing his weight forward, answering her with, "I am here to speak with you, as I have heard you have quite a gift for artistry."

With a hesitant smile slipping across her face, she asked, "Did you speak to Ms. Ebnet at my school?"

El Padre grinned back at the now receptive girl, answering, "She holds your unique gift for drawing rather highly among any of her past students. She believes you have a great future as an artist. Is this what you wish to do, Saffron?"

The young girl jumped off the steps in one giant leap and landed softly upon a small patch of grass near the spool. "I like seeing something in a picture or magazine and being able to draw it by memory, but I *love* closing my eyes and make up a picture I've never thought of or seen before; you know, sort of create it in my head. Those are always my best drawings."

He beamed back at the girl, responding, "They are not simply drawings, my dear; they are works of art."

The look he received from Saffron from such unheard praise rewarded El Padre's heart as much as it achieved a well-deserved compliment toward the young girl. Seemingly uncomfortable with such undeviating attention, she tried to change the subject, stating, "My little brother was just here, but left half an hour ago for his friend's house. He gets to spend the night over there since there's no school tomorrow."

El Padre let the comment drift between them without response, shifting his weight slightly, finally supplying the unfilled gap with, "You take excellent care of your brother while your mother works her long hours. He obviously loves and looks up to you in a way few younger brothers display. He will one day grow into a strong, independent man and carry your strength of hopefulness far beyond the boundaries of this environment. He will be a man of true Native pride, worthy of a great many things, always holding dear the enlightenment gained from his big sister."

A darkness cascaded down upon her face as she struggled to share her deepest concern with the stranger. El Padre felt her inner turmoil and eased her restrictions with, "Your mother weighs heavily on your heart, child; this I know."

Saffron's head snapped up as though her very thoughts had been read, glaring silently, questioningly, at the older gentleman. "I will tell you what I see, but you must promise me to never share what I am about to express. Can you do that for me?" he asked in a manner of secretive bond.

"Yes. I promise no one shall ever know," she countered softly.

El Padre drew a breath and gathered added strength for the task at hand, closing his eyes and directing the focus of his will.

"Many days advance before bonds can be severed. I see a time of suffering, but it is followed by a revelation of truth and justice. I now see your mother smiling and content with eventual outcome and remaining ever near to her son, your brother. Her days are long and difficult, but your love for her and the example you have left for your brother will carry her to a place of happiness and satisfied peace to the end of her days. Her spirit will move with the four winds and remain about the land, along with all of her ancestors."

The distant rumbling approach of a pick-up truck broke El Padre's connection sooner than he preferred. He turned toward the soon-to-be illuminated road and exhaled his deeply sorrowful regret. Surprised from the unexpected physical contact, he quickly turned to see Saffron had closed the four foot separation and was gently holding his hand. She innocently looked up into his blue eyes and asked bravely, "Will I see my brother and my mother again?"

Tears built around his eyes as he reached toward her soft cheek, answering, "My sweet, sweet child. You shall be among a host of angels until they triumphantly arrive."

Walking away from such painful examples of human depravity and not being able to intercede had constantly been the greatest defining battle for not only his enormous undertaking, but also his very soul. A small piece of whom and what he believed in seemed to chip away with every senseless loss. Only his perception of the greater picture kept his one foot firmly ahead of the other, one lasting heartbeat at a time.

CHAPTER 20

By the time Sam returned home after work that day, Katie had transformed their tiny apartment into a sterile atmosphere, void of a single item out of place. Aside from the various cleaning agents used, Sam could smell the lasagna in its infant stage and knew he's in for a great dinner and a much needed fun night with two of his favorite ladies. Katie hollered from the kitchen, "Is that you?"

Sam smiled, answering, "Nope. It's just a hungry visitor following the delightful aroma." Peeking around the corner into the kitchen, he watched his girlfriend focused on the undertaking of perfectly layering the limp noodles into the casserole dish.

She turned to see him and beamed him a big smile, saying, "Well, since I know how hungry visitors love Italian food, how about you open the wine and let it catch a breath?"

Sam set his homework down and began to roll up his sleeves, saying, "She cooks, she cleans, and even politely delegates job assignments. You're hired!"

Katie just smiled her response, not wanting to lose the technique she had going, while Sam grabbed the bottle opener from the drawer and began wrestling with the foil top. "She should be here any minute, so once that's open, you can go and get changed," she instructed after finishing the final layer.

Sam stopped, looked down at his attire, and asked, "What's wrong with what I have on? It was good enough for everybody at work!"

Katie looked him up and down, wrinkling her nose, saying, "Those are your *work* clothes and you've been wearing them all day. Bea will be your first family member to meet me, and she deserves to see you in your *clean* clothes."

Sam stood in place in bewilderment, asking cautiously, "Is this going to be a 'thing' with you and my clothes?"

Katie didn't even look his way, replying, "Not as long as you go and change, so hurry up; she'll be here any minute." Sam decided not to pursue the particular motherly instinct evolving before him and opted to simply obey the instructions and keep the waters calm.

Bea arrived on time, and after introductions and giving her enough time to feel relaxed, the three settled into the living room to enjoy a glass of wine while the lasagna baked. Bea asked, looking around the high ceilings of the living room, "How in the world did you get your hands on this co-op? Walking distance to Central Park, the Met, and Lincoln Center, not to mention the Upper Westside, is a hot commodity. So, what little old lady did you bribe your soul to?"

Sam shrugged ambivalence while Katie cut in, "I asked him the same thing on our second date, but he would only tell me it was luck and perfect timing."

Sam looked at both of the girls staring back at him, waiting for an answer, but Sam only asked mockingly, "There's a park nearby?"

After Sam's offering of dry humor, Bea raised her glass for a toast. The other two joined in as Bea stated, "Well, here's to whatever good fortune allowed you to find this place and brought you two together; may it last a lifetime."

They each took sips from the wine before Bea asked, "So, Katie, Sam tells me you ran the Boston marathon three years ago?"

Katie smiled, looking at Sam, proudly answering, "Yes, though I doubt I could do it again; the first eight to ten miles were okay, but the last sixteen, the same question kept coming back to me of, what the heck was I thinking?"

Bea chimed in, adding, "Seriously, I don't even like *driving* twenty-six miles, let alone hoofing it!" Bea continued getting to know Katie, asking, "So, let me see if I have this right. You work at three different gyms and teach various types of aerobics, is that correct?"

Katie scooted forward to the edge of the sofa and answered, "Well, yes and no. I actually work for a contractor who is employed by the person who owns several Athletic Clubs here in New York. The Contractor hires the trainers, physical therapists, and instructors, like me, and his assistant does the scheduling for all of the staff. We have the freedom to switch our sessions at our discretion, as long as each class is covered. I work at just three of the gyms, but there are some who work every chance they get at all sixteen clubs. And, actually after dinner, I'll need to leave the two of you, as I have an eight o'clock jazzercise class I promised to cover for a friend."

Bea gave Katie an exhaustive look, replying, "Geez, Katie, no wonder you stay in such great shape. Would you ever want to run your own gym?"

Katie smiled bashfully, answering, "I don't think I could compete with these guys. They have so much capital backing them; I just don't think any bank would consider it fiscally prudent. But I've thought about it from time to time. Maybe if it were outside the big city. Who knows, maybe one day." A buzzer went off in the kitchen, and Katie reacted by standing, saying, "Well, dinner will be ready in five to seven minutes, so if you'll excuse me . . ."

Katie headed into the kitchen while Bea turned to Sam, saying, "I see what you mean, cuz; she's an absolute doll. My only question is, what's she doing with you?"

Sam grabbed at his heart, jokingly replying, "Ouch, right in the love shack! A mortal wound straight to the heart by a family member, of all people. It's the stuff of Shakespeare."

Bea swatted at her cousin, pleading, "Knock it off, tough guy. I'm just happy you found someone just right for you."

Sam looked at Bea without expression, then looked down, quietly replying, "Thanks. I hope I deserve her."

Bea started to respond, but Katie yelled from the kitchen, "Okay, you two have enough time to go wash up. Dinner's just about on the table."

Sam and Bea rose together while Sam whispered, "Better get used to this cleaning up stuff. It's like an obsessive-compulsive thing that's crept up recently."

Bea looked at her cousin, responding, "Well, thanks for the warning, but I usually wash my hands before putting them into my mouth."

Sam quickly replied, "Forks, Bea, we use forks!" Bea slapped her cousin again as he led the way.

After the meal was finished and the dishes were washed, rinsed, and put away, Katie hurried to the bedroom and emerged changed, hair pulled back into a pony-tail and ready for her evening class. "Sorry for leaving the two of you, but momma's gotta bring home the bacon! Sam, why don't you take Bea to that pub you like so much? I think she'd love it," Katie suggested before leaning in to kiss Sam and heading out the door.

Once out of ear shot, Bea looked at Sam and asked excitedly, "Pub? Did she say there's a pub? Can we go, Sam, can we, can we?"

Sam smiled at Bea's playful inquiry, declaring, "Fine. We finish our wine and it's off to the pub." Bea looked Sam up and down, asking, "Are you really going to wear *that*?"

Sam looked up to the sky he believed was somewhere beyond the ceiling and asked, "Please tell me she's not rubbing off on you?" Bea just giggled at her frustrated cousin before reaching for her glass of wine to finish off its final sip.

At the pub, Sam and Bea sat across from each other in a cushioned booth in the middle of the bar. Scanning the room, Sam noticed with the lateness of the hour on a week night, the pub had only a few patrons looking for luck, love, or levity while they swilled their various potions in the hope of feeling just a little better about their personal afflictions. Before Bea took a drink from her beer, she broke his destructive thought, asking, "Hey, where'd you go, sport?"

Sam snapped back to reality with, "Oh, sorry. I was just thinking how dismal my existence was before Katie. I'd sit here four, sometimes five, nights out of the week watching whatever game the particular season granted, eating bar food that made its home around my waist line. I was lonely, but in denial, Bea. And, to make matters worse, I didn't have a clue that what I was feeling was loneliness; I labeled it as boredom, so I filled it with taking every lead I could swindle at work."

Sam adjusted his position before continuing. "And when the juicy stuff dried up, I started in on temporary fixes, such as cooking classes, spinning at the health club, and Internet dating. It was after finishing spinning at the gym that I literally ran into Katie. She was late for one of her classes and I was dragging my ass to the locker room when we knocked each other to the floor. She was peeved, and I was laughing so hard that I couldn't speak a word. She stormed off and I didn't see her for two weeks. When I saw her at the gym one night, I had the advantage of surprise and immediately offered her the opportunity to really lay into me for any inconvenience I may have caused her. She didn't have a prayer. I had her without a 'hello'!"

Bea turned sideways in the booth, and put her feet up level on the seat, replying, "You know, nine out of ten relationships that begin accidentally end painfully for one or both parties."

Sam took a drink from his beer and replied, "Sounds like my kinda odds!"

Bea shifted gears with the subject matter from personal to professional, asking, "So, how's my favorite boss in the whole world treating you since your paper stole him from me and left me with a half-witted brunette bombshell?"

Sam chuckled at his cousin's expense, answering, "Fine, just fine. He seems to have picked up right where our last editor left off. You know, other than the lying, back stabbing, and personal agenda scenario. Other than that, he's doing just great."

Bea turned her mood from jovial to thoughtful, saying, "Listen to me, Sam. I know trust comes rarely in this business of ours, especially with what you've had to endure, but Tom is one of the good ones. You can take my word on it."

Sam accepted her advice with a sincere nod, then stated before getting up, "I'm gonna hit the head, then grab two more beers. Be right back."

Inside the bathroom, standing in front of the urinal reading the disgusting messages left by sad and lonely men, Sam's cell phone rang. Frustrated, he reached over with his left hand and took it out of his right pants pocket, pressed a button, and said, "This is Sam."

His editor, Tom Walters, replied, "What are you doing right now?"

Sam looked down, then back up, saying, "Reading. Why?"

"Just got a hot lead come across my desk." Tom replied "You're gonna wanna see this. How do you feel about squeezing in a trip to San Fran?"

Sam checked his watch, and then asked into the phone, "It's nine o'clock in the evening, Tom. What are you doing at the office? They didn't actually tell you that they were paying you by the hour, cuz I hate to break it to ya; you're salary!"

With no sense of humor, Tom just replied, "Be in my office by eight-thirty. Have an overnight bag packed for fog."

After the click from the phone, Sam stared at it for a second before returning it to his pocket. Once finishing his business, Sam smacked the flushing toggle, mimicking his boss's phrase, "'Pack for fog!' Tommy, my boy, I'm already in a fog!" Once Sam cooled down at the bar, he returned to the booth with the two refills, stating, "Well, that was an enlightening trip to the boy's room! While at the urinal, 'one of the good ones' gave me a ring!"

Bea halted in her attempt to take a pull from her new beer and stared at Sam, asking, "What kind of a pub is this?"

Sam replayed his comment in his head and started laughing at himself, clarifying, "No! Tom called me while I was in the bathroom! I have to fly to San Francisco tomorrow morning; some new lead."

Bea showed a look of relief, saying, "Did he say what was up?"

Sam shook his head, swallowing his mouthful of beer, followed by, "Nope, not really. He's mysterious that way."

Bea slapped the table softly, declaring, "Well then, I guess we'll have to just paint the town tonight, cuz! How 'bout we move on to another watering hole, though. Since you told me the story about you coming here every night of the week, it's depressed the heck outta me!"

Sam chuckled at Bea's suggestion, defending himself weakly. "It was only five nights a week; five!"

Bea responded insincerely, "Right, whatever. Let's finish up and blow this joint."

Sam and Bea sat in another similar bar, with similar customers, drinking fresh beers in a new booth. The conversation had gradually developed down to their days of youth as Bea was uncharacteristically laughing from her belly. "No, no, no! I was still in the kitchen when you came downstairs with that water balloon. You totally caught me by surprise with that thing. Remember how pissed my mom was when she got home? The whole place was plastered with wet, rubbery substance everywhere."

Sam laughed along with Bea, adding, "Yeah, I remember, and I also recall you taking the entire blame for the mess, saying you forced me into battle in a way that no man could have resisted."

They both continued laughing at the memory before Bea said, "You know, right until mom died, she never stopped watching the door for you to walk in, drop your bag, and announce, 'What's for dinner?'"

Sam sobered considerably and looked up at his cousin with a pained look, admitting, "Geez, Bea. You didn't have to hit below the belt. It was two years. Two years to the day! I couldn't go through that again, you know that. When mom died, I was a mess. Following her wishes and bringing her out here to New York to be buried near her parents took what little sanity I had left. I couldn't tie my own shoes, let alone eat."

Sam shook his head from the memory. "When Aunt Caroline got sick, it just rehashed everything all over again. I wouldn't have been any use to anybody and I felt I needed to stay away. I regret it more than you could ever know. Aunt Caroline was the only semblance of what a home was supposed to feel like after mom died. The times I spent at your house were the happiest I can remember. There's no way I could have been strong enough to have been there for you or your family, and I'm sorry for that, Bea. I really am."

Bea wiped a long awaited tear from her eye and smiled at her cousin, explaining, "Sorry, Sam. It's just something we've never talked about and something I needed to get rid of, you know?"

Sam looked up from his lamented expression and returned a forgiving smile, adding, "If apologies were pennies, Bea, I could make you a millionaire. You're the last person on this earth who should be asking for *my* forgiveness, okay?"

Bea nodded her compliance as Sam decided it's time for a change toward a lighter fare. "Let's get, as they say in the U.K. 'pissing drunk', shall we?"

Bea sat up in response, yelling, "Bartender, bring me another tankard of swill and a frothy brew for my horse!" Sam leaned over the table laughing at his cousin's outburst as she patted his head, saying softly, "That's a good horse; you've traveled long and hard. Your refreshment approacheth nigh."

Sam looked up at Bea, smiling from ear to ear, and asked, "Hey, do you remember that farm we went to the summer after my eighth grade, so that would have been after your sixth?"

Bea mirrored Sam's smile, answering, "Oh, yeah, the Feldman Farm. They had all of those horses and every other imaginable farm animal. That place was a blast."

Sam made a thoughtful face, asking, "Why did we only go that one time?"

Bea snorted a little beer out her nose before restraining herself enough to reply, "Because old man Feldman got sent away for tax evasion and illegal gun sales. Also, he was seeing two of Mrs. Feldman's friends on the sly, which didn't come out until his last day in court. It made the front page of the *Tribune* back in the nineties!"

Sam shook the thought away, adding, "Perceptions sure can change from when you're a kid, huh?"

Bea focused her foggy, drunken vision to hold her cousin's stare for a moment before answering, "We have to face realities at some point in our lives. Some begin to see it in their teens, others remain naïve until," Bea slammed her hand down onto the table for dramatic effect, adding loudly, "Wham, it smacks 'em in the face. Either way, innocence makes its hasty exit, and pessimism and distrust flood their way into the gap."

Sam just stared at Bea before saying, "That has to be the saddest explanation for the loss of youth that I've ever heard. We can't end our evening on that note."

Bea smiled mischievously back at her cousin before finally supplying, "Well, how about this for a better parting subject? You, my dear cousin, have truly come into your own with this article of yours. I've never seen you write better or with more passion and intrigue. Sure, some of this inspiration could be coming from a certain little hottie you've coerced into your life, but you're absolutely on a roll. You've always had a way with words, but I find myself anxious to snatch your next article to see where you take me. Tell me you don't feel like you're in the zone?"

Sam gave his cousin a wry smile before winking and replying, "Nah, it's just the same old drivel, nothing more."

Bea pushed his forehead back, and he began laughing, sitting up from the force. "Jerk!" she fired at him while chuckling from his response.

Sam took a sip of his beer and relented to Bea's half-serious inquiry, saying, "No, seriously Bea, I find myself in a constant adrenaline rush every time I come across a new tidbit, shift of pattern, or updated lead. This guy I'm chasing is real, and there hasn't been anything chronicled like this before, and each and every morning I wake up to the realization that I'm the fortunate guy writing about him. Sure, I have other columnists nipping at my heels and historians claiming that it's all a lie or that I make it all up, but none of them have the collection of authentic leads that I have, nor do they experience being where this guy has walked so they can all just play follow the leader and keep reading my stories, for now!"

Bea sat back into her booth accompanied by a big smile for her cousin as she blurted out, "Finally! I thought I'd never rub off on you!"

Sam just shook his head at her claim to personal victory before adding, "Between you and me, cuz, I've got a good feeling about this trip out west tomorrow; something huge."

Bea nodded along, replying, "Well, I hope so, too, then. Just don't forget about us 'little people' as they hand you the Pulitzer, okay?"

Sam chuckled at the thought, saying in a mockingly serious tone, "Not a problem. Every time I scrape 'em off the bottom of my shoes, I'll say, 'Oh, hello!'"

Bea squinted at her cousin and replied, "Okay, forget what I said. Now I hope it's a long flight with a close proximity snorer!"

Sam peered back, answering with, "Ouch! You don't fight fair."

Bea drained her beer, offered an unlady-like belch, and stated, "If it's worth fighting for, it's worth fighting for dirty!"

Sam looked around before saying, "Well, first cousin, I've got a long day that starts way too early ahead of me tomorrow. Whataya say we head back so I can get a little sleep before my flight?"

Bea reluctantly slid out of the booth, answering, "Fine, if we must. But next time I come all the way out here, you'd better make more time for me! These trips are at a premium and cost me more in humility than anything else."

Sam opened the door, walking out of the bar together, saying, "Hey, at least you'll have time alone with Katie. It'll be good for you two to get to know each other better. I know she wants to make a good impression, so go easy on her."

Bea laughed at her cousin, adding, "I'm the one you should be worrying about! I think if I accidentally piss her off, she could drop me in three seconds flat! The girl is a lot tougher than both of us put together."

Sam joined Bea in the laughter, saying, "Yeah, I've often wondered whether I'd survive a major blitzkrieg if it ever came to it. Good thing she's on our side, huh?"

CHAPTER 21

Tom was hovering around Sam's work area when he exited the elevator, which immediately made him feel late even though, in fact, he's fifteen minutes early. Sam set his leather case down on his chair while Tom stood silently by, giving his columnist time to settle in. Sam finally looked up at his boss, asking, "Have we switched desks for the day?"

Tom broke in with, "Where's your luggage?"

Sam slapped his forehead, replying, "Left it by the door at home. I was in too much of a hurry to see you."

Tom ignored the humor, continuing with all business, "About this lead," He handed Sam a manila packet, continuing with, "Here's the info we got about this guy and the two witnesses you're going to see. Gotcha booked on the eleven o'clock, so grab the overnight bag from home and head out. Mel has your paperwork, tickets, and hotel info, so grab it on the way. Call when the meet and greet is scheduled, and don't forget you still owe me that follow-up story on the subway thing. Figure you can hammer it out in flight. E-mail it to me when you land so it can make tomorrow's edition." With the arrival of a period at the end of his speech, Tom turned around and headed back toward his office, leaving Sam to replay the instructions at his convenience.

The taxi pulled up to the curb bringing Sam to the airport terminal at JFK and he could tell the place was a madhouse, or at least more than usual. Before he even slipped through the automated door, a fight broke out between two men over the waiting taxi Sam had just exited; not the best beginning for a long trip to the West Coast, but he decided to forage ahead unabated as if his editor had given him a choice.

Inside the terminal, Sam didn't try to hide his displeasure with the length of the line of people waiting to check in. Intimidated by the girth and volume of the irritable crowd, Sam reached into his back pocket to check the status of his departure time, wondering if the long wait in line would cause him to miss his flight. Inside his departure folder was a pink sticky note from Melanie, who set up the flight, that read, "Sam, have a nice trip out West and bring back some warm weather! You are already checked in, so just go ahead to the 'check-in' kiosk at the front and follow the instructions so you can skip waiting in line. Come back in one piece! Mel" Sam said out loud, "Way to go, Mel!" making a mental note to bring back something nice from the airport in San Francisco for Melanie's nice save.

Sam walked past the deluge of morning flyers crushed together in the shape of an angry snake and headed to the little kiosk, noticing the beginnings of a smile taking refuge on his face for the first time since he awoke to his hangover. At the first blaring sound from the alarm waking him from his short, restless sleep, Sam had been struggling with the throbbing headache. The aspirin he took after his abrupt meeting with Tom seemed to have given up the fight and called a full retreat, but avoiding the need to stand in line certainly was a much welcomed pardon.

Once seated on the plane, Sam tried not to make eye contact with the other passengers while they slowly boarded and walked down the aisle toward him, knowing when eyes met, it's perceived as an unspoken approval for someone to sit down. The problem with this approach was that it never seemed to fail that the person he typically made visual contact toward was usually someone who was too needy, too chatty, or someone who just plain annoyed him the entire trip. The seven hour trip to Oakland was too lengthy and the plane too small to actively commit to something so painfully inescapable.

With luck and a puddle of good fortune, an elderly business man slid into the outside seat and immediately began going through a thick file from his briefcase. Sam knew that the only preferred passenger to trump the preoccupied businessman was the enthralled pulp fiction reader who rarely looked up except to respond to a free beverage. Perhaps, he mused, the trip really was looking up, hangover, pain-in-the-butt editor, and all.

When the plane's tires chirped their touchdown and the momentary shake, rattle and roll, passed as the pilot hit the brake flaps, Sam gently awoke to one of the best flights he had experienced. With his headache gone, his subway piece ready for editing, and his arrival ten minutes early, Sam turned to his silent companion until the gentleman returned his stare. Sam finally remarked, "It was a pleasure to fly with you!"

The man in the suit just continued staring, with a look of being unsure if he's required to reply.

Bea arrived back at Sam and Katie's apartment building after her interview on an unusual emotional high, only to be greeted by an out of order sign on the only elevator. By the second flight of stairs, she opted to discard her good mood, beginning to curse the building maintenance crew.

By the fifth floor she included anyone with tools within a five mile radius. Sweating and panting by the time she reached the apartment door, just before knocking, the door opened and she's greeted by Katie and Spalding, heading out. "Oh, Bea, I wasn't expecting you until after five. Spalding and I are heading to the park for a little exercise. Want to join us?"

Bea replied with a look back at the stairs and a hint of sarcasm. "Thanks, but I just got mine. I have some follow-up work to do, then I'll need to send it to my impatiently waiting editor. Thanks for the offer."

Spalding forged ahead, anxious to be free from the confines of the apartment, pulling Katie toward the stairs, explaining, "We'll only be gone about an hour or so. Help yourself to anything in the kitchen. There's beer in the fridge and please make yourself right at home."

Bea hung up her jacket that she didn't need with New York's mild spring weather and made a bee line for the kitchen. After downing the first beer in only four swallows, she opened the second and settled in for the finishing touches to her column in her cousin's living room. The meeting had gone well, and Bea was anxious to get her article fine-tuned and sent off to her boss, confident it'd put a fat smile on the skinny editor's manicured face.

Bea stopped her work on the computer and considered why pleasing her boss seemed to be such a newly acquired desire in her professional life. The mere thought of Gloria in her designer suit and perfectly starched shirt instantly made Bea want to defiantly riot against all forms of authority, but she eventually would have to come to terms with her deep-down desire to impress her.

Bea knew better than anyone that she's capable of reaching much higher branches and that, once she decided for herself to apply her talents, she could easily be the one wearing the Donna Vinci suits and crisp white shirts. It wouldn't be at her current paper; not a chance. Her in-your-face personality and ferocious demeanor had long been embedded at the mere mention of Beatrice Jackson's name. She at one time had been proud of how she made management cringe in fear, but she now realized the futility of her actions.

Pushing aside her personal dilemma, Bea hammered out the final product and zipped it to Gloria before she dusted off her second brew. After a long, triumphant gulp from the remnants of bottled hops, she victoriously pranced around the room before stopping in front of the mirror in the hall. She turned one way, then the other, staring at her reflection. She'd never considered mirrors to be in the realm of close, inviting friends, and checking herself out from head to toe, she recalled the reason, giving herself a disappointing glare before heading to the bathroom to get cleaned up.

Bea applied her finishing touches at the bathroom sink and once again found herself staring at her blank expression in the mirror. Comparing her physical appearance to Katie's, Bea knew she couldn't hold a candle to her cousin's girlfriend. Katie worked long, exhausting hours for that tight little body. Leaning over the sink, continuing the staring match with her reflection, Bea pondered at how she rarely 'sized' herself up to other women, but couldn't deny the fact that it'd become an increasingly annoying thought. Knowing she's confident in who she was and what she did, lately she couldn't help but notice how she'd begun to make small mental notes of how certain women differed. From things like how she dressed, what she considered important in life, or why she preferred arguing over compromise, the list was certainly growing.

Many considered Bea difficult to deal with; something she actually took quite a bit of pride in. Perhaps it was time to reevaluate the reason for her staunch rebellious position. It certainly hadn't moved her up any professional ladders. Only receiving birthday and Christmas cards from the insurance agent each year stood as solid evidence that she could stand to boost her social networking.

Bea exited the bathroom, still holding her damp towel. Katie walked in the front door with Spalding and immediately stopped, looking at Bea, frozen in the hallway by the bathroom door. Katie quickly unhooked Spalding off his leash. After he sprinted for his water dish, she asked, "Bea, what's wrong?"

Bea looked up at Katie sheepishly, asking, "Katie, could you help me with something kind of . . . personal?"

Katie closed the apartment door behind her, set down the leash and keys on the side table, and slowly moved toward Bea. Once there's only three feet between them, Katie held Bea's waiting stare and answered seriously, "What can I do for you, Bea?"

Still unsure what exactly she thought she wanted help with, Bea attempted to put it into an uncomfortable 'girl-talk' dialogue. "I guess what I need is, or what I'm hoping to get help with, is . . ." Frustrated with her lack of ability to communicate effectively, Bea grabbed Katie's arm and brought her to the full-length mirror attached to the wall by the front door. Positioning herself next to Katie side-by-side, they faced their reflection. Quietly taking turns looking at their own reflections, then at each other, Bea finally stated, using her hand to gesture, "I don't want to be just like you, but I'd like to be . . . less like me. Don't get me wrong; I'm not talking about an extreme makeover. I just think it's time for a couple upgrades, both inside and out. I'm thinking it's long overdue."

Katie turned to look at Bea, beginning to smile gently before saying, "Stay here. I'll be right back!" Bea continued her stare of self-criticism until Katie returned with several magazines under one arm. Without a word or even slowing her pace, Katie grabbed Bea's hand, yanking her from her mirror musing, and the two descended upon the living room sofa.

Katie plopped the artillery of female warfare onto the coffee table, scooted forward to the edge of the sofa, and opened one of the magazines, stating, "Now, I saw an article in this one about color tones and proper applications," Still sitting back deep within the sofa, Bea's excited look began to turn into pained curiosity as Katie handed her one off the pile, adding, "Here, Bea, there's an article about waxing versus shaving. See if you can find it."

Bea looked at the cover as the one-dimensional skinny model suggestively smiled back at her before asking, "Shaving and waxing what, exactly?"

Katie looked back over her shoulder at Bea and blushed slightly, answering, "Your legs, as well as anything north of them!"

Bea's eyes became small plates with single black olives in the middle, responding quickly, "Oh, no. Hold on a minute. I said a little upgrade. There's no need to bring out the belt sander and hydraulic equipment!"

Katie grabbed Bea's hand, replying gently, "Bea, we need to work on some of the areas that no one sees to allow you to *feel* the difference first. Things such as the food you eat, how and when you exercise, even what type of undergarments you wear. After that, we'll move on to the areas that others will notice. Once you start appreciating the changes you've incorporated within yourself, the abrasive attitude and social difficulties you face will be that much easier to adjust."

Bea looked blankly at Katie as she continued to hold her hand. Bea finally responded unemotionally, "Katie, I think that was the sweetest insult I've ever received. I bet poor Sam hasn't won an argument since the two of you hooked up!"

Katie returned to her search within the pages of the magazine, answering the rhetorical question with, "Of course he has, my dear. It's simply a matter of preemptively taking the opposing direction to what I want for the outcome. Sam, naturally, takes his usual stubborn contradictory position, so in a way, we both win!"

Bea chuckled, beginning to leaf through her magazine in her own periodical search, adding, "Are you always three steps ahead when it comes to men?"

Katie allowed her guest a quick responsive smile, replying, "With all of their distractions, such as sports, beer commercials, or anyone walking by with breasts larger than a 'C' cup, just being half a step ahead can usually suffice." Bea laughed as Katie forged ahead with, "First, we'll get an appointment for a pedicure for us both, then I have some ideas about what to do with your hair."

Protectively, Bea reached up and touched her mop-like strands, asking, "What's wrong with my hair?"

Katie replied quickly, "Nothing, hun; it just needs some re-characterization."

Bea squinted at Katie and stated sternly, "That is *so* not a real word."

Katie reached for the phone, politely smiled and replied, "Well, I thought you'd prefer it over the one I was going to use!"

Katie stood behind Bea, quietly sitting with a large bib covering from her neck, down. Katie worked on her hair as Bea looked up at Katie in the mirror they both faced, asking, "Where did you learn to cut hair?"

Keeping her focus on the job at hand, Katie answered, "Before I started teaching aerobics and long before I met Sam, I worked at a salon over in Queens called A Cut Before Dying, for about five years. I was taking some step aerobics at the same time when the girl giving the class broke her ankle. I knew the manager of the gym and she begged me to fill in during the instructor's absence. The rest, as they say, is history." Katie gave Bea's hair a tussle with her fingers and moved in front of her to take a good look at her work, asking, "So, what do you think?"

Bea stared at herself in the mirror for a long, quiet moment, and Katie began to think Bea disapproved of the change. Bea finally stated, "I guess getting my hair cut at Bob's Barber Shop for so long hasn't been one of my better decisions. I don't think I've ever had a 'girl' cut before. I like it!"

Katie squealed with the positive feedback and grabbed a hand mirror, adding, "And it looks cute in the back! I tapered it so it flows together at the bottom; here, take a peek."

She handed it to Bea, maneuvering the small mirror to see the reflection of the back. Bea smiled and asked, "Is that really what the back of my head looks like? I need to walk away from people more often! I've got an adorable backside!"

Katie chimed in with, "And with an alteration in undergarments and a size and a half smaller pants, they'll have options to look at!" With that, Bea nearly dropped the mirror and gave Katie a shocked, inquisitive stare.

The table settings and glassware training had all made sense, all in part of Katie's unshakeable patience, but Bea just didn't think she would ever understand which wine was supposed to go with what foods, and vice versa. Regardless, no matter how much Katie stated a wine had tastes of plum, oak, cherry, or pepper, they all left Bea's virgin palette with an acidic aftertaste. The one thing she concluded was if Katie said the words tannin or fruit forward one more time, she would belch out a blueberry.

The crash course on dining etiquette, the head-to-toe make-over, and even the tough love Katie had bestowed the previous day, Bea reasoned as considerate, granted they'd technically just met. Now Katie was moving in to how she thought and viewed her surroundings, and being shacked up with her cousin or not, this was sensitive territory.

Katie came out of the bathroom ready for their walk to the park with Spalding and Bea slipped her hesitation in a disguised form. "Now, you realize if I go walking with the two of you, every man out there will notice you first, the dog second, and me a distant third, right?"

Katie laughed at her humor, adding, "Yes, with an attitude like *that,* I believe you'll be right. All you have to do is hold your head up and push the girls forward and, when they stare, for goodness sake, don't look back. Let 'em wonder!"

Bea smiled on the outside, but only felt trepidation and doubt with the mere thought of her 'girls' being pushed anywhere. At the door, Bea further pled, "Katie, I honestly think I'm maxed out on the self-improvement for today. I like everything you've helped me with, but how 'bout we just go to the park and enjoy the day; you looking like an underfed model from *Glamour* magazine and me as the dog's assistant."

Once at the park, Katie pulled out a blanket from her backpack, stuck a metal spike with a loop on the end of it into the ground, and clicked Spalding's leash onto the loop. "There, now neither of us will need to chase down the little maniac when his girlfriend makes her appearance."

Bea looked quizzically at Katie, then at Spalding lying peacefully for the moment, asking, "This dog has a girlfriend?"

Katie crunched on a carrot stick before handing the bag over to Bea, answering with, "Yup. This has been going on for ten, maybe eleven months. They should be celebrating their first anniversary next month. It started out like any other relationship; you know, a little butt-sniffing, a little playing hard-to-get. But after all the games of curiosity, they decided they liked each other just fine."

Bea let out a gut-laugh from Katie's rendition of puppy love and Katie joined in as the two fed off of each other's laughter. Bea gained control of her laughter first, asking, "Is that how it was for you and Sam? Refrain from any butt-sniffing stories, please."

Katie immediately stopped laughing from the question, replying seriously, "Oh, good heavens, no. When I first met Sam, I wanted to kill him!"

Bea responded with a, "Get out! My sweet little cousin?"

Katie returned to her laughing. "I know! But he didn't appear very sweet when he literally knocked me to the floor!" she exclaimed with pretend sneer.

Bea recalled the story she had heard from Sam and started laughing again, saying in a mockingly serious tone "I know this story! Sam told me his side and, to be completely honest with you, it sounded like your fault."

Katie lowered her head and sternly glared at Bea, replying coldly, "Excuse me? The buffoon ran into *me*, not the other way around. If he'd been in better shape, rather than dragging his sorry butt straight to the locker room after that beginner's spinning course, he could have avoided the incident altogether."

Bea smiled at her next comment, adding, "But then you two wouldn't have met. I guess your tumble must have been kismet." Katie's face turned a shade darker, and Bea picked up on it right away, asking, "I'm sorry, did I say something wrong?"

Katie played it off, mildly recovering, answering, "Oh, it's nothing. I just wonder sometimes if we actually are meant to be together. I swear, there are times when I'm trying to talk to him and

I look into his eyes and know without a doubt his mind is someplace else. It's so aggravating; I can't even begin to explain."

Bea hunkered into her position on the blanket and visually demanded Katie's direct eye contact with no humor to her disposition. Katie responded appropriately, giving her boyfriend's cousin her undivided attention.

Bea looked down, trying to form what she needed to explain before returning to her steady gaze, stating unemotionally, "Katie, what you have to understand . . . no, it's what you need to realize, is our Sammy has a gift. He's a damned great writer; way better than I could ever hope to be. And when a talented writer finds a story like the one he's working, nothing will get in the way. I know that sounds cruel, selfish, and bastardly, but I've seen it more times than I can count. It leaves you with the impossible decision of coping with the part time relationship theory or packing it in. Don't think for a second that I want you to go with plan 'B', but I wouldn't feel like I was being your friend if I didn't mention the small print to this contract."

Katie soaked it in like vinegar, and Bea worried she had overstepped her cousin's confidence, but Katie regained her placid composure, giving Bea a look as though she's about to say, *tomorrow is another day.* Instead, she said nothing and let the subject die quietly. To change the dark subject matter, but remain on their shared denominator, Bea asked, "Does Sam ever talk about his mom?"

Katie gave her a shadowed look before answering, "Rarely, and only when I cautiously ease him into it. I just don't understand why the subject is so taboo. Most guys, you can't get them to shut up about their mothers!"

Bea laughed at her humor, replying, "It isn't that she was mean or anything; in fact, she was a great lady. I think it's just that he carries a lot of guilt for not being home when she died. She was everything to him, and I think he feels like he let her down." Katie started to say something, then caught herself before it came out. Bea, though, was all over it. "What? You were about to say something. What was it?"

Katie held the thought a moment longer before finally asking, "What about Sam's father? If speaking of his mother is forbidden, the subject of his dad is sacrilege. Can you tell me anything about him?"

Bea looked up squinting, thinking back, before asking, "First, tell me what Sam has said about him, if anything."

Katie started to giggle, answering, "He told me he was a talented magician."

Bea started to chuckle, responding with, "A magician? That's the first time I've heard this. Did he say anything else about it?"

Katie continued giggling, answering, "He said he performed an impressive disappearing act shortly after conception and hasn't been seen nor heard from since!" Both girls started laughing until Bea had to brace herself with one arm to keep from falling over onto the blanket. On cue, Spalding's 'girlfriend' arrived with a bark and a challenge, and the grounded constraint was unearthed as he sprinted toward her at break-neck speed, spike and tether flailing behind. Katie and Bea both responded quickly, jumping into action and chasing the incensed dog across the park.

CHAPTER 22

Sam took full advantage of the three hours he gained coming from the East Coast and began working off a list of priorities he'd thrown together before his nap on the flight. After renting a car and checking in to the hotel, Sam started in on his cell phone.

The bits and pieces Tom had sewn together from the two sources sounded a little farfetched. Since Sam had the monopoly on the whole death sentient entity, it was left for him to work out. What Sam figured from the leads was that there's a man living just southwest of San Francisco who claimed to not only know El Padre's true identity, but also the reason for what he did.

The first call was to a San Mateo County Harbor Search and Rescue patrol officer near Half Moon Bay. Evidently the man in question had been hanging around the Oyster Point Marina the past two weeks after allegedly moving to California from St. Paul. Most of the people the man came in contact with had no idea what he was talking about until the officer took some initiative and looked up some of the things the man in question mentioned.

The concern moved to more of a placid interest by the locals, which eventually stirred the Harbor Officer to make the inquiry with Sam's paper. The officer answered right away, but was in training, so Sam made arrangements to meet with him the following morning.

The second call Sam made was for the other contact; a woman who worked at one of the businesses near the marina. With no answer, he left a message on her voice mail and decided to try later in the evening, hoping to catch her once she returned home.

After a late dinner, Sam drove the rental car down to the area of Pillar Point Harbor and parked next to Sam's Chowder House to get familiar with the general area for his meeting with the Harbor Patrolman the following day. With only about half an hour of sunlight left, working the story and watching the sunset on the West Coast seemed like a fitting end to his extended day that began with a splitting headache before sunrise on the East Coast.

After putting together a page and a half of some good background notes of the marina and waterfront, Sam decided to walk along the beach just south of the harbor. With the cool temperature blowing in from the ocean and the oncoming evening, the beach was vacant of visitors and locals, giving him free reign as king of the beach. He took off his shoes and socks and placed them on a large drift log near the path back to his car. Walking barefoot on the beach wasn't something he often got to do in New York. The dark orange sun hovered inches above the ocean as Sam stopped and watched the sea slowly envelope the darkening sphere.

Long after the sun had melted into the water and the vibrant orange and pink hues began to grow dim, Sam was startled by a piercing sound. The shrill cry from somewhere in the growing darkness was not one that he'd ever heard, even in New York. Sam strained his eyes to see the now shadowy public boat launch and adjacent public restrooms, unable to get a visual on exactly where the noise came from or who's making the sound. He turned an ear toward the area as it competed with both the sounds of the crashing waves and an incoming fishing boat, but nothing more cut through the air. Being in unfamiliar territory and realizing he's still barefoot, Sam labored through the thick sand in an effort to quickly backtrack to retrieve his socks and shoes.

Squinting, he made it to within twenty feet of the log where his shoes waited for him before a second shorter screech sounding like a woman's desperate cry for help broke the droning sounds from the sea. Sam stood up straight, facing the public bathrooms behind him about two hundred yards away. Without further hesitation, he bolted for the vicinity where he believed the cry for help originated.

Climbing over the rocky breaker to get to the flat grassy ground, Sam experienced a sharp pain on the bottom of his right foot and started to limp. With his adrenaline pumping beyond any level experienced before, he picked up steam, rushing for the women's bathroom door and with a weighty shove, the door flew open. Even in the dim lighting, Sam could see a man on top of a woman, struggling under his weight.

Sam took a direct line for the man's left arm. As the attacker attempted to muffle the woman's screams, Sam forced his right knee into the middle of the man's back. The shocked look from the assailant almost caused Sam to laugh, before spinning the attacker off the woman and flinging him across the floor of the restroom until he skidded to the far wall.

Helping her off the floor, Sam checked to make sure the woman wasn't bleeding from any injuries before turning protectively in front of her, facing the assailant. The man slowly got up, using the wall for support. Sam could tell the man's left wrist was either badly sprained or broken by the way he favored it. The snap it had made when Sam wrenched on it also served as a clue.

Sam silently glared at the man as the two squared off. Hoping he was going to run for the door, Sam was surprised when the criminal began to slowly move toward him. With clenched fists, Sam held his ground, bracing for the frontal attack. Suddenly, the man stopped and eerily tilted his head, reaching behind him to pull out a medium sized knife.

Holding the blade close to his face, clearly aiming to intimidate, he spoke for the first time, saying calmly and in a whisper, "Hello, hero. Your time has come, too, then. I came here for the girl, but you can join her in death, because that's who I am. The Grim Reaper comes for you both."

The words came out slow and detached, giving Sam the cold feeling they would be acted upon. Just before lunging toward Sam with the knife, two men burst into the bathroom, surprising the attacker. Turning toward the recent arrivals, the self-proclaimed Grim Reaper changed tactics and prepared to defend himself against the new affront.

Sam reacted quickly. With the knife now pointed away from him, he attacked from the man's right side, knowing the two men entering the fray didn't yet know about the weapon.

They converged, with Sam first to get to him. Able to lift the man's right arm straight up, he bent it back awkwardly, until the man released the knife, dropping it to the floor. The force of the two men converging onto the attacker from the front knocked Sam straight back. His head slammed into the middle stall door, and he collapsed into a seated position on the floor. In his murky state, Sam was left to watch as the two men effectively throttled the attacker and dragged him, whimpering, out of the bathroom.

Once the action was taken outside, Sam felt a hand grab his right bicep. Looking up, he stared at the young woman whom he'd originally come to assist, now returning the favor. Sam took her other hand and she helped him slowly stand on shaky legs. Holding the back of his bloodied head while the swelling began, Sam smiled at the woman as she placed his arm over her shoulder in an effort to help him out of the ladies room. Unable to stop smiling, he mumbled to her, "This is just how my day started; with a splitting headache!

Sitting inside an ambulance with the back door open wide, a female paramedic cleaned a nasty cut on the back of Sam's head while a male EMT removed pieces of glass from his foot. The local sheriff approached, carrying Sam's shoes and socks from the beach. His heft, which Sam considered from an angled glance, appeared to be just past well-fed, and seemed to be the purpose for a slight pause between steps, as if unsure the ground beneath would support him.

"I assume these are yours?" the sheriff asked before closing the final ten feet.

Again, Sam cocked his head in the direction of the voice, trying not to disturb the work being administered by the paramedic, replying, "Sure could have used those thirty minutes ago!"

The sheriff set the tennis shoes down on the inside of the ambulance, with Sam's socks tucked neatly inside. He put his left cowboy boot up on the rear bumper of the ambulance, and rested his elbow on his knee. The weight of the man dipped the vehicle a good three inches and the two medical staff both looked up at him with perturbed expressions before returning to their delicate work. The sheriff offered a, "Whoops, sorry, Tina. Sorry, Clyde." Both ignored his apology and continued their focus on Sam's injuries. The sheriff took off his cowboy hat and slowly wiped his brow before returning his hat onto his head, asking, "So, what in blazes is a New York reporter doing way out west, Mr. Noll?"

Sam smiled at the sheriff, keeping his head still, replying, "I thought I was enjoying your lovely sunset, sir; and you can call me Sam."

The sheriff smirked, responding, "Well, Sam, I ain't never been to New York, but I hear there's a good share of crime back that way. Thought you'd fly out here and compare, son?"

Sam thought about it for a second before answering, "No, sir, I was just having one of those days, I guess."

The Sheriff pushed his hat back far enough to scratch his head, asking, "One of my boys said you stated . . ." He pulled out a small notepad for reference. "You grabbed the assailant's arm and 'flung' him across the floor and away from the victim, breaking his wrist or dislocating his left arm in the process." Sam stared silently, waiting for the question. "Would you care to amend your statement for the record?"

Sam looked at the male paramedic for help, but he just shrugged, finishing up with a bandage on Sam's foot. Unsure of what to offer, Sam replied, "Okay, how about, 'accidentally may have broken or dislocated . . .'"

The sheriff didn't smile at the new contribution, but simply closed his pad and stuffed it into his jacket pocket. The sheriff reached inside the ambulance, extending his hand to Sam, saying, "Well, son, I sure do appreciate what you did tonight. And I'd venture to say the little lady in the other ambulance would say the same." Sam accepted the man's hand as they shook. The sheriff started to walk away, but he paused and turned back around, stating, "The two fishermen who joined in on the tussle, Bert and Arnie . . ."

Sam interrupted, inquiring, "Seriously? Their names are Bert and Arnie?"

Not getting the humor, the sheriff just answered, "Yeah, that'd be them. Anyway, they mentioned in their statement they saw you runnin' barefoot into the ladies bathroom, and figurin' something wasn't right, came in after you."

Once again, Sam waited for the question, and when it didn't materialize, he cued, "So, what's the question, Sheriff?"

He looked into Sam's face, asking seriously, "So, how'd you know to go to the ladies room?"

Sam pondered the question for just a moment before answering with a shrug. "Honestly, sir, I don't know. If I had to guess, I'd say it was fifty-fifty, and since it was a woman's scream I heard, my instincts were to check there first."

The sheriff nodded at the good sense of Sam's equation before adding, "Well, once again, son, there's plenty of folk around here awful grateful for your heroics; damned grateful." Sam flushed from the accolade and just nodded his thank you. Before the sheriff turned to retrace his steps back to the crime scene, he stated, "One of my deputies will get in touch with you at your hotel tomorrow and finish things up; just some paperwork is all, if that'd be alright?"

Sam confirmed with a nod and, "Sure, no problem. Thank you, Sheriff" before the sheriff left. Contemplating what the sheriff termed as heroics, Sam had a thought and asked the female paramedic, "I didn't get his name; the sheriff?"

Without stopping her work, she answered, "Sheriff Clayton Boyd. The girl you saved, well, she's his niece." Sam looked back up to where the sheriff had walked into the darkness, but he could only see the red swirling lights from the police and ambulance vehicles as they lit up the small boat launch.

London, 2005

The old bridge spanning the Thames certainly had changed over the years. Like all lasting tributes, a refurbishing from time to time reflected the object's respect and importance to the people around it. El Padre smiled inwardly, realizing once again how he seemed to cling to the things that remained immutable, returning when he's able. There seemed to be a subtle recognition between him and those who transcended explanation. Whenever he found himself in the 'old' world, he took the time to visit his oldest, lasting friends.

Confirming the bridge was going to last another lifetime or two, El Padre slowly parted from his reunion and made his way to the inner calling he often considered as his appointments.

Like a game of 'hot and cold,' he felt the warmth increase with the gentle sound beckoning him deeper into the city. The earliness of the July day gave evidence to the hardworking people of London as every face El Padre passed on the sidewalk displayed an intent and purpose of someone with somewhere to be. Closer, he moved to his intended soul, never straining his eyesight ahead through the throng, knowing it would be revealed in its own time. Into the busy cafe, El Padre waited in line with a host of weary morning travelers in need of a caffeine awakening while they busied themselves reading newspapers or chatting and texting on their cell phones.

After paying for his black coffee, El Padre walked toward the row of window seats just as a man in a business suit rose from his stool to leave. "Perfect timing!" the man said, noticing El Padre approaching.

"Indeed," El Padre simply replied, graciously taking the vacant barstool. The aroma of the hot brew found its escape once the plastic lid was removed and El Padre took in the full sensation. Smelling the grounds upon entering the coffee shop was merely the building anticipation to true satisfaction of experiencing the personalized concoction.

Lost in his appreciation of the little things, El Padre's actual reason for being in the cafe interrupted his first sip. "You must really love your coffee!" the woman declared as she continued to watch him intently.

El Padre turned and looked beyond the warm glow illuminating her being and stared deeper toward the middle-aged woman for the first time, taking in all of her features in a glance. El Padre replied, looking back at his cup, "There are few things in life that are so fleeting, yet so powerfully fulfilling, as a simple cup of well brewed coffee."

The woman chuckled in agreement at his appreciation, adding, "I know exactly what you mean. Sometimes I think I could sit all day and read and sip my coffee. Just one day, with no kids screaming, no husband to make dinner for, and a polite, quiet maid to clean the house around me; just letting me be in a comfortable chair with my coffee and my book. Ahh, now there's true contentment!"

El Padre smiled at the woman's simple desire and looked at the book she's reading, inquiring, "And would that be the book to fulfill this dream day?"

She held it up and laughed again, answering, "Oh, I just picked this up two days ago and can't seem to put it down. Sure, I think it would do!" She handed him the book.

El Padre read the title out loud, *"Even Good People Go to Hell.* Sounds threatening. May I ask what it is about?"

The woman displayed a sign of excitement, starting in with, "I heard about the book from a woman I work with. She said the author, who's a minister of a church in the States, takes a stand concerning what it means to be 'heaven-worthy,' as he puts it in the book. Though I haven't got to this part of it yet, evidently he believes he was visited by an angel who told him he needs to place a little fear into his congregation if he truly wants his believers to grab their faith and follow God. So far, what I've read has been inspirational. The pastor really speaks from a questioning heart, and it's humbling to read how a leader of a big church can have moments of doubt just like the rest of us."

El Padre turned the book over and stared at the familiar face, inquiring of the woman, "May I ask your name?"

Shocked by the question, the woman chuckled once, answering, "Oh, I'm sorry. Here I am blabbering on about myself without a proper introduction. Maggie."

They shook hands and El Padre began forming his will from deep within, like applying an antiseptic before the introduction of medicine. Looking into her eyes, he proceeded. "Maggie, what do you wish for in this life? What would you label as not merely contentment, but pure joy and happiness before you lay your head to rest one last and final time?"

The medicine took its slow, numbing effect as a question that would normally seem forward or inappropriate coming from a stranger was answered simply, honestly. "That my children grow in faith and grace, and their own children with the same. That my husband forgets our moments of hurtfulness and clings to all the many blessings we share together. That he always remembers how much I love him."

Before El Padre released her hand, he leaned in and whispered, "It shall come to pass."

With the separation of their hands, Maggie gently shook herself back to the moment, immediately looking at her watch, saying, "Oh my, look at the time. I'd better be off if I'm to catch the 311 tube. It was nice chatting with you. Have a wonderful day." Off she went to catch her train, leaving El Padre to watch after her, praying for not only Maggie, but for her husband and children.

Once on the busy sidewalk, El Padre observed Maggie halt her progress at the familiar sound of her husband's voice behind her, saying, "I love you Mags. So do the kids." Maggie spun around, saying, "George?" but only saw the unknown faces of other people passing by heading to work or wherever their day took them. Embarrassed, she looked back into the coffee shop in search of the stranger drinking his coffee, but only saw his coffee cup sitting vacated at the table. She shook off the peculiar incident and proceeded to the tube, carrying with her a deep, warm feeling of love from her family.

CHAPTER 23

The deep, dreamless sleep Sam was enjoying came to a slow, groggy disruption as his cell phone continued to vibrate on the hotel nightstand. Without the need of checking the caller identification displayed on the phone, Sam simply answered, "Hello, Tom. Miss me already?"

His boss ignored the humor and fired back, "Sam! Just got your message. Holy crap, son, you alright?"

Sam sat up a little too quickly and gently touched the back of his head, responding, "Well, other than a slight limp and proving I'm not as hard-headed as everyone thinks, I guess I was lucky."

Tom asked quickly with increased concern, "Have you gone to the hospital or seen a doctor or something? You need to get checked out."

Sam pulled the phone away from his ear and stared at it with a confused expression for a moment before returning it to his ear, continuing, "Tom, you've gotta stop sharing this motherly side. It's totally creeping me out! The two EMTs took good care of me last night. I think I'll live."

Tom let the comment go and returned to his usual all-business manner with, "Well, you okay to put something down on paper?"

Sam chuckled at his editor's one-track mind, replying, "There's much to be said for first-hand experience stimulating immediate inspiration."

Tom responded emotionally, "Thata boy! Now, remember the three hour difference, so if you can get me something to work with by three, we can run it for tomorrow."

Sam got up from the bed and stretched his back, saying, "It shouldn't be a problem. I have to meet with a deputy to go over my statement, but they're sending someone over here this morning. After that, I'm all over it."

Tom simply uttered a, "Great. Call me," then he clicked off, leaving Sam to again, in the span of thirty seconds, look at his phone in confusion.

The knock at the door cleared up Sam's indecision of lying back down or getting to work on the story. Peeking through the peep-hole, Sam saw a young officer waiting uncomfortably for a response. He opened the door in his bathrobe and greeted the trooper, inviting him in. The deputy confirmed his greenness by stating, "Um, I'm Deputy Caldwell. Sheriff Boyd, the, uh, sheriff over in San Mateo County, sent me here to go over your statement, if that's alright with you, Sir?"

Sam opted to go easy on the young deputy figuring the sheriff selected him for this assignment so he could get as much experience under his belt as possible. Sam hesitated for only a moment before he prompted, "And is that the statement under your arm?"

The young man blushed immediately, answering while he handed over the document, "Oh, yes Sir. Here you go."

Sam moved toward the small cushioned chair and sat at the table. Opening the manila envelope he asked the trooper, "I was about to order some breakfast from room service. Can I interest you in something to drink?"

The young officer stiffened slightly, answering quickly, "No thank you, Sir, I'm on duty."

Sam tried his best not to smile, rewording his innocent offer, with, "I meant something like an orange juice or soda. I hear the kitchen whips up a delicious fruit smoothie!"

The young man's cheeks flushed with red once more, seeming to loosen just a bit, replying, "Oh, a fruit smoothie actually sounds pretty good."

Sam placed his request over the phone while watching the trooper remove his jacket and move closer to the window looking out over the bay. Once he hung up, he began going over the printed statement from the previous evening's events. Attempting to make small talk with the uncomfortable officer, Sam asked, "Nice view, isn't it?"

Deputy Caldwell continued enjoying the sight without turning away, answering, "Yes, it is. I've been here, California, I mean, for only five and a half months and just can't get over how beautiful it is."

Sam looked up and asked, "Where did you move from? And, by the way, may I call you something other than Deputy Caldwell?"

The trooper smiled broadly, which made him appear even younger, replying, "Timothy, or Tim. I was living in Wisconsin. Actually grew up there in a small town called Pardeeville, about a half hour north of Madison."

Sam turned his chair in interest, saying, "Hey, I was born just outside of Chicago. That makes us both a couple of Midwest boys! Do you miss the muggy summers, ticks, and horse flies yet?"

The trooper moved from the window and sat in the chair across from him, showing his youthful excitement and anxiousness to talk about home, answering, "Not a lick, but there isn't much fishing or hunting around here. I kinda miss going out in the woods with my rifle whenever I wanted. Our family lived on twenty acres. Here, you fart and your neighbor says, Pew!"

Sam chuckled with the young man as the trooper's country boy roots began to show. After the laugh, Sam asked, "Well, I bet you didn't see too much crime in a town called Pardeeville, at least nothing like what happened last night?"

The deputy stood quickly with added enthusiasm, "Man, oh man, Talk about being in the right place at the right time! It's all everybody is talking about. I was hoping I'd have a chance to ask you about it!"

Sam smiled at the inquiry, thinking, I was hoping you would, too!

Sam took on a look of confusion, innocently asking the young deputy, "Who was that guy, anyway?"

The young trooper froze from the question, staring blankly at Sam for a moment before returning to his chair, saying, "You mean nobody even told you?"

Sam retained his blank stare, replying, "Told me what?"

Deputy Caldwell nearly burst before having the opportunity to say his next sentence, sharing, "Holy smokes, mister, you bagged a serial killer!" Sam's face paled immediately as the deputy stood back up, pacing around the room to eagerly tell the whole story. "So this creep-o from St. Paul, Anthony Lloyd Lingham, gets himself released from Cambridge Mental Institution and decides to kill two women before hopping on a bus and moving to San Francisco back in October. He starts reading some article out of New York during his stay in Minnesota about a guy who appears to be the Grim Reaper."

Sam felt the cold chill begin to numb deep within his head before the excess sensation cascaded straight into his heart as the deputy proceeded with his narrative. "So, anyway, he starts believing *he* is Death and gravitates or whatever to California, lucky us, and resumes his self-administered duties."

With a thumb over his shoulder, the young man added, "He's balled up in the corner of his cell sucking his thumb after admitting he killed the girls in Minnesota and two more up in Sharp Park before hitchhiking down Cabrillo Highway to Half Moon. Can you imagine being the guy who gave him a ride? Geez, driving down the coast with a wacko killer; that'd teach me never to pick up hitch hikers."

Sam listened with muted interest. His mind raced through an instant replay of the previous night's incident and the fact of how easily he could have been killed by the madman. The thought that his article provoked the murders was something he couldn't face right now. Better to temporarily move away from that deep ravine of guilt for later therapeutic consideration.

Sam slowly rose in an effort to walk away from any part of the offense, only to be faced with the waiting expression of the childlike deputy standing before him with his hands on his hips. His turn to share, Sam realized; tit for tat. The deputy had filled in most of the gaps enabling Sam to write his story, and now it's time to appease the young man's curiosity with the sordid telling of every little morsel of action that led to the capture of one Anthony Lloyd Lingham.

Once the room service arrived, Sam returned to his seat and slowly began to methodically tell his side of the tale with the trooper on the edge of his seat, sipping his fruit smoothie. "I was unable to meet with the two witnesses I intended to interview, so after dinner I decided to drive down to Marine Park . . ."

Alone again in his room, Sam was unable to stop staring out the window while boats and ships passed through the San Francisco Bay. Dressed in blue warm-ups and a baseball cap, he sat beside his breakfast, cold and untouched where it had been originally placed. Meanwhile, he traveled full speed through the dimension of lamentation.

He never once considered that his article could be mistaken for a breeding ground of the sick, misguided, and demented. That lone, resonating detail, he realized, was incredibly naive of him. In hindsight, it made sense, with the public feeding frenzy on any and all things dark and morbid, from Anne Rice to Stephanie Meyer. This time the tables had turned and the place setting was his, being a firm believer in cause and effect; whatever you sent out, eventually returned.

Over the course of his eleven years of slinging the written truth, he'd seen more than his share of penned justice. He just never thought it would punch him in the gut and buckle him to his knees. His hands felt soiled with being an accomplice to people being killed by a small, unwitting manner; the same way his friend Becklin had been murdered. His ignorance was becoming a liability for too many innocent individuals. Sam dropped his head into his sweaty palms, struggling with the taste of bile rising from his stomach.

Another internal struggle was disrupted by a softer knock on the door. Sam half considered ignoring the visitor, but yielded to his curiosity, figuring he'd seen everyone who knew he's here. At first, when he opened the door, he didn't recognize the attractive woman standing quietly at his door, but when she lifted her eyes and looked into his, Sam realized it was the woman from the boat launch.

The two faced each other, unsure who should speak first or what exactly should be said. Finally, she opened the dialog with, "I had everything planned out with what I wanted to say, but my mind has simply gone blank."

Sam was lost in a swirl of humbled thought and mixed emotions, eventually offering a simple, "Please, won't you come in?"

They stood across from each other as she inspected the disregarded breakfast tray. "No appetite?" she asked, with just a hint of an 'I know how you feel' expression. Sam smiled in response, still uncertain how to proceed with his unexpected visitor. She further tried her best to put him at ease. "My name, if you weren't told, is Makala Vincent. I told my uncle that if he didn't tell me how to find you, I'd never bake him another batch of cookies!" Sam smiled at her threat, continuing, "And everyone in San Mateo County knows that Sheriff Clayton Boyd loves a good cookie."

Sam cleared his throat and found his missing voice before quietly asking, "So, how are you?" The innocent question coming from anyone else could have slipped by as idle small talk, but the two and a half minutes the two shared the previous evening connected them in a way that turned subtleties into volumes.

She stared back and Sam immediately felt regret for asking such a stupid question, yet it truly was something he wanted to be sure of, that she's okay. He watched her expression go through a few changes before settling into a steady resolve before she answered, "I just . . . I don't know how to feel or even how to explain what I'm going through. The attack was stopped, thanks to you, yet I still feel his hands, smell his breath; I still feel the violation. My heart starts pounding like it's going to burst and no one is even around me. When I blink, for that fraction of a second, I'm back in that bathroom, lying on the floor, fighting for my life. Why can't my flashbacks be of being saved and the relief I felt when you pulled that bastard off me?"

Sam paused for just a moment, letting Makala catch her breath before replying with, "Years ago, when I was in my teens, I hated going to the dentist," Makala continued staring at Sam with an intriguing look of someone who thought the other person misunderstood the entire conversation. Sam pressed on, "It was like a phobia thing; sweats, shakes, the whole works. Well, finally the old guy retired and our family started going to a new dentist. Instead of just sticking his hands into my mouth or firing up the drill, the new dentist calmly explained what he was going to do and even let me know when it would hurt. It was unbelievable. Knowing exactly what he was doing and what each stage would feel like completely changed my attitude toward going to the dentist."

Makala slowly smiled, beginning to follow Sam's point as he concluded, "I respect what you're feeling, but I would never try to tell you that I completely understand what you're going through. People say time heals all wounds, but I think they forget about the scars left from the wounds. Having someone to talk to, someone knowledgeable and experienced in explaining what you've been and will be going through would probably be the best thing for you. Family and friends can be encouraging, but sometimes you have to have somebody removed, outside of your support group, to help you all the way down the path."

Makala asked hesitantly, "Do you mean, like a psychologist?"

Sam replied quickly, "Possibly, but I'm thinking someone like a therapist or counselor. Somebody specifically qualified on this subject matter."

Makala hastily interjected, "And what area of expertise is that? Are there support groups for people who were *almost* raped or *nearly* murdered?"

Sam looked at Makala somberly and for the first time she avoided Sam's stare. He continued, saying, "What that excuse for a human being did is just as damaging, because your mind continues to play it through. His vile act was an attempt to gain power over you. Even though he's locked up in a cell and will never see the light of day, the shadows from what he did remain. And that's why talking to someone who understands what all this does to you mentally, physically, emotionally, and spiritually becomes the only way to beat him once and for all."

Makala smiled, only Sam noticed something missing, like a darkness from her eyes this time, making her smile seem less forced and all the more beautiful. She moved in quickly, without warning and hugged Sam, which he returned warmly. As they held each other, she softly asked into his ear, "How do you know so much about this?"

They slowly let go of each other and Sam smiled, saying, "I told you; I had a terrible dentist!" She playfully slugged his bicep as he took the punch dramatically with, "Ouch! I'm fragile!" Sam finally answered, "My cousin. She went through something similar, and since she was pretty much my only family, I wanted to know everything I could to help her through it."

Makala asked tentatively, "And, if I might ask, how is she dealing with it?"

Sam looked toward the ceiling, thinking about it before answering, "Honestly, we haven't spoken of it for years, but she settled back into her typical, grouchy self. Not that you should follow her course; I mean, you don't seem as grouchy!"

They both laughed until there became an uncomfortable pause. Makala took his hand and simply said, "Thank you, Sam. No one has saved my life before, and I don't have any idea how to show my appreciation for doing what you did, other than to say thank you."

Blushing from her sincerity, Sam replied, "It's all you need to say. I'm happy to see you're going to be alright; I know you really are going to be alright." Letting his hand free, she turned and walked out the door, allowing Sam's positive comment to end the visit appropriately.

Sam continued standing there for a few minutes, staring at the door, but with his mind miles away as he thought of Bea and Katie and everyone who mattered to him most. No longer was he thinking about how his actions may or may not have caused certain events to occur in the recent past. It would be like not only attempting to control the weather, but how everyone felt about it. That's the perfect way to fill a life with disappointment.

Sam turned and looked at his computer as if it had called him out for a challenge. He locked his jaw, taking a direct path to it, and pressed the 'on' button. He'd told his boss he had the inspiration to write the story, and now he had the fitting end.

Even his cold breakfast was beginning to look good again.

CHAPTER 24

With the article written and sent off to a momentarily happy editor, Sam learned from Melanie that he's unable to catch a flight out of Oakland or San Francisco until 11:15 that night. Until then, putting off his phone call to Katie and filling her in on his little incident seemed like the appropriate thing to do. Unfortunately, Sam was honest enough with himself to admit that keeping her in the dark was mostly right for him, and the postponement of hearing her concern and belated worries wasn't something he looked forward to.

Dialing her number into his cell phone, he sent a quick prayer up and beyond the ceiling that he caught her voice mail. There was much to be said for the moments between receiving distressful news from a phone message and the time it took for the receiver of news to return the call; a moment to take a breath and calculate the proper response.

As Fate would have it, Katie picked up on the fourth ring, with, "Hey, Sam. I was just heading in for my last aerobics class. Is everything okay?"

The pause was his fatal mistake. "Sam, what's wrong? Tell me now!" she insisted over the phone.

Sam further gave way to uncertainty before uttering, "Okay. Now don't worry, because I'm alright . . ."

Sam heard Katie take a deep, calming breath that proved to be ineffective. Slowly, she asked with more intensity, "Please tell me what happened."

Sam again tried to explain, with less stuttering. "I was down by the marina,"

Katie blurted out, "What marina, where?"

Sam took his turn at a cleansing breath and began to pace around his room, answering, "It's the marina near Half Moon Bay. I planned to meet a harbor patrolman today for my article. Anyway, I heard some screams that sounded like a woman needing help, so I ran to where they were coming from in time to catch a guy attacking a woman in a bathroom near the boat launch."

Katie quickly seized the pause, asking, "Did you get hurt? Are you injured? Are you in the hospital?"

Sam shook his head from the speed of her inquiries, answering, "No. I mean, yes, I was banged up a little, but no, I'm not in a hospital. I'm in my room."

Katie, once again, verbally leapt into the gap in dialog with, "Well, when did this happen, sometime this morning?"

Sam froze from how quickly she came to the dangerous part of his phone call. This was where the lava would most likely begin to spew, but then Sam decided he needed to gain control that'd been absent from the call since pushing the send button. He knew he needed to explain it all, uninterrupted, so that Katie could hear the story in its entirety. Sam closed his eyes and said calmly, "Please, Katie, just listen for a moment. While I was walking down on the beach, a girl was nearly killed last night. As I was pulling the guy off her, two fishermen showed up and helped by detaining him until the police arrived. The girl is okay; just shaken up, understandably. I managed to bang my head and I got some cuts on my foot from the ordeal, but I'm fine, really. I didn't want to wake you up last night and have you worry all night, since I was okay. I'm sorry if that makes you angry, but I wasn't trying to keep what happened to me to myself. It all just happened so fast. I just finished with my statement and I'll be home early tomorrow."

The quiet coming from the other end of the call made Sam think he'd lost his connection, which would really infuriate him, convinced he wouldn't have another opportunity to unload all of the information if he was to call back. Sam finally asked, "Katie, are you still there?"

Katie merely responded with, "Yes. I'm still here."

Not wishing to tip her mood either direction, Sam shot for the middle with, "I'm sorry I'm holding you up from your class. Do you want me to call you after, or better yet, you can call me?"

Katie, sounding exhausted from the short call, simply replied, "I'll call you."

Sam struggled for an appropriate closing comment that would lighten the mood, as well as ensure her he's okay. Before it came to fruition, Katie just hung up, leaving Sam to wish life was as easy for him in the real world as it was on paper.

Sam's chilly reception at home definitely left him exhausted and running on fumes the next day from trying to convince Katie his close encounter with a madman fully intent on killing him would never happen again.

His part in what he believed would be a small story; page three, at best, turned out to catch the country on a slow day and exploded as a lead for several news channels and page one of at least half of the country's leading papers. When someone was saved from certain death, it made for a feel-good sound bite. When that someone was rescued by a member of the media, it became every reporter, freelance columnist, or anchor person's unique opportunity to shed a little positive light on the overall true character of the medium. At the very least it could help tip the morality scale of general census.

Before Sam made it to his office building, he'd received six 'Atta boys,' three lunch date offers, and a request for his autograph. The final request coming, sarcastically, from Ira on the sidewalk outside the office as the two were heading in. After Ira's parting shot concerning 'with great powers came great responsibility' speech, he smugly shuffled off toward his first floor dungeon, allowing Sam to ascend upstairs alone to face his fellow workers, feeling anything but a hero.

Two hours later, sitting outside his editor's office, waiting to be beckoned, Sam enjoyed the five minutes of solace. His co-workers were enjoying showing off their creativity with an abundance of one-of-a-kind displays of hero paraphernalia they'd come up with on short notice. Their ingenuity included a blue cape draped over his chair, non-stop hero themes being played in the background and privately, a personal favorite, his very own action figure that someone from Human Resources had whipped together, although the resemblance was a little scary.

His thoughts were interrupted by his boss yelling, "Sam, my boy, get in here!" Snapping to his feet, he quickly obeyed. Once inside the office, he saw Tom uncharacteristically leaning on the front of his desk before noticing they weren't alone. A tall woman in her late thirties, sporting medium length, dark brown hair and professional attire, stood facing the wall to the left, going over some of Tom's 'wall of fame' pictures. Tom extended a hand for Sam to shake, saying, "There he is. How ya doin', Sam?"

Sam awkwardly accepted the unusually positive greeting, curious as to where the meeting was about to go, replying, "Good. I'm doing alright."

Tom turned his attention to the woman and stated, "Sam, I'd like you to meet Helen O'Day. She's come here from Lancaster Media Group."

As if waiting for her cue, the woman spun and acted like she hadn't noticed anyone else in the room until Tom made the introduction. She strode the eight feet in nearly two steps, shaking Sam's hand firmer than anyone before, stating, "Absolutely thrilled to meet your acquaintance, Sam. Had a little excitement back West, I hear?"

Sam noticed she looked him up and down, making him feel slightly violated, as he answered, "Yes, Ma'am, but, I'm no worse for wear."

She quickly added, "Understand the girl's father is the sheriff?" Distracted by her mannerism of speaking in a short, clipped style, just like Tom, Sam was caught considering how the two must have the shortest conversations ever recorded before she prompted him, "The girl you saved; the sheriff's daughter?"

Sam shifted back into focus, understanding his responses were being timed, like in a chess match, answering, "Niece. The young woman is actually the niece of Sheriff Clayton Boyd of San Mateo County."

Helen just continued to stare at Sam, responding, "Right," before turning back to Tom and speaking as though Sam was no longer in the room with, "He's good looking, which should play well, and if he follows the script, he shouldn't come across quite so . . . off, you know?"

Tom just grunted, "Uh-huh, sure, he can read."

Sam was left watching the discussion about him go back and forth like a tennis match as Helen returned the volley with, "We can clean him up and, if he's as innocent as he appears, we could see a bump in circulation in the neighborhood of six with a nice shares yield, too. Get him prepped and have him there by one." With that, Helen made for the door in three, long steps, saying unconvincingly over her shoulder, "Sam, good to meet you. We're expecting great things!" Sam's attention hesitated on the closed door, trying to catch up with what had just occurred.

Tom cleared his throat, gaining Sam's bewildered look, saying, "Sam, take a seat. We need to talk." Escorting Sam to the sofa with an extended hand, Tom took the seat across from him, sitting forward on its edge.

Sam waited for his boss' illusive form of explanation to develop, but decided to take a preemptive strike, asking, "Just what exactly are you intending to have me do, Tom?"

Immediately, Tom comfortably slid into defensive mode, raising his hands, palms out, in a show of wanting to slow things down, exclaiming, "Whoa, whoa, hold on, Sam. I'm not the one crackin' the whip here. You just saw the same tornado I did. You know as well as I do, when it comes to the news, you lead with your best story and portray it in a way to draw the most interest. Well, if you haven't noticed, you're page one and, you gotta admit, it won't hurt your article's numbers, either. If we don't jump on the exclusive, do you really want somebody else to? What they've got planned is a brief interview conducted by Jackie Powers from our sister station. Just answer her questions about the ordeal from a list they'll be sending me in about an hour and try not to look into the camera. Ya know, just be yourself!"

Sam dropped his head into his waiting hands, asking meagerly, "Did anyone think to ask if I even want to do this?"

Tom just smirked at the question before following it with, "Did anybody ask Lincoln if he wanted to get shot in the head? Heck, no! He just wanted to see the end of the play! But on the road of life, there are curves, and that's why cars have steering wheels, so go with the flow and shift your ass into gear."

Confused by the plethora of metaphors, Sam began to walk out of his editor's office, uncertain if he should get back to work or drive a car someplace, but stopped, stating defiantly, "One short interview, Tom. And I'm doing it because it doesn't sound like I have a choice. But I'm not looking for my fifteen minutes of fame. I'll do the plug, because I want some help finding El Padre, and more people knowing about it, the better the odds."

Tom listened with mild indifference, moving back behind his desk, responding without even looking up, "Then we want the same thing, so there you go. Watch for my email, go over the questions, and be at the studio by 12:15."

Still feeling like he wanted to reemphasize his position on the subject, Sam decided it would only add a taste of bitterness to an already sour atmosphere. Instead, he exited through the door with his usual feeling of discontent when leaving his boss' office, but this time, Sam left the door open in a meager show of defiance.

Sam had never met an actual 'handler' before; not until Brenton introduced himself the moment Sam walked into the studio building, with "Hello, Mr. Noll. I'm Brenton, your handler," he probably wouldn't have known what one did. Sitting in a comfortable chair that he could best describe as some type of over-padded barber chair, Sam closed his eyes while hairs were plucked from between his brows. Brenton warned him early on that he'd be applying light make-up to 'kill the glare,' or so he put it. Sam made a little fuss at the time, but soon realized he wasn't going to have his way on any of it.

"Would you mind if I fix your hair, Mr. Noll?" Brenton lisped, resting a hand on his right hip and extending his left arm, holding a comb, mimicking a teapot, but not at all on purpose.

Sam looked at his reflection in the mirror, decrying, "What do you mean by fix? You make it sound like my hair is broken."

Brenton dramatically reacted as though his feelings were devastated, pleading, "I'm not saying your hair is broken, just, out of order." Brenton leaned in to place his head next to Sam's as they looked at each other in the mirror, adding with a smirk, "Trust me, Sam. I can work with this. How do you feel about A Flock of Seagulls look?" Again, Sam closed his eyes and mentally retreated to his happy place that had nothing to do with make-up, plucking, or tea pots.

Sam sat uncomfortably in the chair across from Jackie Powers and felt a drop of sweat trickle down his back. Jackie looked up from her notes, noticing Sam's greenish hue, and called behind her, "Brenton! He's turning green."

Brenton appeared from the darkness and handed Sam a glass containing a clear liquid. Sam asked, "Is this water?"

Brenton simply answered, "Sure" and waited for Sam to drink it so he could take the empty glass and remove himself from the stage.

Sam downed the fluid, realizing a bit too late it wasn't water, gagged once, then sat back while his eyes watered. Jackie watched the scene play out as though this was standard procedure, until Sam's eyes stopped watering and she said, "Okay, he's back to normal." Shielding her eyes with her pages of notes, she asked someone beyond the cameras, "Can we run through this once?"

A voice from speakers above their heads replied in a deep, ominous tone, "Let's roll on my mark. Three, two,"

Sam sat, staring toward a spotlight, waiting for the voice to say, 'one' until he heard Jackie saying, "Good day, New York! Jackie Powers here with a Channel Nine Exclusive. I'm here with Sam Noll, author of the weekly column Death Comes Easily, who recently found himself moonlighting, as a hero!" She turned to face Sam. "Sam, welcome to the program."

Rule number one; be cordial, Sam recalled from his flurry of advice from Brenton, so he took a breath and replied, "It's nice to be here, Jackie."

Jackie returned with, "And *lucky* to be here, wouldn't you say, Sam?"

Second pointer, Sam thought, keep looking at Jackie as if the cameras, lights, and other people weren't even there, and let the cameras shift if they wanted to see you straight on. Sam answered her leading question, "Luck and definitely a little good timing, that's for sure."

Knowing the camera would fixate on Jackie for the next thirty-two seconds as she briefly told of Sam's heroic activities in California, Sam released the breath he'd been holding as Brenton flew in to mop up the sweat forming all over Sam's face and neck. Before Sam's 'handler' made his exit, stage left, he whispered into Sam's ear, "You're doing fabulous!"

Sam turned back to Jackie just as she finished her informative update for the viewers at home with, "The grateful young woman was unable to be reached for today's interview, but we understand she's doing well, according to her uncle, Sheriff Clayton Boyd of San Mateo County." She turned back to Sam. "So, Sam. We understand the alleged assailant of this crime is suspected in four recent murders; two in California and two more in Minnesota, is that correct?"

Sam only briefly paused, answering, "Anthony Lloyd Lingham has been indicted on the four crimes, yes, but beyond that I can't make any further comment, as I wouldn't want to influence or affect the ongoing investigation in any way."

Jackie eased back into her chair, sliding the questions into cruise control, asking, "So, what brought you out to the West Coast, Sam?" He explained his rehearsed answer of the continuing search for leads on El Padre, as well as the story's background. Sam slowly began to feel more at ease under the scrutiny of the camera and the lights. For the first time he allowed the concept of televised interviews as being something not quite so immoral. Switching gears, Jackie unexpectedly asked, "So tell us, Sam, because, we're dying to know . . . how did it feel?"

Thrown off from Jackie's unscripted query, Sam paused only a moment before asking, "How did what feel?"

Jackie leaned in to Sam and added a hint of bravado to her voice, continuing her probe. "You know, your job is to write about what already happened, then suddenly, to have the opportunity to actually be involved, literally hands on, to personally be the news . . . what was that like?"

Sam, once again, felt the heat of the cameras and his response time slowed. After just two seconds that seemed much longer, Sam looked the reporter in the eyes and held her in check for one more breath. In a cold, honest response, Sam stated, "You simply face the realization that what's happening is wrong; that the person you're defending is good, just as much as you believe the one you face is evil. It all became black and white; right and wrong. There was no option. There was no choice. Once I walked into that public restroom and entered the middle of that situation, I became involved. And, thankfully, Fate favored the good, this time."

Jackie just stared at Sam's response before catching her poor etiquette and turned back to the camera. "So, there you have it, ladies and gentlemen. Sam Noll, an unsuspecting hero in a time of dire need." Jackie turned back to Sam, extended her hand for him to shake, adding, "It was a delight to have you on our show, Sam. Thank you."

Sam accepted her hand in his until he heard the voice overhead again say, "Clear. One and done. Nice job, people!"

Jackie's hand immediately grew limp within his grasp, along with her smile, as she slid her hand out of his. He watched her gather her notes and walk off the set without as much as a glance in his direction, leaving him with the feeling of being used for some purpose he probably would never understand.

Perhaps he and Jackie both worked as members of the media, but they were certainly not on the same team. She's like the high school starting quarterback, while Sam was in the band that played at halftime, probably lugging around the tuba.

Before he allowed her treatment to damage his pride any further, Brenton appeared without a sound to Sam's left. Sam looked at him for further instruction, but Brenton just simply stared back at him. Finally, Sam's 'handler' broke the silence, saying quietly, "Don't let that woman's damaged attitude belittle what you did for that girl in California or how you feel about it deep inside. You did a good thing for another human being, and Jackie has never had that feeling before. She couldn't recognize a decent person if they saved her from cannibals. She'd just call in the story and hope they lead with it before dessert. The only thing she comprehends is sound bites, headlines, and camera lights."

Not knowing whether to comment, Sam remained mute, slowly standing from his seat marked Guest. Sam shook Brenton's hand, saying, "Thanks, Brenton. You helped me through this ordeal without letting me look like a fool. I appreciate it."

Brenton blushed, replying, "It was my privilege to help one of the good guys!"

Sam exited the studio building and walked into the alley. By the time he reached the main street, he decided the entire experience of being an actual news item was something best left behind him. He'd be gracious to anyone who might bring it up, but it would probably be best to let his fifteen minutes end at only five. The lights, headlines, and sound bites were best left for those who needed them.

Burma, 2008

The constant rain seemed to have been falling without break for three solid days. Straight down, sideways, even at times up, the precipitation had such an odd variance to dispense. El Padre watched the small band of governmental military amble by from his elevated place within the small crop of trees. With his hat pulled low, his penetrating blue eyes strained just below the brim toward each face of the bantam representation of the ruling Junta of Myanmar, or as many knew the volatile country, Burma. His gentle suggestion of keeping their heads down, preventing the rain from hitting them in the eyes, was numbly adhered.

They ventured deeper into the forest in search of the white man who continued to evade them. Word had reached El Padre via two missionaries connected to a United Kingdom non-governmental organization, or NGO, that his 'good works' were being tracked and plotted for interrogation, meaning someone on high wanted him tortured and killed. The country was run by small minded men who chose to meet questions and the unknown with a long blade. He came for a great purpose as yet unknown to him, but until the time came there was so much need.

Once assured the band of men had passed well enough away, El Padre turned to the north and headed for the small province near the upper east section of the country. Until now he'd remained close to the Irrawaddy River, as many did, using it like a main thoroughfare or turnpike for unfettered travel. With his pale face and Western features standing out among the populated area of Burma, he considered it better to detour to a less traveled path for the time being.

The other bit of news was the smaller draw he followed to the northeast. The ruling military regime, for some time, had been fighting with the Kokang militia group in that province, and many of the locals were either being massacred or forced to flee into Taiwan or China. One single reason was always found at the root of any fight, battle, or war, regardless of what beautifully poetic words came from the mouths of those watching death from their place on high. Be it land, minerals, ignorance, or a simple misunderstanding, when one dug down deep enough to strike honesty, there, within that pool, was the sole basis for conflict. Without the patience and respect for fearless communication, men closed their ears and turned to aggression.

After three days of remaining away from the beaten path and enduring more difficult travel, El Padre quickly ducked into some bushes as several jeeps sped by carrying many junta soldiers. Once the road cleared, he followed his inner call, as well as the rising smoke, until he reached a small village in the northeastern province in the wake of a blood bath. Twenty to thirty bodies lay before him as numerous injured locals searched with little hope for survivors, while homes and various small buildings burned. He immediately helped a thin, bare-chested Burmese man move a lifeless elderly woman riddled by gunfire into a shaded area, away from the road and the collapse of a small shed engulfed in flames. El Padre attempted to console the man as he kissed his wife for the last time, weeping through his goodbyes. He helplessly watched the man, wanting to take away his grief; wishing to remove his sadness, but he could not. All he could do was hold him tenderly as the small man suffered through his loss.

El Padre looked up at the mayhem all around with similar scenarios playing out in every direction. He watched as children mourned parents, parents wept over murdered offspring, and as other numerous loved ones kneeled over others. All the while, in their expressions of horrific grief, they decried a government that had carelessly taken away one more human being for no other reason than the desire for complete domination.

After giving aid to many involved in the attack and hearing first-hand reports of what took place, El Padre became repulsed with the needless loss and careless slaughter. For eleven hours, El Padre saw to the dying, gave comfort to the survivors, and helped in caring for those lost.

Finally, collapsing to his knees from physical and emotional exhaustion, he lifted his head to the heavens and prayed for strength and infusion of Faith to continue assisting those who desperately required it, even when he knew not how to explain the evils of men. He's left with only the ability to hold their hand in his and weep mercifully with them for what they'd lost. In many circumstances, the sum was nearly everything.

Knowing well the junta's common practice of what was commonly called 'forced venture,' El Padre explained the treacherous path south, with its hidden land mines and array of stingers left buried by the heartless military. The regime's hope was that the remaining would either be exterminated as they travelled south toward the Irrawaddy, or escaped in fear into neighboring China or India.

Left with little choice, most gathered their few belongings not destroyed by the attack, and headed either north or east for China, not knowing whether they'd be received or forced to turn back at the border. The few choosing to remain, elected to rebuild and hope that lightning wouldn't strike twice upon the small village.

El Padre contemplated how chance and hope seemed ever connected with new beginnings. His hand rose to massage his tired neck and shoulders, feeling torn by a strong desire to escort the bulk of the survivors safely into China. At the same time, he wished to enter the northeast mountains where he sensed great evil dwelling. He looked toward the southeast and into the belly of the drug trade, where the borders of Laos, Thailand, and Burma met, commonly called the Golden Triangle. There, he could wreak havoc upon all involved with the drug production, but with a heavy sigh of the long burden of responsibility, he turned southwest, responding to the quiet beckoning he'd followed for so many years gone by. It had neither led him astray nor lost its illumination. The gently lit path was always his true compass, his unsurpassed, sound direction. It exceeded any personal desire or useless need for retaliation in a world of endless atrocity.

CHAPTER 25

Time had slowed for Sam. He began to feel he'd entered what's known as 'writer's rut'; the period between big stories and new leads where one was forced to give birth to pages of blurbs about nearly exciting, almost entertaining reproductions of something already read. The paper had celebrated a nice increase in earnings from the television interview, but things had definitely settled into a slow drip.

Even things at home with Katie had become swept into the tedium factor. At one point, Sam was off on one of his mental excursions when Katie attempted to draw his attention concerning an author his cousin, Bea, mentioned interviewing in Chicago during her recent visit. The book sounded so interesting that Katie had bought it. Near the beginning of her explanation, she stopped and stared at Sam, with an expression of someone knowing they'd lost their audience somewhere near the opening sentence. She leaned into his ear, whispering convincingly, "If you're thinking about someone dying right now, Sam Noll, I swear I'll start bringing some of *my* work home, and I promise after one hour, you'll definitely be thinking about death!"

Sam turned to face her, embarrassed, but managed to hold his own, replying, "Nope. I was just enjoying the moment of solitude before you continue with your summary. I thought you were doing the same and I didn't want to interrupt your creative process of formulation to amply describe your new book."

Katie considered his answer for half a second before Sam realized she figured out his insincerity, responding with a pillow aimed just above his neck. "Okay, okay, so I was off to Never Never Land. But I was *not* thinking about dead people, and you'll just have to take me at my word," Sam shared. Katie nibbled on her lip and simply stared back at him, but didn't reply. Sam got up and headed toward the kitchen, asking, "I'm going to get myself a glass of water before I come back and listen to your book report. Would you like anything?"

Katie smiled, offering her request, "Water would be great, thank you."

Sitting together once again on the sofa, Katie was still talking about the book and Bea's interview of the writer. "After her husband is sentenced for the rape and death of their daughter, she decides to move off the reservation and make it on her own. She loses several jobs, but keeps finding a way to make ends meet for her and her son."

Katie gently rubbed her calf before Sam took the hint and started massaging her leg, at which point Katie proceeded, "At one point, she considers going back to reservation life, but she worries about how it would affect her young son. Working two part-time jobs, she makes the time to start writing down all the reasons she shouldn't return to that life; the terrible influence of drugs and alcohol, the lack of quality education, the increasing gang issue and, most important, the government's unrelenting desire to keep the Native American people enabled, segregated, and dependent on financial assistance. One day, she begins to read her notes and decides to turn it into a book!"

Sam asked, "What's the name of the book, by the way?"

Katie quickly got up, running over to the small table by the entryway, grabbing the book. She handed it to Sam, answering, "It's entitled, *Speaking Through Reservations*. This is its second edition. It was on the best-seller's list for eight weeks!"

Sam turned the book over and took in the picture of the author. Katie leaned in and opened it to the second page. Sam read the dedication, "To Saffron. You were the very best of us. We will miss you, always."

Katie sat back with her legs tucked under her, stating, "Her daughter was barely a teenager when she was killed. When she writes about it in the beginning of the book, I nearly went through a whole box of tissue."

Sam looked up at his girlfriend, gently placing a hand to the side of her face, and softly stroked her hair back. Katie curled into him like a little girl as Sam asked, "So where are you in the book?"

Katie reached over, flipping to the bookmarked page, pointing halfway down the left side. "Right here."

Sam adjusted his eyes to the small print and began to read as Katie snuggled a little closer. "Once viewed as dependent, the image remains locked and affixed around one's collar like a heavy link chain, with no one admitting to having the key. This unfortunate rendering is transferred not only from government to government, but is wide-spread throughout the private sector as well, diminishing any career path before I could even walk through the door . . ."

Tom appeared in front of Sam's desk, unannounced as usual. Sam looked up from reading an article while chewing on the end of his pen. Tom stated dryly, "Think you're supposed to use the other end of that thing. They call it 'writing'!"

Sam sarcastically responded, "But this end tastes better."

Tom turned, walking away, saying over his shoulder, "Walk with me." Sam reacted to the command appropriately, bolting out of his chair, catching up to his boss's long strides. Tom remained silent as they entered the elevator and he pressed the lobby button. Once the doors closed, he leaned against the wall and jump-started the conversation. "That pile of documented sightings Nevins's been filtering through since we ran that artist's rendition of El Padre just mighta given us a possible lead."

Sam perked up, having felt as though he'd been in a holding pattern for the past several months. "What came up? Please tell me it isn't something in San Francisco again!" Sam asked defensively.

Tom hesitantly scratched his chin, replying, "No! I have a special folder for anything we get from California. Um, this one, though, might take a little . . . cultural finesse."

Sam tilted his head, never having seen a pensive side to his editor, but pressed forward anyway. "Okay. So what's the lead?"

Tom paused, reacting to the elevator alerting them it's stopping at the eighth floor. Sam waited, staring at Tom, as two secretaries entered the small box while Tom smiled flirtatiously at them with a head nod. Once the doors closed again, Sam repeated his inquiry to snap his boss back into their discussion. "Tom. The lead?"

Tom returned his attention to Sam and replied, "Ever heard of Tran Anh Tai?"

Sam blinked once before admitting, "No. But I assume he's Vietnamese."

Tom smugly recited, "Not just Vietnamese, but Deputy Prime Minister. But, to be fair, they seem to have a lot of deputies; more than the Sheriff's Department. I'd put his ranking as something like a senator."

Sam squinted, attempting to filter through Tom's partial information before asking, "So, a Deputy Prime Minister of the Country of Vietnam has El Padre information?" Tom didn't adjust his expression from his writer's question, but offered a simple nod of agreement. Sam shrugged, adding, "Well, the way this thing has been going, I guess that makes perfect sense. When do I leave?"

Tom changed his expression from leading the conversation to being caught by surprise as he stumbled over his response. "Whoa there, hold on a minute. I'm not about to experience any de ja vu from your last trip. This can be easily followed-up with a phone call. Amazing invention, the phone; allows people to stay connected without airfare or payable receipts. Let your fingers do the walking and see what he has. Odds are it's nothing major."

The elevator alerted its occupants of their arrival at the lobby as Sam and Tom followed the exiting ladies while the two men continued their exchange toward the front entrance of the building. "Gimme a break, Tom. I'm not going to show utter disrespect to a ranking cabinet member of the Communist Party of Vietnam. If this guy took the time to contact us, he's got something viable. You know it as well as I do. Just attempting to make contact with us could get him in hot water. I need to meet him face-to-face and on his terms."

Unconvinced, Tom continued the shake of his head, replying, "We can't do it, Noll. Each department has a budget, and you're already so red, you look like a crime scene." Swinging his arms frantically, Tom continued his point, "There should be police tape encircling this area!"

Sam wasn't fazed by his editor's theatrics and pushed forward as they both stopped walking and faced off. "You know, Tom, whenever you start talking about budgets and fiscal limitations, there's a side of you that seeps out. It makes you shorter, recedes your hairline, and adds thirty pounds to your waistline; kinda reminds me of the last editor here."

Tom took the insult with a hand to his hip and an immediate glare that raised the hair on the back of Sam's neck leaving him to wonder if he'd gone a little too far. Tom finally cleared his throat before stating in a slow, steady cadence, "Money has limitations, and part of my job is to keep us from over-spending. Is this possibly a strong lead? Yes, I'll grant you that. But don't think for a second I'm going to let emotions of momentary excitement keep me from doing the job I was hired to do. Someone here has to be logical. We can 'what if' scenario this thing to death and still come up empty-handed. Apologize, kiss his behind, or sing his national anthem; I don't care what you need to do, as long as you do it over the phone. You're a pain in this paper's butt, but a creative one; think outside the box and amaze me!"

Tom started to head out of the building, but spun around quickly, adding, "I can't believe you stooped so low as comparing me to

Malcolm! If I had a heart, that would have probably hurt!" With that, he turned and hefted the door open, leaving Sam to stare after him, unable to decide whether he actually liked his boss or hated him.

Katie busied herself between classes attempting to organize her gym bag. It'd been on her 'to-do' list for several weeks, and now was as good a time as any to get that deep, internal feeling of victory for drawing one more line through her ever-growing checklist. Once every item was removed and spread out onto several benches of the ladies locker room, the front desk attendant, Jenny, stuck her head in through the door, announcing, "Katie, there's someone out front to see you." With a defeated drop to her head, Katie quickly collected her belongings, stuffing them back into the black duffel bag. Organization and its just reward would have to be temporarily postponed.

Sam stood awkwardly in the middle of the lobby as she emerged from the locker room. With her immediate look of concern, Sam responded with, "Everything is okay. Nobody's in the hospital. I just need to talk to you. Do you have a sec?" With small, apprehensive steps, Katie approached Sam and took his hand, leading him to one of the three small, unoccupied sales offices. Once the door was closed, they sat across the desk from each other, Sam being the seller and Katie as the customer. Sam started his pitch with, "So, how's your day going?"

Katie easily slid forward on the fake leather seat, put both hands on the desk, insisting, "Don't patronize me with small talk, Sam. What's going on?"

Sam displayed a look of someone mentally kicking himself for lack of planning before admitting, "It's nothing, really. I just need to go out of town one more time, for work."

The slow slide back into her chair was filled with pain-wrenching innuendo as Sam slumped from Katie's wordless rebuttal. With two simultaneous slaps to the arms of the chair, Katie was up and standing over her salesman while a zephyr of anger wafted Sam's face. "I don't get it, Sam. I really don't get it. You pour everything into this damned article, leaving nothing for us. I understand two steps forward, one step back in a relationship, but this is just turning and making a mad dash for the starting line. This article will be the death of you, and it's definitely digging a six-foot hole for us."

Katie didn't wait for any reply, knowing Sam wouldn't have any. Instead, she nearly swung the door off its hinges and stomped out of the small office, leaving Sam to worry about the participants of Katie's next class.

Getting in contact with a Vietnamese Deputy Prime Minister wasn't something Sam had considered ever doing before. His naivety managed to only broker a number for the American Consulate in neighboring Laos, until he gave in to his stubbornness and sought out Ira. Within seven minutes, Ira handed Sam a direct line to the Deputy Prime Minister's secretary, leaving Sam to humbly wonder how one little man could have so many contacts.

Telling Katie he intended to make another trip would be his only admission toward his intentions. Even Ira couldn't know he was about to disobey his boss and follow the lead, in person. He had enough in savings to easily foot the bill on his own, and once he returned, if the results didn't change his editor's tune, he could endure the lack of compensation.

What he knew right down to his very soul was this trip carried a profound piece to the puzzle that Sam could, in no way, explain or fully comprehend until it was perceived in person. He needed to meet Tran Anh Tai, not just pelt him with questions over the phone.

After years of working stories and exposing the truth, he had never felt something so certain or drawing as this lead. He decided to anger or deceive pretty much everyone he knew and cared about, to connect the two unknown dots, and picking up the phone to call the number he'd been supplied, Sam prayed that Katie, this time, wasn't right.

CHAPTER 26

Unable to sleep on the long flight, Sam filtered through an abundance of updated world-wide leads that Ira had collected just in the previous four weeks. The increase of following had started making waves within the other forms of media. Several other newspapers, weekly periodicals and thirty-minute television programs were popping up and jumping on the bandwagon, improvising their own brand of loosely based versions of El Padre, fact or fiction. None of the Groupies, as Tom called them, worried his editor, but it did seem to cause a slight increase in pressure to maximize performance.

The initial awkward phone conversation with the Deputy Prime Minister's secretary yielded little, other than DPM Tran was unavailable, overseeing construction in Norway. Sam had pressed her to make contact with him at her soonest convenience and followed up with a call the very next day. The outcome was that the Deputy Prime Minister would be in Norway for seven more days and relayed to him through the secretary that Sam was invited to join him, if possible. What a Vietnamese dignitary was doing in Norway for building expansion didn't slow Sam's blind ambition to fetter out the connection to El Padre. He packed and booked his flight. If the lead was in Norway, then so was he.

❊   ❊   ❊

Once at his hotel in Oslo, Sam received a message from the DPM at the front desk to meet Tran Anh Tai for dinner the following evening with the apology of not being able to meet any sooner. Sam headed up to his room to prepare his message to his boss. Letting Tom know the 'what' and 'why' would probably remove any form of appetite for dinner anyway. Tom had told him to think outside the box, but Sam knew, in Tom's interpretation, there were definite limits to the box and its vicinity.

The next morning spent venturing about the main hub of Oslo passed by uneventfully for the first hour and a half, as his story's background had nothing to do with the area. In a rare occasion, Sam found himself able to simply enjoy another locale for the mere pleasure of it. His jet lag had worn off sometime after breakfast after a sound night's sleep on the softest mattress he'd ever slept on. The overcast skies and mild temperature allowed him to meander about the area with merely a light jacket, having brought three degrees of coats just in case. The efficient trolley system gave him the ability to see much of the city at little expense, as the taxis were rather costly.

The first comment he'd share with anyone who might ask him about his visit to Norway was its immaculate cleanliness. Other than a rare appearance of graffiti he's unable to notice any discarded litter or even an empty soda can in the street, curbs, or sidewalks. Coming from one of the largest cities in the world, Sam was surprised to be unable to pick up any sort of scent or odor; only clean, fresh air.

At the end of a block, he decided to hop off the public transportation. Turning right and halfway down the sidewalk, Sam stopped instantly, staring up at a large, white structure near the water with an unusual sloped roof. The architecture of the building was impressive, but what'd drawn his attention were the people walking along the ski-sloped shaped roof.

A gentleman in his mid-seventies stopped before passing Sam and asked in English, but with a heavy Norwegian accent, "So then, where ya from?"

Sam broke from his staring of the building to switch his curious look toward the man, responding, "Excuse me? Oh, where am I from? America. I'm an American; New York, to be exact."

The man joined Sam while they both admired the building in question as the older man stated, "Dat would be our Opera House, if ya didn't know already."

Sam continued gawking at the artistic structure, stoically appearing like a glacier gracefully slipping into the waterway. The only statement Sam could express was, "It's simply magnificent."

The man looked at Sam for a moment before smiling and scratching at his scraggly beard, responding with, "Yeah, for sure, but have you seen da Vigeland Sculpture Park?"

Sam turned away from the marble and granite site and tilted his head, asking, "Is it far from here? I'm on foot, and the taxis run a little expensive."

"Nah, not very far at all. I'll be showin' ya then. What is your name, my friend?" the elderly man inquired.

Unaccustomed to such politeness, Sam slowly extended his hand, replying hesitantly, "Sam. Sam Noll. And you are?"

With a tip of his cap and a shake of Sam's offered hand, he replied, "Jorgen Olafsen. Pleased to meet you, Sam Noll."

Tentatively, Sam asked, "I'm not keeping you from anything pressing, am I, Mr. Olafsen? I wouldn't want to be a bother."

The older man smiled as if everything Sam said was humorous, answering, "Oh, no. Not at all, young man. I'd be happy to show ya."

Once at the park, Jorgen assumed the position of tour guide. The pride of his Norwegian culture and history exuded unabated with Sam taking it all in without the need of his notepad; just listening to the older man gush over a country's long past that seemed to have a firm grasp of how to take care of its people's future. When Jorgen took a short break from his historical account, Sam asked, "So I take it your family has lived here for quite a while?"

The look Sam received from Jorgen caused him to feel like he'd just offended the man, as Jorgen turned toward the opposite direction and remained solemn for a moment, thinking. Sam waited the few seconds before Jorgen turned back asking, "How 'bout you join me for some lunch, then?"

Surprised by the change in direction and deflection of subject, Sam gladly accepted, replying jokingly, "Are you sure you know a good place?"

The elder Norwegian laughed aloud, answering, "I think I can manage."

Walking and chatting about Norwegian politics, Jorgen suddenly stopped his forward motion, stating, "And here we be" opening the door to one of the smallest, oldest cars Sam had ever seen.

Sam approached Jorgen, asking, "You mean we've been walking all this way just to get to your car?"

Jorgen chuckled at Sam's sound of distress, responding, "Of course! You don't want to walk all the way to lunch, now do ya?" Sam kept his hands propped comfortably on his hips until Jorgen managed to start the little vehicle, prepared to drive off with or without his guest. Deciding he'd come this far, Sam opted to go a little farther and climbed into the circus ride, checking the cramped back seat for any spare clowns.

The car sputtered with each manual shift of the gear. Sam asked disconcertingly, "Was that third?"

The kindly gentleman chuckled an answer of, "Lost third some years ago. I believe we be in fourth." Sam laughed along with Jorgen as they continued to sputter down the road.

The homes in the area they ventured amazed Sam with their maintained beauty. After several blocks, he asked, "I've yet to see a newer home. They do exist around here, don't they?"

Jorgen smiled replying, "Yeah, for sure. The Vik's house is right there." He pointed with his thumb to a house on the right side of the street. "Had a fire a while back and rebuilt. Guess that were some ninety years now."

Sam stared at the house as it passed by, unable to tell any difference. Finally, Sam asked, "So, just where is this restaurant, anyway? I've seen nothing but residential homes for blocks."

In place of an answer, Jorgen turned into what seemed to be a random driveway, stopped, and turned off the engine. "No needin' fancy dining when the best cook lives right here."

Sam was slow to realize he'd been invited to Jorgen's home and stumbled through his show of appreciation. "Your home? You don't even know who I am or what I do. You don't even know why I'm here, Mr. Olafsen. How can you just invite me into your home?"

The elderly man stopped at his front door and smiled broadly, answering Sam with, "I saw you had a good heart by the way you looked at my country." He looked upward for further explanation before turning back to Sam and adding, "No man of evil or looking to do harm could appreciate Norway the way you do. Now lunch is ready, so best we not keep her waitin'. She's beautiful, but ornery."

The last description Sam would apply to Aase Olafsen would be ornery as her hospitality surpassed her husband's, and Jorgen's brief hint concerning her talent for cooking proved to be understated. The meal of salmon and boiled potatoes was simple enough, but her preparation carried centuries of secrets passed down from many generations. Jorgen sat back after the meal, exhaling a fitting utterance of, "Uff dah. Oye yo yo" loosening his belt one notch.

Almost as though the response was a cue, Aase began collecting the empty plates. Sam rose to assist her in the cleanup, but Aasa gently touched his hand, saying simply, "You're our guest. This is our way. Please sit and be relaxed."

The tenderness of her response to his attempt humbled Sam immediately, and he adhered to her request, slowly sitting back down. Jorgen watched Sam's respectful consideration and scratched at his beard, stating, "Earlier, Sam, you asked about my family when we were at the park. To ask someone about their Norwegian heritage is no light matter, as often the answer can take several days to explain," he said with a chuckle, before continuing. "So, if ya wish to hear a tale, then I have one to tell."

Aasa delivered two slices of rhubarb pie and two forks, then slipped back into the kitchen as Jorgen gave her a smile for either appreciation for the delicious meal or the shared understanding that an epic journey was about to unfold in their small dining room.

With the dessert plates emptied and nearly all of the coffee drank, Jorgen wound down to the Second World War. Sam sat forward, sponging every decade since Jorgen's family arrived by an eight-oared fishing vessel called an 'ottring' in the spring of 1849. With the German invasion and eventual occupation of Norway, Jorgen's father survived as a crofter, or farmer, hiding his three daughters and only son inside the cart under the crop of potatoes he'd harvested. Another farmer stood by, protecting the hidden children, later to be paid for his efforts with potatoes.

Sam slowly shook his head trying to imagine hiding one's own children from the Nazis, leaving them in the care of another while laboring all day just to provide a living. Jorgen, being the youngest of the four, didn't recall the event, but laughed at the story of coming so close to death at such an innocent time of his life. After the completion of his stories, he smiled at his wife with a fondness only a man who had beaten incredible odds could do, as he extended his hand for hers. Sam admired the enduring connection the two had before feeling he was intruding and tried to fill the uncomfortable moment by stating, "What an amazingly epic history you have. Thank you for sharing this with me." Sam closed his eyes, joggling his memory before adding, "Tusen takk."

Both Aasa and Jorgen applauded Sam's correct pronunciation of 'Thank you very much' as they replied in unison, "Vaer sa god, you're welcome, Sam." Jorgen raised his coffee cup and said loudly, "Skol!"

Sam joined in with his, responding with, "Cheers!" All three laughed together, drinking to good health and the saving grace of potatoes.

Jorgen's last contribution to Sam's great adventure was a ride back to his hotel. Once he returned to his room, he focused on prepping for his meeting with the Deputy Prime Minister. One hour into his research on the man, Sam began a list of possibilities as to why the Vietnamese dignitary was in Norway. The obvious conclusion finally came down to the quest for alternative renewable energy sources.

The DPM studied bio-physics at Berkeley and, long before being elected to his present post, had been a leading proponent of aiding in the development of alternative energy sources for his country. Once the reason for the visit was established, the 'who' quickly followed. A company called Statkraft had plans to build the first osmotic plant utilizing pressure-retarded osmosis. The method was beyond what Sam was able to grasp without a PHD, but the technological concept seemed promising, at the very least, on paper. Before jumping into the shower and getting ready for dinner, Sam felt comfortably ready to meet the well-educated, innovative Deputy Prime Minister.

CHAPTER 27

There were hotel restaurants and then there were restaurants within hotels. Walking into the Eik Annen Etage restaurant at the Hotel Continental immediately placed Sam on the defensive. He'd taken Katie to what he thought were pretty nice dining establishments, but this place was perfection at every turn. Even inquiring about the reservation made him feel like he'd be chased out for trespassing. At least he'd been smart enough to bring along his best suit and most conservative tie, but standing there in the foyer, he felt like an imposter.

"Mr. Noll?" the voice behind him speaking his name, spun Sam immediately, as he faced his dinner guest for the first time. The images he'd checked on his computer did the man great injustice; he seemed taller and younger in person, with only the slightest gray beginning to show on the sides of his jet black hair.

"Deputy Prime Minister. It's so good of you to meet me on such short notice and under unique circumstances. Thank you," Sam said with a quick bow.

Tran Anh Tai extended his hand, offering, "Please, let us start with the shedding of formalities; please do me the favor of calling me Tai. Titles, I have learned, are for men who still need to establish them." With their handshake, Sam began to feel much more at ease.

Following the maitre d' and Tai to their table, Sam took in the ornate decor and plush seating as the other guests enjoyed their wine and dinners. His initial consideration of the interior of the restaurant transcended elegant beauty, but the undeniable 'feel' of being aged to a comfortable perfection spoke volumes. Even the walls stood proudly from numerous decades in the making, whispering gentle reminders of every satisfied patron who had graced its welcome.

Seated, Sam stared down at additional silverware he hadn't been briefed on, but quickly grabbed the linen napkin and politely unfurled it onto his lap as though he elegantly dined on a regular basis. Tai was offered a wine list with the arrival of menus, giving Sam a 'second banana' tone from the maitre d'. Even though he'd rehearsed numerous vintage pairings with Katie over the years, yielding tonight's selection was a battle well worth avoiding.

Tai looked up from the list and replied, almost knowingly, "I am often lost in the myriad of choices when it comes to wines and typically let the wait staff select the proper pairing. Is there one, perhaps, you might lean towards? Something you are familiar with?"

Tai handed the wine book to him and the momentary feeling of relief switched to that of a pressure cooker. The intensity doubled with the arrival of the waiter as Sam speed-read the two pages of reds from an endless array of countries represented. When the waiter politely asked, "Is there something from the bar I might start your evening with, gentlemen?" Sam eyed an acquaintance he felt confident about.

"A bottle of Grateful Red Pinot Noir, please." He offered with confidence, handing the voluminous wine list back to the waiter.

Once the waiter departed, Tai stared at his guest, blinking once, before inquiring, "I have found the American Pinot Noirs to be some of the best varietal wines experienced, but I have not heard of this one. Is it named in honor of the band?"

Sam smiled his answer, following it with, "Yes, it comes from a winery in Oregon, and even though my girlfriend, Katie, doesn't appreciate the delicacies of Pinots, I find them ideal for several different types of entrees."

Tai grinned, admitting, "I saw them in concert when I was in school in California. Your unique selection brings back so many happy memories of that time. Thank you for that, even if it was subconsciously." Sam nodded his response as the two begin perusing the dinner menus.

The prices, Sam realized, were a bit high, but nowhere near what he'd expected them to be. The name of each item was curiously deceptive, and he momentarily wondered why every place didn't put pictures of their items, like Denny's. Culture and refinement sometimes dictated one must open one's horizons, so Sam selected the most challenging for his ignorant culinary articulation and closed the menu, placing it to the right, letting the waiter know he was 'ready or not.'

The meal itself, turned out to be pork. It was delicious in its rich gravy and sautéed vegetables, and happily slid down with every sip of wine, but it was just pork with a cool name. The introductory small-talk gave Sam some insight to Tai's position and responsibility and, at best, Sam figured he's something in the vicinity of the American version of the Secretary of Interior. Early on, Sam realized that if the two lived close, they no doubt would be friends.

After dinner and the decline of delectable dessert offerings, Tai suggested they take their wine to Dagligstven, the hotel bar. Sam raised a hand for the waiter, having not seen the bill arrive, only to have Tai wag a finger at him, saying, "You are here as my honored guest. I have looked forward to this meeting for some time and to allow you, or your newspaper, to pay for this evening's meal would be an insult to my invitation and gratitude for your acceptance. I arranged for the bill to be handled discreetly long before you arrived."

Sam lowered his hand and slowly placed his napkin onto the table, trying to come up with a proper thank you. When he looked up, the sly smile on Tai's face caused him to chuckle as he responded with, "I have a friend I work with who would easily bankrupt you with that type of generosity. I, on the other hand, seem to have an issue with accepting things I feel I haven't earned. I very much appreciate your kindness, and though it goes against my nature, I thank you for the wine, as well as tonight's meal. It was absolutely wonderful."

The change of interior decoration in comparison to the gourmet restaurant was subtle, other than the Edvard Munch prints displayed upon the walls and adjusted seating with high back chairs sitting across from the cushioned booths. The soft, unobtrusive music playing gave the room a relaxed ambiance, which remained steady and constant, venturing deeper into the back of the room. Sam loosened his tie, and Tai not only followed suit, but removed his altogether, stating, "Odd, how long this trend of wearing neckties has lasted; such an uncomfortably restricting accessory; completely useless!" stuffing his into his jacket pocket.

Sam laughed at the observation, nodding his agreement, adding while lifting his glass, "Here's to the next great accessory of confinement. May it bring discomfort and consternation to our children's children." Tai joined Sam's glass with his, laughing in response as they humorously cheered the future world of fashion.

The second bottle arrived without either requesting it. Sam shot Tai a look, but he deflected it with a lack of pretension. Swallowing the fact that he'd agreed to be Tai's guest wasn't going down any easier, but the consumption of half a bottle of wine did make things less decisive. Their second waiter for the evening poured their wine into fresh glasses while Tai began to open up about his current business. "Being an investigative reporter, I can only assume you know why I am here in Norway."

Sam's focus kicked in, immediately replying, "Alternative energy, but exactly which, I'm uncertain, as Statkraft is developing several methods, but I would wager my guess on Osmotic."

The slow, agreeable nod and smile from Tai gave Sam a small, inward feeling of vindication. The Deputy Prime Minister continued, "Statkraft confirmed the potential commercial use of

Osmotic Power through laboratory conditions and has begun plans for construction of the world's first osmotic power plant. Tomorrow, my staff members and I are driving down to the location. Would you care to join us?"

The invitation caught Sam by surprise. Meeting for dinner after the completion of his hectic work day was one thing, but intruding on the main purpose for his trip struck Sam as imposition. He politely responded to Tai with, "I appreciate your generous offer, but I certainly would never want to encumber what you hope to accomplish with this visit."

Tai leaned forward in his seat, asking Sam, "Would you not agree that it is important to know where one has walked to truly understand, from their perspective, what one does and why?"

Sam forced away the reflex thought of his mother and her influence before refocusing and answering, "Personal history has been, and probably always will be, a good reporter's best tool. Yes, I absolutely agree."

Tai held his wine glass, swirling it three or four times before replying, "Then, allow me to share some personal insight, as I believe it will help with what I have yet to relay concerning the man you seek." Sam sat back and let his new friend take the floor. Tai took a slow, methodical sip from his glass before setting it down and beginning, "My father was a proud, dignified man; an attorney of law. He very much loved my mother and all six of his children with everything within him. At the end of the Vietnam Conflict and the fall of Saigon, which is now called Ho Chi Minh City, he began to quietly make plans for all of us to escape the brutality of an imposing idealism which was early Communism and move our family away from all that we knew or understood.

"My oldest brother, the first born, bravely gave his life during the war. His loss left an enormous void I saw upon my father's face every day. He refused to allow anymore of his children to die by the hand of another individual's ambivalence. My father realized, under an oppressive regime, his children would not have the opportunity to pursue our individual or educational goals. He arranged for all of us, in the darkness of night, to take a boat to Malaysia, along with many others we did not know, but who wished to leave our home country. Once we were halfway, the owner of the boat demanded additional fees that many were unable to provide. My parents gave up all of their jewelry and many precious heirlooms. By the time we reached America, the only money we had was the equivalent of one hundred dollars my mother hid within her shoe."

Sam scoffed in disbelief, inquiring, "A hundred bucks? How did you all survive?"

Tai pressed his hands together atop the table, explaining, "To come to America, immigrants were required to have a committed sponsor; someone responsible to house and care for those arriving. While still in Malaysia, my father contacted a distant relative who lived in California, which is why we were not dispersed into New York, which was the norm."

Sam asked another clarifying question. "Even still, there were seven of you, yet you've become so successful. Was this relative well off?"

Tai smiled broadly, answering, "No, not by any means. My uncle was a simple, gracious man of sparing income, but carried the burden of a true heart of pure gold. What you must also understand is our culture and its inherent regard for family. When a family member falls or has need, we believe it is the responsibility of the rest of the family to not only pick him up, but take him in and continue to care for him until he achieves or surpasses the other member's level of well-being. This is not an uncommon practice, with many societies responding similarly, such as the Hispanics, who open their homes to another, pooling together their incomes, or the Jewish culture with their Kibbutz communes."

Leading Tai's narrative, Sam asked, "Okay, so your father found a job; then what?"

Tai smiled at the respectful memory, stating, "Three jobs, actually, and my mother worked two. The burden of our additional seven on our relative's household weighed heavily upon my father, so after only three months we were able to rent a small home and moved out on our own. Within the next year we were able to buy a house for ourselves."

Sam returned this information with only a gaped mouth as Tai responded, nodding agreement, before staring at the space between them. "I know. Over the years, I have often referenced this amazing feat and allowed it to be a driving force during some of my most difficult hurdles in life. Both of my parents worked day and night, six and seven days a week, so that all of their children could be afforded an education, a future, and not be hindered by the numerous roadblocks for so many refugees of that time. They paved the path toward our success, and all we were required to contend with was how far we desired to run."

Sam was left to amazement, replying, "You had incredible parents, Tai. I would have been honored to have met them."

Tai looked up with eyes brimming with his thoughts of his mother and father, answering, "Yes, Sam. They were the very best parents. They would have liked you very much, I think." They both sipped their wine and took a breath from such emotional talk. Tai was the first to slightly change the direction, proceeding with, "The theory of gaining knowledge does not apply only to humans." He nonchalantly waved a hand about the room. "Take this hotel, for example; did you know it has been in existence for more than a century?"

Sam looked around the bar, shrugging before replying, "No, I had no idea. It must have some incredible stories to tell."

Tai laughed softly at Sam's response before filling in, "Actually, the story is rather endearing, if I may?" Sam answered the offer by sitting forward, as Tai began. "Opened in 1900, the hotel struggled for most of its first decade to make a go of it. Caroline Bowan, the daughter of a poor family who had chosen not to immigrate to America, which was customary of the time, instead crossed the border from Sweden to Christiania, which is now known as Oslo.

She immediately immersed herself with employment and learned to become an excellent cook. She met, fell in love, and married a waiter by the name of Christian Hansen.

"Together in 1909, they decided to take over the lease of the hotel and cafe. Due to their hard work and firm conviction, they were able to purchase Hotel Continental and Theatercafeen three years later." Tai looked about the room with a respectful nod as he further shared, "The hotel stands as a monument to their love, steadfast dedication, and passion for creating something lasting." Sam silently looked about the room with a renewed appreciation for the enduring creation about him. Tai watched his guest's gaze of admiration, adding, "The hotel was expanded in 1932, then again in 1961, with the current operator representing the fourth generation to Caroline and Christian and carries on the same commitment of faithfulness."

Sam turned back to Tai, impressed with not just the history of the building, but with the entire family's unshakable respect and commitment of honoring their ancestor's vision. With a smile, Tai continued, "You see, walking into a building or room is not unlike passing someone on the street and saying 'Hello, how are you?' and truthfully not really caring to hear their response. We do this every day, you and I, as we become so wrapped up within our own affairs. I wish to learn all that I am able, in the short time I am given, to be meaningful and present in all things, and not to simply get by with a minimal effort of interest. I first learned of this from your El Padre many years ago, and it has carried me through many arduous times. Tomorrow, I wish for you to join me so that you might reciprocate and allow me to learn more about what draws you after the unknown so vehemently."

The following morning, after a restless night's sleep, Sam quietly sipped his coffee dreading one of his greatest fears; the sharing of himself. Learning first thing that morning, that there's no equivalent in Norway for a quick continental breakfast, as any break for nourishment was an opportunity in excess, Sam frowned in disgust at how much he 'participated' in complimenting the cook's breakfast. The breakfast, by the way, had turned out to be more of a buffet with unlimited platters of protein, starch, fruit, and pastries.

He checked his watch, left a tip he believed to be gracious, and waddled out the door to meet his ride. It'd been agreed that Tai would pick him up near his hotel and, over the hour and a half drive down to the future plant site in Tofte, they'd continue the interview. Only Sam knew the first bit of business would leave him grilled and charred.

The reflection that weighed upon his thoughts, shivering from the cold morning while he waited, fell to the previous evening's conversation with Tai merely mentioning a man's driving force having to do with his past. He knew Tai was leading to Sam's article and El Padre, but it's strange how his first thought went toward his mother. Somewhere, Sam considered, Freud was smiling over that one. The two black SUVs pulled up, saving Sam from any deeper analysis.

By mid-trip, Sam managed to gloss over a quick version of his upbringing, college years, and even how he'd lost his mother, but by the last half, Tai, like a skilled interviewer, caught every pause and hesitation in Sam's rendition, exploiting any and all of his tics, exposing the wound to open air.

When Sam began pausing between each question concerning the specifics of the loss of his mother, Tai sat back, letting Sam off the hook, saying simply, "You stated last evening you believed I had been blessed with incredible parents. It sounds as though we share this same fate, my friend." Sam silently looked back at Tai with a mixture of personal connection and appreciation for not pushing the subject any further. They both sat back, contemplating what each had learned from the other, with Sam feeling less enlightened, but no longer wondering what it was like to be a barbequed rib.

CHAPTER 28

The entourage awaiting their arrival was respectfully impressive. The already formed foundation to the main structure rested within view of where a large river flowed into the Skagerrak Strait. Sam was slow to exit the car, not wishing his new friend, Tai, to include him in the introductions as he mixed into a group of lower-level technicians wearing white coats and hard hats.

Listening from a distance, Sam observed the Norwegian host attempt to explain the basics of producing emissions-free electricity by mixing fresh water and sea water through an ion specific membrane. In the process of explanation, the host chose to give his narrative while walking backward. Only, each time the speaker stopped to turn and navigate the group's direction, Tai politely finished every sentence of the narration.

After thirty feet of shared dialog, the Norwegian host stopped, looked at Tai, and began to laugh, humorously inquiring of the group, "Is there anyone here who doesn't understand Pressure Retarded Osmosis or Salinity Gradient Power?" Sam refrained from raising his hand and uncomfortably laughed with the rest of the crowd, feeling as though he's back in high school and accidentally walked into advanced chemistry class.

The tour lasted three hours, but Sam felt certain everyone's watch stopped early on. He nodded comprehensively and offered appropriate 'hmms' and 'aahs' retaining the stagnant face of intelligence throughout the tour, but when the guide released the phrase, "And for our grand finale . . ." Sam just about grabbed the nearest lab coat for a short jig.

Back in the vehicles, Tai was on the phone with several of his colleagues back home for about forty-five minutes, going over what had been learned from the outing. Once finished relaying the day's events, Tai opened a bottle of champagne and filled two glasses, returning his attention to Sam, waiting patiently in the seat next to him. "So, what did you think of the prototype and their commercial utilization?"

Several quick jests blundered toward Sam's forethought, receiving one of the glasses, but after a cleansing breath, he answered honestly, "Tai, that informational tour was so far over my head, I think I severely lowered the IQ curve by at least eighty points."

Tai began laughing at the candid response, replying "I stole a glance from time to time and thought you carried yourself with a complete understanding of the informational tour; I was so impressed."

Sam shook his head, embarrassingly admitting, "Sorry to disappoint, but I was spending that time attempting to recall every Kevin Bacon movie."

More laughter erupted from the back seat as the driver began staring questioningly at the two through the rearview mirror. Once the laughing eased, Tai patted Sam's knee in an encouraging manner, followed by, "Oh Sam Noll, you have made me laugh like I did when I was back in school. I cannot remember laughing this hard for many years." Another short burst of chuckles, before he continued, "Tonight, I insist on dinner. It is the least I can do for putting you through such torment. Will you do me the honor and accept my offer? I promise to tell you that which we both are eager to speak of."

Sam nodded agreement, adding, "Yes, I accept, and I very much look forward to hearing what you know about El Padre.

But don't think today was a complete loss for me. It was intriguing to watch you at work. The way you speak so compassionately about the future of your country and its environment is moving. I can't think of ever listening to anyone talk with such pride and willingness to do absolutely whatever it takes to improve their homeland. It's admirable, yet humbling at the same time. You're uniquely authentic."

Tai smiled at the compliment, returning it with, "Well, thank you for your kind words. I hope to one day bring sustainability to last several lifetimes."

Sam saw the conviction within Tai's countenance, as well as through his words. Sam leaned in and asked what he considered a sensitive matter, "Tai, coming from a man who's witnessed first-hand the offerings of a Communist dictatorship and a Democratic nation, how would you describe the variance?"

Tai turned to his champagne glass for the answer, returning the question, asking, "We share many attributes, you and I. One of which is preparation, as we both see much profit from intensive research. During my studies of your writings, I have come to understand your affection for similes and metaphors, so I offer one in return. Ruling governments are not unlike preferred laundry service. Yours simply accepts a slightly more relaxed *comfort*, where ours opts for the application of a little more starch." Sam couldn't help but appreciate the analogy, tilting his glass toward Tai's uncomplicated explanation.

At dinner, the two sat comfortably in the bar, deciding to skip the elegant dining of the restaurant, opting for the lighter menu of appetizers and wine. This time, Tai took control of ordering which turned out to be nearly every appetizer on the menu, as well as a bottle of Duckhorn Merlot. "My wife and I visited this winery during my return visit to California six years ago. That trip through Napa has been one of my favorite experiences," he stated proudly. The wine, indeed, was pleasing as were nearly all of the appetizers, outside of the snails that Sam couldn't force himself to try.

The evening conversation remained light with Tai relaying how he came to the reasoning about renewable energies for his country. Sam, in exchange, shared his new understanding of Norway and its uniquely accommodating inhabitants as Tai took great pleasure in listening to Sam's educational outing, thanks to Jorgen Olafsen and his lovely bride, Aasa.

Sam noticed Tai push the final plate aside and took it as a signal he was prepared to speak about El Padre. Giving the Vietnamese representative the luxury of unlimited time and lack of pressure, allowed him to become more comfortable around Sam. The amount of time spent together gave Sam a deeper understanding of the man he came to interview, as well. Tai stared at the center of the table for a moment before asking reflectively, "Have you ever, on any occasion in your past, been faced with something so unexplainable, so unbelievable, that your mind simply pushes it aside as though the matter is rejected for complete lack of common sense?"

Sam followed the dignitary's train of thought, replying, "Never exactly to that extent. I've experienced some amazing occurrences and incredible feats of humanity, but with my investigative fortitude, I've made it a priority to make sense of the incomprehensible."

Tai nodded his understanding of Sam's varying perspective before moving forward. "In the business I have chosen, being able to recall names at will has never been my strength. When it comes to faces, I have yet to not recognize one that I have met. Even after much time has passed and many years have taken their toll, there seems to be enough of a consistency for acknowledgment.

"During the American and Vietnamese Conflict, I crossed paths with a man touring throughout Vietnam during this violent time. His features appeared to be Western, but his accent seemed slower and uniquely pronounced; more likely European. He assisted me with my injuries as I had been wounded during a short skirmish of gunfire with an American reconnaissance unit where my brother and four others had been killed. He not only spoke excellent Vietnamese, but even my dialect with perfection. He displayed uncharacteristic concern for my well-being and gave me food and water as he saw to my wounds. One of my injuries required he extract a bullet from deep within my leg, and though I lost consciousness, he remained with me as guardian until I awoke."

"What more can you tell me of this man who assisted you; anything about his physical appearance?" Sam asked at the pause.

Tai looked past him and considered the inquiry for a short moment before answering, "You already know about the scarred hand and penetrating blue eyes, but I have not heard anything mentioned about his necklace."

Sam looked up at Tai and smiled, asking, "No, but I'd certainly like to hear about it now."

Tai sipped his wine, then smirked a response of, "I only mention it because, when I saw this man that you seek for a second time in 2005, he not only appeared unchanged, but he was still wearing it."

Burning the midnight oil wasn't a new experience for Tom Walters. The drive still firmly ignited within him easily could keep that lamp aflame for years to come. Keeping his expectations at a satisfactory level for his staff and subordinates without applying too much pressure was easily his most daunting task. The realization that not everyone was willing to sacrifice their home life, three marriages, or any form of connection to their children for the momentary gratification of beating another paper to a big headline was something he seemed to slowly comprehend.

Before the cusp of the thought could be administered, a knock at his office door drew him out of the negative and hoping for a positive. "In!" he hollered without getting up. Ira slowly opened the door, giving his boss a look of either disgust or dread, neither of which Tom cared about. "Whataya got, Nevins?" Tom bellowed while resting his elbows on the desk, waiting for the small man's response.

Ira shuffled in with a rather large stack of papers, leaving Tom to wonder if he'd decided to take up writing a novel or two. "I've been working on the El Padre sightings, as requested, between the numerous phone calls from every schizophrenic in the Eastern United States. The incoming data is pouring in every day since we ran the sketch, but this is what I've compiled as of today, minus the previously mentioned unreliable ones." Ira whined as he laboriously placed the pile of papers onto Tom's desk for his perusal.

Ira started for the door, but Tom asked, "Is it in any sort of order? It looks like it's just been thrown into a folder."

Ira closed his eyes, clenched his jaw and took a deep breath before turning around, answering, "I've taken the liberty of filling out a chronological list which may be located on page one of the file. I cataloged each sighting using small, easy to read language, so that even a second grade child can grasp, so if you know one, perhaps he or she can assist you."

With a contented spin, Ira made his way for the exit, but Tom stopped him in his tracks, stating, "When you hear from your little Norwegian friend, and I know that you will, let him know I'm simply dying to speak with him." Without looking back, Ira continued his silent escape as the evening seemed to have found its completion on a sour note.

Sam pushed his wine aside and leaned onto the table in an effort to not miss any detail Tai was about to offer. In a controlled, yet excited offer, Sam suggested, "Please, go on."

Tai chuckled at his friend's exuberance, but complied, beginning with, "I had just learned of my opportunity for promotion to my present position that morning, so my spirits were quite high. It was March 11 of that year. I was on my way to meet my wife for lunch and share with her the wonderful news. I recall strolling down the block, completely distracted by the hopeful advancement. I began to turn left, but in my blissful state, lost which direction I intended, and when I spun around to get my bearings, I saw your El Padre not ten meters from where I stood."

Sam asked with eyes wide, "Did he see you? Did he say anything?"

Tai lowered his head just an inch or two, replying, "Yes and no. He looked directly at me, and I saw immediate recognition, but he simply, calmly, turned toward the opposite direction and stood there, looking toward the south."

Sam blinked at the plain answer, then pressed onward, "What part of Vietnam were you in?"

Tai replied immediately with, "Hanoi. I had just left from my meeting with the Prime Minister."

Sam scratched his head, returning to a nagging detail yet to be satisfied. "Okay, so you followed him, right? I mean, you must have been curious how after thirty-plus years he hadn't changed?"

Tai responded to Sam's questions uncomfortably, shifting and adjusting his napkin and silverware before finally answering, "To be quite honest, I became distracted from a loud sound coming from the street behind me. I turned to see what it was, and when I looked back toward El Padre, he was no longer there."

Sam remained sitting forward, not wanting to let Tai off the hook just yet, following with, "Gone? You turned for just a second, and he disappeared? Did you run after him or check the various buildings?"

Tai pursed his lips together, answering, "No, I did not."

Sam tilted his head in lieu of acceptance, asking further, "I mean, this wasn't some old school buddy we're talking about; this was a guy who may have saved your life during a brutal war and, by the way, hasn't aged a minute since you last saw him! You didn't chase the direction you last saw him?"

Tai stared at Sam with a pained look in his eyes of wanting to offer Sam something more concrete, but then turned away, answering, "I do not know how to explain what took place at that moment. It was as though . . ." Sam slipped back into his chair, alleviating the intimidation factor, allowing Tai to return to his steady, confident gaze to finish the sentence, "It was as though I forgot about him for that short span of time."

Sam's open flight had a small inconvenience on the back end. Due to the immediate need to be in Norway on short notice, his schedule for the flight home had to be best described as 'receptive and patient.' The evening with Tai had produced ten questions with every new revelation, but his curious mind hadn't so much as quivered from the challenge. The one, lone fact Sam held firmly to from the time spent with Tai was that no one in the world had come forward with two separate El Padre sightings; at least, to the best of his knowledge and not without dying soon after.

Not having any concrete availability for a flight home, Sam found himself stranded in Oslo for another day and a half. He smiled at the thought that there were certainly worse places to be marooned. He heard some guests talking about a stone pulpit well worth the long hike. Having brought his tennis shoes, a light jacket, and idle time on his hands, Sam decided a little exercise would be just what his over-fed body needed.

The comical sneer he received from the cook when he requested a small sack lunch for a hike actually placed a little fear in him, leaving Sam wondering if he'd need his suitcase for the 'light snack.'

Sitting in the airport bar the next day, Sam made further headway on his article, spreading his notes onto the bar table. He began with the beautifully manicured country of Norway and the people's amazing love for food, with the unparalleled ability for lack of weight gain. Contributing the Olafsen story as subplot, he smoothly transitioned into the background concerning Tai, after confirming that his new friend wouldn't experience any repercussions from his tightly controlled, socialist government.

On a hunch, Sam explored the timing of El Padre in Hanoi. To his horrified amazement, he uncovered an accidental train derailment that killed eleven passengers. The train had left the station in Hanoi on its way to Ho Chi Minh City approximately the time of Tai's sighting. Sam stopped his typing as a curious thought slipped in; had El Padre offered Tai a clue of why he was there with his turning toward the south? Why else would Tai recall which way El Padre faced, unless it was with intention?

Sam winced at the swerve from sensibility. The last thing Sam needed was his editor to start worrying his writer had turned into a conspiracy theorist, leaping toward any conclusion. Before he's called to the gate podium, Sam nearly had the first installment satisfactorily complete, or, at the very least, polished enough to impress any furious editor-in-chief.

CHAPTER 29

The rain pouring down onto the roof of the taxi plodded Sam's ungracious welcome home while the driver cursed in Farsi at the stagnant traffic. Sam smiled to himself, picking up only the words 'dysentery' and 'goat' from the emotional man in the front, but they're enough to get an idea of his displeasure. His week away from the city seemed so much longer than it appeared on his stamped visa. He missed his girlfriend and his dog, as well as their small, cluttered apartment, and the stalled progress only increased the final moments of anticipation.

He distracted his impatient thoughts with the nagging riddle that continued to be his boss. The two messages left on his phone while in Norway were angrier and more threatening than usual. The progress achieved in Norway, though primarily self-indulgent, wasn't exactly viewed as a priority with his editor. The new piece to the El Padre puzzle would spark a noticeable interest with Tom, but Sam feared his editor's patience was growing thinner with every edition. He decided to send his boss a pacifying text that he'd be in first thing the next morning, but the single word response of, 'FINE', continued Sam's growing apprehension.

The cab pulled up to the curb in front of his apartment building and he paid the driver, along with a healthy tip, saying in Farsi, "Thank you for the safe journey," surprising the driver with hearing his own language. Once inside his building, Sam was immediately confronted with a large sign on the single elevator door reading, *Elevator Out of Order.* The only thing missing to correctly complete the words on the sign was the word 'again,' as this had become a regular occurrence. The prospect of climbing the seven floors to get to his front door with his bulky luggage seemed to be one more obstacle in a day with already far too many, and sadly, it wasn't yet noon.

Sweating and frustrated, Sam finally entered his long awaited destination of walking into his apartment, celebrating the feat with a deep, satisfying breath of familiar air. After setting his bags aside in the entry, he noticed Katie's large travel bag opposite his own luggage. Not giving it much thought, he called out, "Honey, where are you?" When no response came, he ventured into the dimly lit living room to find Katie sitting quietly on the sofa as the familiar air immediately escaped his lungs, and he was faced with the suffocating density of trouble on the horizon.

Katie heard the key enter the lock and her body tensed from the awaited sound. Her voice caught in her throat, unable to respond to his beckoning. She had checked the clock on the wall every few minutes until this moment, yet it still left her feeling unprepared. Katie had turned out most of the lights to set the tone and watched Sam slowly enter the room, adjusting to the lack of lighting. She closed her eyes and held the final innocent moment for one breath before she turned the page of the next chapter in her life. When she opened them, she saw Sam staring down at his feet, unable to face her, lost in the inability to form an appropriate opening question. At last, he finally asked all the wrong ones.

"What's with the bag at the door? And where's Spalding?" Sam inquired without raising his chin.

Katie bolted from the sofa like a phoenix springing from the flames. She crossed the span from sofa to within eight inches of Sam's face with lightning speed, her slender body tightened and flexed from years of training, jazzercise, aerobics, and tie-BO. If her wish had been to harm him physically, Sam would already be a crumpled heap lying whimpering next to his newly arrived luggage. His innocent questions surprisingly triggered a host of emotions she didn't expect along with subjects he was unprepared to face.

Katie stood before him with a thousand angry words ready to slide off her tongue, but it was the hundred hours of therapy that allowed her to stand down her arsenal. She turned her back to Sam, reminding herself she wouldn't cry; not a tear. The absentee relationship had taken more than its share of wasted tissue. Unsure of where to begin, she turned to face the innocent, beautiful man she fell in love with three years ago. Her voice started out shaky, but she drew strength from the commitment to her decision, knowing where their future path would lead. "The bag at the door is mine. I'm moving out, Sam." she uttered with little emotion.

She watched for his reaction and wasn't sure if she's grateful or disappointed when his hazel eyes welled with tears. Mercilessly, Katie pressed forward with what she realized would be a very long, heartbreaking speech, "For a long time now, I've tried to express how I feel about where we're going in this relationship, but every time we come close to a step forward, you're gone for weeks at a time, and I'm left to wonder if this is what you really want."

She glared at Sam, who remained idle, still fixated on the floor by his feet, so she continued to fill the silent gap. "Since you started following this ghost, I've watched you change, and it hasn't been for the better; not for you, and not for us. Your life is being slowly drawn out of you because of all of this . . . death. You eat it, you breathe it; it's all you talk about, and it hangs between us like a suffocating vacuum." Her timely pause was again met with Sam's incapability to utter the slightest interjection. At this point, she'd even try to read something of an effort from him clearing his throat, yet he remained silent, which pained her deeper than if he were to become defensive and angry.

She inhaled a hard, incomplete breath knowing the worst had yet to escape her lips before resuming the painful onslaught. "There was a time, before this assignment came your way that I believed in us and a future for you and me, but then, like the sad song goes, you let a stranger come between us."

Finally, Sam looked up and into her eyes for a moment and she thought he might take up the argument, but the moment slipped by too quickly, once again returning to his downward gaze. Katie became angry again and channeled the resentment to finish all she intended to say regardless of any further interruption. "Unfortunately, it's someone I can't even blame or call by name. If it were another woman or playing video games, I'd have something to beat the crap out of. But an apparition you're convinced is real that will either drive you to utter disappointment or complete insanity, I can't stand by helplessly holding your hand and watch it play out. This is a road you're determined to follow; I'm just unable to continue being a passenger in the back seat."

Katie admired her strength thus far, but she bit her lower lip, knowing the subject she's about to enter would be the true test of emotional control. She had decided an entire minute ago she wouldn't let him avert eye contact for what she's about to say, because it would end things far too cruelly. No, she had to look into his eyes for him to know she did everything out of her love for him. It's her final message of what he meant to her, and hopefully, after time, her respect given to him at this moment would outlast the pain and loss.

Finally, Katie drew the last bit of her strength, saying, "Sam, please look at me." Instinctively, Sam raised his head in response, knowing she so infrequently asked and only made the request out of utmost importance. Katie took a delayed breath, awaiting the final knife with tears falling down his gentle face before her words began to slowly tumble. "It's Spalding. He . . . oh, Sam, I'm so sorry. He had a seizure in the middle of the night, and . . ."

Sam's face paled with immediate concern. Grabbing both of Katie's arms, he cut in, yelling, "When? Where is he, Katie?"

She broke free from his grasp and began to lose control, putting a hand to her mouth, answering, "He's gone, Sam. He died." Sam froze from the words. His hands remained raised where she left them from breaking away. He continued to stare, unfocused, at the place she'd just vacated, as the switch of emotion was slow to catch up to him.

Katie, now openly sobbing, tried to proceed, knowing Sam had to hear all of it. "Eight days ago, Spalding woke me up whining. I just thought he needed to go outside, but then, he laid at my feet and started growling. I was so scared; I didn't know what to do." Katie crossed the room to retrieve several tissues from a pastel box as she continued. "Then, he laid so still for about half a minute, before he started shaking and convulsing. Oh, Sam, I couldn't stop crying, and I kept saying his name over and over, and I tried to hold him, comfort him, but he just kept shaking. When he stopped, he wasn't breathing. I carried him down to a taxi and rushed to the emergency vet clinic, but . . . he was gone. There wasn't anything they could do."

Sam crossed his arms in slow motion and turned around to face Katie. In an accusatory manner, Sam demanded, "Why wasn't I called? Why in the hell didn't I get word?"

Katie immediately stepped back from the blame directed at her, but quickly realized Sam needed to go through all the emotions before the pain of losing Spalding flooded in. Knowing she had to be strong enough for both of them, she collected herself as best as she could, closed the space between them, and calmly took his hand, saying, "Let's sit down, can we please?" She led him to the sofa as Sam sat stiffly, unemotionally, next to her. He stared straight ahead, still attempting to get his mind around which loss to address first. Katie began to whisper softly next to him in a soothing, gentle voice, continuing to hold his hand and fill in only what he needed to know.

She'd never tell him how long their dog actually convulsed and shook, nor would she mention how many times she screamed for Sam to come and help her. Katie would keep all of the additionally painful details that haunted her sleep to herself. His dog was gone and she was leaving him. His emotional plate was stacked, and in this case, less simply had to be better.

What seemed like several hours of lying on the bed turned out to be only ninety minutes. Katie had left, but not after offering to stay one last night. Sam declined, knowing in her mind she was already gone and there was nothing left but the crying. One thought continued to reverberate in his head, something he read once, perhaps a poem; 'I can't remember when love entered, but I know just when it left . . .' The second stanza he was pretty sure ended with something that rhymed with 'left.' but it didn't matter, as the first stanza said enough.

He's on his third beer and was feeling all of them. Katie wrote down where Spalding was laid to rest; a small pet cemetery, ironically, not a half mile from where his mother was buried. Sam stared at the slip of paper on the nightstand for a full minute before deciding there's no time like the present to force the painful dagger all the way in. He stood on shaky legs, walked to the bathroom to wash his face and, without looking at it, stuffed the piece of paper deep into his pocket and headed out the door. With the rain finally dissipating, he figured the walk would do him good.

Katie had class, and if there ever was any doubt, looking at Spalding's graveside plaque would answer the subject, once and for all. She knew there was no way he could have emotionally dealt with making arrangements for Spalding; their bond had ventured far beyond pet and master the day he brought home the rambunctious little puppy. Sam knelt before the small stone and brushed away some newly cut grass that had inadvertently stuck within the engraved letters, as he read out loud, "Our Spalding. He was the best of both of us. You will, forever, be by our side."

Sam bent farther down to kiss the picture Katie had selected to be laminated next to the words on the headstone, one with Spalding responding to their request to look into the camera, with his head cocked. Sam began to kiss the picture as a surge of emotion caught in his throat, and he began to cry from a depth he didn't know was there. Whether the tears were for losing Spalding, Katie, or both, he wasn't sure. He didn't hold anything back and just let it all out in the hope of communicating his goodbyes to anyone who'd listen. Once the tears subsided, Sam stood and looked down one last time before saying, "Goodbye, my friend. You'll be missed, so very much."

Walking down the sidewalk, Sam snapped himself out of his daze of memories with Spalding, only to realize he's about half of a block from the cemetery where his mother was buried. Not since her death had he ventured anywhere close to this place, yet here he was, and he couldn't help but blame Fate. Sam dropped his head, muttering to himself, "Well, why not, as long as the blade is still sharp?" He walked up the sidewalk and entered the graveyard. Other than a few additions and the trees being larger, the area she had been laid to rest beside her parents pretty much looked as he remembered.

Within the last week or so, someone had visited the gravesite, as flowers that looked to be somewhat recent lay at the base of her gravestone. Katie, no doubt, Sam considered. She had gently pushed him to talk of his mother, with disappointing results. She obviously had chosen to go to the source, leaving Sam to wonder if she'd ever found her answers.

Standing over his mother's grave, Sam tried to focus on what, exactly, he wished to convey to the ground beneath his feet, but was unable to do so. The word closure, to Sam, seemed to be such a contradiction of terminology for something having to do with emotions. By definition, closure meant concluded, no longer open, or to bring to an end, though, nothing truly ceased when emotions were involved; they simply evolved from one state to another.

Sam had long given up trying to determine which of his 'feelings' seemed to rise to the top when he thought of his mother. He didn't blame himself for her death; it was the cancer that took her away. Nor had he felt any anger toward her for dying; that would be like cursing the clouds for dispensing rain. He simply failed to see any connection his mother's premature death had to do with his willful disregard for sustaining and maintaining a close relationship.

Without any further composed thought, consolatory expression, or even a word of prayer, Sam turned and walked away from his mother's gravesite, heading toward his empty apartment. It'd been a long, heart-wrenching day, only to be followed by a painfully exasperating morning once his editor got his hands around his neck; best to retire to the comfort of the last three beers of his six-pack. Tomorrow would do whatever tomorrow intended, so Sam thought, why not greet it with a slight hangover?

Sam entered his newspaper's building the next morning, crossed the lobby, and entered the elevator. Begrudgingly, he pressed the button for the thirteenth floor for the showdown in his boss's office. His head hung low, contemplating the recent string of disappointments, both romantically and as a pet owner. He felt the surge of the elevator rise and the building anticipation of facing his condescending editor with his emotions already wrung to shreds. He mulled over the preparation of having to listen to his editor's lack of respect for the proper use of pronouns, beginning his sentences with verbs as he morbidly played out the ensuing conversation in his mind.

His thoughts were interrupted as, mid-flight up, the elevator sounded its 'ding' and halted, opening the doors to none other than his editor. When Sam looked up and saw his boss, he dropped his head again in further defeat, thinking, Geez, Tom. I thought I'd have six more floors before having to bend and spread 'em!

Tom entered, tapping a brown folder against his leg, extending his six foot four inch frame to its maximum, towering over Sam in the corner of the elevator. Tom's expression failed to mask any of the pleasure he extracted from the tense moment of superiority, but he quickly ended the silent face-off. Leaning into a comfortable position against the back wall next to Sam, they both watched the doors slowly glide shut, erasing any escape for Sam. Tom didn't wait long before easing Sam off the plank, asking, "Calvin Hoffman from legal, ya know him?"

Sam, still paying homage to his shoes, paused briefly before grunting. "Uh-huh, yeah, I know Calvin." Sam stood straight, curious where the conversation was about to go, adding, "He used to work at Bingham, Collins, and Wertz before defecting to us."

Tom cut in, "Photo nut; big time. Says he's been into it since his college days. Likes to 'vaca' across the pond over there in Southeast Asia. China and Thailand, there about. Just got back two days ago. Guess he loves their countryside. Not sure. Don't care. So, there he is, traveling around with a guide, taking loads of pictures. Crosses into Burma one day and comes along a recent skirmish, say, an hour or two after the shooting stops. Many injuries, burning huts, lotsa blood spilled, and Calvin there just snappin' away like a tourist." Tom paused, removing an 8 X 10 photograph from the brown folder and looked at the picture before resuming his narration. "Takes one with a guy caring for the injured. Later, the guide mentions the man has been seen at many of the worst conflicts, always tending to the dying."

Sam jumped at the break with a qualifying guess. "A priest or some local healer?"

Tom turned to face Sam's eager, waiting expression, and without any emotion in his tone, stated, "Calvin asks the guide the same question, and the guide tells him matter-of-factly, 'No. That one is the Reader of the Bardos.' Pretty much, the Buddhist equivalent to our Grim Reaper."

The elevator dinged again opening the doors to their floor. Tom handed Sam the picture before exiting the elevator, leaving Sam to scour over the photo. Scanning the eight by ten, his eyes fell upon the top right corner, showing the side angle image of a man of about fifty years of age with dark, curly hair, kneeling beside a man on a makeshift cot with a bloody bandage on his head. The kneeling man was holding the injured man's hand with his left hand, pressing a wet cloth to his mouth with his right. Sam squinted from the poor lighting of the elevator, but couldn't see the right hand clearly enough.

The doors began to close as Sam jumped through in time, immediately searching for Tom's progress. Not seeing him, he bolted toward Tom's office across the floor, passing numerous staffers pouring their complete attention at whatever was before them, in the wake of their boss just passing through. Turning a corner, Sam sprinted down the hall, passing the conference room with its door wide open. He screeched to a stop to backtrack to the open room to find Tom sitting forward in a chair, leaning over the conference table.

Next to Tom stood Ira who simply nodded his greeting, while Sam leaned on the door jamb, attempting to catch his breath from the short chase. Tom continued looking at an enlargement of the photo Ira made available through a lens magnifier eyepiece, continuing his conversation with Sam. "Looked up this whole Bardo thing on the Internet. Turns out there are actually six bardos in the Tibetan belief for the death process during the period between the two planes of living and dying. The fourth bardo, the Chikai Bardo, evidently is the Transition Process from the Bardo Thodol." Tom looked up at Ira. "Did I get that right?" Ira nodded, yes.

Sam quickly cut in with, "The Tibetan *Book of the Dead.*"

Tom turned to Sam, who remained in the doorway, while Tom continued, "Not bad, and without a computer. Anyway, best as I can understand it, this Bardo Thodol is like some sort of *Dying for Dummies* instruction manual that's read to the passing soul, assisting in liberating itself from samsara, or the physical plane."

Sam continued once Tom finished. "In following the Buddhistic doctrines, reciting of the bardo text can last forty-nine days, but it's widely believed that forty-nine, or the number seven squared, is how long the soul spends in bardo. The reciting of the first bardo, the Kye Ne Bardo, allows the soul recognition of the Clear Light, offering it the chance to free itself from the samsara, the wheel of reincarnation, or what most Christian faiths would label as . . . Salvation."

Tom fell back into his chair, tossing the eyepiece onto the table and watched it roll onto the photograph. He rubbed his eyes and sighed heavily, then stared darkly at Sam. Sam slowly entered the room and fluidly took a chair at the table to Tom's left, sliding the picture and eyepiece in front of him. He paused, looking to Tom for approval before studying the evidence. Tom half smiled his consent before Sam hungrily studied the picture using the eyepiece. Under better lighting and the enhanced image, Sam could feel the building excitement of discovery until he saw it; through the eyepiece he could clearly see a large scar on the kneeling man's right hand.

Tom stretched, turning to Ira. "Ya know, Ira, when I first took over and heard how Sammy here was placed on this whole ridiculous endeavor of chasing ghosts around the world by my predecessor, I thought, Why not yank the kid? Better off exposing dirty politics! But then I thought let's see if he finds an audience interested in the theories he was slingin'. When circulation jumped four percent after his fifth column, and another nine after that incident in California, I knew we were on to something."

Ira deadpanned, "Dread sells."

Tom rose, chuckling, "Damn straight it does. Took all this Dr. Death crap with a proverbial grain of salt, but gotta admit . . ." Tom peered over Sam's shoulder at the picture. "He's lookin' more and more interesting in glossy color."

Sam looked up at Ira with a look of contempt for his lack of empathy toward his cause, but Ira just shrugged his response. Tom moved away from the table and headed for the door, calling out over his shoulder, "Sam, let's have a chat in my office."

Sam slowly got up, still fixated on the photographed image of the left side of a face he'd scoured the world for. Ira removed his glasses, saying before beginning to clean them, "You do realize chasing a ghost can only lead you to where it's been, right?" Sam studied his friend without responding and waited for him to continue while Ira held his glasses up to the ceiling lights to see if he missed any spots.

Finally, he looked at Sam, saying, "Don't get me wrong, it makes for interesting reading and frightful bedtime stories, but at some point . . ." He gestured toward the door leading to Tom's office with a nod. "Someone is going to want the man under the white sheet." Ira walked past Sam, picked up the photograph, and looked at it a moment before continuing. "My suggestion, which you no doubt are waiting for, is this; one must learn where the ghost intends to be if one is to meet said ghost." Ira placed the picture in Sam's hand and looked at him over his glasses before leaving Sam standing in the room alone.

From down the hall, he heard Tom yell, "Noll! You lost?" Sam snapped out of his musing and hurried out the door and down the hall.

Once Sam was comfortable, sitting on the sofa in Tom's office, he waited patiently as Tom made himself a drink at the bar. After dropping several ice cubes into his tumbler, Tom stopped, looked at the wall straight ahead of him, and asked over his shoulder, "You still a beer drinker, Sam?"

Sam jerked his head up, surprised by the unexpected question, and finally replied questioningly, "Yes?"

In response, Tom reached into the small refrigerator to his right, and with his right hand, retrieved an imported bottle of beer, slipped off the top with the bottle opener attached to the bar, and at the same time with his left, filled his own glass with his favorite brand of whiskey. When he approached the chair adjacent to Sam, he said, "My predecessor, may he hopefully rest in peace, was a scotch man, I hear. Never touch the stuff. Sissy's drink, if you ask me."

He extended Sam the beer, which he timidly received, and noticed Tom hesitate with his glass. Sam, not sure if Tom was waiting for someone to say, *To Malcolm!* froze in an uncomfortable, bent over position holding his beer before taking a leap of faith and met Tom's glass with his own drink. As the sound of the 'clink' broke the uncomfortable silence, Tom finally offered a simple, "Cheers."

Both sat down and took slow, thoughtful pulls from their respective poisons. Tom cleared his throat and started right in. "Listen, Sam. Nobody knows how badly you got screwed over by Malcolm more than I do. Losing grip of that whole ship terminal business to that Mexican at the *Times* had to hurt like a Mother. And then to not even get so much as a nod of appreciation for breaking it, well, it would be an understatement to say you didn't get a fair shake. Let's fast forward to the here and now, and focus on the story you *are* on. The public has seen more than their share of dirty politicians and want something else to fill their moments of boredom. They've grown weary of things to complain about or take a side on. They hunger to be pulled to the edge of their seat and wonder about something other than whether their taxes will increase and their stock portfolios dwindle."

Sam set down his beer and cut in defensively. "First of all, I've never cared about personal glory. My gratification has been, and always will be, in the offering of my own perspective of the factual clarification of the world we live in, regardless of its content."

Tom brushed aside Sam's speech as if it were a gnat, cutting back in with, "Fine, fine, fine. But the effect of how this Grim Reaper story has captured the yearning public and the direction it's taken us can't be what you expected, now, be honest? Hell, even I catch myself looking forward to reading the next article!" While Tom wet his throat with a long sip of his drink, Sam kept his grimace, as well as his silence, wondering where the heck Tom was going with this. Finally, Tom dropped the other shoe and unloaded his plans. "We're runnin' the pic tomorrow, naturally, with one of your thunderous soliloquies as only you can deliver. And, then you, my friend, are on the first plane for Burma to chase down your Incarnation."

Sam got up quickly. "I just walked in the door from Norway, Tom! I haven't even unpacked nor had time to decide whether to wash my whites or my darks first! Heck, we haven't even confirmed the photo is El Padre! What, do you want to send me to Burma with a photo in my hand, asking everyone I run into, 'hey, have you seen this guy'?"

Tom stood as well, yelling, "Yeah, it's called investigative journalism. Sometimes we're inconvenienced by timing, but we go when it happens to where it happens. If it was easy, everyone would do it. But this is what we do, Sam. We follow leads and track down the truth, *regardless of its content*! Calvin put together everything you need concerning the area, and I don't need to tell you that time is of the essence."

Sam stood defiantly in front of Tom with his hands on his hips, unable to put any further energy into the battle. He knew Tom was right, even before Sam opened his mouth and had his own words thrown back at him. The story was his and he knew there were responsibilities attached to that claim. Sam slowly sat, trying his best to save face in the presence of his boss and the 'tough love' speech was the last thing Sam needed to hear at that moment. He's tired from his trip and a little on edge from his break-up with Katie, not to mention he's emotionally drained. Even he was surprised by his own knee-jerk negative reaction to Tom's plan.

Opening up to Tom and filling him in on his welcome home would only show weakness, so that wasn't an option. Sam knew his boss placed about as much interest in his staff's personal lives as he did in his second wife's children, so he decided to switch gears on his boss with an attempt at some transference. He slowly reached forward, grasped his beer, and in a controlled deliverance, stated, "Well, let's talk about my raise, then."

Tom, still standing at this point, returned to his seated position as his expression changed from anger to shock and finally rested on serious. Sam watched him intently while Tom took a short, respectful sip from his drink before proceeding with, "So, that's what this is all about? Not feeling appreciated or compensated enough?"

Sam continued forcing a dry demeanor, tossing some of Tom's offensive game plan back at him, declaring, "Well, as you've mentioned, the story has a following from the 'yearning public,' and you've also stated that you, the editor of this respected circulation, anxiously look forward to each segment. I believe this places us at a fork in the road. When I was reporting on stories within our borders, I was content to do so. But now that this story has me, literally, on multiple continents in a span of three days, renegotiation is long overdue to be conversed."

Tom placed his hands on his knees and returned to a look of shock, saying loudly, "Conversed!"

Sam sarcastically quipped, "It means to discuss, exchange thoughts or ideas."

Tom raised his voice another octave with, "I know what the hell the word means, and I wasn't asking." Tom quickly slid forward and leaned into Sam so there was only two feet of air between them and nothing else before continuing sternly, "Okay, Sammy boy, here's the way this works, and it's a onetime deal; I'll present an offer to the owners on your behalf. It's gonna be a bump in the ten to twelve percent ballpark, depending on my mood at the time. Whether it's yes or no, you're on that plane tomorrow. I'm not gonna waste our first opportunity to nail this ghost just cuz you're forkin' around!"

Sam held his expression, though he only wanted to laugh uncontrollably. After a slow, long drink from his beer, Sam couldn't help himself before asking, "So, no bonus?"

Tom rose quicker than Sam expected he could, yelling, "Get the hell outta my office!" Sam nearly sprinted out the door, feeling, overall, that the meeting had gone pretty well.

Washed, folded, and repacked, Sam looked about his empty apartment trying to pretend something was missing or forgotten other than his dog and his girlfriend. Many professionals had lived through tougher losses than he and struggled to find some form of empty solace by casting themselves completely into their work.

This would be his mantra until the vacancies filled or became less painful. His flight for Burma was for seven o'clock the next evening. The time spent between now and then would be filled with setting up an English-speaking guide, making hotel reservations, and deciding whether he'd fly from locations or rent a small boat to travel up and down the Irrawaddy.

Time for research was a luxury he wasn't familiar with, but knowing his trip to Burma carried some dangerous pitfalls, cramming every bit of cultural knowledge could end up being his saving grace. Ira left him a message to swing by the office for what he called a 'care package' for his flight. Knowing his friend as well as he did, odds were against it being a fruit basket.

CHAPTER 30

Settled in his seat once the plane was in flight, Sam opened the thick, manila envelope from Ira. The bulk of updated data from the El Padre sightings was overwhelming, thanks in part to the artist sketch. With the seat empty next to him, Sam attempted to divide the 'book' into several sections before checking the envelope one more time and locating a three-page summary from Ira, explaining everything for him.

Sam chuckled over his friend's constant need to be an efficiency expert in all matters, to the degree of martyrdom. Ira's helpful summary sheet easily allowed Sam to quickly reference exactly what he needed in seconds rather than filtering through the entire volume. The overview was broken down chronologically, but Sam was just happy someone else had taken on the enormous task. He smiled at the thought of, but hey, that's what assistants were supposed to do! knowing Ira would definitely offer him one of his angry stares at the insult.

After three hours of too much reading, too much water and not enough exercise, Sam stood and slowly walked past the sleeping passengers toward the bathroom in the back of the plane. After washing his hands and splashing some water on his face, he offered his reflection an appreciative smile for Ira's dedicated, hard work on the collected data. He wondered how frustrated Ira had to have been, choosing whether to file the sightings chronologically, alphabetically, or by region. The last thought snapped Sam up straight, careening further down the train of thought. He quickly dried his hands and face, pushing open the door, eager to follow what he thought was a possible breakthrough.

Shuffling back and forth between the computer-generated information and the summary, Sam scribbled comparison notes. After forty-five minutes of furious referencing one section to another, Sam began to work the math. Albeit, never being saddled as much of a mathematician, rudimentary addition and subtraction managed to fall into his comfort zone.

Once his basic mathematical result was complete, he gleamed at it as if it were the Emerald Tablet of Hermes. At a glance, Sam thumbed through the mass of possible sightings, never believing he could follow-up on each and every one of them even with a team of thirty assistants. What had stuck with him from his quick glance was a repetition of particular sighting locations, particularly South America, Vietnam, and Israel.

If Ira had completed his work by region, anyone would have picked up on it, but since he'd chosen to go with chronological, it'd been missed. With sightings in the vicinity of Peru in 1923, '57 and '91, Israel in '40 and '74, and finally with Tai's help, Vietnam's addition of confirmed sightings in '71 and '05, the simplicity of the solution was elementary; El Padre was following a visitation cycle of thirty-three to thirty-four years.

The math never lied, Sam recalled someone stating. He'd never referenced the phrase before, because he avoided anything beyond simple subtraction and division, and that only had to do with his checkbook and love life. According to his calculations, El Padre would be due in Israel somewhere near the beginning of May to the end of August of that year. Sam could barely sit still from the revelation, double, then triple checking his figures until he couldn't be further convinced. Ira suggested to Sam that he needed to figure out how to place himself on the mystery man's path, but at the time, the thought was a mere pipe dream. The dream, though, was looking him dead-on, but the excitement turned bittersweet, realizing he had no one to share it with.

Sam forced his attention away from Katie and refocused on work, which was preparing for the job at hand, which was Burma, and possibly finding his target within its borders. But comparing the size of Israel to Burma was the same as comparing New Jersey to Texas, and he wasn't exactly excited to have to mess with Texas, figuratively, of course. Something, though, had drawn El Padre to the country also known as Myanmar, and until Sam figured it out, Israel could wait a few weeks.

When he picked up his notes at work, having the time to speak with Calvin from the legal department about his trip and itinerary produced several additional pages of 'do's and don'ts' for Sam to reference concerning the Republic of the Union of Myanmar. One of the first misunderstandings Sam needed to clear up was the confusion of the two names for the country. Calling the country Burma was the norm, but he'd also heard it named as Myanmar. Learning of the military coup in 1988 and their declaration of renaming the country back to its original name the very next year cleared up part of it.

The reason for so many other countries, including America, to remain using the name Burma disturbed Sam. Admitting his point of view coming off as simple or, perhaps a bit naïve, he figured whoever presently ran the country had every right to call it whatever they chose. He understood that the Burmese democracy movement hadn't accepted the present regime's legitimacy nor right to change the name. Even though the country was under serious pressure from the UN and many powerful nations advocating against numerous human rights violations, what the country called itself had little to do with exemplification.

Referencing his co-worker's notes, Sam went over preparation for his arrival at the airport and finding a proper hotel. He had stopped by the bank before departure for crisp, new twenty, fifty, and hundred dollar bills after learning few places in Myanmar accepted wrinkled or imperfect American currency. Calvin flew into China and crossed into Myanmar with a day pass, but had to have a guide and return to the same border crossing. That allowed him to happen into a restricted area in an extremely rare opportunity, as the northern Kachin region was a hotbed for insurgent fighting with tensions exceedingly high after government troops were deployed to the area.

Sam's planned arrival to Yangon was agreed to be the safest, most sensible point of beginning and seemed to be the preference of the government of Myanmar. But, hearing that journalists were being denied entry and, if they managed to get in, had been harassed by the abundance of military representation at the terminal was a big concern for him. Sam sat back in his seat, taking in a deep breath of recycled cabin air while a growing concept began to brew within him that perhaps this country was a bit more than he bargained for.

Rubbing his eyes, Sam let his head tilt back, closed his eyes and pushed aside preparation, registration, and trepidation, not to mention military junta opposition. Sleep would be the focus, for tomorrow was promised to no one. He just hoped he wouldn't have to deal with any cobras. He jokingly cursed Calvin under his breath for highlighting the existence and possible run-ins with the scary serpents in his notes. Sam had faith he could charm an angry monk, but he wouldn't have a chance against a cobra.

The voice of the pilot letting the passengers know they'd be landing in Yangon on schedule in about thirty minutes was Sam's gentle wake-up call. He stretched his arms and yawned, looking around at the other passengers in various modes of returning to semi-consciousness after such a long flight. He shifted back into business mode and started to mentally prepare for what Calvin could only best describe as an interrogating gauntlet of ridiculous bureaucracy.

Getting into Myanmar, it was explained, was difficult enough, which was why Calvin opted to enter via the Chinese walking border, but the truly daunting task was upon leaving the country.

That's when the redundancy boiled to extreme. Not having much choice in the matter, Sam decided he'd revel in the experience, making use of any oddities as material for side stories in his article. When he's told by Myanmar customs that he's forbidden to bring his laptop into the country, he gritted his teeth and allowed them to confiscate it until his departure.

The two official-looking terminal patrolmen stared at Sam as he glanced over their shoulder toward the three armed military officers who didn't hide their open animosity toward him. They continued watching his every move while he filled out the proper claim paperwork for his computer, hoping for a grimace or show of hostility toward their laws and fluctuating rules. Sam refused a smile or even hint toward one emotion or the other, signing away his livelihood with the hope and prayer he'd get it back.

The hotel Calvin suggested was located down the street from the Bogyoke Market, where he thought it best for Sam to 'slip a toe' into the unique Burmese culture. After checking in and taking a short power nap, Sam changed clothes for a stroll through the market and the humid Yangon atmosphere. Before he entered the open-aired market, he's welcomed by a row of several men and women offering food samplings on trays. Sam peered at each delicacy, taking in their individual aromas, not having a clue as to what they were or whether he's supposed to actually eat them.

A voice of British accent startled Sam from his inspection with, "The one that you keep coming back to is an excellent choice." Sam turned to face a good looking man in his mid-thirties with short, blond hair and muscular tone.

Looking back at the tray of food, Sam asked him, "But, what am I about to sample, though?"

Sam turned back to see a flicker of a smile from the man as he replied, "Its jengkol beans in coconut milk. The one next to it is called Mote-Lake-Pyar. That one is a rice-based local snack, embedded with a bean paste."

Sam extended his hand. "Thanks for the helpful save. It would have been tragic getting food poisoning my first day here. I'm Sam."

The Brit received the introduction with, "Good to meet you, Sam. I'm Robert; Robert Jordan. Are you just going in?"

Sam nodded apprehensively, replying, "Yes. I have it under good experience that visiting this market will instantaneously alter me into a native."

Robert laughed, responding, "I'm not so certain of that, but it'll no doubt be an experience you won't soon forget. May I join you? Perhaps I can sway you from any erroneous souvenir purchases."

Sam smiled broadly, answering, "That would be great. I could use the company and help!"

The display of primary colors was seemingly endless. From beautiful water-color paintings to rows above rows of vivid articles of clothing to numerous jewelry shops with so many varieties of sapphires, jade, and rubies that Liberace would have probably moved in. The two slowly made their way down the opaque tile floor, experiencing an inundation of amazing scents that nearly caused Sam to become lightheaded. With a slow, complete spin in place, Sam commented, "Never in my life have I experienced so many sensations in such a short span of time. This place is absolutely incredible. How many times have you been here?"

Robert picked up a jade turtle for closer inspection, coming back with, "The market or Burma?"

Sam replied, "Pick one."

Robert chuckled, returning the turtle to its proper home among the rest of the little bejeweled creations, considering the question before answering. "Let's see, I believe this makes my seventh trip to Burma."

Sam turned, surprised by the answer, asking, "Really? What brings you here so often? Is it the cooking?"

The Brit laughed, replying, "The food is certainly one of a kind; nothing like what you find at home. For me, it's the people. Even through despair, extreme violence, and less than acceptable living standards, there's a beauty and kindness I haven't witnessed anywhere else; and let me tell you, I've seen the world."

Sam watched Robert as he spoke and couldn't figure who he reminded him of. Something in his demeanor or the way he carried himself nagged for recognition, but he just wasn't able to make the connection. "So, tell me, what made you decide to come to Burma? Was Acapulco closed off for you Americans?" Robert inquired with a look that lacked an appropriate level of humor.

Sam smiled, lying, "Just wanted to take a vacation someplace uniquely amazing. Like I mentioned, a friend visited not too long ago and sold me on the idea."

The extended look Sam received after his answer caused him to wonder whether Robert believed him. Not accustomed to purposely deceiving someone else didn't sit well with Sam, but until he knew better, letting anyone know he's a reporter possibly might not bode well for him down the road. If Robert was experienced with the country, as he seemed to be, letting him know later shouldn't harm their new acquaintanceship. Sam moved on with, "I understand the government here considerably limits visits."

Robert sneered mischievously at the comment, saying, "Yes, only two week stays and no less than six months apart."

Sam could tell the Brit was holding something back, so he asked, "And you seem to find that funny for some reason?"

Robert stopped their progress and looked into Sam's face for an instant before saying nonchalantly, "This country's governmental control is firm, but it definitely has its limits." He turned to his left and beckoned for Sam to follow his lead, walking over to one of the many jewelry shops. He approached a large bowl of semi-precious, uncut stones. "If my hand is a typical country's government . . ." He shoved his hand into the bowl of stones and pulled it out tightly holding a fist of gems, "We'll say it would look like this. But Burma's government . . ." He opened his hand. Nearly all of the stones escaped through his fingers, leaving only a few in his palm. "struggles with their grasp of dominance."

The tiny female store operator walked up to them, appearing irritated with Robert's hand in her cookie jar and barked at him in Burmese. Robert cordially smiled at the clerk, releasing the few stones back into the fish bowl, answering politely, *"Ka mya, zey beh lout le?"* pointing to the gems in the bowl.

The clerk's expression immediately changed from agitated to courteous, responding, *"Tit-ya kyat."*

Robert made a sour face, responding, *"Zay-chi-ling-de"* and started to lead Sam away with a gentle touch to his elbow.

The shop clerk followed a few steps, calling after them, *"Kueh-na-seh kyat?"*

Once far enough away, Sam asked, "I understand Burmese is probably one of the most difficult languages to master. And after only seven visits here, you can speak the language?" Robert offered a short glance with no other response, so Sam let it go. "So, what was that about, anyway?"

Robert sneered nodding toward the shop clerk behind them, answering, "We were haggling. It's a national pastime here, like baseball for you Americans. The only problem is, in your country, when you pay to go to a game, the money doesn't go straight to the regime. Here, most of the seemingly public operated businesses are government run or, at the very least, shelling out a large portion of their income to fund the military junta."

Sam listened as they worked their way down the collection of small, overloaded stores. "While you're here, best to limit any purchases to small, off the beaten path places; the larger cities and towns definitely are under government control. And, when you meet the locals, don't encourage the begging by giving them money or candy; rather, try to learn some of their language and let them show you if they can speak yours. The children, especially, love to try to speak English."

Sam asked, "Why not give them candy? I thought every kid loves candy."

Robert stopped, looking around, and as he halfway extended both hands up, answered humorously, "Do you really think these people can afford a dentist? They can barely pay for food and clothes!" Sam, too, looked around him at the display of hardworking locals and imagined if three-quarters of his pay went to fund something he didn't want nor believed in. The outcome was hard for him to swallow.

Outside the market, Sam and Robert sat at an outdoor table of a small restaurant a block down from the busy stores and quietly watched the traffic of locals go by. They sipped Yenwejan with laphet thote, which Sam found to be, basically, Chinese tea. Robert watched Sam try his best to become accustomed to the flavor, while Sam broke the silence, saying, "I appreciate the pointers, Robert. Reading notes from another person who's been here isn't anything like the actual experience. Thanks." He clinked his tea cup against Robert's.

With a stretch of his arms, Robert replied, "No problem, ol' chap. I had a bloke do the same for me on my first visit; I guess you could call it a circle of life sort of thing!" Sam smiled his response, while they returned to their people watching. Robert took his turn at filling the gap with, "Say, I'm heading up-country tomorrow; would you care to join me?"

Sam sat up, thinking for a moment, before asking, "What time, because I'm supposed to meet with my potential guide for a game plan at around nine?"

The Brit scratched his head and replied, "I was going to head out early, but we could bugger off after your meet; say around ten?"

Sam nodded agreement, answering, "As long as it isn't any problem, I'm in! Where do you want to meet?"

Robert pointed toward the entrance to the market, saying, "Right over there. Maybe give you another try at the fish cakes and damson preserves!"

Sam laughed at the joke, replying, "I love the smell of fish cakes in the morning!"

CHAPTER 31

After the meeting with his guide and the decision they wouldn't be able to communicate with each other, a disgruntled Sam headed for the market to meet Robert. Standing at the entrance in his dungarees and long sleeve shirt, Robert waved his greeting when Sam came into view. Robert immediately noticed his new friend's irritable mood, asking, "What gives, ol' boy? Did your hotel double-book your room, leaving you with an unexpected roommate?"

Sam didn't mask his open contempt, responding, "No, I just wasted the last hour trying to explain that I need a guide who can understand English. But I didn't have an interpreter to explain it! I think the guy believes we're still on for tomorrow."

Robert laughed at his expense, stating, "I wouldn't worry too much. I'm sure he'll catch a drift after the third hour of waiting. Shall we shove off?"

Sam nodded with an ornery glance back toward the way he came, answering, "Yeah, sure, let's head out."

The small truck Robert drove seemed to be missing shocks as the road did more than rise up to greet them. A heavy mist engulfed the terrain, limiting Sam's first opportunity to survey the not-so-traveled parts of the country. Sam listened while Robert gave him a vague explanation of what he's doing in Burma, leaving Sam to only focus on the spaces between the limited information. There's something interesting and mysterious concerning Robert, but Sam felt safe enough to agree to travel to parts unknown with the man. He's courteous, respectful, and polite to a fault, but definitely had an underlying firmness about him. His presence in Burma had a serious purpose about it, regardless of how obscurely he wavered on the matter.

The first two villages Robert took him to, the general census from the people was best described as extremely guarded. Robert allowed Sam out of the truck for the first stop, but by the second, he simply said to Sam, "I'll just be a minute." Robert delivered a full backpack to someone from each village, shook hands, and departed.

"Are you hungry yet?" Robert half-yelled over the noise of the truck with both of the windows open.

Sam squinted through the fog, answering, "I could eat. Why, is there a Burger King coming up past that yak?"

Robert laughed, responding, "Better than that. But don't joke about the yak. He's the road marker for where to turn." With that comment, Robert jerked the wheel sharply, making an abrupt left turn down an overgrown dirt road Sam hadn't even noticed until it was almost too late. Sam stuck his head out of the window to make certain they missed the yak. Before he could bring his head back in, he got slapped in the face by several thin branches jutting over the narrow road. He blankly stared at his pilot as Robert informed him, "I wouldn't suggest doing that again!" Robert burst out laughing at him while Sam tried to keep a straight face, but finally gave in to the humor of the situation.

The surprise of their destination left Sam with his mouth gaped. Not even out of *National Geographic* could a village be characterized. From the small, smoky grass-roofed huts to the delicate stream trickling beyond, if Norman Rockwell had been Burmese, this was what he would have painted. Once parked, Robert leaned over the rear tire and thrashed around in the back of his truck while Sam exited the truck and slow-stepped around the vehicle taking in the little village from varied angles.

Eventually, Sam requested, "If I ask you how you came across this place, are you going to give me another load of useless non-information?"

Robert found what he's looking for from one of his backpacks and as he stuffed several items into his leg pockets, answered dryly, "Yes, most likely."

A Burmese boy near the age of five and missing his two front teeth sprinted toward them from one of the huts. In route, he yelled at the top of his voice, "Wobut! Wobut!"

Robert spun in time to scoop up the fast approaching little boy as Robert's face lit up in a way Sam had yet to see before. "Tom-Tom! How's my little soldier? And just look at who's lost his front teeth!" he said, easily lifting the boy up and over his head, spinning him as though he were as light as a cheerleader's baton. The child returned to earth giggling and beyond happy with Robert cradling him in his strong arms.

The boy noticed the new stranger for the first time, with his face becoming serious, asking Robert, pointing toward Sam, "Who dis?"

Robert eased the boy back onto his own feet, looking into Tom-Tom's face, saying slowly, patiently, "Who-is-this. Now, try it again."

Tom-Tom watched Robert's lips form the words and made a second effort, "Who-this."

Robert laughed out loud, giving in with, "Close enough. This," He turned the attention to Sam. "Is my friend, Sam. How do we greet people we haven't met before, Tom-Tom?"

The small boy considered the question for only a fraction of a moment before replying, "What shakin' bacon?"

Both men laughed vigorously as the Burmese boy smiled proudly. Sam recovered enough to say, "I see you've been applying a rudimentary foundation of the English language; well done!"

Robert held out an open hand and Tom-Tom slapped it as he uttered a trailing, "High-fie!"

Robert asked the boy something in Burmese, and after a short response from Tom-Tom, sprinted off for his hut.

Sam asked, "His name is Tom-Tom?"

Robert tilted his head, answering, "Not really. Burmese names are extremely unique, requiring the collective input by the monks and astrologists to include the day of the week they were born; even time of day is recorded into something called a Zar Tar. It's their form of a birth certificate. It's created from a stack of palm leaves smeared with residual oil and folded into, sort of, a package."

After buttoning his leg pockets, Robert proceeded. "Nicknames are much easier for non-locals to use, and the people tend to appreciate the affectionate nicknames almost as much as they revere their given names. My first time here, I met Tom-Tom when he was two. He wanted to show me everything, pointing here, pointing there. His given name started with a 'T,' meaning he was born on a Saturday, so, respecting their traditions, I came up with Tom-Tom. It's kind of stuck."

Tom-Tom returned with what appeared to be his parents on each side of him. Both smiled broadly, receiving Robert with affectionate hugs; a striking contrast to previous welcomes at the other villages.

Khin Au Wai and her husband Mar Tun Han warmly greeted Sam with handshakes and smiles while Robert appropriately handled introductions and interpretations for all. Khin, whom Robert called 'Winnie' and Mar, who went by 'Marty,' rattled off an excited dialog to Robert who then explained to Sam that lunch was ready and waiting for them.

"We had reservations?" Sam asked, while the five made their way to the small hut.

Robert looked back over his shoulder, replying, "They expected me sometime today, yes, but you'll find that once these people befriend you, you become welcome at any time."

The meal filled the angry void Sam had been ignoring for over an hour, and once his plate was empty, Winnie forced him to eat more. After everyone was finished eating, Robert arm wrestled with Tom-Tom in the corner, something that seemed to be a regular expectation with the visit. Once Tom-Tom was declared the victor, Robert gave Marty a quick glance, and the two moved to the doorway. "I'll just be a minute, Sam. Give a try with the reigning champion. He may best the both of us before we leave."

Sam watched after the two as they began to speak softly, heading away from the hut, toward Robert's truck. The seriousness of their subject matter added to Sam's growing suspicions of Robert's motives. A disrupting tap on Sam's arm called him out for a match of strength and dexterity as Tom-Tom stared down his new challenger with a gravity well beyond his five years. Sam smiled at the lad, pleading, "Now, you're going to go easy on me, right?" Tom-Tom just turned, unemotionally leading Sam to the small table and his eventual ultimate humiliation by the hand of a child.

The five walked the small village, introducing Sam to each family. Winnie and Tom-Tom kept Sam preoccupied with showing him every little nuance to their village, while Robert spoke to each of the men with the same solemn expression as with Marty. The news was one-sided, and Robert didn't appear to like what he was hearing.

On the way back to Yangon, Sam kept the conversation light, talking about the closeness of the families, as well as the unity of the entire village; then there was Tom-Tom. Sam could easily tell by how he spoke of the young Burmese child, that Robert was under the little boy's spell in a way only a deep, unconditional love could express. "His real name means, 'courage' or 'fearlessness,' and I believe his parents couldn't have chosen a more appropriate name for him," he gushed.

Sam chuckled at his friend, asking, "So, a better name than Tom-Tom?"

Robert shot a quick look and then a smile at Sam, responding, "Absolutely."

By evening they returned to Yangon, and the main street was still bustling with locals. Sam asked, nonchalantly, "Can I buy you a beer? It's the least I can do for such an astonishing day of meet and greet with the locals."

Robert cheerfully accepted the offer with, "Sounds like a perfect end to a good day. I know just the place!"

The small bar had only seven tables and a mismatched pairing of metal chairs. Sam took a long sip from his beer, beginning to adjust to its unique flavor, preparing for some distracting and inquisitive small talk before trying to squeeze some truth from his smooth new mate. After chatting about the weather, sports, and specific areas for sightseeing, Sam decided it's time to go deeper. "Robert, just tell me you're not supplying them bad drugs, and we can leave it at that," he offered in a convincing fashion.

Robert ceased his approach of beer to lips and lowered the bottle back to its place on the table. The pained look from Robert nearly forced Sam to scrap his inquest at its opening, knowing Robert would never be involved in anything that could harm the people he met today. "Seriously, Sam; you think I'm some sort of drug smuggler?"

Sam kept the charade for a bit longer, replying, "Let me tell you something about me, first, and maybe you'll forgive me just a bit." Sam leaned in and continued in a softer tone and slower cadence, "I'm a reporter. And I'm from New York, so basically I distrust everything I see or even wonder about. I don't take someone's kindness at face value, and when I see something that appears to be too good to be true, I typically go at it from a pessimistic point of view. I'm here looking for . . ."

Robert cut him off with, "A mysterious man named El Padre. Yes, I know who you are, Sam!"

The surprised look on Sam's face immediately turned the table on his plan of attack, slipping back into his chair, while Robert took the moment to return to his slow sip of contentment. Sam yielded a humbled scratch of the head, gingerly pressing on, "And just when exactly did you figure all of this out?"

Robert was next to lean in, informing Sam smugly, "When I took a slip and borrowed your passport at the market, ol' chap! Ran your info and, I must say, you've been quite busy as of late, haven't you?" Sam swallowed the comeback like plywood as Robert kept his thumb firmly on the pulse of the conversation's heartbeat. Sam crossed his arms with some attitude, and Robert fell back into his own chair, adding with a much lighter delivery, "Listen, ol' boy, if I didn't feel I could trust you, do you really think I would have taken you with me today?"

Sam thought about the question, realizing Robert must have deemed him safe early on to have spent as much time as he had with him. Sam, still a little hurt by the deception, shrugged his response. In the uncomfortable silence that followed, Sam started to feel guilt-ridden for going down his own path of deceit and immediately decided to remove all the walls. "Robert, I'm not here for any other reason but my story. Not knowing who you were made me feel as though I needed to protect the fact that I'm a reporter in a country that's severely unfriendly to people in my line of work. For that, I apologize."

Robert offered his turn at being unsure where things were going, but accepted the admission with a heavy nod, but then, Sam lowered the boom. "I'll feel greatly relieved if you can tell me, honestly, something about what *you* are doing here in Burma. I don't need every little detail; just in general. No, I never really thought you were dealing drugs, but know this, I can be trusted. If you've read anything remotely accurate about me, you know that I can be trusted." The slow, contemplative nod in any other circumstance would've made Sam feel victorious, but from Robert he felt he'd opened a possible huge can of worms, or cobras.

With the minutes and hours drifting by like the ease of a boat down a slow river current, Robert began the story with his youth as the son of a pastor. His checkered history in the military followed with an amazing story of conviction and reaffirmed faith that had been suppressed for decades. He joined the American Special Forces, and after ten years and multiple clandestine operations, was honorably discharged from the service. During one of his missions on the western border of Thailand, in the summer of '97, he was first introduced to the plight and ruthless violence in Burma. Moved by the oppressive handling and violent displacement of its people, Robert had little second thought in joining the good fight for the internally displaced people of Burma.

In a chance meeting, he met a like-minded, ex-military American and with Robert's faith-based background and determined need to help the democracy of Burma, he quickly joined the man's worthy cause. Without offering too many particulars or exact details, Robert shed some light on his main purpose being junta military reconnaissance concerning the armed influence and protection of an oil pipeline running through the Karen State. In a multitude of excruciatingly graphic examples, he gave Sam a hint of how the villages were being torched, women raped, and the way innocent people were being killed, and that didn't bode well with Robert at all.

Sam had listened to so many interviews in his life that they were a blur to his senses, but Robert's explanation and shocking story of what's really taking place in Burma made Sam sick to his stomach and angry enough to spit fire. Unable to verbalize anything appropriate, he simply looked about the small bar and the street beyond at the people he'd never view the same way ever again. His heart literally ached for them.

"Basically, my assignment is to observe and report how this dictatorship and attempt at ethnic cleansing is throttling this country and the locals; the true people of Burma. Our group delivers humanitarian relief, to include frontline medical treatment in war zones, provide the pro-democracy villages with leadership training, and educational and medical supplies. We assist with the Internally Displaced People by providing food, shelter, and clothing and create and sustain open lines of communication to document all incidents of forced labor or any other human rights violations. But most important, we pray for their freedom from hostile tyranny. Our hope is for our message to shine a big, bright spotlight on what's going on here."

Sam was hesitant to ask the next question, but felt he needed to know, "Does your group engage the enemy?"

Robert rubbed at his jaw from the stickiness of the inquiry, then leaned farther over the table, saying, "We're not to engage the enemy, but we won't back down when they come to kill our friends. The organization doesn't provide us with weapons, but they don't prevent us from arming ourselves."

Sam smirked at the disclaimer, adding, "For personal protection, of course."

Robert sat up straight, responding before taking a sip from his beer, "Naturally."

Sam considered the selflessness and danger in the work that Robert and his entire group of faithful humanitarians performed and couldn't help but compare it to his own life. What Sam had preoccupied his life and career with, he now considered as incredibly self-absorbed by comparison. Knowing that not everyone was cut from the cloth of heroes and martyrs, Sam mentally reflected over the twisting path behind him. He shivered from humiliation, repulsed from the squandered recognition of so much need around him. The moment of chastisement stirred the beginning of an idea, though, and before he allowed it to form completely into a full-fledged plan, he asked Robert, "So, where are we off to tomorrow?"

After two and a half beers, the semi-plan made enormous sense, as most things do in that particular mental state. Sam needed a guide, and Robert could use the help. They enjoyed each other's company well enough, and Sam figured trekking around the 'hot spots' would be his best avenue for running across El Padre. With Robert's resources and an already set-up channel of real-time information, Sam figured Robert was his best bet.

The brokered deal had some requests from Robert, and he forced Sam to swear to follow them. First, if any fighting broke out or a village they happened to be in was attacked, Sam was to grab as many of the children that he could and lead the people away from the oncoming affront as fast as he's able. Second, write about what's happening to the people of Burma. Get the word out in every way possible. The main reason Robert was agreeing to the pact was because Sam had sources Robert hoped to take advantage of.

The transaction was deemed fair and equitable for both parties and with a handshake, the deed was signed. Robert smiled mischievously at Sam once the bond was in the books. Sam froze in place, asking, "What's so funny?"

Robert continued smiling, answering amusingly, "Tomorrow we cross into Thailand to pick up more supplies."

Sam didn't get the joke, asking while he placed payment for the beverages onto the table, "So?"

Robert whispered softly, "That's the easy part. But sneaking *back* into Burma . . . now, that's the tricky part!"

CHAPTER 32

The fifty-pound backpack pushing Sam farther into the mud while he lay frozen in motion became his greatest foe. Watching and waiting for Robert to change from fist to an open-hand sign for Sam to proceed up to his position, Sam began to think the fist sign was alright for now. When the signal was eventually updated, Sam grunted from the extra weight he had to counter pushing with his arms and legs off the soaked ground. A sharp look back from Robert let Sam know he needed to be absolutely silent, for fear of the seven members of a junta border patrol camped a mere fifty meters away.

Sam had never understood the concept of face paint before the trip, considering it only for theatrical purpose when filming war movies or something someone like Arnold Schwarzenegger would wear. At the time, it was uncomfortable having another man apply make-up to his face, but seeing what the dark lines did for Robert in the dense jungle, Sam confirmed to himself its necessary measure.

Once safely beyond the border, moving deeper back into Burma's Karen State, Robert let a controlled level of conversation open up between them. "So, you train the ethnics in communications, to better prepare for possible attacks; what else do you provide?" Sam asked.

Robert remained focused, looking through his binoculars, studying the terrain ahead for the unexpected. Once satisfied, he turned his head, answering, "One of the most difficult pinnacles, after proving to each individual ethnic group that we can be trusted, is for them to work with each other. The strengthening of inter-ethnic unity has been one of our greatest allies. We're here for them, but need each of them to corroborate with each other for this to get off the ground."

Sam considered the answer a moment before further inquiring, "The first two villages we stopped at before Tom-Tom's; they seemed pretty hesitant, even with you."

Robert nodded his understanding of where Sam was going, satisfying his friend's curiosity with, "We're always building our contacts and connections; the more we gain, the greater our chances. The first two villages are fairly new to what we're offering and have yet to confirm their allegiance. Bringing an unfamiliar face along with me was a test of their direction. They didn't question who you were, so I believe much progress can be expected."

Sam stopped his advancement through the jungle as Robert turned, noticing his tail was no longer wagging behind him. Sam stared at Robert, waiting for either an explanation or apology, and when neither was offered, asked redundantly, "So, I was used and didn't even know it?"

Robert wiped his face with a handkerchief from his leg pocket and replied seriously, "When I first saw you at the market, I decided to approach you to be certain you weren't CIA, NSA, or another merc or hired mercenary. After two minutes, I confirmed you as harmless, but something didn't jibe about you, so that's when I 'borrowed' your passport. I'll admit, my curiosity got the better of me, bringing you in thus far, but it's worked out just fine, wouldn't you say?"

Sam contemplated the fifty pound addition strapped to his backside and the mud dripping from his front-side and stated sarcastically, "I feel like the Hunchback of Notre Dame after a mud bath, and if you consider I'm basically being used as a pack-mule carrying who-knows-what to who-knows-where, I'm rethinking our agreement." Robert took Sam's grievance with a slight shrug and a hand wave to keep moving.

Sam remained in place as the constant seriousness of Robert's personality finally broke his stubborn memory. The obvious comparison to his friend and inside connection to Senator Sinclair's demise, the mysterious Becklin, and how he carried himself with the same solemn confidence, was the same as Robert. Both being trained by the military and further educated in the art of espionage or whatever super-secret preparation handed down from unknown organizations etched a darkness about them that could never be understood by a mere civilian.

Sam firmly acknowledged the sacrificing price for the freedoms he enjoyed. Starting with the signing of the Declaration of Independence and every war thereafter, Sam never made light of those who fought and continued to fight so bravely for his life of comfort. He greeted every veteran of any branch of service with a heart-felt appreciation for doing what he, himself, was unable to do.

Now the realization of what each person truly sacrificed in the name of democracy came to complete fruition for Sam. Giving one's life for what he or she believed to be right and good was the ultimate sacrifice. Losing one's innocence and allowing the simplistic joys of life to be marred with the shadow of actually knowing where evil lived and what it's capable of had a tendency of drowning every good thing with black paint. The rest of us were left to simply accept them for what they were; the unsung heroes of our freedoms.

Sam moved off his direction of needless complaining and switched to a more productive line of conversation. "I couldn't help but notice when you spoke with Marty and the other men of the village the report wasn't favorable."

Robert took Sam's deduction without any look of surprise, replying, "I guess I need to remind myself that I'm dealing with an investigative reporter who doesn't miss much. Well, other than being bloody well pick-pocketed, that is!"

Sam scooped up a handful of wet leaves, balled them up, and threw it at Robert. The shot nailed the back of his head, but Robert didn't stop or even acknowledge the good aim. After a few more meters of cadenced hiking, Robert continued on the subject. "You'd be correct in your assumption, ol' chap. Things look grim. The army is moving south as they pursue their scorched earth policy in our region. I fear it won't be long before they make their way to the villages we visited."

The disappointing news hung between them with only the sounds of their footsteps and noises from the deep forest to comfort them. Sam felt the raw anger of injustice and wondered what Robert must be thinking, being so close to the people in harm's way. A firm believer in everyone else needing to release bottled emotions for the good of their sanity, Sam engaged an edgy line of inquiry. "So, what are we going to do about it?"

Robert stopped and turned around, speaking a bit emotionally. "There's bloody little we *can* do that we haven't already done. It's like preparing for a tidal wave. You gather what you care most about and run like hell in the opposite direction. There's nothing you can say or do to stop the wave. You can't talk to it and try to reason with it, because it will only blow right through you." Robert caught himself and took a step back from Sam as the forest sounds returned without the beat of the footsteps.

Sam let the moment go without interruption, giving Robert a second to regain his composure, even though Sam silently shouldered the blame for inciting him. Robert eventually gave Sam a look of boyish guilt as Sam asked jokingly, "Now didn't that feel good? You should let off some steam more often, Robert. You're way too polite when you get angry, though. They would eat you alive back in New York! Better stick to the jungles and mountains!"

Robert became serious once again, spinning around and returning to bear the lead. "Let's make double-time so we can get back to the truck before nightfall," Robert stated, speeding up.

Sam joined the increased pace as the burn in his legs and shoulders beckoned for a Jacuzzi tub and bottles of ibuprofen.

The wind and the sky had been changing for several days as the rainy season for Burma quietly slipped in. The soft hum of the largest choir of needed attention refused El Padre sleep while he made his way from township to rice field to village, offering his words of peace and comfort in a country that discriminated both. He led with his gift while his exhausted body followed, allowing his unique ability to guide his mind to where it required direct focus.

For three days, he'd traveled south down the Irrawaddy on a borrowed narrow, motorized canoe called a launghle, until he reached the heart of his calling. The spectacular views of various stupas and temples as he entered the lowlands were worthy of further inspection, but his responsibility was becoming immediate.

El Padre, at last, sat for a time, taking a working break. He faced a small, older Burmese woman sitting in front of a bamboo hut held together with dried grass as she continued to chew with the blood-red juices from the Piper betel leaf dripping from the corner of her mouth. In her language, El Padre asked if she could spare some of her betel, which she wordlessly handed to him. The two sat quietly enjoying the flavor and a moment of shared fellowship.

The woman, who had avoided eye contact until now, looked into the face of the man and stated casually in her heavy northern dialect, "A storm is coming."

El Padre responded with a slow look upward before once again returning to face her, answering, "Yes, I believe it is."

"The weather forecast doesn't look good, Sam. They say heavy rain is expected," Robert called out over the voice on the radio, competing with wind as well as the noise from the truck.

Sam asked loudly, "Do you want to scrap the plan and try for the village tomorrow?"

Considering the dilemma for only a breath, Robert responded, "Let's take a run at it. You won't mind a little nasty weather, will you?"

Sam chuckled at the challenge, answering his friend, "Just as long as I don't have to haul anymore of your voodoo jungle medicine or witchcraft literature for the entire village of children to digest."

The surprise explosion tossed both driver and passenger from the vehicle, effectively flipping the truck off the road. The detonation, from either a mortar round or rocket-propelled grenade, landed a mere fifteen meters away on Sam's side of the truck. If it hadn't hit a slope and impacted out, both Sam and Robert would have likely been killed. Two of the four backpacks of educational supplies were shredded, but the rest of the items seemed to be still intact.

Without prompting, Sam followed Robert to grab the remaining bags and both got off the road to the safety of the deep jungle. "Was that intentional?" Sam asked breathlessly, while inspecting two new minor injuries on his arm and struggling to control the adrenaline.

Robert was already in reactionary mode, scanning toward the direction he figured to be the source with his binoculars. "Not sure exactly, but let's just wait a moment and see who pops up." It didn't take long before a worn-out jeep pulled up to the wreckage and three Burmese men in military uniforms inspected the truck and discarded backpacks. Robert strained his ears as the men discussed the small victory and stared off into the dense vegetation, with a hesitation of knowing better than to enter it with the bad weather approaching and without another thirty soldiers and a tank. Once satisfied with the day's progress, they jumped back into their jeep and headed back the way they came, which Sam was convinced to be just slightly north of Hell.

"Looks like we're walking again, ol' chap," Robert straight lined, getting up from his crouched position.

Sam shook his head at him, replying, "Well, since we're lucky to still be breathing, I'm going to consider walking a luxury!"

Robert turned around and gently slugged Sam in the shoulder, followed by, "Now, there you go, Sam, old boy. You're sounding more and more like one of the ethnics with every near-death experience! Around here we call that perspective!"

Sam promptly quipped, "I call it trial by fire . . . and explosion; a really, really big explosion."

On their eight mile jaunt to their first stop, Sam and Robert joked and opened up with each other in a way only people who had skirted recent death could do. Sam pressed his friend, "No, seriously. What's the best place you've ever eaten at, I'm dying to know?" Robert gave him a disconcerting stare at his poor choice of wording. Sam caught his error, correcting it accordingly with, "Okay, *nearly* dying."

They both laughed at the modification while Robert thought hard for an answer. "This won't impress you in any way, but it's simply being the guest of any number of the locals from the countless villages here in Burma."

Sam gave him a shocked look, saying, "Really? After traveling the world in the military, sampling so many foreign cuisines, you'd prefer Mohinga in fish gravy?"

Robert stared off in an attempt to accurately explain his selection. "It isn't the particular meal they serve or even the different styles they use to create them. It's the affection and acceptance they offer freely, once they know you're their true ally. It opens a door to their hearts, allowing you to feel . . . as one. Their strife becomes your strife; your pain is their pain. It's a collective consciousness I haven't experienced any place else. In a strange way, I believe these are my people."

Sam smiled at Robert's honesty and humbled answer, before submitting his answer, "Well, for me, it has to be Bob's Burger Barn at the corner of Third and Quinn. They have this monster burger you have to stretch your mouth wide-open and it still barely gets in!" With a dismissive wave of the hand, Robert shook his head at Sam's humor, as Sam added, "With all of this talk about food, I sure hope 'your people' have something cooking when we finally arrive; and a fire. This weather is starting to get worse."

The smoke could be seen rising above the jungle from about a mile from the village and Sam could tell immediately by the intensity and speed in which Robert left him in his tracks; it was Tom-Tom's village.

The smoldering cinders of what was once a collection of huts, forming a community, lay in ruins, with only the gentle sound of the creek beyond. Six or seven bodies lay strewn carelessly about the flat, burned ground as Sam arrived to see Robert inspecting the last of the victims.

"Gunshot, point blank," he said angrily and through tight lips as Sam watched him walk in a circle, appearing unsure which direction to follow.

"Is it . . ." Sam couldn't even let himself finish the painful question, not knowing how his friend would react.

Robert turned to Sam; the anger welled up to a boil. "No," he said, "it's five of the men from the village and one of the women, but it isn't Marty or Winnie."

Almost as a prompted release of pressure, Tom-Tom emerged from the jungle running toward the waiting open arms of Robert. He hugged the little boy for an exaggerated duration as the child cried within his arms during a brief emotional question and answer. Robert looked up at Sam, saying, "They took Winnie. The bastards took his mother."

Marty came out of the forest with two other men and one of the women from the village. Robert moved toward him to console his friend as Marty slumped slightly, fighting back the tears. He looked up and tried to offer Robert a forced smile, but it's broken off as Marty looked over Sam's shoulder and pointed beyond him, shouting desperately, "*Ho beht. Ma ho bu!*" Sam spun quickly to see a lone junta soldier lowering his rifle directly at Robert. The first shot dropped Robert to the ground, hitting his right leg.

The weapon was then turned directly at Sam.

Not having time to react in any other manner, Sam grabbed Tom-Tom, pulling the boy into him tightly while protectively turning his back to the soldier. His last vision before clenching his eyes shut was of Robert scratching and clawing the scorched ground, frantically trying to reach for his backpack.

Time slowed as Sam waited for the bullet to strike him in the back. He could feel the young boy's heavy breathing and the hastened pace of his heartbeat against his legs. The sound of rifle fire, followed by a shotgun blast, forced Sam's eyes to tighten even harder. After five seconds of silence and no bullet to the back, he opened his eyes to watch Robert, holding a sawed-off shotgun from a prone position, being helped off the ground by Marty; then, a young, slender Burmese woman came out of the jungle holding a high-powered rifle tightly within her grasp.

Sam turned around, still protecting Tom-Tom, and saw the soldier lying motionless on his back with blood escaping from the center of his head. The serious young woman walked past Sam with a surprisingly affectionate caress to the little boy's back. She stood over the body, confirming it wouldn't attempt to harm anyone further, ever again. She spoke a few words in Burmese in a low, sultry tone to Robert, who wisely nodded his agreement to the woman with the sniper rifle still under her arm.

Once she dragged the corpse into the jungle and out of ear shot, Sam asked, "What did she say?" finally letting go of Tom-Tom as he ran to his father.

Robert watched until she disappeared into the foliage, answering, "She thinks the soldier was ordered to remain here as a sentry, in case anyone returned for the dead."

Sam looked back toward the place she entered the jungle and further inquired, "What's she going to do with the body?"

Turning to limp his way to speak with Marty, Robert answered over his shoulder, "You really don't want to know."

A short moment later, Sam jumped in place at an explosion from the direction the woman took the soldier. Before Sam could ask another question, she calmly walked out the way she entered, minus the extra hundred and twenty pounds of dead weight. Sam became a spectator, a bit shell-shocked from the over-abundance of recent stimulation watching Robert attempt to tie a tourniquet around his thigh with the insistent help of Tom-Tom.

Robert looked up and recognized Sam's blank stare, calling for him to hurry and grab their things and follow the group away from what had been the village. Snapping him out of the delayed state, Sam quickly slung the two bags onto his left shoulder and immediately felt a sharp pain, dropping the backpacks to the ground. The blood soaking through the top of his sleeve wasn't much, but when he peeked under his shirt to see the source, he noticed two small entry wounds in his left shoulder. Each was about the size of individual buckshot from a discharged shotgun. Sam looked up to the sky and offered a thankful prayer for near misses.

CHAPTER 33

At one of the organization's training camps, in the Southern Karen State, Robert sat up on a makeshift gurney, watching, as one of the 'medics' tried to remove the bullet from his thigh. Sam laid on his side facing Robert, but his gurney was only a table top, and his 'surgeon' was the quiet Burmese sniper lady called Lilly. Robert explained on the way to the safety of the camp that her Burmese name translated to 'delicate flower,' so the leader of their group had nicknamed her 'Lilly.'

The increasing winds from the storm shook the bamboo walls while she gently dressed Sam's two small wounds with matching 'Sponge Bob' adhesive bandages. He asked Robert, "Do we try to get Winnie back?"

Robert clenched his teeth from both the pain of the wound and the medium size tweezers being stuck inside him without a painkiller. Robert shook his head no, taking several short, quick breaths. With her work done, Lilly handed Sam his shirt and walked out of the multipurpose room that appeared to serve as chapel, training room, and mess hall, as well as an operating room. Sam peeked after her, asking Robert, "How do I say, thank you in Burmese? It's the least I can do for her saving my life, back there."

Robert replied, "*Kyeizu tin ba de*, but it isn't necessary. She probably already forgot about it. She's a tough gal, that one. Her entire family was either killed or raped, then murdered when she was only sixteen.

She managed to get away and hide in the jungle for two years before being taken in by a village up north. She's been with us for six years; trains most of our ethnics into great soldiers, too."

Sam looked back toward the way she left with a gained respect from such an enormous cost. Turning back to Robert, as the worker cleaned the leg wound, now free of shrapnel, Sam asked again, "I'd like to know what she did with the body."

Robert looked at the young man finishing up on his leg. He returned Robert's stare and gave him a shrug, so Robert turned back to Sam, stating, "When we're cornered and have no other line of defense but to engage the enemy for the safety of whom we fight for or for the protection of ourselves, we do what we can to . . . cover our tracks, so to speak."

Sam tried to put it together, concluding with, "So, the explosion was . . ."

Robert completed the explanation with, "The poor bloke, slipping on his own feces and unfortunately landing head-first onto one of their landmines."

Sam flinched from the mental image, replying, "Ouch! What a way to go, if you can excuse the pun!"

Robert sneered, adding, "I believe the appropriate term is classic irony"

Within the next two hours, the storm somehow found a way to accelerate. Several trees began to fall, and a quickly thrown-together contingency plan was adopted and ratified. The only news source made available to the group was the state-owned weather station, but one of the team members had recently been in contact with one of the group's advocates near the Ayeyarwady Region and reported cyclone conditions with severe loss already. Unsure of the direction the storm would take or whether it might weaken as it moved inland, the decision to move everyone south seemed like a gamble, but with no one offering up a more logical plan, it's implemented with expediency.

Sam was placed in charge of being accountable for the seventeen children and keeping them toward the front of the mass exodus southward. Tom-Tom was recruited by Sam to assist in child verification, but mostly to keep the young lad from worrying about his mother. Sam understood there's nothing that could be done for Winnie, and it's an impossibly painful fact to bear, but in a world unlike he'd ever experienced, his learning curve was catching up quicker than he cared. Tears would be spared for Marty's beloved wife and Tom-Tom's mother, but now the immediate concern was to ensure each person in his charge didn't follow her unfortunate fate.

The worst of the fierce storm had moved east; so many lost, so many swept away. El Padre closed his eyes and recalled, only hours prior, the lush, beautiful hills with its trees, rice crops ready to yield, and the happy people of the Labutta Township. He opened his eyes to the wake of destruction in every direction, the damage so angrily invoked, and the death that had been left behind. Bodies laid in various positions, as sobbing, unbelieving survivors desperately drudged among the dead, looking for traces of life left behind, but sadly, their search was in vain.

El Padre inhaled a deep, sorrowful breath and swallowed hard with the unbearable task ahead. The storm had passed, this was true, but greater loss was weighing heavily upon the days ahead, with the second wave of casualties from disease, lack of medical attention, and governmental resistance of any form from international relief efforts. So many people who could be saved, yet the selfishness of an inhumane, volatile government insignificantly opted to sign the death warrant of hundreds of thousands of Burmese.

Not in over sixty years had El Padre witnessed such a grand scale of casual indifference for human life. Judgment for such atrocities, though, could not be his focal point. His attention had to be for the patiently waiting, for they spoke to him a language only he could translate, only he was left to decipher. It's the summoning for completion, for the words that allowed them to lay their head for the final time and leave all they knew behind with contentment. El Padre lifted his face toward the heavens and nodded with the heavy acknowledgment of responsibility. With the gravity and enormous depth of the circumstances in front of him, he gathered his faculties and began to see to the dying in the way he'd been allowed to perform for more years than any other.

That evening, after all who traveled south were temporarily set up with food, clean clothing, and beds, the band of humanitarians gathered to figure out the next step. Robert invited Sam to join them, not only because of his helpful and much needed assistance, but for his creative thinking and level headedness during intense situations. The small group happily accepted the addition, agreeing one more perspective would be appreciated.

The first subject to be voiced was the concern for moving deeper into such volatile terrain. With several military encampments previously scouted through southern Karen state, the likelihood of running into junta soldiers increased tenfold. The issue of minimal supplies and not having enough food or water to last more than two days was mentioned. Also, the suggestion of crossing into Thailand and leading the group to the safety of the neighboring country was promoted. Sam remained silent, as the decision of responsibility for many lives fell clearly above his judgment level.

Finally, Lilly spoke, and her foreign words came out slow and calm while the rest remained solemnly attentive. Sam didn't understand what she proposed, but by the appearance of the others, her advice was highly regarded. Once complete, she turned and walked away toward the resting villagers. The rest of the group continued to quietly absorb the plan while Sam tried his best not to interrupt their mulling. Robert was first to look up, to see Sam waiting for an explanation.

With a heavy sigh, Robert interpreted, "Lilly says we move them into Thailand. There's a refugee camp about thirty clicks due east from this location. She says they'll be willing to take on the additional displaced villagers." Sam recognized that there's something else Robert wasn't relaying, but rather than ask, he continued staring at him patiently. Robert kicked at the ground before finally adding, "She also strongly suggests I lead them the rest of the way, due to the fact that I'll have to head home for the next six months for rehab."

Sam looked down at Robert's leg, tilting his head from nearly forgetting his friend had been shot. The emptiness from no one wanting to say anything to acknowledge the unsatisfactory situation was how the conversation and meeting ended, disbanding to their various duties. Sam followed Robert as he walked to the edge of the clearing, where he stopped and stared into the density of the jungle. He waited, letting Robert get his mind around the fact that he must temporarily leave the people he loved and a mission he's willing to die for.

Sam eventually cleared his throat and tried to find a silver lining. "I'm certain with your determination, you'll finish recovering in half the time, Robert. You'll return quickly to lead them back."

Robert spun around and showed his angry side, seething as he spit out, "You don't get it, yank. They can't come back. I'm leading them out of this hell-hole that they call home; the country they were born in and the only place they know. We're doing exactly what the bloody government wants and there isn't a damned thing I can do otherwise."

Sam took a step back, partly from not realizing the true fate of the villagers and also to allow enough separation, just in case Robert decided to fling him and his ignorance into the forest. Robert inhaled a lung-full of angst before calming his emotions enough to explain to Sam in a much more controlled tone, "Lilly's decision is right; it's just not one any of us, especially the villagers, want to do. It's the last option, chap. And the disappointment of my being benched," Robert's shoulders slumped and he looked down at the ground between them before finishing with, "just feels like defeat."

Uncertain of what to say, Sam struggled with the desire to remove the feeling of failure he knew his friend was dealing with. Without over-analyzing how it might appear, Sam closed the gap between them and placed a consoling hand on his friend's shoulder. Sometimes, Sam considered, words could only say or do so much. Robert was smart enough to know them already, anyway. What he needed, Sam believed, wasn't someone to tell him they felt his pain or empathize with his situation. What Robert needed was for someone, anyone, to *show* him they're there with support, no matter what that meant. The two stood quietly looking into the perilous jungle together, sharing a moment of understanding without any need for words.

With every bit of spare food and water collected for their journey into Thailand, Robert and Lilly quietly discussed some final arrangements before the group began their emotional trek. Sam approached, watching Lilly place a comforting hand on Robert's shoulder, then turning and silently walking away.

Robert was first to speak, and Sam could tell immediately he wasn't the type who cared for goodbyes. "Now, don't come over here with a face like that, ol' chap. It'll only make this harder than it already is."

Before Sam could reply, Robert pulled from one of his pockets a small, clear container with a cork stopper and tossed it toward Sam. He caught it and held it up, asking while staring at it, "What the heck is this?"

Robert began to slip the straps to an over-stuffed backpack onto his shoulders, answering with a chuckle, "Consider it a farewell gift," Upon closer examination, Sam could see two small caliber buckshot rolling around inside, as Robert continued, "From me to you!"

Sam chuckled at the humorous gesture and replied, stuffing the gift into a pocket, "Now I wish I would have gotten something for you, like a new leg!"

Both laughed and clasped each other on the shoulder before Robert turned serious, "Now, follow Lilly, old boy, and do exactly what she tells you. She's sharper than both of us put together and won't let anything happen to you, but stay on her six and keep your head on a swivel, got it?"

Sam nodded, replying sternly, "Got it. And you stay strong and get that leg taken care of, as soon as everybody is safe; God speed, my friend."

Once the large group began to enter the fray of the jungle, Tom-Tom left form and ran up to Sam, saying, "Hug?" Sam picked the little boy up and spun him as they hugged, causing the young Burmese child to laugh one more time for Sam. He gently landed Tom-Tom's feet safely back onto soil, before he scurried back into line with his father. Robert turned one last time and waved at his American friend before slipping out of sight within the dense foliage of the storm-tossed jungle.

CHAPTER 34

The small, remaining group of six quickly gathered to pack up what's left of the bedding, medicine, and various pieces of equipment that weren't sent with the displaced villagers. Sam tried to follow every instruction he received second hand from Jack, Lilly's Burmese interpreter. In his attempt to correctly fold and tie down one of the bundles of tarps in preparation for mobilization, Lilly mutely pushed him aside to reassemble the tarps on her own and fasten them correctly. Sam swallowed his pride and simply accepted her obvious display of belittlement, reaffirming to himself that this was her country with rules and customs he'd never wholeheartedly comprehend.

Once the last items were packed, each member loaded what they're able to carry and fell into line behind Lilly, the obvious choice for lead. Sam looked to Jack for his suggestion on his placement, which ended up being second from last, ahead of Jack, who brought up the rear. Lilly's pace turned out to be considerably hastened, compared to Robert's, and even when they were nowhere in the vicinity of enemy encampments, she allowed no talking. Sam's thighs and calves felt like they'd ignite at any moment, yet they maintained the blistering pace for hours at a time. On one of their few abbreviated stops, Sam only desired to remove his backpack, utilizing it as a large pillow and lie down for an hour. Before he could even consider a thought to ask, the entourage was up and moving on.

Sam had just been contemplating how odd it was that he could travel such great distance without requiring food, when the small village appeared. Almost on cue, his stomach growled loud enough to make Lilly turn and scowl at the unauthorized noise. Several happy villagers appeared, welcoming each arriving member, as Sam's confidence immediately climbed concerning whether the village was an ally or not. One of the men from the small community even helped Sam remove his heavy burden and carried it for him while they all walked toward the center of the village.

Water to drink, a basin for washing their faces and hands, and towels were delivered as the villagers showed their hospitality and appreciation for the group's endeavors to free Burma from a way of life to which so many turned a blind eye. Sam found a place to sit away from the center and watched while the villagers treated the freedom fighters like deserving local rock stars. A young Burmese girl about Tom-Tom's age cautiously approached Sam and delivered a rolled-up leaf filled with sticky rice. Never one to refute local courtesy, Sam took a bite of the offering, smiling gratefully to the little girl. Suddenly overcome with shyness, she giggled and ran back the way she came, leaving Sam to devour the appetizer in two, ravishing bites, leaving him to wonder about the next course.

Bathed, fed, and rested, Sam sat before a fire with the comfort of safety engulfing the moment. Sitting among the contented villagers and band of humanitarians, Sam shook off the disbelief that only hours before he'd been immersed in the activity of dodging several units of an immoral army, starved beyond natural limits, and somehow attained the hefty aroma of yak dung.

Observing the true people of Burma, and not just some of what they're forced to endure, but all of it, Sam recalled his early assumption of indifference in how the country's name had been officially changed to Myanmar. This country was Burma, he resolved deep within. No illegitimate, self-appointed government choosing to involve themselves in the act of forced labor of their own people, annihilation of entire villages, and the destruction of any and all forms of freedom deserved an ounce of satisfaction or resolution in the realm of how it ran its government. Sam could feel himself getting worked up reflecting upon the plight of the majority.

His fire and anger leaned him toward casting aside his previous life of self-absorption and taking up the fight for the worthy cause, but as he rose from his position, a folded item fell from his pocket. He stared at it as it waited at the edge of the fire light, begging to be retrieved. When he picked up and unfolded the photo of El Padre, he gazed at it like a wake-up call from a past, long forgotten. So very much had occurred since his arrival to this unusual, forgotten country; not only around him, or to him, but also deep within him.

No longer could he look at a person and assume anything about him or her. Only speaking with and understanding where that person came from could one truly know another. It's exactly what his friend Tai had tried to explain in Norway, but comprehension often required experience and an open mind. The door to Sam's mind, he believed, had finally come ajar.

Watching the villagers in a moment of serenity amidst the continuing fight for not only basic freedoms, but often mere survival, Sam humbly conceded how before two weeks ago he'd never regarded their plight. He shuddered at recalling his bad days consisting of returned Calamari because it was too cold or discarding a morning's latte due to not having enough desired foam. Dealing with an irritable boss didn't compare to losing a home, a beloved family member, and a country in the span of forty-eight hours.

A hard truth settled in, that each of us had our own responsibility, and Sam's had just applied a gentle reminder. Truly assisting the people of Burma required years of training and a physical and emotional endurance he sorely lacked. To attempt to go at it unprepared could endanger the worthy mission and possibly the lives of others. One's own function in life could be assisting another in a small way or doing something on a grand scale, like what this team was accomplishing. There were also those left to witness the big and small feats, and the capacity of offering documentation about it so that people halfway around the world could know what's going on. Sam would be the one to try to shake the masses hard enough to remove their blinders.

He stared at the picture for an extended moment, studying the silhouette of a face he already had memorized. Just before he refolded the picture to return it to the safety of his pocket, he frowned at something he hadn't noticed before in the left portion of the photo. Behind two men who stood over a kneeling El Padre, observing his handy work, was a young, slender Burmese woman who could only be Lilly. Sam looked up in amazement as his eyes fell directly upon her. Surprising him, Lilly was staring right back from the other side of the fire.

"Please, Jack. Ask her one more time to look at this photo and tell me if it's her," Sam pled. Jack gave Sam an obvious look of displeasure, as none of the men in the group were comfortable 'asking' Lilly anything. After a long, paraphrased translation, Lilly stubbornly looked toward Sam, then down at the picture in his extended hand. She snapped the photo quickly from Sam and turned her back to the fire to better see the image. Without speaking or looking his way, she extended an open hand toward Jack, who placed a small black pen light into her waiting hand. She studied the entire photo for several moments before handing it back to Jack instead of Sam.

When she began to walk away, Sam tested a theory that'd been growing for some time, asking her directly, "Is it you, Lilly? Is that you in the photo?"

She turned to him, making direct eye contact before stepping into his comfort zone so that she's only inches from his face. "Yes, woman in photo is me. So why you care? Is dis man no good?"

Sam framed his appearance with a renewed confidence, lifting his chin accordingly. Jack stared from Lilly to Sam and back to Lilly until she nodded her approval for him to depart. He didn't need Sam's second opinion to make haste his exit. Lilly rested her hands on her hips challengingly, waiting for Sam to reply, but Sam let the small amount of confidence reignite the investigative reporter inside and opted to draw it out, partly for her inferior treatment toward him, thus far. He paced in front of her, peppering her with questions. "Did you speak with the man in the picture?"

She shook her head no.

"Were you close enough to hear him speak and did you know what language it was?" he pressed.

Lilly crossed her arms, answering, "He first speak a Northern Burmese, din he switch to Mon."

Sam quickly asked, "I was told by the man who took this picture that this village was just east of Bhamo in the Kachin state. Why were you so far north?"

She darted him a look of intrusion and held Sam in check for just a moment. Sam didn't back down, though, competing quite well with the intense young woman. Her eyes lost some of their hostility and softened just a hint, lowering her voice, answering, "What I do, I no answer to you. What I do, it for my people. Village attacked, I go help. Shan Providence once my home, and I go when I hear junta invade. So I go warn them. I follow army north to village in picture . . . but I too late."

The intensity he saw in her face and the tension in her body spoke clearly where her broken English lacked. Sam took a breath, understanding Lilly for the first time. Her only desire was to fight back and be there for the ethnics in the aftermath of brutal fury. Without any compensation expected or even genuine words of appreciation required, she fought with, for, and against all in the same effort. Every life she saved, every person she helped bury, and every ounce of assistance she offered allowed the reason for her surviving somehow bearable. At some point, she crossed the line of caring what happened to her physical body and eternal soul, and she dove head strong into a lake without bottom. There would be no end to the war she battled inside.

Sam stared at the young woman for a length of time before he realized he hadn't asked another question. Lilly, though, didn't seem to notice. He scratched at his unshaven face and quickly contemplated how to proceed. Taking him by surprise, Lilly broke the silence first. "What is you want from me, Sam Noll? Ask me. I do best to tell you."

Sam gave the sincere request a moment of consideration before smiling at her, answering, "Honestly, Lilly, I haven't a clue."

The slow, advancing smile that cascaded across her face didn't strike Sam as beautiful, but rather a breathtaking event. Even the brief sight of her flawless teeth practically caused Sam to giggle. The occurrence was but fleeting, as the evening shades collected once again upon her face, returning with it her accustomed appearance of the weight of a nation.

Sam shook the exhausted confusion of the moment, saying, "Lilly, how about we both sleep on it tonight and hopefully tomorrow will enlighten one of us with profound direction." With a firm nod of agreement, she turned and headed for her evening's arranged quarters, leaving Sam to stare up at the moving dark clouds that blocked the stars of guidance.

The deep sleep Sam had been enjoying was restlessly ended as Lilly awakened him to a sunless morning. "No sleep the day. We have direction." Sam rubbed his eyes while a dream dissipated that had something to do with Katie being disappointed with something stupid he had done.

Once properly dressed, Sam sought out Lilly to hear the latest plan. He found her arguing with Jack in Burmese, and Sam remained at a distance, not wishing to intrude or be blamed for something. Jack stormed off without looking back in a way Sam had witnessed from every other member of the group after a short chat with Lilly.

"Everything okay?" Sam asked, approaching her with caution.

When she turned, she actually greeted him with a hint of a smile, giving Sam a morning rush like that of three coffees. Her expression then turned sour, nodding toward the direction of Jack's exit, stating, "He no like plan. He wish to go with us, but rest go north to train."

Sam tried to catch up with her explanation, realizing something pertinent was missing from the equation, asking, "I don't understand who's the 'us' and where's the 'go'?" The humor in his inquiry was lost on her as she stood all of her five foot six inch frame and tilted her head in question. Sam walked up to her, asking softly, slowly, "Who's going where?"

Lilly slung her heavy pack over her shoulder, answering, "We, you and me, go to Delta Region. We help those from great storm."

Riding in a similar truck like the one Robert and he were blown out of didn't settle Sam's already fraying nerves. Lilly's driving was terrible, urging his manhood to suggest she let him drive, but Sam managed to keep his ego checked in the glove box, along with anything else small and fragile that might get bumped out of the truck.

Before their hurried departure, it was explained a call came in on a satellite phone the group carried. There were heavy fatalities in the Irrawaddy Delta, and the regime was blocking any and all outside assistance. Lilly knew Sam wanted to be there nearly as much as she, so the two would make the trek together.

Trying to time the larger bumps in the road, Sam scanned a map, asking, "Where exactly do you think we can get in the easiest?"

Lilly quickly skimmed over the map, knowing her country better than the map maker. She responded, "There a place ten kilometers northwest of Yangon. Road few use. We try there."

Sam watched the road for a while until he decided to make an effort to simply chat with Lilly to see if she's capable of speaking of anything not immediate or dire. "So, Jack seemed more than just a little angry about not coming on this trip. Is there anything I need to know or watch my back over?"

Lilly glanced once toward him, then twice, before answering, "Jack has idea, not like me. He better off with rest of group right now. Better focus with me far away."

Sam nodded his understanding of her wisdom of the male thought process and let the matter be, then, suddenly irritated by a topic not yet cleared up, he asked, "So, why wouldn't you speak English to me and lead me to believe that you didn't understand what I was saying?"

Without taking her eyes off the road, she replied unemotionally, "People speak lies when they know someone hear. Truth be heard when they believe nobody listen."

Sam soaked in the wisdom, asking, "Who said that, was it Ghandi?" Lilly ignored the dry humor as she tried to smear some of the condensation off the inside of the windshield.

With barriers being quickly set up in many locations heading west out of the city, getting through Yangon proved to be a quite test. Lilly stopped at an intersection, bit her lip, and forged quickly east, picking up speed in hope to beat the onslaught of military deterrence. After zigzagging their way for what seemed to be twenty or thirty miles, she slammed on the brakes as a military vehicle pulled forward, blocking the narrow road ahead.

Both Lilly and Sam froze in their seats as two armed soldiers jumped out of their jeep and approached the truck. Sam sensed Lilly slip her arm down to her left side and feared she was about to go Rambo on the two unsuspecting men. Ready to follow her lead, Sam slowly unfastened his seat belt in case he had a chance to help clear their path. When she removed her papers from a side pocket, Sam visibly deflated from his imaginary action of guns blazing and followed her example of not making any sudden movement, presenting his papers as well.

Sam listened as one of the uniformed officers moved to Lilly's door, ignoring her documents. A heated verbal exchange began between them, with the officer pointing repeatedly back the way Lilly had come. Sam remained facing forward in an attempt not to antagonize anyone for any reason. The second officer remained at the door of their jeep, directly in front of him, holding his weapon low, but not low enough to adjust quickly to spray the small truck and its occupants with rapid fire.

The soldier talking at Lilly had the last word, which Sam was assured didn't sit well with Lilly. The result seemed inevitable, though, that neither Sam nor Lilly were going to get through the roadblock.

Lilly shifted the vehicle into reverse and launched the truck back down the road at breakneck speed, leaving Sam to refrain from asking, *So, how did that go?*

Back on the wider road and driving forward again, Lilly began speaking in some form of accelerated Burmese. Sam let her vent over the real conversation she wanted to have with the regime soldier, simply content that her ire wasn't directed at him.

After several miles of silence, she turned to Sam, saying, "You know when to speak and when not to. Thank you, Sam Noll. That rare in men." Sam smiled at the compliment, leaving her perception unruffled.

When they began to get close to Yangon, Sam asked, "So, what do we do now?"

Lilly sighed with the dwindling prospect, responding, "You go back. I try again tomorrow. I know many way to sneak past bad junta. Where I go, no white man can follow. Junta no let outside know what happen. You is outside, head-to-toe, Sam Noll. They kill you if they see you. They save their money and power, and no let different country see what go on inside borders. Robert tell me when you come, and junta no like when people stay past there time . . . so you must go."

Sam swallowed hard, not ready to give up the fight he felt inside. The pain of not being allowed to even try to save some of the people struck an angry chord he's unaccustomed to experiencing. His two weeks in Burma only felt as though he'd just arrived, but his experiences could fill a novel. Sam didn't know what penalty would be administered if he remained beyond his two weeks. Unfortunately, he had to trust Lilly's knowledge on the matter.

Entering the city, they moved closer to where he's staying as Sam turned to Lilly, requesting, "At least come up and rest. You can shower and take however long of a nap. We can have a meal together and allow you to gain some strength for what you must do tomorrow."

Expecting the offer to be refused immediately, Sam was amazed when she simply nodded her consent. Whether it's the enticement of a hot shower, the nap, or the extending of his company, Sam didn't care. All he knew was his opinion of Lilly had taken an abrupt modification, along with a country he knew little about.

Many of the buildings and homes showed disruption from the passing storm, and even the market appeared to be working at limited capacity. The hotel Sam had spent only two nights at didn't seem to notice his absence, as everything in his room was exactly how he left it. Before she slipped into the bathroom, Sam offered Lilly one of his t-shirts, at which she smiled briefly before graciously accepting.

With neither hungry, Sam busied himself laying out and folding clothes to be repacked for his returning flight, while Lilly took full advantage of the rare shower and dispensed the hot water accordingly.

Packed and ready for the morning, Sam moved the suitcase to the floor and turned toward the sound of Lilly emerging from the steaming bathroom. "I think I use up hot water," she said with an uncharacteristically shy smile. Seeing her in his shirt with her hair still wet, Sam couldn't keep the smile off his face and thought the cold shower might just be appropriate. Sam wordlessly pulled back the corner of the covers and let her be, grabbing his bathroom kit, change of clothes and taking his turn in the bathroom.

When he came out, Lilly was fast asleep lying on her side, facing away from the middle of the bed. Sam stood over her from his side of the bed and just watched her in her rare, comfortable state. He observed her body rise and fall with the slow, steady breathing of one who had entered the deepest of slumbers, and he hesitated to join her in fear she'd be awakened. Sam quietly moved to an upholstered chair away from the bed and sat back into it, still refusing to take his eyes off Lilly.

He fell asleep that way, wondering what might have happened if he slipped under the covers next to her and she *did* wake up. Would she be receptive? Would she say yes? He drifted away toward his own dreams of abstract scenarios that only the subconscious thoughts could curiously invoke.

Sam startled awake to find Lilly dressed and standing over him. He rubbed his face and yawned, asking, "What time is it?"

Without referencing a timepiece, she answered, "Seven. We go soon." The return to her commanding ways was more of a wake-up than Sam cared for, but he understood her need to get underway. He stared at the made bed and momentarily grieved the missed opportunity before rising and going about the task of fully waking up.

With visa, passport, and other forms required to depart, Sam and Lilly stopped for a quick breakfast of some pungent spicy Mohinga and tea. Sam noticed Lilly was avoiding casual eye contact and stated nonchalantly, "I wanted to join you last night, but you were sleeping so soundly, I couldn't get myself to bother you."

She looked up, startled by the comment, before returning her attention to her breakfast, replying, "There was more than enough room for you. You no need to sleep on chair."

Sam accepted her answer, digging his regret an inch further, responding jokingly, "Also, I didn't want to find out the hard way that you keep a knife hidden somewhere for emergencies."

The stare she directed at him caught his breath as she replied blankly, "Last thing you get be my knife, Sam Noll." With his face flushed from her unique form of flattery, Sam had to remind himself his brain still needed oxygen, exhaling and returning to a regular pace of breathing.

Sam reflected how so many times his brief hesitations had saved many a train-wreck over his past. Now, he cursed his indecisiveness and its complete lack of respect for spontaneity. With no positive way to respond or explain himself accurately, Sam simply let her comment encompass his regret, allowing his flustered expression be the most appropriate counter.

The minimal exchange on the way to dropping Sam off at the airport was filled with small talk, which Sam could tell neither was comfortable with. The unbearably approaching departure stifled the cramped space inside the cab of the truck. Just beginning to get to know her, and having to leave before seeing its potential, Sam desired to say so much, with so little time or right words.

They pulled up to the drop off zone and Sam slowly got out while Lilly exited to help remove his suitcase from the back. Standing there, facing each other, Sam tried to conjure up all that he wanted to express in one perfect sentence, allowing him to make a dramatic exit, leaving the heroine contented, yet yearning for more, but it's Lilly who grasped the chance. Leaning into Sam, she kissed him deeply on the lips, holding him there, leaving Sam to play catch up and engage his response.

As they ended their kiss, Lilly held his stare, stating with sincerity, "You come back someday, Sam Noll." With that, she stole the show in spectacular form, jumping into the truck and driving off without looking back.

CHAPTER 35

Sam watched the Israeli, speaking his broken English to a husband and wife from Australia. From his angled position, Sam listened to the sales pitch become more fevered before the two finally agreed to a price for the walking tour of Old City Jerusalem.

Leaving Burma had been more difficult than he imagined, emotionally. Lilly's unexpected influence caught him daydreaming of fighting the good fight by her side, but the prospect of such an extreme life change from his present occupation left him arguably divided. Retrieving his laptop and wrestling the hordes of people trying to leave or being forced out of Burma actually made his physical departure easier. At several stations, maneuvering to the proper exit terminal, he was reminded that his return wasn't recommended for quite some time. Even switching his return flight from home to Israel was accommodated, for a small fee, just as long as the end result was his exit of Burma.

Deciding where to start his search in Israel, Sam followed recent news reports of tension building near Tel Aviv and began speaking to people around the city. After four days of wandering aimlessly showing both the picture and sketch without any luck, he packed it in and made his way south.

His new plan was to continue his search in Jerusalem for a few days, then head north to check out the small skirmishes near the Gaza Strip, if he could. With a cease fire firmly in place and

346

somewhat adhered to, there'd been little trouble occurring within the last several weeks there, so he'd have to rely on a great deal of positive luck if he's hoping to cross paths with El Padre. The disappointment and time lost in Tel Aviv had his spirits low and, with time running out, he lamented over poorly choosing to start with the capitol. After Gaza, he questioned whether he would try another city or head home with his tail between his legs.

Patiently, Sam waited for another couple to be drawn in to the dealing salesman, all the while observing the man's gestures, tone and particular subtleties. Once the second set of customers left after payment for their tour, Sam turned and stared at the Israeli until he had his full attention, saying harmlessly in English, "Quite a deal you offer. Strange, though, how much the price varies among your customers. Do they know the amount fluctuates depending on their dress, accent, or your particular mood for the day?"

The man's grin faded quickly in the conversation, but when he turned away, Sam was quick to step in his path. "Perhaps someone should check with a few of your patrons and see just what the average amount rounds up to. What do you think?" he asked with the man beginning to look around the busy street.

No longer did the speech come forth with any effort, as his English transformed miraculously with great improvement. "Don't bust my balls, I'm only the seller. If I wasn't here, these morons would be giving these trips for free. I provide food on everybody's plate, so don't have a cow." The man looked Sam up and down, adding, "So? What do you want? Cuz, we both know you won't tell anyone. You just have a need, so spill."

Sam reached into his pocket, handing the Israeli his picture of El Padre while saying, "This man isn't a criminal, nor is he in any sort of trouble. He's simply a man I wish to speak with, and I wish no harm to him. Can you help me?"

The man stared at the picture long enough to get Sam's hopes up. He handed the photo back to him, answering, "Yesterday, walked the tour. He didn't haggle the price one bit either. That's why

I remember him so well; even tipped the guide pretty well." Sam looked around for a second, not expecting this kind of progress. Impatiently, the Israeli began to leave, stating, "Listen, you're costing me money. If there isn't anything else . . ."

Sam held out a twenty dollar bill, which froze the man in his step, with Sam adding, "I want the full meal deal, and don't insult me by saying you need more."

The man took the money and handed Sam a paper stub, replying, "Ten-thirty, by the stone stairwell outside the Omar-iye Upper School for Boys. If anyone asks, you paid twice this." He waved the money once before it disappeared into an inside pocket and he immersed himself among the hordes of people looking for bargains.

While Sam anxiously awaited his upcoming tour, he wandered around the Muslim quarter, admiring the entrance of Lion's Gate from every angle. Moving toward the El-Wad street vendors, the selling began to become more heated and invasive. Sam tried to avoid the shop owners feverishly attempting to lighten his wallet with multiple souvenirs, t-shirts, and enticements of scents of strong coffee.

Simply stating "No thank you" to a Muslim vendor was much like saying, "Please try harder!" as he tried to ignore the hands-on approach of salesmanship. Just getting past the first three carts turned difficult, moving to the center of the street, Sam tried raising his voice, thinking that might let them know he wasn't interested in purchasing their wares.

Just as Sam broke free from one particularly stubborn salesman, two adjacent carts collapsed from their weight on each side of the market, spilling their goods into the narrow street. The throngs of shoppers, some trying to help the vendors, some not so much, collapsed upon the dispelled fortune as the owners frantically tried unsuccessfully to control the situation.

Sam stared at the unexpected exhibit before him, and his mind flew directly to a relevant conversation with Tai. He immediately scanned the assemblage of visitors seeking out one in particular within the mass. A quick moving blur caught his attention half a street farther up. Sam bolted for the stairs, his adrenaline soaring, slipping between shoppers, thieves, and somewhat holy men. Once at the top of the stairs, he scanned the rooftops and streets below, not seeing anyone attempting to avoid his detection. After a prolonged visual search, Sam concluded he's mistaken and descended the rocky stairs.

At the base of the staircase, he's met by a thin Muslim vendor holding up a t-shirt of a yellow, smiling face. The seller asked, smiling, "You like, no?"

El Padre watched the reporter walk away from the t-shirt vendor as the American continued to occasionally glance upward toward the stone walls that shaded the sun from both their eyes. El Padre considered the near miss as far too close for comfort by any means.

Making his way for the Damascus Gate, he glanced toward the bee's hive of activity he created in the street. The two shop owners glared and cursed at each other, blaming the other for both of their support beams breaking simultaneously, not to mention their unexpected losses. El Padre inwardly grinned, looking up to the heavens, whispering, "For you, my good shepherd, for it has been far too long since a table has been turned in this place. But forgive me for the pleasure I take from it."

He'd visit the Garden Tomb and take leave of Israel. His tenacious shadow was beginning to alter his freedoms. No one knew as well as he that to tempt Fate often caused it to surprise him by simply turning around to stare his way.

A small man quietly announced to the thirty-five to forty waiting tourists in three separate languages, last being English, "The Via Dolorosa shall begin shortly, if you'll all gather in and present your receipts." The push Sam experienced from all directions surprised him, since the tour was considered by most as a pilgrimage and way of displaying intense respect.

The path, known in Latin as 'the way of suffering,' would take Sam and the others through the fourteen stations of the cross, loosely depicting the path of Christ's Passion, from condemnation by Pontius Pilate to His entombment at the present location within the Church of the Holy Sepulchre. The guide explained in dramatically explicit, if not slightly biased offering, the walking of the very footsteps of Jesus Christ and how any person who followed the route couldn't deny a sense of responsibility or moral persecution. Sam listened to the rehearsed lines and canned feelings, expecting nothing less, considering the salesman he encountered earlier.

Midway, near the fifth station, Sam began to notice a deep emotion building within the small Israeli, contradicting Sam's previous assumption of a feigned performance. The group grew nearer to the church, while Sam managed to maneuver his position closer to the tour guide. Once he's only a few feet from him, he noticed tears falling from his face. Astonished, Sam took the open show of emotion thoughtfully, believing the man was truly torn by conviction rather than an incredible actor.

After the crowd dispersed, Sam approached the Israeli guide. The man saw Sam coming and greeted him with a smile. "Shalom, my friend. Did you enjoy the journey back in time?" he asked, never easing his genuine show of endearment.

Sam reached out with his hand and, as they shook, responded with, "Yes. I was moved by how it still affects you after so many guided tours. At first, my hesitations led me to doubt your display as mere theatrics. But I'm humbled by your obedience and pure heart."

The sudden embrace took Sam by surprise, being unaccustomed to such grand demonstrations of appreciation. Giving in to the gesture, Sam finally put his arms around the man, not wishing to insult any local custom, but mostly due to just enjoying the friendly embrace from someone so spiritual. In the midst of the hug, the little man whispered into Sam's ear, "All things are borne out of divine purpose. You are here for a great reason; do not fear the path, for the Lord lights the way." Sam pulled away, staring into the man's gentle, smiling face, looking for any substance of affirmation. The man adjusted his appearance to that of concern, asking, "Do you not search for that which shall console thee for eternity?"

Sam took another step back, beginning to chuckle, stating, "Would you not agree that consolation is wrought with various opinions?"

The man smiled again, answering slyly, "Opinion of the people is not often agreeable. I prefer adhering toward a more heavenly representation. It has led me, without regret, thus far."

Sam allowed the man to have the last statement in their philosophical exchange before politely changing the subject. "I understand a man I've been looking for walked this same tour yesterday. Is this something you can help me with?"

The guide took another reflective glance at him before answering, "Is this man in any type of danger by you or anyone you work for?"

Sam quickly responded. "Not in any way. He's simply a curiosity to a great number of people, and what I truly 'search' for is only his identity." With that, Sam pulled from his pocket the picture and sketch of El Padre.

The man looked at both for a respective moment before handing them back to Sam. He again stared into Sam's eyes as if trying to confirm a lack of deception from the strange American. Sam filled the space of doubt, saying, "I believe this man has many answers I've sacrificed nearly everything to understand. Please help me, if you can."

The release of breath and slight drop of the little man's head gave Sam his inner confirmation of success. "Yes. I noticed this man you seek from the early expedition yesterday. He remained in the back, but I noticed he listened with great intent at every word I expressed. His hawk-like blue eyes never swayed from each and every turn, building, or station, leaving nothing to be dismissed. I paused as we were leaving the fifth station when I saw him hesitate there, bending upon one knee. Many travelers, pilgrims, and believers are often extraordinarily moved at different points of the Via Dolorosa. But rarely do they react in a way that leaves me feeling so incredibly humbled. This man carries within him pools of emotion the likes I have never seen."

Sam took the information with a firm lip, not knowing where it would take him or how it would help. Struggling to come up with a following question, the man offered the unsolicited information, "This man you seek; we spoke, just as you and I, after the completion of the walking tour. He told me you would come. He told me you would seek him out. He said one day he will meet you, but that day has yet to pass."

Sam felt the immediate rise of a plethora of mixed reaction with what he heard. His mouth exceeded his brain to the punch, answering with a hint of anger, "What do you mean, he knew I would be here? How could he know that?"

The Israeli took the response calmly, placing a hand on Sam's left sleeve, saying comfortingly, "Sit, my friend. Let us speak of this so that you might achieve enlightenment." Sam followed his instruction unable to function in his usual reactionary manner, with his mind swirling into a level of unvented terrain. "I will share with you everything he relayed to me, and I will answer all of your questions, but please understand our entire exchange lasted nothing more than three or four breaths," he admitted to Sam, slowly sitting next to him.

Sam remained silent, letting the man offer what he could, not knowing what to interject even if he could. "Your friend whom you seek carries himself like a man with the weight of the world upon his shoulders and displays a wisdom I have yet to entirely measure. Nothing I spoke entered his ear for the first time, and when he spoke of you, he did not mention your name, but described you amply enough that, when you approached me after the tour, I was quite certain our encounter was about to commence as he had predicted."

Sam looked up, asking, "Did he say how he knows me?"

The tour guide pressed both hands onto his knees and pushed upward giving the impression to think back, answering, "The only thing he mentioned was that he was strongly aware of you, and, as I said before, that one day the two of you would meet."

Sam locked his jaw, repeating, "But not this day!"

The man dropped his head reproachfully, adding, "The most agonizing virtue of all is that of patience; it is also the most rewarding."

Sam faked a rueful smile, countering with, "Virtues are for those with meager expectations. Those with a realist's concept of reward have little virtue."

The Israeli lowered his head slightly, thoughtfully replying, "Then, perhaps, it is best for both of you that he has taken leave."

Sam grimaced his response to the news. "He told you he was leaving Israel?"

With a nod, he answered, "Not in so many words, but yes, he suggested with much sadness that he would be departing soon."

The wind that had momentarily inflated Sam's sail was suddenly usurped into nothingness. With great effort, he stood on uncertain legs, wondering which direction he should follow before sitting back down and looking for any type of support from the Israeli. In response, the gentleman took Sam's hand into his and, in a show of genuinely unconditional acceptance, bowed his head and began to pray, "Our Great Messiah, give this man the strength and courage to face that which you have placed before his feet. Light his path, so that he might follow your will in all things, as you have intended since the beginning of creation. Amen."

CHAPTER 36

El Padre sat at the bar of an Israeli restaurant bustling with staff and patrons during a busy evening rush. An attractive American woman in her early forties wearing a black evening dress and carrying a matching black clutch entered the bar and quickly scanned every patron, then dramatically dropped her head in obvious disappointment. She took a seat beside El Padre, obviously frustrated, checking her cell phone before turning to watch the door when someone entered.

After taking a sip from his glass of wine, El Padre leaned toward the woman. "I am certain whatever has held him up will not keep him much longer."

The woman took notice of the man to her right for the first time, giving him a curious stare, then quickly smiling, easing onto her bar stool. When the bartender approached, she met his unspoken inquiry. "I'd like a glass of the house Red, please; something full-bodied."

Once the bartender left to fill her order, she took out a cigarette from within her purse and searched for her lighter. El Padre, on cue, lit a match for her, cupping it with his hands until he's certain it would remain lit, then extended the ember toward her. She leaned in, allowing the flame to ignite her cigarette, looking into his clear, blue eyes. She quickly moved herself back into her seat appearing self-conscious for gazing at him a moment too long, nearly burning one quarter of her cigarette.

She smiled briefly, collecting herself before saying, "Thanks. Sorry for interrupting your quiet evening with my inappropriate behavior; it's just that my husband chooses the worst moments for his tardiness to kick in."

El Padre returned his attention to his wine glass, responding, "I am certain your husband's heartbeat quickens simply by the anticipation of seeing you, even when he has just seen you an hour previously."

The woman turned her full attention upon the stranger sitting beside her. As she often did when men paid too much attention to her, she began to size him up in her preparation to tear him down, but hesitated for some reason, instantly believing him to be harmless. When her wine arrived, she paid the bartender and returned to her exchange with El Padre. "And what do you know of the heart of man?" she asked before taking a satisfying sip from her wine glass. "Do you retain some insight or knowledge that has escaped all others, or do you simply attempt to bear witness for the defense of the brotherhood of men?" She smiled at her own repartee, taking a slow drag from her cigarette, then returning it to its proper place on the glass ashtray.

El Padre slowly turned to face the woman, closed his eyes briefly and waited for her returned attention. When no response came from the stranger, she turned to see if her witty retort had been wasted upon deaf ears, only to fall under El Padre's intense gaze which froze her instantly.

He began to speak to her deepest hidden secret. "The doubt and fear you long to escape are of your own creation. Previous transgressions from long past relationships do not transcend to your present bond of commitment. This groundless manifestation that preoccupies your idle thoughts and restless sleep must see its end. The man that you married and share your bed with remains faithful to you and you alone. His heart knows no greater joy than the moment you agreed to his marriage proposal five years from this day in this restaurant. He runs late this evening due to his inability to select only one bouquet of numerous choices of beautiful flowers, when he desires to present you them all. Fear not your forthcoming business trip, for it will only make his heart desire you more."

His words drove deep inside her, reverberating through her guarded heart, releasing a pain long entrenched that had festered for decades. The woman wiped tears that had been absent of emotion for as long as she could remember. El Padre handed the woman a white handkerchief with thin, blue pinstripes, which she graciously accepted. Once she finished dabbing away the tears, El Padre stood in preparation of his exit, stating, "Tonight should be about new beginnings and introducing your husband to a part of your heart he deserves to know. You have a depth to your love that can now be fulfilled. Cherish every moment together."

Walking toward the door, the woman stopped him, extending the return of his handkerchief. "Sir, I can't thank you enough for your insightful words. Thank you."

El Padre gently returned a smile, saying, "The words and the handkerchief are my gift to you. It is my prayer that the first gift might be used more than the last."

Exiting the restaurant and turning north, a dark-haired Israeli man carrying a bouquet of flowers was rushing down the sidewalk toward him with a frazzled look upon his face. Once they're about to pass, El Padre greeted him. "Those are beautiful flowers. She will no doubt forgive you for the delay." The man just looked at him strangely before continuing toward the restaurant.

Sam removed a shoe, sitting on the edge of the bed, staring at the floor of his hotel room. In a fit of rage, he threw the shoe at his luggage innocently sitting against the wall, but the shoe missed and hit the wall. He fell back onto the bed, laughing mockingly, saying out loud, "I can't even be angry right!"

He sat up and tried to find peace in his failure to locate El Padre. He contemplated the reaction from Tom once he returned empty-handed, other than a feeble offering of more pretty, written stories of near misses. He tabulated the growing expectation and excitement from the last eight articles he'd sent since arriving in Israel. The response from Tom was building him up for either great reward or disastrous failure of epic proportion, with the later becoming more and more applicable.

His inner pride touched momentarily on his written expression in regard to the inner fight for Burma, wondering how Lilly would react, if she ever had the chance to read it. With his flight set for the next day, Sam tried to clear his mind of wrestling with wants and desires far too difficult to consult at the moment. Better to save that battle for the long flight home, where escape was severely limited.

Sam paid the sherut driver and exited the taxi van still mentally lost in his disappointment. Slinging his bags over his shoulder, he asked himself how he could honestly wait another cycle before having another definite opportunity of crossing paths with El Padre? The answer was painfully obvious; he couldn't. The only option available was to follow any and all leads concerning areas of growing conflict where there could be a high probability for death and the dying, and hope for the best.

He shook his head with what a miserable optimist he had become. What kind of life was that? Sam felt like he'd sacrificed everything already. Was he to commit the entirety of his life without any real place to call home and, should he completely disregard having someone, anyone, waiting for him to call or return from a faraway assignment?

Entering the sliding doors to the airport terminal, he realized his feelings of frustration ran deeper than just missed encounters. After his abbreviated feelings were cut short with Lilly, Sam began to consider that maybe he's having some delayed regret from recently losing Katie, too. Once in line to check in for his flight, Sam decided to go at the subject of Katie from an objective point of view. It's only fair to admit that he wasn't the most romantic man in the world, though he certainly did have his moments. He believed that growing up without his mother seemed like an excuse or cliché he had chosen to deny, but perhaps there's some connection to his lack of allowing anyone in, completely.

He couldn't hold any ill feelings toward Katie, and that in itself was hard for him to swallow, because it left only himself holding the blame. He ventured in and out of their relationship only offering half measures, with Katie being the one making the sacrifice, always being the anchor. She deserved someone who wouldn't only appreciate all that she afforded, but also someone who could verbalize that emotion and give just as much in return. From his position of hindsight, Sam mentally skipped through a painful array of failed opportunities to be the man he should have been, rather than the guy Katie was dealing with, and that took the air from him like a kick to the stomach.

Standing there in line, he committed to calling Katie and explain to her that he's sorry for all the wrong things he said, all the times away when he should have made a better effort to contact her, letting her know he was thinking of her. He'd tell her what he truly felt inside about how she deserved so much better than him and let her find closure from their break up. She deserved that, at the very least.

Sam suddenly reflected on their last conversation together and how he was unable to look at her or even try to defend himself whatsoever. Recalling how given the opportunity to express a variety of deep emotions, such as sorrow, regret, or even a simple thing such as gratitude, that he folded like a lawn chair, Sam changed his mind and decided that perhaps a letter would be the better plan.

The speed in which the long line of hopeful travelers was moving toward the check-in counter could easily have been eclipsed by a glacier. It appeared that every person successfully reaching the counter was deciding to make the very most of their feat by sharing their entire life history.

After eventually checking in and receiving the discouraging news that his flight was delayed by three hours, Sam exhaustively picked up his bag and meandered away from the counter wondering what he'd do to fill the time. He slowly turned a complete circle, taking in the high ceilings in the terminal of Ben Gurion Airport with its enormous opaque pillars. He began counting the police officers and IDF soldiers within view and wondered if they outnumber the actual passengers.

About to head to the departure hall, Sam noticed a young girl about thirty feet away wearing a bright red dress. Within her arms was a pure white teddy bear that looked to be twice her size. Uncertain which caught his eye first, the bear or the bright red dress, Sam smiled on behalf of the shrewd child's parents, figuring the dress and comically over-sized bear would make it difficult to lose the child.

Surprisingly enough, there she was appearing lost, being aided by a gentleman obviously giving her directions toward the . . . Sam's breath immediately caught in mid-passage, freezing every part of his body's functions at the sight of the man's extended hand. There, on the back of the man's right hand, was a large scar.

The man remained in place, respectfully watching after the little girl departed, looking downward and facing away from Sam while he cautiously moved into position directly ten feet behind the man. The gentleman with the scarred hand slowly lifted his head as if hearing Sam breathe and informally said, "Hello, Samuel" slowly turning to face Sam.

El Padre had a worn, tired face with kind, yet piercing eyes that seemed to take in everything at once. Sam just stared at his long awaited 'holy grail,' feeling a sensation of familiarity as El Padre turned toward the direction of the concourse, picked up his small leather shoulder bag, and extended his arm in reception, asking, "Shall we walk together?"

Sam and El Padre both faced toward the terminals with El Padre the first to present a suggestion. "Perhaps we could talk a moment. I have some pressing business and I must not miss my flight, but I have waited a long time, just as you, for this chance meeting." Sam, still unable to find sufficient words, simply nodded his agreement, once again taking his position as follower.

In the short time it took to find a table in the openness of the rotunda area of duty-free shops and for him to pull out his laptop, voice recorder, notepad, and pen, Sam regrouped and managed to organize his first five questions with little preparation. Motioning with his digital recorder for consent, he was met with El Padre's gracious nod of approval. After nearly three years of anticipating the moment, he's pleasantly surprised with his focus and ability to set aside the anxiousness to recall some of the inquiries that had crossed his mind during his search.

With El Padre now seated across from him, Sam couldn't help but steal a long look into the peaceful face of the man. A nagging inquiry popped into his thoughts that he couldn't help but blurt out, asking, "You had your back to me near the departure counters, so how did you know I was there or who I was?"

El Padre scratched his dark, three-day growth shadowing his face, giving the question a breath of respectful consideration before saying, "With focus, I am able to pick up on another person's emanation, or perhaps aura, if you will, whether they are simply across the room or on the opposite side of the world. It is not unlike a beacon or lighthouse, only each person's soul is the light that summons my attention. When a person places attention solely upon me, the aura's light increases tenfold, allowing me the advantage of, shall we say, misdirecting any unwanted curiosities?"

Sam continued this path of questioning with, "So, you could have 'misdirected' me away from your presence?" El Padre simply smiled in replacement of his answer. "Were you in the market yesterday at Old Jerusalem when the two carts collapsed?" Sam quickly asked in the hope to satisfy an earlier assumption.

El Padre shrugged his answer, followed with, "I thought the shirt the vendor offered you would have been a nice souvenir." Sam squinted at the mysterious man, moving forward with how to best present his list of burning questions, but El Padre was the one to administer the first draw, inquiring, "I assume there are questions? Since time is not our friend, perhaps you could relay to me a list of these inquiries and allow me to clear some or all of them up for you."

Sam stared back in the direction of the perfect solution and calmly sat back before responding, "Very well. That would seem appropriate, and . . . helpful." Sam took the deepest breath he could ever remember consuming before diving head-first into the uncharted body of water. He sat forward, a bit giddy, almost expecting a starting pistol to fire before disclosing, "I have five questions off the top of my head; One, how did you come to be immortal?"

Sam hesitated before continuing to look for any signs of argument from his interviewee, but El Padre simply appeared content in hearing the list, so Sam proceeded with, "Two, how and why are you drawn to the dying? Three, what is the significance of the scar upon your hand? Four, what's your name? I doubt very much your passport reads, *El Padre*. And last, are there others like you walking the earth?"

El Padre smiled at Sam, which curiously warmed Sam's heart for some strange reason. El Padre studied the imperfection upon the back of his right hand, appearing to contemplate the list. Finally, he looked back up at Sam, who patiently waited as if he were someone who had more than three hours to wait for the answers. "These are all excellent questions, Samuel. I believe I can answer each of them, as well as others not yet conceived." El Padre slid forward to ensure the volume he projected reached no farther than the two of them before continuing, "Allow me to share with you a story that begins a long time ago."

El Padre looked upward in the direction of the water feature dripping from the ceiling, though his focus delved far beyond the artistic fountain, as he began, "I was a simple, angry man. I believed I was owed something that I was unable to justify, so I sought refuge for this angst within a group of like-minded freedom fighters which I led for many years in numerous attacks against the governing body. Eventually, I was captured by soldiers and quickly tried for numerous offenses such as thievery, rioting, and for attempting to overthrow the government."

Sam interjected mischievously, "Sounds like you were something of a revolutionary in your youth."

El Padre only hinted at a smile before continuing, "Branding was a favorite pastime with the guards who held watch over the prisoners, so I was marked for being a thief upon my left hand, and for acts of rebellion against the state, I was branded on the right. While imprisoned, word came that someone had been killed during our riot. Of this, I was completely unaware, but my penalty was . . . adjusted to fit the added violation."

El Padre briefly took pause allowing Sam to digest the story's direction, but Sam quickly asked, "You were tried for murder?"

El Padre returned with a serious look and simply replied, "I was."

Sam immediately followed with, "And what was the judgment?"

El Padre's expression remained unchanged, simply answering, "Death."

Sam continued staring at the self-declared condemned man across from him and indicated, "Well, this story is getting really interesting unless the next part is, 'and then I died. The end.'"

El Padre smiled and tugged on his shirt, proving his existence, as he joked back, "We are far from the end, as you may have already guessed, my friend."

Sam jumped back in, saying with a chuckle, "So? Did you escape or did you find a talented lawyer?"

El Padre once again became somber, saying unceremoniously, "My sentence was commuted and I was set free."

After a look of inquiry into the poker face of El Padre, Sam scoffed, "Commuted; for all of the crimes? How did you pull that one off?"

Ready for the question, El Padre answered, "During that period of the year, it was the custom for the governor to select one prisoner's death sentence and set him free as long as the crowd that gathered approved. It showed compassion on behalf of the government, also allowing the people to feel as though they were part of the selection process."

Sam cut in, "So, you're telling me that the same governor that you and your political liberators were trying to oust selected you to be freed in a celebratory act of kindness?"

El Padre proceeded slowly, "No. He intended for another to be freed; a man who had been arrested the previous night. But he underestimated the crowds, not knowing they would be filled with servants and employees of those seeking death for the other man, and they rejected his release and began calling my name as the one to be set free."

Sam's face began to pale; his mind racing further and further back into the past while he wrestled with the conclusion slowly dawning upon his thoughts. With dryness to his mouth, he asked the implausible, leading question, "And what name did they call for?"

El Padre looked up into Sam's eyes before speaking a name that hadn't passed his lips for nearly two thousand years, "Jesus Bar-Abbas. A name, over the years, that has been known to you as Barabbas."

CHAPTER 37

Sam often considered the hopeful moment of finding himself face to face with the one he knew as El Padre, but this wasn't playing out as he'd scripted. The man walking in the shoes of 'his' El Padre was going to be an average Joe with an amazing story of how he came to cheat death. Sam's readers would eat up every word he profoundly shared, his boss would praise his tenacious work, and a Pulitzer Prize would be gently lit upon his desk for all to admire.

This 'zig,' though, in the road he had 'zagged' for so long would most likely prove more than his readers, his editor, or the entire Pulitzer Prize selection committee could probably swallow. Even he was noticing a questioning lump in his throat. Sam proceeded staring bleakly at the man now known as Barabbas and found himself once again at a loss for words.

Sam started to speak, hesitated to clear his throat of an imaginary constriction, and finally asked, "So . . . you would be *the* Barabbas?" Barabbas smiled broadly in response when suddenly behind Sam, almost if on cue, the skylight dome in the middle of the ceiling began to release water. Startled by the light roar, Sam turned to watch as the stream relented to gravity, cascading from the ceiling to the round pool below.

Sam admired the water feature as a light waft of mist and cool breeze began to circulate through the air around them from the display. Sam instinctively considered his open laptop and turned quickly to close it, not wanting it damaged from the condensation. When he looked up at Barabbas, who continued to marvel at the waterfall with the look of a delighted child, he wondered just what first question was befitting for a man more than two thousand years old?

Finally, surrendering to the moment, Sam returned to his original five questions, retracing which were yet to be covered before respectfully proceeding, "You mentioned both hands were branded, yet only your right bears a scar. I assume there is an explanation for this?"

Barabbas returned his attention to Sam and shook his head with a look of disgust from the memory. "I was suddenly free again, but the well of hostility still ran deep within me. That very night, I drank for seven men, stumbling through the streets, encumbered by my own good fortune. My compatriots pleaded for me to retreat into the hills in fear of reconsidered disposition. But I arrogantly rebuked them, ignorantly screaming for the heads of my captors. At last, exhausted from rebellion and malevolence, I collapsed upon the edge of the street.

"Slowly, crowds began to gather about me, and it fell upon my drunken ears that the blood-thirsty Romans were to bring forth the one to be crucified in my stead, the Nazarene. He was to be led past 'His people' on his way out of the city to the place called Golgatha."

Barabbas paused briefly and looked into Sam's eyes, adding somberly, "The irony of the situation, at the time, drew me to uncontrolled laughter. There I was, the one who was freed, about to watch the man who took my place on His way to be crucified."

Barabbas reached out and grasped Sam's hand resting atop his computer. He winced more from surprise than pain, with the grip being so sudden and forceful as Sam could feel the strength within each of Barabbas' fingers. They stared into each other's eyes while Barabbas began to well up with deep emotion before taking a breath and proceeding. "It was the custom for the condemned to be handed over to the soldiers, and they were allowed to torture and further humiliate the prisoner before his execution. They would play sadistic games, which resulted in the victim to be beaten beyond recognition.

"There, from my place on the street, I saw the Nazarene for the first time being led past the hordes that had gathered, while many of those around me screamed for His death. His face did not look like that of a man. The closest of His disciples would have difficulty recognizing Him from the beatings at the hands of the soldiers. He bore the cross upon his shoulder, slowly making His way toward assured death. When He stumbled before me, I was motionless from self-reproach and struck with an inability to move or even attempt to assist Him.

"His head slowly rose from His kneeling position and He peered directly into my eyes with a look . . . of pure forgiveness. It drew me in and bestowed a gracious comfort to my very soul. With everything that was within me, I began to weep for this man and for all of my wasted years of wickedness and sin."

Barabbas paused again, and Sam could only hold his hand and look on in silent empathy of a man who had carried the unspeakable weight of a crucified Christ who surrendered Himself in his stead. Barabbas lifted his somber expression and continued dryly, "The thorns within His crown of contempt were driven so deeply into His brow that blood ran down His stricken face. Gazing upon me, holding me in my place, a drop of His blood purposefully fell upon the back of my left hand. With His forgiving expression still lit upon His gentle face, a soldier grabbed Him forcefully from the ground and yelled for a Cyrenian man standing next to me to gather the cross and carry it for the Nazarene. The Cyrenian did as instructed, then . . . Jesus was gone."

With the last word spoken, Barabbas released his intense grip of Sam's hand, collapsing into his chair from the spent emotion of telling the painful story of so long ago. Sam not only acknowledged the release of his hand, but also received a glimpse of the lost opportunity for Barabbas to further connect with Jesus before He took his place on Golgotha.

Sam allowed Barabbas the precious moments of recovery, watching him with awe. Unsure just when to continue with the conversation, Sam realized that he had moved to the edge of his seat and scooted back in a feeble attempt to appear at ease with the break in dialog. Before Sam could fill the gap, Barabbas reengaged his dialog. "History remains uncertain of my exploits beyond my release; of this I have had time to research; odd, reading about yourself written by someone born two thousand years after you." Barabbas broke the seriousness with a wry smile, returning the twinkle back to his eyes, before asking, "What knowledge do *you* possess of my life once I was released?"

Sam looked to the high ceiling recalling his studies from college before answering the test, with, "Let's see, all of this is, of course, speculative, but one belief is you returned to your rioting ways only to later die in a revolt against the Romans. Another is that you lived out the rest of your days in quiet solitude. I've heard the theory that since none of the Apostles were actual witnesses to this event, some believe the existence of Bara . . . I mean, you, was another biblical parable or metaphor concerning Jesus taking our place on the cross."

Barabbas smiled briefly, interjecting, "I did not know I was considered a metaphor; how intriguing."

Sam smiled at the now defunct explanation, but pressed forward, adding, "Another theory is the dramatic event moved you so deeply that you went to be near Christ as He died upon the cross. That's the one I choose to believe. It gives me . . . affirmation that we can all find redemption."

Barabbas smiled softly at Sam's honesty, adding, "Then feel sanctified in your choice." Barabbas adjusted himself in his chair, returning to his narration, "I remained back, following the angry crowd to the hill called 'the place of the skull' and shaded my face so that no eye fell upon me given my recent exoneration.

"The seriousness of the predicament had an immediate sobering effect upon me, causing me to become resolute in my desire of being witness to the atrocity. I, as so many, heard the stories of great miracles performed, and I believed, with simply a word, He would cast aside the cross He bore and walk upon the crumpled heap that once was the mighty Roman Empire, proving to all He was the one true Son of God."

Barabbas touched his cheek as though he became lost in thought, but slowly, almost reluctantly, continued with, "And yet, He did none of these things, except lift His head toward the heavens and, with a powerful cry, released His Spirit with the word, 'Tetelestai,' meaning, 'It is finished!' And then He died before my disbelieving eyes."

Catching Sam by surprise with the sudden burst of vigor, Barabbas continued the story. "Suddenly, the noon day sky grew black as coal and, upon His death, the ground began to shake with such great magnitude I have yet to experience again. Many said the ground opened up and released its captive saints who arose and walked among us. I did not witness this miracle being unassociated with such holy believers, but I will say the tremor was not like any other. It shook with purpose, rather than haphazard manner. It was as though its very intent was set toward a singular objective. At that moment, my eyes met with the centurion whose charge was that of keeping peace during the crucifixion, and I saw not only fear, but also unmistakable recognition that the one who had just died was like no other.

"At the time of His passing, when I was watching for one ultimate miracle, I missed something amazing that I only came to acknowledge after centuries of experience. When I say His death was like none other, I struggle to explain in a way one might truly fathom. I have been on hand and witnessed many people die; this I wish not to express as an objection, but rather, a blessing. All deserve to die peacefully and with dignity, and this has become my life's continuing contribution." Barabbas stated, punctuated with a tap of his fingers on Sam's notepad.

Proceeding, he added, "Upon many final breaths, not all mind you, I have seen so many fight with all that is left within them or attempt to sustain for one more moment, one more intake of air, as they die unwillingly. Jesus relinquished His spirit willingly. It was not His body giving in to injury or from loss of blood or from internal damage; He *allowed* Himself to die for a greater purpose. And that fact alone, realized so many years after I witnessed it, has guided my path for all of these years, teaching me how the word *sacrifice* has seen no greater example, nor shall it ever again.

"You must understand, Samuel, I was a difficult individual; hard-headed, argumentative, and constantly angry. Upon my being captured, jailed, and sentenced to death, my only thought was that of defiance. When Jesus fell before me, tortured and beaten and looked into my eyes with forgiveness . . ." Barabbas paused from the emotion and wiped his eyes before proceeding, "The man who chose to take my place, to be nailed to that cross . . . and He offers me peace and forgiveness. Any thoughts of defiance turned to humility. All of my anger was eclipsed by love. I had never been humbled before that day. I have lived my life humbly, since."

Sam was left speechless from the magnitude of Barabbas' first-hand narrative. Barabbas chuckled pensively, commenting to his singular audience, "Just as you had imagined, I assume?"

Sam returned the inquiry with a tilt of the head, replying, "What do you mean?"

He sat forward, indicating Sam's computer with a nod. "Has this not been the answer to that which you have been searching; who it is that I am?"

Sam released an uncomfortable laugh as Barabbas enjoyed Sam's response of complete lack of confidence. "Yes, just as I had anticipated. But then, that's why they put me on the case!" They shared a brief laugh at the unfeasible improbability until Sam finally sighed heavily with the rapidly approaching burden of parting before addressing his notes to ask another question, "Oh. What about the cycle?"

Barabbas was caught with a blank-faced return, inquiring, "And what cycle do you refer to, Samuel?" Sam set down his notepad and reworded the request, "The thirty-four year cycle that you seem to follow and return to particular regions; it's how I was able to narrow the search."

Barabbas smiled with Sam's simple explanation before telling him, "Ahh, so it was *that* repetition that was the nub of me. It never occurred that I inquire, as I am a firm believer in Fate." Both smiled at the concept before he continued addressing the matter. "It is quite simple, really. My inspiration and the role model I have looked toward is quite naturally the one who saved me. I am certain you have heard on occasion the phrase 'Jesus died for you,' I do not dispute this fact, being a true living witness to the reality, but from my perspective, the phrase carries with it a lifelong accepted burden and depth that no man can glimpse nor fathom."

He shifted in his seat, before answering, "The time interval you inquire about is the ultimate life cycle of thirty-three and one half years. That was how long it took our Savior to be born, grow to be a man, and die for all of us allowing the gracious, undeserving gift of salvation to billions of souls. If that is not the greatest example of a perfect life cycle, I do not know what is."

Sam nodded his agreement and, after a respectful pause, asked, "Will I ever have the opportunity to speak with you again?"

Barabbas looked up and smiled at Sam, stating, "I would suspect one day I might appear upon your doorstep, but that visit is for another time down the road."

Sam chuckled at the grim subject before restating his query, "What I mean is, I have so many more questions to ask; so much I still want to know."

Barabbas looked toward the ceiling in consideration before turning back to Sam, offering, "Through my years, I have placed many of my experiences onto paper. Well, it is more of a journal and has evolved into several books. There have been many, many changes in the world, changes in customs, in languages, beliefs, as well as changes in me . . ." El Padre looked down, hesitating before he proceeded, saying, "I would like for you to have these stories as a gift for the world. I will be in your vicinity in several weeks, and I will make them available to you."

With an unbelieving expression, Sam responded, "Your journals? Seriously? You'll let me read the entirety of your existence? What do you wish for me to do with the information within them?"

Barabbas slid his satchel from between his legs and displayed a solemn look, continuing, "Some may not believe them. Some may doubt you. Many will deny my existence. But you, Samuel, you will be my voice." Sam knew the expression on his face displayed his continued skepticism, but couldn't seem to allude to any other expression.

Barabbas slowly stood, slinging his satchel back over his shoulder, almost slumping with the heaviness of a life-long burden, adding, "I have been delegated as an observer of earth's worst atrocities. I have witnessed plague, uncountable war, famine, senseless acts of terrorism, genocide, and the holocaust of my own people. I have stood by, silenced by my commitment, watching thousands of souls select a path resulting in their demise or the end for numerous others." Barabbas continued to his point, lowering his head from the weight of years of exhaustive disgust and without looking up, he offered, "Free will must have been God's second most unbearable gift to us."

Sam held an anxious breath for him to continue. At the opening of Barabbas' shirt, Sam caught a glimpse of a small medallion on a gold chain. Before he's able to ascertain the design, Barabbas finally looked up at Sam and proceeded with, "My perspective perhaps may appear biased at times, but my resolve has been steadfast. I wish the world to remember where they came from; to know who they are and what matters most. I hope for so much, Samuel, and within that hope my words are all I can offer to those who persevere."

The man now known as Barabbas turned to walk away. Sam stood, asking another question. "I met a woman some years ago who spoke of your pension for the dying as a Holy Sacrament; an act of Last Rites. Would you agree with this rationale?"

Barabbas stopped and slowly turned back, staring at the polished floor for a moment before lifting his head and facing Sam once again. "I thought you might have understood from at last hearing my story, my dear, patient friend. What it is that I do, all of which I hope to achieve with every step, and with every blessed breath I am granted, is for penance. If my life's work need be wrapped up within the confines of a Sacrament, it should be that of my continuing search for Atonement."

With little more to say on the subject, Sam sheepishly looked up at Barabbas and asked, "One last question; one on the personal side and nothing to do with my article." Barabbas faced him, fully prepared to field the question, before Sam asked. "You've seen the very best of us, as well as the absolute worst. I was wondering, before you go, if you could relinquish just a smidgen of your wisdom concerning love?"

Almost instinctively, Barabbas reached up and touched the medallion around his neck as his thoughts ventured somewhere in the past. How far back his mind traveled would most likely be impossible to know. Before long, in his typical slow, methodical response, Barabbas reached into his backpack and withdrew a small loaf of baked bread wrapped in white paper.

Sam straight-lined, "If you say, 'man cannot live by bread alone,' I'm gonna ask for a refund!"

Unwrapping the bread, Barabbas quickly retorted, "No. That line has already been used by someone I very much look up to, but I was unable to follow in His footsteps." Barabbas smiled briefly before proceeding, "One of the many things about bread is this," He broke the loaf in half. "There are countless ways to make it, in numerous textures, tastes, and even sizes. After hard work and much consideration, it comes out of the warmth in whatever form the maker had intended." Barabbas took a bit of the center, chewed it, and continued with a smile, "And it is good. Even though the bread is delicious on its own merit, it desires to be with something else. Be it cheese, meat, fruit, or vegetable, and even Jesus himself utilized bread with wine, but my point is that bread is incomplete until it is paired. The options seem endless. So much thought and preparation should be respectfully considered. Once one has found the other, both should find delight in the uniqueness of their pairing."

Sam shook his head with the metaphor and chose to smile through his response of, "With an example like that, I can understand how so many decide to stick with just the wine!"

Barabbas heartily laughed out loud and looked to the high ceiling for his response, stating as he remained looking upward, "You certainly have your mother's sense of humor, Samuel. She, too, bore a quick wit about her."

The emotion from hearing Barabbas speak of his mother built an immediate lump within his throat and his eyes reacted by welling up. With prolonged hesitation, Sam took a nervous step toward him before asking from a shaky countenance, "You . . . you knew my mother?"

Lowering his face, Barabbas, too, displayed wrought emotion, simply answering, "Yes, I had the great pleasure of meeting her."

He took another uncertain step forward before Sam pressed on with, "When? When did you meet her?"

Barabbas continued his penetrating stare toward Sam, answering, "I believe you have already deduced as to the when, Samuel."

With a hand to his face, Sam physically tried to hold back tears, but his emotions far out-strengthened his attempt to grip any form of control. His knees began to buckle from the all the years he'd refused to express any feelings about the loss of his mother, but Barabbas was there, holding him up as they returned to their table.

Assisted into his chair, Sam asked through the gentle sobs, as any child who had lost his parent, "Why did you take her? Why did she have to die?"

Barabbas kept his hand on Sam's shoulder, attempting to rub the overdue grief and sadness from deep inside, replying, "My sweet child, it was simply her time. Your mother was suffering, and there is nothing more agonizing to observe than one of God's children in pain. Her strand had come to its intended end, and for her to remain any longer would have only inflicted needless misery. She found peace and contentment in all things. I gave her everything she required to go gently into her final slumber."

Sam looked up, not at Barabbas, but once again at the face of what he perceived as the Incarnation of Death. Through gritted teeth, Sam started to rise, saying angrily, "So, you took my mother's soul and took her away from all of us; you took her away from me?"

Barabbas tightened his hold on Sam's shoulder, but his expression softened even more, holding him in place, responding with, "Samuel. Do you wish to know what your mother wanted me to tell you?" The roller-coaster of emotion didn't seem to end as Sam's rising anger faltered, leaving him to fall back into his seat, emotionally rung out. Immediately calmed, Barabbas moved his hand to Sam's knee, patting it, continuing, "Your mother loved you with everything that was within her. Her biased pride spoke of your achievements and of your strength of character, and fearlessly pestered me to relay to you, one day, what I am about to share . . ."

Sam once again surged to the edge of his seat, anxious to hear his mother's dying wish from the man who was with her in her final moments. Not to keep his eager audience waiting, Barabbas went on, "Let it go. Release the useless pain you have inside for words, both said and unspoken, and let it all go. Allow yourself to be forgiven for not coming home when I asked. Remember me as you remember best, of us laughing with each other and holding you and kissing the top of your head, telling you how the greatest thing I ever achieved in life was you. Open your heart to love unconditionally, without restraint, and you will feel so much more than you could ever imagine. Let it all slip away, melting into the ground beneath your feet, so that you can be left with the cleansing feeling of freedom from all sadness, fear, and regret. This is my ultimate wish for you, my son; the ability to truly love once again. Release me, and let me go in peace. I'm ready."

At some point unbeknownst to Sam, he had subconsciously taken Barabbas' hand into his and now held it with both of his. Tears openly flowed down his face as Sam rubbed his eye with a shrug, not wishing to let go of Barabbas' hand just yet. Between soft gasps, Sam stated, "You were with her. You really were there for her when she died."

Barabbas sighed heavily, responding meekly, "I was with them both, Samuel."

The reply hit Sam surprisingly, returning Barabbas with a questioning look, asking, "Both? Who else do you mean?"

Barabbas offered him a compassionate look, answering, "I held your friend Becklin's hand as he lay upon the gurney and looked into my eyes while he fought so bravely."

Hearing the name of his friend only intensified Sam's already scoped emotions, dropping his chin and, with his eyes clenched shut, he let Barabbas continue, "I let him know you would see it through. And you did, Samuel. Perhaps not as you had hoped, but you made certain your promise to your friend was fulfilled. I showed him, and he was able to join his parents with a pride and peacefulness deserving of one who had battled long and hard and came through victorious."

Sam let go of everything he had held back emotionally. He began to weep; not out of deep sorrow or loss of loved ones, but for the resolution that things that happened were not his fault. It rolled over him like a cold splash to the face before quoting Manuela Esperanza, "There is purpose in all things . . ."

Barabbas simply nodded agreement before adding, "I believe you are on the right track, my friend." With that, Barabbas leaned over and kissed Sam atop his head, touched his cheek, and headed toward his terminal without looking back.

CHAPTER 38

Watching El Padre walk away, Sam remained in place for a long time attempting to get his mind around what had just occurred. At last, he grabbed his luggage and lumbered toward the men's room to splash actual water onto his face to make certain he wasn't dreaming. Bent over the sink staring at his reflection in the mirror, a frown slowly yielded to a smile, admitting, "Story of a lifetime!"

A man exited a stall, looked at the odd puffy-eyed man smiling at himself in the mirror, and left the restroom obviously deciding to wash his hands later.

Sam looked up to a voice over the terminal intercom announcing, "Passenger Sam Noll. Passenger Sam Noll, please see the attendant at terminal Gate 33." Sam finished drying his face and hands and grabbed his bags to check on the latest delay information he'd have to deal with.

At the terminal front desk, Sam approached stating with a smile, "Hi, I'm Sam Noll. There was a page for me to see you."

The attendant referenced a sheet of paper, replying, "Ah, yes, Mr. Noll, we see your already postponed flight has been delayed another thirty minutes." Sam dropped his head in expected disappointment, before she continued, "But, we do have a flight leaving for Newark airport in twenty-two minutes that appears to have available seats. It should arrive thirty minutes after your original ETA. Would you be interested?" Sam lifted his head as his bathroom smile suddenly returned.

On the plane, Sam quietly typed on his computer. He stopped, taking a deep, long overdue breath, before reading what he had written: *What if the incarnation of death wasn't the dark and menacing Grim Reaper we've depicted from dozens of movies and years of scary bedtime stories? What if he was just a man, hand selected by God, to assist us through our final difficult phase upon the earth; chosen to grant us pride, companionship, and most of all, peace. For over three years, I've accounted for the wake of a manifestation I often chose to disbelieve, but delved further, in the hope to prove myself wrong. I allowed myself solace in the unrestrained fancy that no one should die alone, and at last I have looked into the face of death incarnate and found him merciful.*

The last words I said to my mother the night before she died were those in anger, and since that day, my entire life has been a path toward absolution. On the night she died, someone knelt beside her in the place I should have been. Someone took her hand, wiping away her sadness, and bestowed to her peace and comfort from the limitless love of her only son. The truth, before dying, was her final gift on this earth and that endowment empowers me to face a new future, leaving guilt and regret, at last, behind.

I have always considered death to be greeted as an uninvited guest; a momentary inconvenience with an outcome not yet determined. I have emotionally stiff-armed life's final experience to the point of denying myself and my loved ones the opportunity of telling them how much I loved them and how desperately they would be missed. I have carried these beliefs with such conviction that I allowed them to taint the writing of this article, and I beg for you, the reader, to forgive me. I believe I can now comprehend this article's true path. My previous theories, as well as my doubts, have now and forever more, been eclipsed by the gentle, white light that is Salvation.

Sam paused from writing to reflect on the enormity of his article and how it would be viewed by the world. He then further considered the impact on the literary world with the eventual

Book of Barabbas, Christ's Continuing Disciple, and shook off the excitement from within. Sam moved the cursor on the computer to *Save*, tapping the touch pad to retain what he'd just written to his thumb drive, but the computer screen indicated to *Insert Flash Drive*. Checking the back of the computer to no avail, Sam then went through his bag trying to locate his *Best of Mozart* thumb drive.

Farther down the aisle, a pure white over-sized teddy bear slipped off its seat and onto the aisle, before the flight attendant gently returned it to its companion. The bear's owner, a young girl in a red dress with her head resting against her father's side, remained contentedly in her slumber.

One row behind her, an attractive woman stared out her window into darkness, deep in thought. Within her hand, she clasped a white handkerchief with blue pinstripes.

The plane's cabin speaker softly carried the calm voice of the Captain's request, "If everyone could return to your seats and fasten your seat belts, it looks like we're moving into a patch of bad weather and we'll be feeling a little mild turbulence . . ."

Barabbas slowly walked into the entry of an assisted living home, past the elderly residents watching the news on the television in the lobby, with the voice of the anchorman following Barabbas past the nurse's station. ". . . as there still are no answers to Flight 1203 going down over the Atlantic Ocean, and crews attempt to ascertain its final location, in the hope to find any survivors of the three hundred and thirty-eight passengers aboard . . ."

Barabbas walked down the carpeted hallway with wooden handrails on either side, with his head tilted up and to the right. His pace slowed until he stopped at a room with the door open. He stood in the entry, looking around the room, taking in a slow, deep breath in a manner of someone preparing to complete an enormous task. At last, he entered the room and moved to a chair next to the bed, sitting. Quietly, he leaned toward the bed, reaching over to gently take a man's frail, thin arm from its resting position atop the comforter. Taking the tiny, disfigured hand into his, he tenderly submitted to the man, "Hello, Efram, my dear friend. I thought we might, at last, finish our conversation."

END

CPSIA information can be obtained at www.ICGtesting.com
Printed in the USA
BVOW07s1021021214

377418BV00003B/7/P